Tribes of the Vampire Book 2:

THE JADED HUNTER

By

Michelle M. Pillow

Dark Paranormal Romance

New Concepts   Georgia

Be sure to check out our website for the very best in fiction at fantastic prices!

When you visit our webpage, you can:

* Read excerpts of currently available books
* View cover art of upcoming books and current releases
* Find out more about the talented artists who capture the magic of the writer's imagination on the covers
* Order books from our backlist
* Find out the latest NCP and author news--including any upcoming book signings by your favorite NCP author
* Read author bios and reviews of our books
* Get NCP submission guidelines
* And so much more!

We offer a 20% discount on all new Trade Paperback releases ordered from our website!

Be sure to visit our webpage to find the best deals in e-books and paperbacks! To find out about our new releases as soon as they are available, please be sure to sign up for our newsletter (http://www.newconceptspublishing.com/newsletter.htm) or join our reader group (http://groups.yahoo.com/group/new_concepts_pub/join)!

The newsletter is available by double opt in only and our customer information is *never* shared!

Visit our webpage at:
www.newconceptspublishing.com

The Jaded Hunter is an original publication of NCP. This work has never before appeared in book form. This work is a novel. Any similarity to actual persons or events is purely coincidental.

New Concepts Publishing
5202 Humphreys Rd.
Lake Park, GA 31636

ISBN 1-58608-716-9
© copyright 2004, Michelle M. Pillow

Cover art (c) copyright 2004, Amber Moon

NCP books are available at special quantity discounts for bulk purchases for sales promotions, premiums, fund raising, or educational use. For details, write, email, or phone New Concepts Publishing, 5202 Humphreys Rd., Lake Park, GA 31636; Ph. 229-257-0367, Fax 229-219-1097; orders@newconceptspublishing.com.

First NCP Paperback Printing: 2005

Dedication:

To Leah, for all the wonderful translations you do for me. To all
the readers who support my work. To the editors, proofers,
family, and friends who help that work see print. Thank you.

Prologue

New Orleans, Louisiana, May

"Ye dinna understand, lass!"

The cryptic call pierced through the night. A frown creased Jaden MacNaughton's features as she concentrated on establishing the position of the voice. When she lowered herself to the rain soaked concrete, her hand slipped over the grainy texture. Irritated, she steadied herself.

Luckily, the sky had stopped its midnight torrent long enough for her to track her prey into the old graveyard. Narrowing her eyes, Jaden peered around the crumbling stone pillar at the entrance. Her gaze darted over the grounds, moving towards the dirty crypt the vampire apparently called home.

"Lass?"

The vampire's Scottish accent fell thick through the dark night. Jaden had an eerie feeling something was off. Duncan was of Scottish descent, but according to her file he was human-born in the American old west. His accent shouldn't have been so strong. Shrugging off her suspicions, she focused her feelings. Her logical assessment had been off before when she hunted. She needed to trust her instincts now--and her file. Tonight was just another night in her life. No matter how much Duncan protested, one of them wouldn't be leaving the graveyard walking.

The moonless sky made it hard to see, and the street lamps didn't shine on this part of the old city. She couldn't detect more than the stretches of shadows cast by weathered tombstones and mausoleums. Scowling, Jaden pulled back. It wouldn't do for her target to see her before she was ready to strike. Vampire eyes didn't need the benefit of light, but unfortunately hers did.

Why couldn't it have been, Jaden, the poltergeist stalker? I'll rid your family crypt of pesky, ethereal relatives or your money back! Jaden grimaced, trying not to get distracted by the sarcasm invading her thoughts. Unable to resist, she added, *At least I would get paid in cash for my services, and a damned ghost would be like fighting a gust of wind instead of being swallowed whole by a walking, immortal snake.*

"We know what you've done, Duncan. Last week you tried to change a woman in labor. Even your beloved tribal council has rules. Besides, you've been killing innocent people," Jaden said. She refused to think too deeply about it. It had been her job to terminate the life of the child and mother. The infant had been in too much pain to try to save. Besides, once the vampiric disease was in your veins, there was no turning back. There was no cure. Dispassionately, she said, "Care to come over here and read what happened to the mother in my file? Care to hear what happened to her baby?"

"But that is what I've been tryin' to tell ye, lass. I'm not this Duncan," the vampire returned. His voice was nearer. The nightstalker had drawn close to her hiding place. Vagueness stirred in her senses, a remembrance she couldn't place. Ignoring the déjà vu, she swept her lashes low over her eyes in concentration.

"And I dinna care what ye wish to be called, laddie," Jaden growled under her breath, mimicking his soft burr. She knew the vampire could hear her as if she shouted, just as she could detect his whispering chuckle at her defiance. His arrogance was no surprise. Immortality tended to convince the vampiric beings that they were Gods upon the earth. And like the ancient Gods, they wielded their power with pleasure and contempt.

Closing her eyes, Jaden reached out her senses to feel for him. With the help of her uncle she had tracked the vampire from New York. Her uncle was methodical in his business. He wouldn't have made a mistake. Not in something like this. It was too important to her. She needed to avenge his victims.

The father of the baby came to her mind—his face contorted in grief and pain, his limbs flying in desperation as he ran helplessly through the alleyway next to the hospital. The poor guy was lost without his wife, with no evidence to bury, no idea what happened to them. And he would never be told the truth. Besides, what could she tell him? *Hi, I assassinated your vampiric wife and baby? Want to go get coffee?*

"Which one of the bloodstalkers are ye, lass?" the vampire asked calmly, breaking into her thoughts. He wasn't afraid. Jaden could feel his emotions swirling thickly with her own. It was her gift and her curse. It was the reason she could track. It was the reason she was alone. She was a *dhampir*, daughter of a mortal woman, daughter of an undead father.

"I just want you dead," she muttered, without compassion. She found the mother and infant in an alleyway where they were left to writhe in pain. Duncan had left them. She put it from her mind. Emotion always distracted her. That is why she never let herself feel anything for those she stalked or hunted. She couldn't afford to be weak. One mistake and she could end up dead, or much worse—she could end up a vampire.

Jaden slowly ran her hand over the leather satchel at her waist, clutching a wooden stake. The light weight felt comfortable in her palm as if it had been carved to fit there, when in fact it was her hand that had grown around it. She'd held her first stake when she was two years old.

What a game it had been to her then, striking the weapon into a feather pillow to see how high the feathers would flutter. She had danced in them like snowflakes. Now, her target was much harder and instead of dancing, she was bathed in warm blood. The stake wouldn't kill any but the youngest of vampires, but it would slow this old one down so she could capture him. She bounced the wood thoughtfully in her palm.

Reacting on instinct more than sight, Jaden spun up from the ground, twisting around the stone post to strike the vampire in the center of his chest. Her muscles moved with the ease of frequent use. The vampire hesitated. Jaden could feel him holding back. Duncan stopped his counter-strike to let her come at him. It was as if he waited for her to hit him.

Jaden had little time to wonder at the creature's hesitancy. In an instant, she could feel that the vampire was powerful, that he could've easily put up a fight, and yet he held back. Unable to stop her motions, she felt the wood meet with the unforgiving steel of undead muscle. Her palm brushed next to a cold chest as she let go.

Duncan gasped in surprise. Jaden didn't falter, not seeing his face as she whipped around to punch his jaw. Once he was away from her, she could better sense him. If she had made a mistake in her tracking there was still time to right it. The vampire's head snapped back and he fell to the ground. Instantly, two men clad in ninja black were at her side, one carrying a claymore. The weapon's large blade gleamed dangerously in the moonlight.

Jaden turned to the men, automatically knowing they were mortal. Without thought, she kicked her foot through the air, hitting the unarmed one in the chest. The man deflected the power of her blow before returning one of his own. His fist snapped across her jaw, bouncing off to leave a trail of blood on her lips.

Jaden fumed, but she hid it beneath a hard smile. A red trail trickled down her pale chin. She didn't bother to wipe it away as she turned upon the man with the full force of a fanatical demon, slashing the air until she pummeled him to the ground.

Spinning, arms held before her, she confronted the man with the blade. His sword lifted over his head, coming through the air to hack off the vampire's head. Jaden stopped him with a whirling kick to the abdomen. His sword barely missed her arm as it whizzed past. The man stumbled before whirling to face her. He jerked the mask off. His short brown hair matted around his irritated face.

"Damn it, Jade! What'd you do to Tom?" the man asked in breathless anger, ignoring his own injury while motioning to the man on the ground.

"This is my job, Rick," Jaden said angrily. "I warned you if you came on my turf again, I'd beat the living--"

"Damn it, Jade! Mack sent us!" Tom growled from the ground, cradling his arm as he stood. He too had pulled the mask from his sharp features. His expression fell into a sulk but his chin lifted proudly. Jaden pressed her lips together in irritation and ignored him.

Directing her stare at Rick, she said, "So you're the one that's been following me for the last two nights. I should've known."

"We were following orders," Tom said, coming to stand beside Jaden. She continued to ignore him, concentrating on Rick. Rick's look was just as harsh. They clashed in a silent battle of will, neither backing down. Most women would've been intimidated by Rick's handsomeness and cool, militant demeanor. Jaden wasn't a normal woman.

"Why would my uncle send you?" Jaden questioned in disbelief. "It's been a simple enough track. The cocky bastard didn't even run."

"I don't know," Tom said, still angling to get his say in. "We're just following orders."

"How many times do I have to tell you? This is not the military." Jaden scowled. Finally, she drew her eyes away to glance impatiently at Tom. When she looked back at Rick his stance had relaxed but he was still angry. "I work alone. I can't be responsible for your lives. This was my capture. I'll handle it."

Rick stepped forward. Lowering his voice so no one else could hear, he whispered hotly into her ear, "No one is asking you to be responsible for us, Jade. You're not the only one out here fighting the good fight. And no matter how much you want to be alone in this, you're not."

"I work alone," she said bitterly. She wasn't as discreet as Rick, leaving her voice audible. "You didn't even give me time to sense him."

"What is there to sense? He's a demon," Tom hissed from behind. Jaden turned to him, ready to begin fighting anew. Rick grabbed her elbow to keep her from pummeling the man. Duncan gave a slight moan, reaching for the stake protruding from his chest next to his heart. Their attention turned briefly to the ground, distracting them from another skirmish.

Jaden didn't have an answer for Tom's question. He was right, of course. Nightstalkers were all demons and she should've been killing the vampiric scum as indiscriminately as they killed humans. Perhaps it was her father's blood that drove her to be sure, to sense their crimes for herself before finishing them off. And maybe it was her punishment, her need for self-torment that forced her to feel the victim's pain, to remind her what vampire blood was capable of.

Lifting a walkie-talkie to his mouth, Rick kept his eyes trained steadily on the slender woman before him, as he ordered, "Send in the sunlight. We've got clean up."

"What are you doing?" Jaden rotated back to Rick. Placing her hands on her hips, she glowered at him. Rick latched the radio back to his waist. Jaden snorted in disgust. She didn't carry anything but her phone and a few simple tools--a stake, a knife or sword, her wits, and on rare occasions a rope. The militant ninjas that her uncle employed brought an arsenal of uselessness out with them--their electronic files, two-ways, swords, blades, vehicles done up like tanks, artificial lighting, backup. Seeing the handgun at Rick's waist, she grimaced.

"Mack ordered this one done to death immediately," Rick acknowledged. He knew better than to test his luck against a dhampir. "We all heard what this creature did and we know what you were forced to do. You're too emotionally involved. It only takes one mistake and you're dead."

Jaden's jaw dropped. To her thinking that was the overstatement of the century. She couldn't afford to be 'emotionally involved' in anything. Rick should have known that little detail better than anyone.

Duncan began to sit up. Blood pooled around the wound in his chest, running down his sides and staining his cotton shirt a dark red. Rick kicked him absently in the chest to knock him down. The vampire wheezed, showing pointed fangs. His eyes filled with blood as his body fought to survive.

Turning, Rick motioned his men to bring forward the large circular light. They stumbled under its cumbersome weight. The light only imitated the sun. Its rays were not as powerful against a vampire unless he was completely drained of energy and blood, like Duncan on the ground before them.

Jaden seethed. Something was definitely not right. Mack had never sent his boys to help her out before. Not on a routine slay. She walked over to the fallen body. Looking at the creature fully for the first time, she froze.

"Jade," the cold, blue lips began to mouth with a rasp. His red hair was slicked back from his pale features. The vampire's deadened gaze glanced over her shoulder in warning.

Jaden spun into action, her arm coming across her shoulder to strike out as she turned. It was too late. Tom anticipated her move before she even made it. Her arm met with the hard crash of metal. The man held a riot shield. She winced violently, shrieking in pain. Her shoulder popped out of joint with the force of her blow. Instantly one of the faceless men who dragged the light was next to her, shooting her side with a tazer. The metal hooks bit into her flesh and the heavy electric shock brought her instantly to her knees.

"No," Rick hollered. His cry came too late. The man had already brought Jaden low to the ground with his assault. "She's one of us, fool!"

Tom stood defiantly over Jaden, smirking at her helpless form as she shivered. The other man dropped his tazer, yanking the hooks from her skin. He glanced around in confusion. Rick glared at the both of them, waving his hand back. The men obeyed the silent order, disappearing into the graveyard the way they'd come.

Jaden groaned, recovering quickly from the attack. She panted for air, unable to breathe, unable to speak. Her lungs felt as if they'd been crushed by a wrecking ball. Her arm hung limp at her side as she pulled up on her one good hand and knees. She looked to the fallen vampire, really seeing him for the first time. The old eyes stared back at her. A bright light flashed behind them, mimicking the rays of the sun. The face began to wither before her, its lips opening slightly as if to scream her name.

"Bhaltair?" Jaden whispered weakly in disbelief. It wasn't Duncan. She had tracked the wrong vampire. Yelling at the men, she ordered hoarsely, "No, stop! Don't!"

Jaden's head reeled from the pain shooting in her shoulder. She dropped faintly to lie on the ground. Her mind swam in threatening blackness. The vampire shrieked, turning slowly to ash.

Jaden coughed, breathing in the grave dust of vampiric death as it swirled up gently in the night breeze. It fell over her, blanketing her body like the tender falling of feathery snow. It was too late. The vampire was dead.

Chapter One

New York City, New York, August

"Over eight million people in this damned city and not one vampire," Jaden fumed with a growl, as she looked down a nearly abandoned street. A large rat ran by the flattened figure of a drunken bum slouched against a brick wall, surrounded by the wind's collection of garbage, but no creatures of the night. The dark alleyways were starting to look the same. She could hear the soft melody of jazz in the distance, reverberating out of the club a block behind her. She could feel the presence of the crowd gathering, their liveliness beginning to trample out onto the city streets as the hour crept closer to dawn.

Picking up her pace, Jaden tried to ignore the annoyance of a humid night. She wasn't scared of being alone. She much preferred the solitude of darkness, keeping a vampiric schedule of her own. She hardly ever went out during the day. There was no point--her work was at night.

Jaden's tight cotton shirt was beginning to stick to her skin. It blended perfectly with the loose black pants covering her legs and short army boots. She could easily slip into a corner and disappear from sight if needed. But tonight she wasn't trying to disappear. She wanted to be on the vampire's radar. Pulling at her low ponytail to tighten the strands of her dark reddish-brown hair, she paused to look over her shoulder.

"Come on," she hissed to herself. "Is there a conference I don't know about? Are the undead gathering in Chinatown tonight?"

Jaden felt like she'd walked most of the city. Almost ready to give up and leave Greenwich Village to the partying mass behind her, she came to the end of a block. Her skin prickled with a familiar sensation of warning. A grim smile lined her features. Turning the corner, she peered down the darkened alley leading behind numerous shops.

She could see nothing but the normal shadows stretching over the hot cement and wooden crates. Closing her eyes, she concentrated. It wasn't hard. She felt an instant rush of sensations flow through her. It wasn't her emotions swirling inharmoniously in her calm blood.

The music faded behind her. She detected a young vampire nearby. In a flash, her throat began to shoot with pain and the edge of her gums pulsed lightly. The vampire had a victim. Growling, she rushed forward. She could feel the steady beat of two hearts. The victim was not yet dead, but by the weakened rhythm, would be soon.

Jaden came to an abrupt stop as the sensation strengthened. Lowering her jaw, she casually continued forward as if she were strolling through the park. She allowed her boots to fall heavily on the pavement in warning. Behind a crate she detected vampire shoulders hunched around the hapless writhing of its prey. Its large arms wrapped about the thin body of a man, trapping him to his chest like a steel clamp.

If the vampire was surprised by her intrusion, he didn't show it. In fact, his icy gaze was placid as he casually turned it to her. The streetlight illuminated the creature's pale face. The yellowish cast formed eerily over the bluish skin of the undead, adding intimidation to his strong nose and square jaw. His lips closed leisurely over his fangs, covering the light bathing of blood on his teeth. His eyes found her with chilling precision. He didn't move--just waited to see what she wanted.

Jaden's first reaction was to shiver. Instinctively, she grabbed a stake at her waist. Her fingers slipped over her hip. There was nothing there. Clearing her mind, she recalled in weighty numbness, *You're not here to kill. You're here to die.*

"Let him go," Jaden ordered, barely turning to the victim caught up in the vampire's grasp, her words low and steady. The man's feet hung above the ground, kicking with renewed force at her heated words. To her great surprise, the vampire released his hold. The victim darted away, his shoulder hitting Jaden as he sped back into the lighted street. She ignored the mortal. When they were alone, she said wryly, "That was the right decision."

The vampire straightened to his full height. Jaden's stomach tightened in unease. Crouching over, the creature wasn't so intimidating. However, with his broad stature directed completely at her, he became quite daunting. In a fight, this creature would have the benefit of natural strength behind his vampirically enhanced abilities. Only, Jaden wasn't there to fight him.

The vampire waited patiently. He kept his hands folded in front of his chest, not in intimidation but in easy repose. His face showed nothing, no fear or reprisal at having his meal interrupted. He wasn't reacting like a typical young one. Usually the newly turned--especially those from the more elaborate boroughs of New York--bared their fangs with animated hisses and growls.

Jaden forced herself to ignore the truth of her eyes. Sight was not her strongest gift. Even though she had perfect vision and could navigate the night with ease, she couldn't make out the details of those things hidden within the shadows. This one appeared much older and more confident than she first sensed. But, no, she had never been wrong before. Her senses never failed, they might waver but they never failed. She had long since learned to focus on her emotions and inborn talents. And right now, her senses said this one's blood was new.

Seeing large empty crates and garbage bins trapping the vampire's escape, Jaden took a step forward. She moved easily, used to confronting his kind. Again her wrist brushed near her waist, seeking the comfort of her meager weapons. Again she remembered she brought nothing. She didn't want to change her mind. She didn't want to alarm the young one before her. If he ran from her, she would have to start her search anew.

No, Jaden bemused in silent apathy, *this is what I came for. At least he seems to possess some dignity. I would hate to be bitten by an idiot. How degrading of an end that would be for a legendary hunter.*

Jaden studied the vampire for signs of curiosity. His eyes didn't travel over her form. His attention didn't take in the lines of her face. He waited for her to speak with the silent patience of a statue. The icy blue of his striking eyes didn't reveal any emotions beyond watchfulness.

When the vampire merely continued to stare at her, Jaden said without preamble, "You are a nightstalker, are you not?"

One brow lifted halfway up the vampire's smooth, pale face. It was a small effort, the only one he made in acknowledging her. If Jaden couldn't see his gaze trained on her face, she would've doubted he paid attention. Once more, she started to distrust her senses, but again the sensation of newly turned blood was overwhelmingly strong. If she had to venture a guess, she would say he was maybe fifteen years made at most.

With a groan, she realized her first impression of sight was probably really off. This creature wasn't cold and calculated. By his age, she could only assume he was dumb. Some sick, undead fiend picked a poor, helpless mental patient with the size of Hercules to be its child. No wonder the vampire only stared. No wonder he obeyed her order to release his victim without question. The creature was just another reason to prove she was doing the right thing.

She was tired of seeing and feeling such things as the atrocity before her. She knew what she had spent her life doing, seeing. Jaden wanted to live--in theory. But her life was never a life. She was tired of sensing death, causing it. The grim hold was an apathetic noose around her neck, tightening but never releasing. She was already one of the walking dead in spirit. She wasn't frightened by her own death. Death was her only release. It was her only out. It was the only way she could shut herself off and find any rest.

Shaking her head, she continued in sarcastic disgust, "You are a nightstalker, are you not? A benighted child, a damned soul, possessor of the dark gift?" Jaden paused, waiting to see if any of her words brought recognition to the immovable face. They didn't. With a sigh, she whispered in dejection, "*A vampire.*"

"Nightstalker is a bloodstalker term," the creature answered at leisure. He moved his head a hairbreadth to the side.

Jaden froze at the low rumbling of the vampire's rhythmical voice. His soft words were extremely coherent if not a little bored. They took her by surprise. She saw a swirl of color begin to enter his eyes. It slivered green and then faded. Something that she hadn't felt in a long time threatened to awaken in her--curiosity. Jaden suppressed it. A whirlwind of confusion endangered her senses. She felt him trying to enter her mind, to put thoughts into it. She fought it, focusing herself once more. Maybe this one liked to play games. Maybe he liked to pretend he was older than he truly was. She had seen the arrogance before.

"So it is," she said easily, surprised that he knew the old term. Very rarely was she referred to as a bloodstalker. Still, this creature couldn't possibly sense what she was. Only the old could smell the parentage in her blood.

"Are you hunting me?" A small smirk of amusement tilted the side of his mouth. The very idea seemed to fascinate him. Jaden froze. She still wasn't so sure about her choice in vampires, no matter how she convinced herself she was. Her legs screamed at her to run. Her heart's heady rhythm echoed the plea. This one's confidence compounded by his size was alarming. Jaden's determination took over, refusing to listen to the treacherous urges of her fear.

Without the assuredness of her previous statements, she forced the bitterness from her tone. "No, I don't wish to kill you. I am no hunter."

Silently she added, *not any more.*

The old vampire studied the brave woman before him. He knew what she was, could feel the strength inside her veins. Just as he could tell she wasn't there to try and harm him. Upon turning to greet her interruption, an interruption he felt long before she spoke, he had taken a brief glance over her frame. She was pretty but not glamorous. Her body was athletic and well used.

However, it was nothing he hadn't seen before. What captured his attention the most was the peculiar shade of deep jade that glittered dispassionately in her eyes. And, at his age, that anything captured his attention was unusual. Those eyes were the only thing that kept him from abandoning her for the sovereignty of the night.

Narrowing his gaze, he unleashed his powerful thoughts, trying to pry into her mind. He could feel a well of passionless emotions inside of her. He saw her shiver, becoming entranced within his gaze. In the brief second he was inside her thoughts he detected one word drowning out all the others, *death.* And then she kicked him out. He hid his humor, knowing that if he wanted to he could force himself back in, but he found waiting for her to reveal herself much more diverting. Beside, he didn't like to feel inside of humans. They were too messy, too unorganized, too *alive*.

"Then why do you seek me out, mortal?" he queried enigmatically, showing the first hint of interest at her intrusion. It was clear she wasn't merely trying to save his victim from the bite. She hadn't given the man a second glance.

The vampire's body moved with all the enthusiasm of a faded marble statue anchored to a slab of stone. A slight turn of his lips indicated he smiled more than frowned. Jaden felt a dim sense of loathing awaken in him. He was disgusted with her. He despised her taking up his time, as endless as that time was for him. The insult stung slightly, but she refused to allow herself the luxury of caring. Lifting her chin proudly, she directed her boldest stare.

Choosing to ignore the pointed question he directed at her, she shifted her weight on her hips. With false sweetness and concern in her voice, she muttered in a coquettish sulk, "You haven't eaten. I just scared away your meal."

The vampire's smile faded just as deceptively as it had formed.

Jaden trembled as his gaze finally moved from their fixed position to take her in. Even fully clothed she felt violated by the concentrated inspection. So intense was his probing, she was sure he could see through her clothing. Was she mistaken, or did his eyes linger too long on her breasts?

Before she had time to cross over and slap him, he said, unconcerned, "So you have. I'll find it again. Good eve."

He turned to leave her. Jaden's heart leapt in her chest at the hasty dismissal. She couldn't wait any longer. She couldn't last another day. Crossing forward in growing desperation, she stopped him from leaving.

The vampire's gaze again found her as she drew close. He could've escaped her if he truly wanted. But, he didn't. He would never fully understand why he didn't. Perhaps it was her bravery in facing him. Perhaps it was her acceptance of his existence--acceptance without trembling or fear.

Pulling back her collar, Jaden offered her neck to him. Tensing, she said, "Here's your meal, vampire. Drink it and be done."

His eyes darted naturally to her slender neck. He focused on her artery, protruding from under the thin veil of skin. It was a tempting offer, one that his teeth were capable of taking. It would take no effort to pierce the flesh. He could hear her blood rushing. He could smell its sweet scent-- alluring, proud yet tainted by her emotions. But, to Jaden's surprise, he didn't instantly bite her. He held back as if he cared not to taste her blood. His brow lifted vaguely.

Unbidden, her hand dropped to her side. Her body stung considerably at the blatant rejection of her offer. Her cheeks flamed in anger. Damn him! Her blood was the best thing he would ever be offered--strong, pure, half vampire!

She smelled faint musk on the air--the scent of death and decay--but the stirrings of it were so faint that she only imagined she could smell the grave on him as she had with others. With this creature there was more. There was a hint of freshness and breeze to his odor and the impression of freshly churned earth, not dust.

Meeting his eyes as they bore into her, she shuddered. Her head was forced back on her shoulders to accommodate his height. She felt dwarfed by the girth of his body. His form did something wicked to her senses, awakening them with the stirrings of longing and suppressed desires. Her mind screeched in warning that all was not as it should be. She ignored the reasoning, concentrating desperately on her intuition.

The vampire wore a long dark jacket. Its ordinary lines weren't spectacular, though it had an older look to the style. Small buttons worked their way down the front, hanging open from their holes. Beneath the coat was a simple burgundy knit shirt over dark pants--too tightly made by Jaden's critical estimation. In the shadows she couldn't make out if they were constructed from leather or denim.

He was a handsome creature--well formed though intimidating. He seemed bred for battle. *Or for other things,* her treacherous mind entered. Jaden gulped, instantly thinking of silken sheets on a large, thick bed. A wave of sensations flooded her, like the forbidden caress of cooled silk and velvet to heated flesh. A fog threatened as she looked him over with a more discerning eye than before.

Her gaze flitted over him with the concentration of a wine taster examining a glass of port before bringing it to his mouth to taste. Thick arms connected to the crowded muscles of his shoulders, bunching to a neck worthy of an All-American football player. By the snug burgundy, she could see the outline of muscle as raw and unyielding as formed steel. Shadows hid his waist. Jaden didn't need to see his stomach to tell it would be just as muscled as the rest of him. His very presence was pure potency. Blinking heavily, the fog lifted. All of his kind was picturesque. If her head were easily turned by beauty she would've been killed long ago.

His dispassionate eyes studied her for long moments, unhurried by time. To him, he had an eternity to answer her bidding. At length, the creature began to chuckle. The sound was cold and heartless. Jaden's head snapped up, alarmed to be caught studying him so long. She sneered. He watched in silent ridicule, as if he knew the images that filtered inside her imagination--as if he had purposefully put them there for her.

"You seek me out, but you do not like me, do you?" His voice came to her lighter than a whisper. For an insane moment, Jaden thought to only hear the words in her head. She didn't see his lips move. She had no time to wonder, as he said, "You wish me to turn you. That is why you have come, eh, conceited mortal?"

"No," she responded without hesitation. The vampire's tone was soft, never rising above a whisper. Jaden couldn't make out an accent on his words though she detected there might be one if he spoke louder.

The vampire drew back in obvious wonder. Emotion trickled for the first time from his expression. His initial shock was only overshadowed by his obvious doubt. She waited for him to speak, disinterested as he seemed. His lips didn't move.

"I want you to kill me," Jaden stated without remorse. The hard set of her jaw told the truth of her words. Once more, she offered her throat with a slight turn of her head. "How often is it your meal comes to you? Take a night off from hunting, vampire. Do me this small favor. My blood will be your reward."

If her statement surprised him, he didn't show it. A lazy smile curled his mouth. His lips parted slightly, revealing the sharp point of fangs, two on top, two smaller on bottom. Jaden took the detail in stride, automatically narrowing down in her mind what tribe he may be descendent of.

Moving to pull insistently at her collar, Jaden paused. Without thought, she questioned, "How old are you?"

"Eternally twenty eight," he answered in a low grumble.

"That's not--" she began.

"Would you like me to mesmerize you?" the vampire interrupted. He lifted his hand with an easy elegance to hover near her face before leaning in to cup her cheek. His touch was gentle and cool against her flesh. He stroked her with a deceiving tenderness. "I could take the pain away. I could take everything away."

Jaden shivered at the self-confidence of his touch. He had come so close so quickly. His nearness overwhelmed. His contact took her by surprise. Not even her uncle dared to lay a hand on her with such tenderness. Tears threatened her at his gentle hold, welling up from her heart. She blinked the moisture away. But why wouldn't she cry at this moment, this most intimate moment of death? And why shouldn't it be tender? It was after all the most intimate of acts for her--more so than sex or love.

For when you killed, you took a part of that being with you. The blood, the moment couldn't be rid of. It jaded your thoughts, your soul. It marked you and marred you. It tore out a piece of you, carving a home deep inside. Jaden knew it, felt it as sure as anything each time a vampire ashed by her hand. So she supposed that when she died, part of her would forever stay in this silent, mocking creature before her.

Instinct told her to fight him, to push his hand away and strike him. But she had brought no weapons. There was no turning back, and Jaden wasn't one to easily change her path once the decision was made. She knew what she was doing this night, seeking out the killer. She wanted to die. She wanted the curse of her life to be over.

"You have that power?" Jaden questioned in mild astonishment, suddenly remembering his offer to mesmerize her. "But you seem so young."

"I have that power," he acknowledged quietly. Jaden made the mistake of searching his ice-chipped gaze. She felt herself easily drawn into the mysterious, enticing power of him. She felt her will slip. Her emotions calmed. Her heartbeat slowed to an easy thump. The vampire invaded her thoughts, probing and prying to open her mind. Her limbs went numb with a strange lethargy. Gulping, she turned her head to the side to expose her neck. He let her eyes escape the depths of his mind's hold.

"Just get it over with. My blood is strong. You'll enjoy it."

At that the creature grinned. Huskily, he murmured, sending chills over her flesh, "I'm sure I will."

A wave of torment overcame her at the promise in his words. Her body ached and pulled towards him. If he had been a man, she would've done her best to attract him. She would've used him and discarded him. Her hands fluttered up, finding hold in the barrier of his chest. He was as brawny as she first imagined. Her fingers trembled in frightened anticipation, so intimate was his nearness. It was strange to be so close to someone and not try to fight them, especially if that someone was undead. His closeness made her quiver. Jaden knew there was no affection in his cold limbs. She knew that he cared nothing for her, but she drank in the comfort of him anyway.

Death didn't frighten her. His potent, masculine nearness did. She waited for the first sting of his teeth, knowing it must be the worst. She had prepared her whole life for this moment, knowing it to be a hazard of the job. It was why she chose to end this way rather than a faster method. At least by this death, she was saving one last innocent life--the man whose death she interrupted.

The vampire renewed his hold on her face in a stroking caress. His fingers brushed over her ear to tilt her further to the side. Jaden closed her eyes, waiting for the draining of her limbs.

Slowly, and with drawn out precision, he pulled her forward. Muscle folded around her body as he loomed over her, pressed intimately against her. She felt the brush of lips on her skin, pulling across the tautness of her sweating flesh. The summer's heat engulfed them, but the chill of his body sent a pleasant coolness over her.

Just a few more seconds, she thought. Her heartbeat sped once more. He pressed a kiss to her throat. Jaden jolted in surprise at the softness of it. When she inhaled, her breath came in a staggered pant. He kissed her again, his tongue dragging over her flesh. Desire flooded her limbs, a quick outburst that put strength in her weakened knees. When he didn't claim her blood, she pulled indecisively back. She gazed at his mouth, expecting to find it stained crimson. It was not.

Instantly, the soft glowing haze of his eyes caught her. For a moment, she thought she felt desire within him--so soft and gentle was his gaze on her. She could almost believe he cared for her, desired her, loved her.

"One last kiss before death," he whispered. His breath fanned over her cheek with the caress of a man. Passion awakened in her limbs, where before she was sure she'd been dead. As she heard his voice, she wasn't sure if it was him speaking or her imagination conjuring up words. "I always kiss those as precious as you before I kill them."

Jaden couldn't find her words. The pleasure of what he said befuddled her mind. She was lost in the haze of a dream. Her voice became locked inside her chest. With a pant, she watched him come towards her with great care. Stiffening, she awaited the brush of his mouth on hers. His mouth parted as if to deepen the intentions of his kiss. Jaden instinctively pressed her lips together in denial. It was the only way she could fight him.

But, as the soft velvet of skin touched her, she gasped in wonder. His mouth was not as cold as she imagined and his lips did not taste of blood though she had seen him eating. Her hands traveled easily up his chest to the sides of his face in pure acceptance.

The vampire leaned over her, overwhelming her with his size, his strength. His fingers found hold, twining beneath her low ponytail. Taking advantage of her parted mouth, he rubbed his lips along hers twice to test her resolve before opening his mouth wide. With the precision of a surgeon, he cut his teeth deep into her lip with a needle-like strike to draw blood.

Jaden released a sharp breath of dismay. Her eyes rounded in horror at the pain. She pushed viciously at him. The vampire let her go and she stumbled back from him in confusion. The strength she borrowed from him brutally drained from her, leaving her numb and disoriented. Watching the iciness of his eyes, she saw the light fading from them. He had mesmerized her to his will, tricked her into kissing him like a pliant fool. Jaden's face turned red in anger. Touching her lips, she growled furiously.

Flicking her tongue over the injury, she said incredulously, as she tasted blood. "You *marked* me!"

"I did," he said with annoying self-possession.

"Why? That wasn't the deal!" She caught the amusement filtering his gaze. He was laughing at her. And no wonder! She had made it easy for him.

"There was no deal," he flung back effortlessly. "You sought me out. I never said I wanted you." Licking his fangs in a drawn out show of tasting her blood, he added purposefully, "Mmmm, *dhampir*."

"How?"

"Your blood tells your story." The vampire gave her a wide smile. She would've thought him overjoyed if not for the threat of boredom shading his eyes.

"But you're not old enough to know that. I made sure that you weren't!" she hissed. This couldn't be happening. He couldn't know what she was. But, somehow, he did. And he marked her as his own! Now no other would dare to touch her to finish the job he started. This one would be able to track her wherever she went. His affront was worse than death. It was a death sentence without the release of an ending. She felt the noose tightening around her.

"Mayhap you mistook--" he offered, his look harboring on the outermost edge of repentance.

"Finish it," she commanded fiercely. Hatred bubbled within her as she looked at him. She wanted him dead for what he dared to do to her. If he let her go, it would impede her job. Now, she had no choice. "Finish it now or--"

"Or?" he taunted.

"I'll kill you," Jaden retorted hotly.

"You will try," the creature countered, never losing composure.

"I'll succeed," she threatened. "I always finish my task."

"You will assuredly fail if you come after me."

Jaden growled, realizing his banter was just another way for him to toy with her. No matter what she said, he would respond in kind with his overbearing contempt and disdain. Not wasting any more of her night on words, she darted forward. Her foot struck the creature in the chest. She was enraged, and the desire to spill blood overtook her.

The attack caught him by surprise. His face contorted from amusement to annoyance. He stumbled back slightly from the force of her assault. Stiff as her kick had been, it didn't faze him. With a weary sigh, he stood. Brushing the dusty footprint from his chest with the back of his hand, he shook his head.

Jaden ignored the warning in his eyes. Flinging her wrist at his throat, she attacked. Quickly, his annoyance faded and he smiled at her--an aggravatingly handsome expression that drove her to distraction. The vampire blocked her with an elegant lift of his arm. Jaden turned with another sweeping kick. It missed its aim, but hit his stomach. She was rewarded with a satisfying grunt.

The vampire blocked several more of her blows with easy movements of his body. He had the gift of speed on his side as he moved from her path. Jaden's kick ended on a trash can, denting the metal bin. Spinning on her heels, she backed him into a corner, knowing deep down that he didn't return upon her with full force. She became more aggressive in her desperation. If he wouldn't bite her, then maybe he would beat her to death.

Landing a punch on his jaw, she jeered, "Scared of a little mortal? Scared of fighting back?"

The vampire snarled at the series of annoying stings that she dealt him. With one controlled flick of his hand, he smacked her cheek, sending her flying backward into a brick wall. The breath oozed from Jaden's lungs as she landed prone on the ground. With that one blow, the fight was over. He had won.

Jaden rested motionless on the concrete, gulping for air. Wet pebbles pressed into her skin and the smell of dirty streets entered her nostrils. When she finally managed a feeble push up from the ground, the vampire was standing above her. His eyebrow arched in question. Jaden shook her head.

"No," she panted, falling back to sit against the wall. She brushed her cheek on her shoulder, knocking loose the dirt and gravel. Her spine ached as if it had been snapped. She couldn't even muster the will to glare at him, though she hated him enough to do so. "I'm done fighting you."

"Good," he whispered. The vampire turned on his heel to leave. He was completely unharmed.

"Wait," Jaden called breathlessly. When he turned to her with an exasperated sigh, she said, "Just one thing, nightstalker."

"What?" he rumbled. The dawn was drawing near.

"Your name," she sighed. "At least tell me your name so that I may know who bested me this night."

The vampire was not fooled by her false modesty. They both knew she didn't consider herself bested. She would just bide her time before coming after him again. He could see the pride shining in the jade green of her eyes, though she turned them down and tried to hide it. This was not a woman who liked to admit defeat.

"Tyr," he whispered as he jumped into the air. His body seemed to dissolve into a strange mist as it filtered over the dank alleyway. In an instant he was gone, disappearing into the night.

Jaden shuddered in disbelief over the whole tragically horrible experience. For a long time she didn't move, staring after him into space, the back of her head pressed against the brick wall. Her legs wobbled when she moved them. Her body was numbed from his punch. A throbbing angered her cheek. She did not move to touch it. Finally, as the lightness of dawn loomed, she pushed up from the ground and swore, "Next time I'll be ready for you Tyr. And I'll make you regret not finishing what you started. This is one dhampir you should never have marked."

Chapter Two

"Gentlemen," Alan 'Mack' MacNaughton acknowledged good-naturedly as he stood from his large oak desk. His very presence demanded attention. He smiled politely, giving the two men before him a confident tilt of his head. "There is nothing to worry about. I assure you that you and your wives will be perfectly safe within one of our specially developed vehicles and one of my men will be with you at all times to assure your well being."

Alan MacNaughton was a slender man with unmistakable elegance and grace. He embodied everything that those with money and affluence strove for. His soft features were carved without the stone cast of hardship. His dark brown hair, sprinkled only lightly with gray at the temples, and light eyes added an amiable appeal to his complexion that belied the cool confidence of his true nature. He was a charming man, pleasant to be around. If he wanted you to like him, you most likely would. He used his charm and grace to his fullest advantage. Mack, as he was called amongst his peers, was a ruthless businessman. His business was vampires.

"That is good to hear, Mack," a swarthy man answered. He had dark hair and eyes. "Marianne insists this is what she wants. It's our second anniversary and I don't want her to be disappointed. Cynthia Rothwell told her what you did for them. And I'll be damned if I'll be showed up by Henry Rothwell."

"She won't be, Sizemore," Mack answered with confidence. His smile invited their trust. "You have my full assurance."

"Good," the swarthy Sizemore said. He motioned to his companion with a small grin and said, "Hell, Stevens, if our wives like it maybe we should bring out those two girls we met in Vegas last week. I bet the four of us could have one hell of a time."

Stevens, a tall slender man with a long nose and hawk-like eyes laughed in return. With a slow blink, he nodded in agreement. He didn't speak much, leaving words to his blustering friend.

Sizemore glanced back at Mack and explained, "My wife would never go for your more 'elaborate' packages, but what this wildcat redhead I picked up couldn't do...."

The man left his words unsaid, but the sexual implication behind his eyes as he winked knowingly told more than his words could have. An obscured chuckle escaped his lips, joined by his companion's lighter laugh.

"What do you say, Mack? Will you give us a discount for the second trip?" Sizemore asked. By his clothing it was obvious he and his companion had no concern about money. Like most rich people, he enjoyed negotiating a bargain.

Before answering, Mack leaned down and pushed a button on his intercom. No voice answered the soft buzz. Lightly, he indulged, "Sure. But just because I like you."

The men laughed in reeling excitement. The library door opened to acknowledge the summons. Mack waved his hand.

"Gentlemen," Mack began. "This is Tom Carter. He will be going with you on your little adventure."

The men reached out, shaking Tom's hand with enthusiasm.

"If you'll follow me," Tom said. "I'll go over the details of what you would like to see. And," he paused with a pointed grin to Mack, "if you desire I might even arrange for you to pull the trigger yourself, so to speak, for an additional price."

The men murmured in agreeable excitement.

"What about Champagne for the ladies?" Sizemore asked. "And scotch for us men?"

"And dinner afterwards," Stevens added quietly, talking more to his friend than to the group.

"All will be taken care of," Tom assured with a bob of his fair head. "If you have any preferences feel free to tell me as we go over the final details."

"Yes," Mack acclaimed with a wave of his hand. "Follow Tom. There are just a few forms to fill out and then he'll help you transfer your payment to my account."

The two men quickly took their leave with many thanks. As they were departing, Sizemore boomed, "So you actually do this for a living, son? By George, what an adventure! If I wasn't born so damned rich, I like to think that I might have become a vampire hunter. In my college days I was quite the experienced boxer...."

When the door closed behind his clients, muffling the blustering man's words, Mack smiled in self-satisfaction. His eyes narrowed. His face became less charming now that he was alone. Slowly, he walked back to his large oak desk.

The tall ceiling of his library curved high overhead with Renaissance women painted on the wooden panels. The dark wood of the shelves housed endless volumes of books and artifacts. It was the pinnacle of his written collection. Large drapes hung from ceiling to floor, covering the crosshatched panes of gigantic windows. Tastefully expensive artwork decked the walls. A sculpture nestled on the planked wood floor and a thick Oriental rug gave relief to the dark wood.

Lifting the lid on his cigar box, Mack helped himself to an imported cigar. Smoke curled around him as he made his way around his desk to his computer. With a click of a few buttons, he brought up his account. Then, sitting at the leather chair before his desk, he flashed a wide, dreamlike smile as he waited patiently for the money to transfer.

* * * *

Jaden stretched her arms over her head as she wearily climbed the steps to the second level of her uncle's Upper East Side apartment. Mack owned the building, reserving many of the rooms below his penthouse for the men who worked for him. He liked to keep his employees close and being above so many talented vampire killers was an added perk in his line of business.

On the first level of the penthouse was the open main hall, showcasing the curling staircase and railing along the upper hallway. The marble covered floor gleamed with understated elegance, the swirling cream pattern and dark wood was an ongoing theme in the apartment. To the right, the servants worked and even lived on the first level alongside the kitchen and utility rooms. Jaden never went beyond the hall in that direction.

Next to the kitchen was a large entertainment room. No one ever watched television in the house. Their lives were too interesting without it. But the large flat screen and a leather couch were kept there nonetheless. If not for the servants they would've accumulated dust long ago.

To her left was the dining room. Mack often held dinner parties for those of higher rank who worked for him. Jaden made a point of being unavailable on such occasions. Those of his men who didn't know her would frequently gain too much encouragement in drink and find themselves asking the rudest questions about her heritage and every one of them wanted to see what she was like in bed. She made it a rule never to be with anyone who knew what she was. She wouldn't be a game to the lot of immature boys Mack employed.

Jaden made her way quietly up the stairs. She ignored the long windows at the top of the staircase showing the brilliance of the familiar New York skyline. She had lived with her uncle for many years, growing up in the luxury of his many homes. But to her the luxury wasn't what it would appear to most. To her, it was a place to crash after endless nights of training and working had taken its toll.

Nowadays, she rarely stayed in the same house as Mack. Her work carried her all over North America and occasionally overseas. She lived out of hotel suites and boarding houses. She didn't mind. She liked the travel and she was left to her own, which she preferred. And if she ever decided to have a meaningless affair then so be it. The men she picked rarely spoke her language. If they did it was usually broken and she would be gone before they woke up the next morning. Not that she did it often.

In the highest level of the penthouse were the bedrooms--hers and Mack's only. Her uncle didn't invite guests in the house. He liked his privacy too much. There was a library and each of them had their own bathrooms off the hall. There was a small room resembling a study. Jaden knew her uncle sometimes used it for business.

However, her preferred area was the gym. It was an empty room with a wooden floor and a wall filled with weaponry. Mack had them installed in all his houses for her when she was a girl. Jaden favored the openness of space. If only the penthouse had been out of the city, it would've been her favorite home.

Jaden frowned, slowing her steps as she came to the top of the stairs. She heard voices, but couldn't make out the words. Seeing Tom coming from her uncle's library, she moved out of sight. It was too late. Tom saw her. He gave her a polite nod of acknowledgment, but the greeting didn't erase the coldness in his eyes. She didn't bother to return the pretense.

She waited until he led the two men with him away, not wanting to be forced into smiling for her uncle's friends. No doubt they would wish to impress her with their bank accounts. She shivered. When she heard a door close above her she moved to the library and wearily pushed her way in.

Mack's eyes met hers instantly. Jaden didn't even pretend to smile.

"Who was that with Tom?" she asked in distraction. For the hundredth time since picking herself off the alley floor she flicked her tongue over her stinging bottom lip. The mark was still there. She grimaced.

"Just a couple of men who lost their sisters to a vampire. They wished to donate a large, anonymous sum to the organization," Mack answered easily. He did not elaborate and he knew Jaden wouldn't ask him to. He leaned forward in his chair and stroked his keyboard with a decisive punch of his fingers. The computer screen cleared.

Jaden shook her head. She always knew her uncle's venture was well funded. She just didn't know how. And, frankly, she didn't care to ask.

"Do I need to take care of it?" she asked, distracted.

"No. I'll put the guys on it," he answered. "It's simple enough."

Mack studied his niece for a long time. He couldn't ignore the large bruise forming on her jaw. It wasn't a spectacular sight seeing her thus. She always came home a little banged up from her fights. Luckily, due to her unique bloodline, she had a high tolerance for pain and quick recoveries. Beyond the bruises, Jaden was a beautiful woman just like his sister had been. She had strong, Scottish cheekbones, a smooth pale complexion and hair of luxurious dark brown with just a hint of red. But what made his young niece striking was her eyes the color of precious jade. Those she had been given from her father.

When Jaden was a girl, he and a small group of scientists had tested the limits of her abilities. It was ironic that the one feature she carried from her father--her magnificent eyes--was the one feature on her that was practically normal in function.

Seeing his unusually long perusal, Jaden frowned. "What is it, Mack?"

"You look so much like you mother, Jade," he murmured with a shake of his head. He kept his real thoughts from her.

Jaden ignored his words. She didn't like to talk about her parents. Instead, she crossed over to his desk. Taking a seat in a comfortable leather chair, she asked indifferently, "Tom still angry?"

"Do you blame him?" her uncle asked. He reached over to pour a glass of scotch. He offered it to Jaden. She took it gratefully. Gulping the contents down in one swallow, she set the glass down on the desk with a decisive clink.

"No," she grumbled. And she wasn't sorry for it. "I would be pissed off too, if I'd been beaten up by a girl."

"Jade," Mack scolded lightly. His scowl couldn't last. His eyes turned fondly over her emotionless face. With a sigh, he whispered, "You've been insolent since girlhood. I remember your tutors nearly pulling their hair out at your quick, sarcastic wit."

"Hum," she mumbled, showing no particular fondness for the same memory.

Mack cleared his throat. "You still haven't given me a full report of what happened in New Orleans. If you told me, maybe I could talk to Tom and smooth things out. He is one of my best men and I would like it if you would work together."

"And I won't give you a full report either," she answered evenly with a yawn. "The vampire is dead. That is the report. Type it up yourself. Or hand me a pen and I'll write it down for you."

Mack chuckled, "All right, Jade. You win. I'll stop asking. But will you consider working with To--"

"No," she broke in before he could finish. Wryly, she added, "I would be too tempted to let the vampires have him."

"Then what about Rick? You seemed to like him when I first lured him away from the Marines," Mack continued to try and persuade her. Jaden smiled ruefully, shaking her head in denial before the words were completed. Mack sighed and let the matter drop.

"How's the shoulder?" her uncle asked instead of prying. He suspected something happened between his niece and the man. Jaden never had much to say when he mentioned Rick Fletcher. And Rick was just as uncomfortably quiet.

"Doesn't hurt." She shrugged, shifting awkwardly. After what happened in Louisiana, she wasn't sure she trusted her uncle completely. But she wasn't about to admit it to anyone.

"And your jaw?"

Jaden scowled at the reminder. For a moment she had forgotten. Lightly, she touched her face. Wincing, she drew her hand to fall back on the arm of the chair. Wrinkling her nose, she said, "It's nothing."

"Need a doctor?"

"No," she answered just as wryly. A small smile threatened her lips but never surfaced. A flash of ice blue eyes flickered through her mind, disturbing yet calm.

"Who were you tracking?" Mack asked, busying himself with the papers on his desk. Casually, he placed them in a folder and turned to put them into his safe hidden beneath a decorative sundial. Jaden watched him curiously, but couldn't see how he opened it. "I haven't given you an assignment for months."

"Just felt like a bit of a spar," Jaden lied. Before he could call her on it, she rushed, "Have you ever heard of a vampire named Tyr?"

"Tyr what?"

"Just Tyr." Jaden again shrugged.

"I can't say that I have," Mack answered thoughtfully. Shaking his head after silent deliberation, he asked, "How old? It is so hard to log all the new ones. It seems like someone is going about building an army of late. The guys have been running into a lot of newly turned."

"I'm not sure how old. I just heard his name mentioned and wanted to know if he was worth worrying about." Jaden stood, crossing over to the expanse of old books lining the wall. Running her fingers over the volumes, she stopped at a thin leather bound record book. Pulling it down, she flipped open the yellowing pages. After careful searching, she sighed, "I don't see him on this list."

Jaden snapped the book shut and slid it back into place.

"If he's one of the old he more than likely would be," Mack answered. "That list was taken directly from the vampire tribe's own records in the 1700's. If he isn't listed, he must be a young one. I'd say he was nothing to worry about."

"I'm not so sure. Maybe it is a nickname for one of these others," she said quietly. She again reached for the book and carried it with her to the chair. She flipped through it, ignoring the crossed out names signifying the vampire was confirmed dead. Seeing the name of Bhaltair still boldly displayed, she ran her finger over it lightly before moving on. "And I really have doubts about the thoroughness of the tribal council's record keeping ability. How do you know this list is an honest account?"

"The source is fairly reliable," he murmured.

"I doubt it," she clipped. "The only source I would call reliable is one of the tribal leaders themselves. And they wouldn't turn on their own kind."

"Let's just see." Mack sat at his desk and started typing. He ignored her words about the council. "Tyr, you say. T-I-R. Nothing."

"Try Tyr, T-Y-R," Jaden murmured in distraction as she turned another page.

"Ah," Mack said. "Here we are. You're right. It must be a nickname. It says here that Tyr is the Norse God of war and justice, son of Odin. He carries a spear in his left hand and is missing his right hand. It was bitten off by a wolf, Fenrir."

"That makes no sense," Jaden muttered coming to her feet. She thought of the vampire in the alley. He did resemble a Viking God of sorts, though he still possessed two hands. "None of the young ones would pick such a name. They always call themselves so-and-so the bloody or the mace, the hammer, whatever weapons have you."

"Someone must be teasing you, Jaden," Mack mused, leaning back. "Maybe one of the guys is playing a prank to cheer you up."

"I don't think so." She scratched behind her ear. She licked her lip. It was no prank. She was marked.

"Wait, Tyr." Mack suddenly sat up. He pressed his forefinger thoughtfully to his lips. "I think I have seen that spelling somewhere before."

Within moments Mack pulled a large tomb of a book from the highest shelf. Dropping it on the desk, he pulled it open.

"What's this?" Jaden asked. She eyed the French words she couldn't read.

"An old book of myths that I bought several years ago in India," he explained. Mack flipped through several more pages before finding the one he wanted. "Here. The Dark Knights."

"Dark Knights?" she repeated with a doubtful chuckle.

"Yes," Mack murmured before translating. "The Dark Knights are a legendary band of enforcers created by the vampire council in the year 888 AD. They number eight, one from each of the existing tribes. It says that if the vampire council of elders is the political force behind the vampire nation, then the knights are their elite military. Not much is known about these dreaded soldiers of the darkness except that their numbers were chosen by the council after rigorous testing, their existence is well guarded and they are feared by not only mortals, but by vampires. They are the only creatures, aside from the council, that are allowed to feed on their own kind."

"A cannibalistic knight?" Jaden questioned in bemusement. She rolled her eyes in disbelief. "Vampire's can't feed on their own kind. I thought you said the dying blood would cause them harm. Besides, it contradicts all we know of the council. They would never allow it. By all accounts, they are too greedy for power and would never permit such a creature to exist. One of their sacred laws is that no vampire can harm another vampire, especially from the same tribe."

"Ah," Mack argued for the sake of being controversial. "In theory, if the council chooses them, then they might be allowed special privileges."

"But to break a sacred law?" Jaden countered skeptically. She shook her head, "What else does it say?"

"It references some old text. It is said that they act with ruthless force and that their decisions in any matter are final, unless overruled by the council elders for some spectacular reason. The existence of the knights is widely accepted as a myth between vampires and mortals alike. They are generally not believed as anything more than an old folklore created in the superstitious times of the Middle Ages to get new vampire children to obey their creators. See attached list for names and known descriptions."

Mack turned the large page. Jaden leaned over for a closer look. Touching the small print, she found a word she recognized. "This is a list of the eight tribes. The *Moroi* tribe must have created Morana. The *Myertovjec's* knight is called Chernobog." With a smirk, she added sarcastically, "That's a pretty name."

Mack chuckled at her cynicism as he walked over to his computer. He began typing in the names she read.

"Ah, the *Llugut* knight is Aleksander," Jaden continued with a deepening frown. "*Vrykolatios* is Hades. The *Vrykolakas* is Ares. Are you getting the feeling these were all named after Gods of some sort?"

"What about the name Tyr?" Mack asked.

Jaden gulped, freezing as her eyes picked out the name. Weakly, she whispered, "Yes, he is the *Drauger* knight."

"It would make sense. The tribe is said to be of Nordic decent."

"Ah, Shiva is of the *Rakshasa* and Osiris is of the *Impudula*." Jaden looked up from the book, hoping her last words didn't quiver too tellingly. "What do you think?"

"I think someone is playing with you. In all my research I have never heard mention of a Dark Knight actually existing. Occasionally they are blamed for a vampire's death, but nothing is ever proven. And in the old superstitions it was said that they killed hunters amongst the gypsies. But really, the deaths could be linked to any number of things, not necessarily a Dark Knight."

"You mean *dhampirs*," Jaden said as quietly as possible, thinking of the gypsy myths. A fear gripped her heart. She knew the stories of the old dhampirs. She knew what had been done to them--especially the hunters.

They were tortured for days and saved each time they were brought near death. When aided by the healing properties of vampire blood drops, the process could last for years--decades. When he didn't answer, she added, "Like me."

Mack swallowed uncomfortably. Not meeting her eye, he nodded. "Yes, but it has to be a joke. It isn't as if your profession is low profile in the underworld. They probably revived the old name to scare you."

"Can you translate this description here, just in case," Jaden asked. She pointed to the short paragraph following Tyr's name.

"Sure." Mack came over to her and read. "Tyr is known as a heartless and cruel warrior. He uses his strength to execute his duty and to obtain whatever information he was sent to acquire."

"That's all?" Jaden asked in sinking dread. She stared at the foreign words, wishing she could translate them herself. A suspicion crept over her as she noticed the word *vampijorivic*, little vampire. It was another name for dhampir. There was more her uncle wasn't telling her. Memorizing the page number, she turned her eyes away.

"It pretty much says the same thing for all of them," Mack answered soothingly.

Jaden wasn't concerned with the rest of them at the moment. Wearily licking the wound on her lip, she thought in dejection, *Boy, do I know how to pick the good ones. It seems I can't even get my own suicide right.*

Even as she thought it, she wasn't as ready for death as she had been at the beginning of the night. She knew it should have shaken her how close she had come. But not being as eager to end it didn't mean she wanted to continue on. She was thoroughly exhausted--tired of the isolation, tired of being forced to hunt, tired of feeling too much of the wrong thing and especially tired of living with the guilt of what she had allowed to happen.

Seeing she was unconvinced, Mack laid an arm around Jaden's shoulders. In a low whisper, he murmured, "You know I would never let you get hurt. You are my only family and I love you."

"I know." Jaden pulled away, unused to the affection. Mack let her go. "So you think it is a hoax?"

"I would stake my life on it." Mack gave an assured nod.

Jaden sighed. "All right then. I'm off to bed. I've had enough excitement for the night. I'll see you at dusk before I go out."

"Jade," her uncle said, stopping her from retreating. "Why don't you stay in tomorrow? Or maybe we could go out together--catch a play. I can get tickets to anything you want."

"No," she said.

"You should take a break," he said gently. "You've been working yourself too hard."

"Have you no assignments for me? You mentioned the guys had their hands full with an army of young ones."

"It is nothing the guys can't handle on their own," he denied her request for work. "Although, if you would like something to do, some scientists in Russia have come up with a new weapon for us to test. It's like a flash bomb. It is lighter to carry than our current light and stronger. I'm thinking of testing it out in the field. If it works, we could all possibly retire. And the good news is that it doesn't harm mortals--just gives them a terrible headache."

"Hum," Jaden mused. Such weaponry seemed like cheating to her. Dropping a light into a den of vampires took the sport out of the hunt. She much preferred hand to hand combat.

"You could help me test it, if you like," he offered again.

Jaden shook her head. Seeing that she wasn't interested, Mack frowned.

"I think I'll go to Europe," she decided. In truth she wanted to run as far away as she could from the man who marked her. If he was a Dark Knight, she knew she should be afraid. If he wasn't then he was most likely a lunatic and she still should be scared. Either way, he would be able to find her. If he so chose, he could haunt her shadow for the rest of her nights.

"Great!" Mack exclaimed. "Which house would you like me to ready for you?"

"I don't care. Could you just make the arrangements?" Jaden forced a smile she didn't feel. It would be better if she didn't know where she was going. If she ran into Tyr again, he wouldn't be able to find it in her mind. "And I'll need some cash this time. American is fine. I can exchange it when I get where I'm going."

"The jet won't be available for a few days," Mack said.

"Fine." She yawned noisily, putting on a good show for her uncle. "Then I'll just have to leave in a few days."

Mack waited for her to close the door. When he heard her footfall shuffling away, he picked up his phone. He didn't have to wait long before his call was answered.

"Yeah," came a tired yawn on the other side.

"Rick, Mack," Mack stated. "I want you to trail after Jaden tomorrow night. This is top priority. See where she goes and if she talks to anyone."

"Want me to bring the men?" Rick's response sounded more awake. His military training brought him to quick attention.

"No, go alone. I don't want anyone else knowing she is followed."

"She won't like it," the man answered. Mack could hear the phone being shuffled about as Rick adjusted his headset.

"Don't let her find out," Mack commanded sharply. "There is

something she's not telling us. What the devil happened in New Orleans?"

"Nothing unusual, I told you," Rick defended to the harshness of his employer's tone. "It was completely routine. Duncan didn't give us a fight. Jaden wasn't happy with our intrusion and she beat up Tom. Nothing unusual."

"She didn't say anything about it to you?" Mack queried.

"We don't talk." Rick's voice was hard with what he wouldn't allow said.

"You've got two days to find out what is happening with her. Then I'm sending her off to Europe."

"Done."

"You know, Rick," Mack said. "I think you could use a vacation yourself. How about going with her? I would be pleased if you got close to her."

"She'd never invite me--" Rick began doubtfully. He did not like spying on Jaden. It would be nearly impossible for him to hide his presence from her.

"I'll take care of it. Just be ready to leave." Mack smiled into the phone, not bothering to say good-bye before hanging up. Shaking his head, he whispered, "I'll take care of everything."

* * * *

Jaden couldn't sleep, but she lay in bed anyway. She could sense her uncle's servants moving across the hall outside her bedroom. She could feel them dusting, scrubbing, sighing, scrubbing harder. Their presence was one of the reasons she didn't stay with Mack too often.

Unable to keep up the pretense of falling asleep, Jaden pushed up on the bed and glanced around in the pitch-blackness that surrounded her. Her shoulder shrieked and popped in protest. Gingerly, she rolled it, ignoring the pain the best she could. She couldn't see in the dark, but knew she was alone.

Throwing the covers off of her legs, she crawled out of bed. The sound of her footfall was muffled as she crossed over a thick Persian rug. Instinctively sidestepping a chair as she blindly moved thought the darkness, Jaden didn't break her stride. Reaching out, she grabbed the heavy velvet drapes and gave them a stiff yank. The room was instantly blanketed in daylight.

Jaden blinked in the heavy rays, holding her hand before her face as her eyes adjusted. Turning away from the light, she felt the warmth of the sun on her bare shoulders. It outlined her, eerily casting her shadow over the floor in a long ghoulish stretch of distinctive darkness.

Jaden pulled absently at the string near her waist. It bound the silken pajama pants she had stolen from her uncle's unused collection of clothing. Yawning, she winced as she stretched her hands above her head. Her body was sore from being thrown against the wall, although the aching was nowhere close to matching her injured pride. She couldn't believe the strength of the arrogant vampire. And his speed! She had used some of her best moves on him and Tyr had been completely unaffected.

Jaden's bedroom was decorated to her specifications--a large comfortable bed, a vanity and dresser, plenty of open space and heavy drapes that blocked all traces of the sun when closed. All of her rooms were the same, with a small variant in design and color. Half the time, she didn't even know where she was.

Her uncle paid for everything, allowing her to work. Beyond her credit cards, of which she never saw a bill, she hardly carried cash. She didn't even concern herself with money. She knew that some of the jobs she pulled where paid for by injured parties and Mack kept all of it. The arrangement suited her just fine. Not once had Mack denied her a request. When he died, she was to receive everything--not that she wanted it.

Sitting before the vanity of dark wood, Jaden sighed in frustration. She leaned forward on her elbows, poking wearily at the bruise on her jaw. Already the skin was beginning to yellow around the edges. Suddenly, her mouth began to throb. Leaning into the mirror, she pulled down her bottom lip. Just along the edge were two distinct punctures starting to scab.

Jaden blinked. When she again looked at the mirror, a face glinted before her in the smooth reflection. Jolting back in terror, her chair tipped back, knocking her onto the floor. Her aching back pressed into an uncomfortable combination of chair and carpet. Her breath came in heavy pants. The image had been distinct. It was Tyr. He had found her already.

In the following moments, she felt him next to her as he had been in the alley. His muscled hands gripped to her weaker flesh. She could smell the musk of his body. She could detect the blood in his veins, thick with unspeakable passions, with lust, with death, with horror, and a never-ending need to take. Her skin boldly tingled.

His eyes stayed with her, blinding her to the ceiling, daring her to try and move, daring her to defy his will. She shook her head to whisk the image away. Tears came to her eyes. She was scared. Tyr terrified her. He was nothing like he seemed. She should have known his power the moment she saw him. It coursed through him--bold and taunting like its master. But he had tricked her somehow. He had masked his true self from her, making her believe he was young. Or was she just confused?

Pushing the unkempt waves of her hair back from her face, Jaden tried to calm her thundering heart. It was daytime. There was no way he could come for her now. She assured herself that it was just an illusion, a trick of her overtired mind. Unbidden, her eyes searched for his face again, looking at the arches above her, studying the wood grain for his features. A dark part of her wanted another glimpse, another rush of feeling--even if that feeling was fear. The fear was more real an emotion than the sweetest happiness ever could be.

When she saw nothing, and realized it was for the best if she didn't, Jaden crawled from the floor. Her movements were labored as she righted the chair. Rolling her neck, she avoided looking at the mirror, anxious of what she might again find in it. The yearning inside her, throbbing with temptation in her lip, had to be ignored--like a recovering addict ignores the root of their addiction. She must not think of him. To do so would be to summons him to her. She knew enough of the enigmatic vampire to know that her imagination didn't need anymore fuel tossed onto its raging flame.

Had he been waiting for her in the alley? Did he know she was coming? Was that why he let his victim go so easily at her approach? Was it a trap?

"No," Jaden reasoned to herself. She always talked aloud when nervous. It made her feel not as alone. "It was a coincidence. I'll probably never see him again."

She didn't believe it for a moment. Feeling as if whoever was outside her door had finally gone away, she closed the curtains and ambled back into bed. Her limbs sunk down into the stiff mattress. The tension eased its way out of her unmoving body. Within moments the exhaustion of the long night wore on her and she fell into a labored sleep. But the slumber brought no rest, only erotically charged dreams of a handsome pair of strong hands and tender caresses. And somewhere in the darkness lingered two dangerous eyes, glittering in blue enchantment.

Chapter Three

The consoling shadows of night were not so pleasant in the city. Bright lights from windows glowed like eerie suns through broken panes onto the hard asphalt earth. The yellow, green and red casts of luminescent billboards blighted the already pockmarked street. Cars sped past, honking everywhere until their loudness deafened the sensitive caverns of vampiric ears. The air was foul with rat droppings and smog and human sweat, clouding inside fine-tuned noses with their stench.

Some vampires loved the city--usually the young ones. They loved the blood, the flavor of life, the smell of existence. Tyr hated the city. He hated being around so many blood beings at once. Easily, he could block them from his mind but he needed to search through them to find his *indicium*, his marked one.

Tyr easily picked up the woman's scent at dusk, though her presence never really left him in sleep. His mind searched for his connection to her, waiting for the moment her thoughts were lenient enough to let him in. For a brief moment, his dreams had found her and he had awaken motionless in the confines of his coffin. Now, he streamed through the maze of endless buildings with ease to get to her.

Tyr had to admit she intrigued him--as much as he could be intrigued after so long. In all his many years roaming the earth he had seen many things. But never had he been begged to end someone's life that was not already eaten away by human illness. This dhampir was strong. Her strength and power flowed aromatically through the sweetened perfume of her blood. It was blood he would enjoy drinking.

And, unlike many of her kind, she was not completely run down. Often the dhampirs he found were mind-numbed on mortal drugs--unable to take the gifts they had been given. They were moody and raw, passionate and reckless. He was sure his indicium would possess some of these traits. She did after all seek out death. But the fact that she resisted the pull of degradation meant she was to be feared by his kind. She would be strong and determined in her purpose and, to vampires, she would be most lethal.

Tyr detected instantly her honed skills, even before turning around in the alleyway to acknowledge her intrusion. He knew she was a hunter-- trained to go after his kind. That was why her total defeat piqued his interest. For out of all the vampire clans, he was the most adept at dealing with a dhampir. He had judged, had punished, had read into more vampire children than any other.

Stopping beneath a large stone building, Tyr ignored the doorman who vied for his attention. With a brief, absent wave of his fingers, he ended the man's half-spoken inquiry. The doorman turned away and stood once more at his post completely unaware of the large stranger standing only a few feet away.

Tyr lips curled into a cynical smile. His cold gaze traveled over the building showing little interest in what he saw. He clearly perceived the gargoyle stories above his head. He knew this place well. He scouted it out upon first arriving in the city a couple weeks earlier.

Tyr frowned. Why hadn't he known who the dhampir was? He should have sensed it. His frown did not last as curiosity again pulled within him. Jaden and Alan MacNaughton were the main reasons he found himself in the city. He was sent to watch them and to judge.

The tribal council already had several complaints about Mack MacNaughton. His 'business' dealings were well documented amongst the tribes. He would've been killed years ago, if not for his shifty ways. He surrounded himself constantly by vampire hunters and it was well known that his apartment complexes, along with his many houses, were highly secure against the undead.

Such things did not frighten Tyr. Although younger, less skilled vampires had a right to be anxious. Many had tried to kill Mack and just as many had failed. Yes, Mack MacNaughton's reputation preceded him. All Tyr had to do was to clarify and confirm the reports for the council. Nevertheless, it was not solely Mack who Tyr was sent to investigate. It was his niece.

Jaden was more of an enigma. There were many reports of her killings--very numerous compared to other dhampirs. Yet there were just as many reports of her leniency towards the vampire race. With so many conflicting accounts it was debated as to what they should do with her.

During her early years, Jaden's progress had been well tracked. But, as she grew, Mack kept her hidden away within his fortresses. When she emerged, she was a lethal killing machine--but with a benevolent mercy? It was unlikely.

Usually he wasn't bothered with such mundane cases involving mortals. Their lives ended so quickly that they rarely gave vampires pause. The council had been content to wait on making a decision about Jaden, but that was until two months ago. A report came from New Orleans that Bhaltair was dead by the girl's hand. It seemed the girl was finally going to take after her uncle. That is when Tyr had been summoned.

New York was a city infested with undead problems. He had a whole list of vampires he was suppose to pay a visit. Most of those on that list no longer existed. The MacNaughton's were the only mortals.

Old enough to control his blood hunger, Tyr hadn't eaten. Waiting patiently, he scanned the upper levels of the apartment building, moving his gaze from window to window until he felt the strongest pull.

A slow smile formed on his mouth. How lucky for him that his marked one was also the one he needed to speak with. It was an amazing chance of fate that his task was made all the easier by circumstance.

With a speed born of centuries, his body dissolved to look like mist. His fog clung to the side of the building, curling over the sun-bleached stone. The movement took little effort, merely the will of his mind that it should be so.

He swirled high above the ground, his body becoming elongated and small as to fit in the crack of Jaden's window. He slipped from behind the heavy drapes unnoticed, his body solidifying in an instant as the mist gathered and grew.

His eyes adjusted to the pitch-black room. Tyr could smell the heady scent of her on the air. It was a strange mix of cinnamon and spice-- exotic and old. It reminded him of the Turkish temples of long ago.

Through the darkness he saw her form beneath the thin layering of sheets that donned her bed. The satin molded effortlessly over her body. The smooth material swept every muscular curve like valleys and peaks of desert sand--shifting yet forever flawless. Her face was softened as she slept, hiding the hardened stare of her jade eyes. Briefly, he wondered why the mystical orbs hadn't been in the accounting of her. When he thought of the dhampir, it was the first thing that came forth in his thoughts. Asleep, she looked so soft and feminine. His hand wanted to see if her skin would be as silky as the sheets that cradled her. Tyr resisted the urge to touch her.

He crossed through the room with effortless grace. His feet made no noise as they pressed over thick Persian carpet and hard wood. For as rich as she was, the room was amazedly bare of finery. Tyr detected the faint scent of old sweat on the air, knowing she must use the space to exercise more than sleep. It would make sense. Most of her kind was known as insomniacs.

Tyr made his way over to the bed. Lightly, he sat next to her. The mattress didn't shift. Beyond her bedroom door was silence. His hand crossed gracefully over her form, keeping distance between their skins, urging her face to turn to him. It did with no protest. A mumble escaped her lips on a sigh.

His ears picked up the steady beat of her mortal heart. So easily could he reach into her chest and pull the organ from her. His sharpened nails would cut her flesh with the ease of a sharp knife to warmed butter. She would be dead before she had a chance to gasp in horror. No one would stop him, question him. He could deliver her heart to the council and tell them she was judged. They wouldn't care. But Tyr didn't make a move to harm Jaden. In all the centuries since his human birth, he had never unjustly ended an assignment just for the sake of ease. As a human he was bred with honor. As a vampire he was bred with prudence.

As he watched her, his fingers drifted before the softness of her breath. He allowed time to slow and flicker. He felt her life hitting his palm in soft gushes of stirred air. He let the sound of it fill his ears. Her breath caught around his fingers, intertwining them in a tickling caress. His skin tingled and pricked at the warmth.

He looked at her bared arms stretched beneath her head. His fingers dipped to touch her honeyed cheek. Instead he denied himself the pleasure of her sleep-warmed skin as he hovered his hand above her. So corpselike were his tapering fingers, his extended white nails. The sight of them didn't bother him as they had long ago when he was first made one of the benighted children of darkness. The vague memory of his rebirth was more of an impression than it was an actual tangible thought.

Curling his pale hand into a light fist so that the nails scraped his palms, he withdrew his fingers. With a small wave, he parted the drapes behind him. A thin thread of light passed over the room.

"Miss MacNaughton," he whispered matter-of-factly. His face revealed no compassion, only reflected a passionless well. It wasn't so much the sound of his voice that stirred her but his nearness that he allowed her to feel. Tyr knew he could've kept quiet, letting her sleep, letting her dream. He wanted to lay next to her, listening to the fragile beat of her heart and the soft fall of her chest. It was the basest of rhythms--the song of a human.

Tyr's face remained an impartial mask as her eyes fluttered open to meet with his. He knew the instant the jade orbs recognized him. He sensed the deep hatred she harbored for him, and for herself, before she shaded her gaze beneath the sweep of her lashes. He didn't move, watching and waiting for her to speak. Somewhere deep inside he longed for her to smile at him, to laugh as she said his name. No one ever smiled at him willingly. No one ever laughed with him anymore.

Tyr wasn't disappointed when her lips refused to curl up for him. He hadn't expected them to. He waited patiently, eternally still as the lashes lifted and the jaded eyes continued to glare at him.

* * * *

Jaden sighed. Suddenly, within the canvas of her dreams, her fight with immortality dissipated into air. Her fist turned from a ball of anger into a gentle stroke of kindness. Her fingers searched the darkness, eager to feel and be felt. A hand brushed over her face, not touching her skin. The fingers were old, but looked so achingly young. Her cheek turned to lean into it, but the hand always stayed just beyond her reach. With a jolt, the hand disappeared into a mist. She was awake.

Jaden's eyes found the source of her disturbance. She blinked heavily, waiting for Tyr to disappear as he had in the mirror. The fog of her dream faded. He didn't. Her heart fluttered with caution. Her breath caught. She was outraged to find that the insolent creature could be leaning so casually next to her. And in her uncle's home!

"You're a surprise, Miss MacNaughton. Had I known it was you in the alleyway I wouldn't have left," he drawled sardonically.

Jaden shivered at the use of her name. It rolled effortlessly off of his tongue, mechanically efficient and precise. If not for the slight movements of his lips as he spoke, he would've looked like stone. Jaden knew that this vampire might act and feel as hard as rock, his skin may be as cold and unforgiving, and he might even try and crush her with his very whim, but he wasn't stone. He was a killer--an undead virus sent to plague humankind with his disease. And, like a psychopathic mass murder caught up by the hand of justice, he deserved a swift and final execution.

The ghost of a smile wafted on his features as he read the analogy in her thoughts. It was so angry, so violent and full of a conviction he didn't feel in her depths, as if it was a trained response she had hammered into her brain over the years to convince herself in a purpose. It contrasted the numb pain she buried from the world--maybe so well that she didn't even realize she carried it.

Glaring at him, she said, "Get up."

Tyr bowed his head, a mocking gesture of acquiescence. He stood with grace. There was a stinging melancholy in his languid movements as he backed away. He kept his eyes steadily on her.

"How did you get in here?" Jaden hissed, forcing annoyance. Her voice was harsh compared to his low murmurs. She threw the sheets off her body with a rough toss. Self-consciously, she tugged her white tank over her tight stomach. "You must be a true imbecile. Do you know what this place is? You'll be killed."

"I had no idea you cared for me so deeply," he said with feigned astonishment. The look ended as swiftly as it began. He didn't move to touch her, but Jaden felt as if he was all around her. A sliver of green tinted his blue eyes. She blinked, darting her gaze away from him. She stared at the wall.

"Don't try to read me," she demanded hotly. "I won't be mesmerized so easily again. I know your vampire tricks."

"All of them?" he goaded.

"Yes," she sneered, unamused. "All of them."

"Tell me," he questioned. Her mounting rage was prefect to his task. It would give him a chance to test her knowledge. "What am I trying to do now?"

Jaden's eyes cautiously shifted to watch him. He didn't move. His eyes bore steadily into her. She swallowed before meeting his gaze. But how could she back down now? The icy blue stayed the same, though a glint of silver threatened inside. She could see that he purposefully put it there. A wave of hot desire washed over her before she could block it. Her breath panted with marked shallowness, her lashes fought to dip demurely over her eyes. She could feel her loins heating with a potent fire as they violently tweaked close to orgasm. Within an instant the feeling was gone, leaving behind a dull ache that her body produced naturally to aggravate her.

"You are trying to annoy me," she said instead of telling the truth.

Tyr's lip threatened to curl up. She was right. He was trying to annoy her and he enjoyed doing it. However, that was not his test and he knew she knew it also.

Feeling vulnerable in the middle of the large bed, she moved with purposeful leisure to the floor. Her limbs tried to hurry, but she held them at bay. She wouldn't let this creature know he scared her.

Jaden winced as her lower back cramped. Lifting her arm over her head, she stretched the tight muscle. Then, seeing Tyr watching her, she dropped her hand to the side. Pride came over her face and she refused to let him see her pain.

"By the way, I don't care what happens to you. I would just as soon see you dead," she muttered arrogantly. Tyr grimaced.

"And should I worry about what will happen to you?" Tyr began to take pleasure from their banter. The feeling was very rare and never lasted more than a brief moment. However, with the feisty hunter, he found himself paying more attention than usual to the words of another.

"What do you mean?" she asked in confusion. Seeing the intensity in his eyes, she stepped back suspiciously. "Why would you worry about me?"

"You are mine."

Jaden shivered at the firm finality of his words. They left no room for argument.

"You are my indicium," he continued. His low tone curled around her like a warm blanket in winter--safe and enfolding. She was not deceived. "You are marked, my familiar."

Jaden couldn't find the voice to speak. His words were so possessive, as was the look he gave her as he said them.

"You are my slave and I your master," he continued, low, dark, seductive.

Jaden wasn't sure if his lips were moving, but the last caught her attention. "No, I'm not your slave. Slaves obey their masters and I'll never obey you. Aside from a scratch, you have no claim on me, nightstalker."

"I saved your life," he answered. Tyr didn't touch her, but he knew that she could feel him. He let her feel him caressing intimately along her skin. His eyes narrowed languidly, urging hers to do the same. A breathless moment passed between them, stretched out in a cloud of immeasurable time. The world faded until they were the only two in it.

"No," she managed at last. Her words were a husky defiance. Jaden's nerves jumped from her skin to his. She didn't fight the sensations of her body, needing all her power to fight the pull he had on her mind. Weakly, she said, "You only spared it. My life cannot be saved."

"Why do you seek death, dhampir?" A spark of honesty moved past his face as he released her from his hold.

"I...." Jaden couldn't continue. She shook her head, not able to answer. Moisture crowded her eyes and burned her nose. The dull ache that haunted her unfurled beneath her ribs, offering its pain to her heart. She blinked it back before he could see what he was doing to her.

At her silence, he closed some of the distance between them. His face, though mainly devoid of expression, beckoned her to finish her answer. His hand lifted to gently cup her cheek.

"Enough," she growled in anger, stopping his progress before he could get to her. Tyr's hand dropped to his side. Jaden could feel the kindness he tried to force on her. She was no fool. She knew a creature like him couldn't feel what he was trying to offer her. It was all a deceitful lie. Knowing it as such did not make it easier to resist. Her hands balled into fists. Abruptly, she said, "I do not belong to you. I may be marked, but I am not yours! All you will find here is a fight. Now, tell me your business or leave. I have no interest in speaking with you further."

"My business?" he repeated.

"Do you even know who lives here?" she asked with a discourteous roll of her eyes.

"You mean your uncle?" Tyr's lips curled. He wasn't scared. It had been an infinite time since he felt fear. At her pointed look, he whispered, "Yes, I know all about your uncle. This is his home."

"Then you know what he is capable of," she said with a gallantry she didn't feel. "You know what he will do to you if he finds you."

"I know," he murmured. *I know more than you'll ever realize.*

A chill crept up her spine. She backed away from him, moving towards her vanity. Tyr's eyes followed her with ghostly precision. She stared violently at the icy orbs--so cold was his look compared to hers. There was no fire in him. She could feel the morbid calmness of his soul swirling in her blood. It was like a euphoric drug--mind numbing with its potent aloofness. This creature was beyond feeling, beyond regret or redemption.

"Leave or you'll be sorry," she stammered. "I'll call my uncle's men."

Tyr chuckled at the idle threat. He could detect her fear, her rage, her helplessness.

"I thought you would be happy to see me," he answered her. He shook his head slowly, never tearing his gaze away. "You did seek me out."

"I wasn't looking for you," Jaden said. "I was looking for...."

"For death," he supplied when she faltered. The words hung in the air between them. She could see the dark angel of death himself within this large vampire. In a whisper, he asked, "And in a way you did find it, did you not? So what do you want with death, m'lady?"

"My life is none of your business," she growled. Her breasts heaved as she gulped for air. He opened the dam in her chest a bit more purposefully, bombarding her with sensations her mind couldn't interpret. Little explosions snapped on her skin, tingling the roots of her hair. The cords in her throat strained, as she shakily commanded, "Leave at once. I demand that you never come back here. You are not welcome."

"You might not have been looking for me, but you did find me. And I was looking for you." Tyr finally drew his gaze away, taking his disruptive feelings with them. He looked around the room for a chair. Seeing only one, he crossed over to her vanity. Jaden stiffened at his approach. He glanced briefly at her before pulling out the chair. He sat.

"You're insane," she voiced. Jaden stalked away from him, her body desperate to put distance between them.

"I've been called worse over the years," he remarked without censure. His words still rolled out in a whisper.

"Like a Dark Knight?" Her eyes hardened as she remembered herself. She was not going to give him the pleasure of her fear. She took a deep breath, concentrating on her anger. Her fingers ached, wanting to fight him.

Tyr smiled at her. He knew she was a woman used to resolving matters with her fists, avoiding the emotion it took to speak. He could feel her desperately wanting to disconnect herself from him, from his feelings. Reclining in the chair, he moved with liquid grace to rest his hand in mid-air.

Jaden crossed over to the window, pulling hard at the curtains to let in more light. Almost instantly, she was sorry for it. She gulped. The blue rays, which permeated from outdoors, bathed over him. The vampire was clothed the same as the night before, in a long antiquated coat that flowed when he moved. His back was to her, but she knew he sensed her every movement. Even if she had the advantage of a surprise attack, she knew she would fail. His size alone gave her reason to pause. Only too well did she remember the breadth of his shoulders, the gladiator height of his form, the feel of his hand slamming into her jaw. And not a single one of her punches had fazed him.

The Viking blond of his hair flowed freely over his shoulders, long and golden, touching down his back close to his waist, draping over the chair like silk threads. Jaden could detect the stroke of his long, pale fingernails as they moved absently over the wooden arm of the chair. The fingers that controlled the stroking were long and tapered. Veins rose beneath to fabric of skin on his pale hands. They were hypnotic and blue as she stared. The action seemed too gentle for such strength.

"You know your vampires, m'lady," he spoke at length. His words rushed over her like the sprinkling of fine, watery mist, just before one would jump into the full stream of the waterfall to be crushed over the rocks.

"It's my business to know," she whispered. He sighed and nodded in appreciation.

"And what else do you think to know about me?" he wondered.

"I know you are crazy," she endeavored hotly. Suddenly, seeing the coolness with which he spoke, Jaden wasn't so sure this man was a myth or a joke. Despite the feeling of newness in his blood, she began to doubt herself. This creature knew too much, saw and said too much. "And you are trying to frighten me. It won't work. I can tell how old you are. I can feel it in you. You are insignificant–a little vampiric worm crawling through mortal dung."

She did not receive the outrage she expected. Instead, he seemed almost to chuckle. A vague sense of enjoyment flooded her. Finally, he muttered, "It matters not what you believe me to be. I am what I am. And if I wanted you frightened of me, I could show you fear."

"Spoken like a true wannabe God," she taunted. Her eyes relished the very idea of her words, as she said, "Careful or your ego will fill up this room and push you out the window. That is unless I throw you out of it first. It won't kill you but it should hurt."

At that declaration, he did turn to eye her. Jaden's breath caught. The ice blue of his gaze softened with tender emotions. For an insane moment she thought he would declare his love for her. His lips parted as if to breathe. Her breath caught. Her heart stopped beating. But the insanity passed and in the confines of a mere second heat passed over her skin, burning and scorching her flesh. She felt bugs crawling on her clothing, biting with the prickling of needles, crawling up her nose and into her mouth to stifle her breath. She tried to fall, but her legs couldn't bend. She was frozen. Blinking, he took the sensation away.

Jaden coughed and wheezed for breath. Bending over, she steadied herself. She closed her eyes, the darkness helping to stabilize her panicked brain. Eyeing her skin, she saw her flesh was unharmed. But the pain had been real and it had hurt worse than anything she had ever felt.

Tyr waved his hand in dismissal of her threats. "Naturally your nasty tongue is learned from your loathsome uncle."

Her eyes rounded in horror. Her mouth opened to protest.

"No, do not take offense, Miss MacNaughton. I am used to women with a sharpened, unrefined speech." Tyr knew that he was purposefully goading her and wondered at it. His interview could've been finished before this conversation ever happened.

"What do you know about my uncle?" Jaden whispered. His barb hurt. He was comparing her to all the vampiric low-life trash that he knew. She definitely didn't need a reminder of how she lacked as a feminine woman. It was not by her choice that she was what she was. Her chest tightened. Through tense lips, she declared, "He is a good man. You have no right to speak out against him, just because he does something about the evilness of your kind. You are a plague and you need to be destroyed."

"Strong sentiment, m'lady," he whispered. Slowly, he came to his feet. "We have the tribal council to attend to our own. Your uncle should stay out of it and so should you. You have no business meddling in the affairs of vampires."

"One of your kind made it my business," she whispered, thinking of her father.

Tyr paused, cocking his head to see if mention of the man brought her any concern. Her feelings on the matter were closed to him. When he didn't speak, she hastened on.

"Your council does nothing. They should regulate their own. Force them to use blood banks or at least let the mortal's live. But, no," Jaden growled in reckless anger. She charged forward to face him. Leaning up to yell in his face, she hollered, "You feed and spread yourselves around like a virus. You slaughter innocent--"

"And what of your uncle's crimes? What of your own?" Tyr seethed in return. His voice rose, revealing a smattering of an Old Norse accent. "Are they no worse than some of those committed by vampires? Do you not seek to eradicate us? We who perhaps understand this world as your kind could never? And do not speak to me about the slaughtering of innocents. We hunt for food, as does your kind. I can smell the meat of animals in your veins. And I daresay the charges against Alan MacNaughton are worse than a mere killing of a mortal for food."

"What crimes? I call what I do justice," Jaden fumed.

"Do you little one?" His voice once again dropped to a passionless whisper. He shook his head, feeling her lie. His own outburst surprised him. "That is why you sought me out to kill you, because you know you are right and just?"

"You could never understand it." Jaden stiffened, hating him for mentioning her failed suicide and continually throwing it back in her face. She became aware of his nearness. He was too close. She could feel the chill of his body, hitting her like an open refrigerator. Taking a step back, she shook her head. How could he ever understand the dilemma her soul went through? He had no soul.

Tyr leaned forward at her words, only slightly but enough that she could feel him looming in. Jaden edged back.

"You couldn't possible understand anything I think or feel. You are a walking, talking virus. A disease. A curse. An evolutionary mistake." Jaden paused. She lifted her chin into the air. She could feel the mild rousing of anger in him. It would seem the vampire wasn't an emotionless void after all. He still had the bestial stirrings of rage. Finding it in him, she exploited it. "And, like a virus, you live long and are hard to kill. But, give us mortals time, we will find a way to cure you and your kind. And if there is no cure, we will eradicate you."

"Your part in your uncle's scheming is still to be determined," he decreed. His emotions settled once more into a bottomless pit, devoid of everything. Feeling the blackness, she wondered if it had only been her emotions she had felt mistaken for his. His soul was too long dead.

"What do you mean? Are you here to judge me?" Jaden gasped in bewilderment at his audacity. "How dare you?"

"You did say that we should regulate our own," he reminded quietly. Tyr was glad that they were finally coming back around to the point of his visit. He wasn't sure he liked the emotions he felt coming from her. They were a strong blend of hatred and anger and determined strength. Though she spewed nonsense about viruses and eradication, he could tell she didn't believe her own words, but flung them out of a curious mix of desperation and helpless outrage.

Beneath the shield of hate she built around herself, there was more. Tyr didn't want to discover what that was. He didn't need the confusion. It had taken him centuries to determine who he was and he didn't need her shaking him up with human feelings.

"I am not your own. I hate your kind. You have no power over me," she announced with a toss of her head. As she said the words he glanced at her lips to the mark he gave her, reminding her just how much power he wielded over her. She didn't even lift a hand to fight him off. Tears threatened her controlled poise. She forced her anger to the surface, but it was hard to hold onto.

"Deny it if you wish, dhampir. But you are what you hate. Half of your blood is vampire. It is what you are." Tyr watched her face pale at the harsh truths. Intentionally hurtful, he added, "*You* are the evolutionary mistake--a half-breed. You don't belong in either world and you know it, don't you? Humans will never understand you and vampires will never want you."

"I am none of your concern," she sneered in heated breathlessness.

"Ah, but the crimes against my people are my concern. Come with me to be judged, *dhampir*." As he insisted on calling her dhampir, Jaden shivered. There was no pleasure in the hard, crackling sound. As it whispered past his lips, it was a curse. She knew he was right. Humans looked on her like a curiosity, something for her uncle's men to place bets on. Vampires looked on her as a menace, a half-breed, to be destroyed if not a little feared.

Tyr stepped forward. He lifted a hand as if he would cradle her face. Jaden was pulled towards him. Her body ached to touch him. Her eyes ached to gaze upon the beauty of his face, the handsomeness of his blank expressions. There was a serene peace in the void he radiated. This was not the disorder that exuded from most vampires and mortals.

"It won't take long," he said, not touching. "If I find you innocent I'll let you go. So long as you stay innocent, no one will harm you. I'll give you my word on that."

"The word of a vampire?" she whispered, doubtful. She pulled back from his hovering fingers.

Shaking her head, she moved away from him. Tyr followed her with his eyes. Slowly she leaned back on her vanity. She placed her palms thoughtfully behind her, hitting her finger instantly to the silent alarm button beneath the edge. Without changing her expression, she whispered, "What crimes do you claim to be mine? And what crimes are my uncle's? I would hear the charges brought up against me before I go to be judged, for I doubt my idea of a crime and yours are the same. You say vampires do not want me then I do not recognize their authority over me."

Swiftly, Tyr's head darted to the door an instant before running footfall could be heard on the outside stairway. He smiled ruefully, knowing she was trying to distract him while she waited for her uncle's men. Part of him was disappointed she had called them.

With a slight bow of his head, he answered, "Mayhap you should ask your uncle, Miss MacNaughton. If you truly do not know what it is you have done, then you should find out."

The footfall skidded to a stop and the door to her bedroom crashed open. The thick wood reverberated against the wall but did not break. Jaden spun, seeing Rick's form in the entryway followed by a handful of partly dressed men. Confusion passed over the man's face as his gaze darted instantly to her window.

Jaden followed Rick's gaze. But instead of Tyr all she saw was the soft dissolving of mist left in his wake. The window remained closed. Her emotions pulled her to the mist, bidding her to jump after it, knowing if she did he would catch her and sweep her away with him. She held firm and didn't move, resisting the urge to run. The thick curtain fluttered softly.

"Who was that?" Rick demanded. Seeing Jaden in her nightclothes, he waved the other men out of the room with a stiff command that was immediately obeyed.

Jaden detected their eyes on her--questioning. It was as Tyr said, they did not understand her. Humans loathed with a peculiar terror what they couldn't comprehend. They might respect her, but they never understood. Slowly, Rick closed the door behind him so that they were the only two in the room.

"No one," she said.

"Jaden--" Rick began in obvious disbelief. His eyes moved to the window and then back to her pale face.

"It was nobody," she hissed through tightened lips. She hated that she had to call him for help. "Just an overbold vampire."

"I know you, Jade. You're frightened," he murmured quietly. "You're shaking."

"One misjudgment and you think we're friends?" she questioned incredulously. Tyr's words echoed in her mind. *Half-breed. Humans will never understand you and vampires don't want you.* Misdirecting her rage onto the unfortunate man in front of her, she snarled, "You think you know me, Rick? You know nothing about me. You're my uncle's lackey--that is all. And make no mistake. *Nothing* frightens me."

Rick stiffened. In short strides his muscular body was across the room, confronting her. His hand shot out to grab her about the arm. Gruffly, he stormed, "You didn't think sleeping with me was a mistake when it happened."

"I was high from the hunt," she lied.

"If I remember correctly it was more than one time," he said in grim victory. Jaden grimaced. "If you don't remember it, love, I would be happy to remind you."

Her eyes searched his coldly. In fact, for a fleeting moment, she had been attracted to him. He was strong, smart and witty. He had an easy smile and a good heart. He was loyal in a business when loyalty was to be prized above all else. But their affair was before she discovered he was her uncle's hired gun. With deliberate slowness she pulled her arm from his grasp. The movement showed no effort as she lifelessly glared at him.

"You're afraid to feel. I know what you are and that scares you. You liked it when you thought me a civilian. Hell, you didn't even mind when I told you I worked special ops for the government. It was fine for me to kill other men in combat. But step on Jade's precious territory and that changes everything." Rick's cheeks became red with anger. His breathing deepened. "You can't stand that I accept you as you are!"

"You should have told me you worked for my uncle. You lied to me," she said with ease.

"You never asked," he said hotly. Rick's bitterness was palpable. "And you better than anyone should know the secrecy that our lives demand. It isn't like I could just blurt out what I am over coffee. In fact, you never told me who you were. You abandoned me in the middle of the night without so much as a goodbye letter. It was only by chance that I discovered who you were when I came here to meet with Mack."

During the silence that followed, Rick studied the hard countenance of her face. Her eyes, though focused on him, didn't see him. He could've left and she would never have known, never have moved to stop him. Slowly, his gaze fell to her lips. Narrowing his gaze, he was hard pressed to hide his frown. Carefully, he said, "You haven't said how that vampire got into your room or why for that matter."

"The same way he left I would imagine," she sighed, her eyes clearing from the fog. Slowly she turned, walking over to her dresser. Pulling a cotton shirt from her drawer, she tugged her tank off and pulled the fresh one over her head, unmindful of Rick's watching gaze. She kept her back to him. Rick was not so unaware of her, as he studied the strong line of her back marred by thin scars from her work. He saw the bruise fading from her shoulder.

"I have never seen a vampire dissolve into mist," Rick said. "It must be some sort of trick."

"No," Jaden said. "He's just a bit different than the others."

When she turned to him, Rick asked, "And why did he come to you? What did he want? For this is a long way to climb for a meal, especially when there are so many sheep below us grazing the city streets. Did he bite you?"

"You saw that he didn't." Jaden sucked her bottom lip in slightly.

"Then what did he want with you?" he probed. His hand lifted to examine the bruise on her features. She jerked her head away. "Is he the one who did this?"

"You'd have to ask him what he wanted. Why don't you go find him and try to figure it out? I don't really care," she answered with a flippant toss of her head. "If he comes back, I'll be ready for him."

Rick read the lie on her face. Her eyes lowered, unable to meet his probing gaze. In that moment, she looked vulnerable--like a real woman.

"I know you are an indicium," he whispered under his breath. He knew she could hear him. Jaden bit her lip automatically feeling the puckering marks. She should have known Rick would see it. He never missed a detail, no matter how slight. "Was that the one who did it to you?"

Jaden refused to answer. She turned her back on him.

"Does Mack know?" he insisted.

Still she remained quiet.

"Damn it, Jade!" Rick leaned forward, grabbing her roughly by the back of her head, tangling his fingers in her hair. With a heavy tug, he spun her around. He couldn't hold back any longer. He had seen her strength waver as he mentioned her mark. In a rough kiss, the first he had dared since their affair, he pulled her into his embrace. His thick arms wound possessively around her. His intent was clear. He didn't try to hide what he wanted from her. He knew Jaden would accept nothing less than pure honesty. She could detect a lie.

Jaden could feel the comfortable press of him to her skin. Her heart raced. But when she closed her eyes it was not Rick she saw. It was a dark evil with piercing blue eyes filled with ice and terror. It was emotionless lips taunting her with mocking disdain. She hated those lips--those undead eyes. Jaden came to her senses, tearing herself away.

"It's been five years. We are not going to happen," she panted.

"You felt something." His look dared her to deny it. She did with little effort.

"I feel nothing," she said quietly. She gazed at him with wide green eyes filled with pity and sadness. "I am dead, Rick."

Rick's protest died on his lips. The fight slowly drained from his limbs. He saw she believed it to be true. There was no passion in her gaze. Angrily, he spun away. He didn't want the emotionless creature before him--the hunter tired of the hunt. He wanted the young, adventurous woman she had been when he had met her--hot and determined in her place in life. She had understood him like no other. She knew the thrill of the hunt, the glory of doing one's duty, the satisfaction of ridding the world of evil. She understood the sacrifices they had to make.

With a stiff nod, Rick stalked away. He vowed to help her out of this mess with the bold vampire and then he would devote himself to making her feel again--to become the woman she once was.

Stopping at the door, he said, "Get dressed. Tonight we hunt together."

Jaden didn't have time to answer. Rick was gone before she could collect her thoughts. Wearily staring at the window, she crossed over to the glass. She could sense Tyr wasn't there waiting for her. No, there was no hurry with Tyr. He would come for her again when he was ready. And no amount of protection would be able to stop him.

Chapter Four

"You told my uncle," Jaden said with mild accusation. She stared forward, not trusting herself to look at Rick as he moved effortlessly by her side. The city was pleasantly quiet as they made their way. The loudest sound was their gentle footfall as they walked along the hard, abandoned sidewalk. A cool breeze nipped at the night making the air smell clean. "I know you did. His eyes didn't move away from my lip."

"He is worried about you," Rick defended. "And he has a right to know--"

"He has a right to know only that which I decide to tell him," she broke in with a harsh frown. She didn't break stride as they passed a row of stoops. "And *only* what I tell him. You might be employed by him, but I am not."

"Who are you kidding, Jade?" Rick grimaced at her hard tone. "Who pays for everything? Who gives you assignments? Who tells you where to go and what to do? You may be his niece, but you are still employed by him."

Jaden bit back the curse that threatened to pass through her lips. She thought of Tyr's mocking of her vulgar speech and hated herself for caring what he thought. And she hated Rick for having a point.

"What's the assignment then?" she grumbled. Jaden noticed he wore a comfortable pair of blue jeans and a sweater, not his usual scouting attire. A waft of cologne stirred every time he moved. It was a strong, seductive scent. It made her want to rip at his clothes in a most primal way.

"There is none. I am supposed to take you out and show you a good time." At her suspicious look, he added with a charming smile, "Mack's words, not mine."

"It's a good thing I stole this address from the top of his desk, then," Jaden smirked. She felt herself softening against Rick. He wasn't such a bad guy. And, if truth be told, he was the closest thing she had to a friend. She lifted a small piece of paper from her pocket and handed it to him. "Or else we would have nothing to do."

"What's this?"

"I thought we'd crash Tom's party tonight," she said dismissively.

"How--?"

"How did I get it?" Jaden broke in with an impish smile. She shook her head, her eyes saying he should know better than to ask such things. "I have been trained by the stealthiest of thieves and the most successful of criminals. I could steal Atlantis from the ocean if I wanted to."

"Jaden, you heard your uncle. You know he wouldn't like this." Rick glanced at the address before stuffing it in his pocket. He peered around the street, ignoring the few pedestrians trailing opposite them and the bright headlights of the occasional car.

"I believe he ordered you to show me a good time. And I can think of nothing I would like more than to piss off Tom." Jaden purposefully shot him a naughty smile. Rick was surprised by the look and said nothing. His heart sped a little at the mischief he read in her. "Come on, it's about two blocks this way."

Jaden's pace hastened, forcing Rick to keep up. Without quickening their breath, they reached the end of the second block. Suddenly, Jaden stopped. Her skin prickled as she looked around. Within an instant, she was crouching to the ground behind a parked Suburban with Rick at her side.

"What?" he whispered. Without his normal weaponry he was uncomfortable. When Jaden looked at him, her eyes held unspoken merriment. She pointed into the distance, over a clearing of trees near a little park.

Waving her hand, she took off across the street. Covertly, she moved over the concrete to the fenced yard. Jumping over the wrought iron fence, she landed neatly on the ground. Rick was right behind her.

Sprinting to a tree, she ducked behind the old trunk. Her expression turned serious as she squinted into the night. Instantly, she took in her surroundings.

"Can you see that?" Jaden asked, pointing to a black van parked on the side street.

"What about it?" Rick asked. His body tensed on full alert. "Is our vampire in there?"

"No, I don't feel any vampires. Look at the roof. What is that?" Jaden peered at the strange protrusion.

"It's a surveillance vehicle," Rick whispered. He shot Jaden a confused shake of his head. "But it's hardly stealthy with that scope on top."

"Police?" she asked.

"It could be but I doubt it. It's a little too obvious, even for the police."

"Should we go check it out?" Jaden moved, not waiting for an answer. Rick grabbed her arm, pulling her back. His chin jutted, directing her attention to the clearing within the trees.

Seeing a lone woman walking along an earth path, Jaden froze. The soft floral pattern of her schoolmarm sundress and perfect bun were sorely out of place in the darkened park. Tilting her face towards Rick, she kept her gaze trained on the woman. Silently she mouthed, "Vamp."

Rick nodded in understanding. The vampire stumbled as if drunk or confused.

Jaden sensed another presence around them. Looking at Rick, she leaned closer to his ear and whispered, "We're not alone."

"Something's not right," Rick said, voicing both their worries. He frowned, his gaze narrowing as he peered around them.

"She is newly turned. A few days at most," Jaden said in a whisper. Such a creature was not a usual target, at least not one requiring more than one person to track. However, by the way her nerves jumped, the small park was filling up fast.

Just then a man jumped down from the tree, tackling the vampire to the ground. Several more followed him, ganging up on the creature. The vampire screamed--an awful, crazed sound. She fought gallantly, throwing off several of her assailants as she tried to regain footing against the onslaught. The men made a dramatic show of struggle against her-- falling too far when punched, rolling into the dirt when lightly kicked. To the untrained eye, it looked as if the young vampiress would thwart the attackers. Jaden knew they were holding back, which she expressed in a glance at Rick.

The fight took much longer than it should have, considering the skill and strength of the men and the newness of the vampire. With one strike of a stake, the battle would've been over and the vampiress defeated. Finally, one of the men took out a tazer and shocked the vampire into submission. The creature howled and shook as she fell to the ground. Descending upon her the men spared her life, but bound her limbs with rope.

With a screech of tires, another van came bounding forward. The men carted the weakened vampire away, stuffing themselves and their captive into the second van. Within moments it was over. The second black van left as quickly as it came. The park was all but cleared.

"Is that how you usually do business?" Jaden asked. She glared at Rick.

"No," Rick murmured, disturbed. "We never take prisoners."

"Is that...?" Jaden began.

"Tom," Rick finished for her with a hard jerk. "Come on."

Coming out from behind the tree, Rick stormed forward. Jaden was quick behind him. Tom, hearing their approach, spun on his heels. Seeing Rick, he sighed in relief. He pulled the black mask from his features. Seeing Jaden, he grimaced, a small sound of displeasure escaping his throat as he rolled his eyes in a show of great annoyance.

"What's going on here?" Rick demanded gruffly.

"Routine capture," Tom answered with a deceitful smile. His eyes glanced over Rick's street attire before training on Jaden. He could smell the man's cologne. Seeing Jaden dressed as she always was, he was hard pressed to hide his smirk. His eyes darted over her athletic frame, unable to help the manly appreciation he felt, as he continued quietly, "All finished."

"Who's in the van?" Jaden asked with a hard set of her jaw. She pretended not to notice the way Tom was staring at her or the way he licked his lips thoughtfully. She didn't trust him and she definitely didn't like him.

"What van?" Tom smiled. He gave his most innocent look at the two. "Oh, that van. That is just some of the new trainees. Mack wanted to revamp the training program a bit. He thought it would be best for them to see what they were up against before setting them out into the field."

"Oh, yes," Jaden muttered wryly. "And that was such a vicious creature. Was she giving the vampire children too much homework?"

Tom glared at her. His nostrils flared but he bit his tongue.

"And the capture?" Rick probed, hoping to break into the impending fight. "Why the big show? You could've handled that one alone."

"Talk to Mack. I'm just following orders," Tom answered. He gave Jaden a curt nod and began walking towards the awaiting vehicle.

"Hey, wait a minute. I would like to meet some of the new trainees," Rick said suspiciously. He followed Tom. The man hesitated. He kept his back to the two intruders. Jaden shared a concerned glance with Rick. "I wasn't aware we had any."

"Mack thought it best to replace the two I lost last weekend in Florida," Tom delayed. His hands gripped nervously at his black mask. Hearing a noise by the surveillance van, all eyes turned towards the opening door. A man's head poked cautiously out of the back. Jaden squinted, trying to place the overly slender face. The man looked too old and too thin to be in their business. He disappeared behind the door as quickly as he popped out. Tom glanced at Jaden and then Rick, shifting uncomfortably on his feet.

"I see," Rick expressed thoughtfully. He leaned closer to Jaden. To his pleasure, she didn't back away from him. Tom eyes again moved over Rick's layman attire and then focused on Jaden curiously.

"On a date?" Tom smirked. Jaden's chin jutted into the air. Rick felt her stiffen and frowned. Tom snorted in merriment at the very idea. Giving a blatantly lewd glance over Jaden's plain attire, he winked at Rick. "You two kids have fun."

"We are patrolling the streets," Jaden snapped. It was Rick's turn to stiffen at her waspish denial. He didn't have to have her innate abilities to sense the discomfort Tom's implication gave her.

"Well, we are running late. I've got to get the trainees back," Tom said quietly. He knew that his planned barb had successfully taken the couple's minds away from his purpose. He made haste towards the vehicle only to call over his shoulder, "But I'll be sure to bring them by the penthouse later. We'll have a meet n' greet."

As soon as the van was gone, Rick turned to Jaden. His hand began reaching for her shoulder as he stepped closer to her. With a grim look of assurance, he said, "He was lying."

"Tell me something I don't know.…" Jaden's words trailed off. A shiver worked its way up her spine. She backed away from Rick's oncoming hand to look around.

"What is it?" Rick questioned sharply. He knew that look on Jaden's face. Instinct taking over, he peered around in the darkness. He found nothing. Not even the hairs on the back of his neck stood on end.

Jaden narrowed her gaze in agitation. They were being watched. She could feel a purposeful stare peering at her through the darkness. It boiled her blood and consumed her skin with a fire. She knew who it was. Tyr.

"It's nothing," Jaden muttered, suddenly very glad Rick was by her side. She pulled lightly on his arm to get his attention. "Let's go."

Jaden led him back the way they came. She refused to turn around, knowing that Tyr would come to them if he wanted to be seen. Quickening their pace, Jaden moved towards a more crowded part of the street, hoping to lose their stalker. They walked in silence for sometime, both of them lost in thought. The feeling of an undead gaze haunted her and the aloof woman at his side haunted Rick. He kept his eyes casually away, all the time aware of her movements.

"I'll ask Mack what was going on as soon as we get back," Rick began when she refused to speak. "I'd bet Tom is up to something."

"I don't think you should. Let me do it," Jaden said softly. The presence slowly disappeared from her senses. She sighed in relief. "Let's call it a night and go home. There is nothing going on in the city anyway."

* * * *

Tyr scowled. Perching on a limb, he watched Jaden from the height of the tall park trees. Only his eyes moved, glinting a dangerous red-black as he looked at the cozy scene unfolding in the night. The rest of him froze, encased by the rattle of leaves in the wind.

The man Jaden was with leaned into her, giving her a meaningful look. He didn't hear what they said, but he saw the possessive way the one called Rick stayed close to her side. The human's eyes always strayed to her with a longing Tyr could sense easily from across an ocean and his mortal body was always inclined to lean in. It was the same man who interrupted his conversation earlier in the night. Who was this mortal to her? And why did he care?

Tyr cursed himself for being affected by the dhampir. But, try as he may, he couldn't deny he was fascinated. When it looked as if Rick would reach out and touch her, the knight dropped the cloak he carried over his emotions to block himself from Jaden. He watched her shiver, feeling his nearness. He saw her eyes dart around, searching. A grim smile spread out over his features when she hurried away from the park.

Following them for some time, he glided behind them, invisible. He ignored their words but tried to feel what Jaden was feeling. Without seeing her eyes, he couldn't read into her thoughts. He found himself edging closer, reaching out to touch her. Suddenly, her head snapped around to look back. It was as if she pierced him with her stare. Tyr knew it was senseless to lurk and pulled his emotions away from her. Jaden visibly relaxed, her walk becoming lighter now she believed him to be gone.

Tyr silently tracked her location until he felt her arrive at Mack's building. To his displeasure, the man was still beside her. With a scowl, he fled into the blackness of the city night. Jaden was safe--for now. But, as soon as the man left her side, Tyr would go for her again. And this next time, he wouldn't be as indulgent with her.

* * * *

Mack was gone. Outward, Jaden stayed calm. Inside, she cursed the blackest string of profanity she knew. She wanted some answers and she didn't want to have to wait for them.

The penthouse seemed empty without her uncle's dynamic presence. The servants faded into the background until they became part of the walls. Jaden could feel them around her, but tried to ignore them as she always had.

Mack left a message with the butler that he would be back in three days. He didn't say where he had gone--only that Jaden should be ready to leave when he got home. Jaden grimaced, scanning over the note. He bid her, *most insistently,* to stay in until he got back. Jaden made no such plans.

For Rick, Mack left a different message. He found it slipped under the door of his apartment. Rick lived directly beneath Mack's home. The loft style suite was simply decorated with an industrial type of feel to the metal bar walls and black furniture.

Mack warned that Jaden might be in danger and ordered that Rick should stay by her side. Whatever happened, he was not to let her leave the house. Attached to the note were two forms of tranquilizers--a dart and a vial filled with powder. There were enough drugs to keep Jaden sedated for a week. Rick frowned. Shoving the package into his duffel bag, he packed to go up to Mack's apartment to stay.

In the penthouse, he was met with as warm a welcome as he could imagine getting from Jaden. She sneered, looking with haughtiness at his bags, before turning to go to bed. Rick sighed, dropping his bags as he went to follow her.

Catching up to her on the stairs, he said, "It's only for a few days."

Jaden paused halfway up to turn her needling eyes at him. "I don't need a babysitter, Rick. I can take care of myself."

"Mack is concerned, is all. You're his niece. He worries about you," Rick said. Giving her a sheepish grin, he offered, "We can train if you like. I've been working on my swordplay and could use a worthy partner. Not many of the guys are interested in the old styles."

It was the only offer he could've made that would've piqued her interest. Jaden allowed herself a small smile. Studying Rick's handsome face, she nodded. "All right, Mr. Fletcher."

A boyish grin spread over his face. His eyes sparkled with mischievous intent and hope. Jaden turned from him, her smile fading when he could no longer see. She saw the look in his eyes and was sorry for it.

Once she was alone in her room, the door safely latched behind her, she allowed herself to breathe. Her head hit against the frame of the door with a heavy thud. She thought of Rick downstairs in the den watching television on her uncle's couch. He really wasn't a bad guy. He was generous and kind, athletic and smart. He was a gentleman. And in bed, if memory served, he was quite the inventive lover. Why was she fighting him so hard? Sure, she didn't love him, but why fight animal nature? And it would seem she had enough pent up animal nature inside of her to fuel the most indecent of vampiric fantasies.

If she made her intent clear to Rick in the beginning, why shouldn't they resume their affair? And maybe if she released some of the tightly wound tension Tyr created in her body, she would be better apt to face the irritating vampire. It wasn't the first time she thought about resuming her meaningless affair with Rick, but it was the first time she considered it.

Jaden lifted her head to stare at the door. Her fingers trembled slightly as she reached for the lock. A nervous flutter came to her stomach. It had been a long time since she allowed herself to get close to someone. Two years, nine months and twelve days to be exact. Life had just gotten too complicated to make time for men. And being with Rick tonight would beat being alone.

Her decision made, she unlocked the door. The latch slid easily beneath her fingers. Pulling on the knob, the door didn't move. Jaden frowned. She looked at the lock. It was still undone.

"What…?" she began. A puzzled frown edged her face.

"Do you really think he can make you happy?"

Jaden froze. She heard a match strike behind her and the slow puffing of a cigar. She dropped her hand from the knob. Slowly, she turned around. The lock slid into place as she moved, untouched by human hands. The red glow of a cigar tip floated eerily in the darkness as her eyes adjusted to the low light.

"He'll never understand you," the voice continued uniformly. Tyr sat in her chair by the vanity as if he'd been waiting for her all evening. His coat lay over the side of her bed, draping over the edge with an odd possessiveness. His legs drew forward from his body, clad in tight black leather, as he rested. Sitting, composed and at ease, he dominated the room, made it his own. She felt like a stranger in her own home. His arced lips drew over the tip of the cigar in a slow caress as he tasted it with leisurely enjoyment. Jaden shivered at the deliberately idle action. She recognized the cigar's smell as one of her uncle's.

"I should have known you'd be here," she grumbled sharply. She glowered succinctly at him. His brow raised on his face reminding her of the still creature she'd met with in the alleyway. What a fool she had been that night, so off her game. Any imbecile could see him for what he was--a strong, willful vampire. As if to prove her point, his fangs peeked out from beneath his lips. Swallowing, she forced her attention away from his sensually kissable mouth.

Jaden walked over to her bed, sitting as she pulled off her boots. She threw them haphazardly onto the floor. Smelling the smoke crossing her face, she coughed and waved her hand through the air. "That thing will probably kill me. Could you put it out?"

"Isn't that what you wanted?" he asked with a tilt of his head. His lungs didn't move, never needing air. He waited as she studied him. His middle finger smoothed over the chair's arm, the fingernails moving in undulating circles that reminded her of a naughty caress.

Jaden felt a fire in her limbs, stirring in her belly to weaken her will. She kept her gaze trained on his hand, letting her eyes travel up the breadth of his pale arm when his fingers ceased in their movements. She took in the gladiator girth of his chest constructed of steel and flesh. His shirt collar curved around his neck like a crimson colored noose. The sinewy lines of it held in timeless motion like the contours of an ancient statue. After a long moment of silence, he let the smoke escape his parted lips.

Jaden watched in a curious state of awe as the smoke left his firm mouth, riveting around his fangs as it passed by in curls. Even the elements of that simple action seemed controlled by the vampire who allowed it to be. When the last of the smoke dissipated above his head, he finally moved. Taking his dry fingers to the end of the cigar, he smote the burning tobacco without a flinch. Jaden feigned a look of proper awe and bowed over her feet.

The sultry sound of his low chuckle rode over on the air, twirling and twisting like a cartooned storm from her childhood. The voice it held was old and familiar, begging her acceptance with each blithe note. The creature called forth her most primal of desires, her most blatantly disobedient needs--the kind of need that didn't seek permission or logic, only a reason to be. And Tyr exploited it. He used her human weakness of the flesh, causing her to shiver and tremble like a virgin maid set before her would-be impaler.

"I'm not going with you." Jaden tugged off her socks before moving across to her vanity barefoot. She didn't like coming so close to him, especially after her wayward thoughts. Her mind reeled to think of what all his power would be capable of if put to a more passionate aim. It was said vampires made excellent lovers. They had years of experience and the bodies to back it up. They could make a human woman believe anything. Jaden was no fool. She knew that for the vampire it was an illusion, another way to stir the blood before tasting it.

She refused to let him see her apprehension. Glancing at the table, she took up a brush. Then, allowing time to sneer at him, she straightened defiantly.

"That button won't work," he said easily. Jaden hated the amiable light in his eyes, the bored set to his jaw as he watched her.

For all the care he seemed to exude, she could've been a pile of pig droppings sitting in the middle of a grassy field--a small annoyance that must be considered for only a passing moment before being stepped over or swept away. She wondered which fate he would chose for her. Would she be released from him, left behind as he went onto ageless centuries? Or would she be snuffed out, swept away beneath the heel of his boot, forced into the stirring of his whims?

As he spoke, she instinctively knew her answer. "You cannot call for help this time. I promise to kill any who answer. Besides, I disabled your little button. I should hate for another rude interruption."

"Why are you here, Tyr?" she sighed in frustration. She stood proudly before him, watching him carefully through the slit of her eyes. Like most vampires, he hadn't changed his clothes since before the alley. Vampires didn't sweat. The burgundy sleeves were pushed up to his elbows. Jaden saw the markings of a scar on his right forearm. Her eyes narrowed, delicately trying to make out the branded symbol. Tyr rotated his arm down, hiding it from her view.

"We weren't finished talking," he said easily. Drawing forward, he placed his elbows to his knees. His head came dangerously close to her side. Jaden looked down, meeting his eyes peeking out from beneath the top of his silky lashes. With a small sound of derision, she strode to the bed.

"I have nothing to say to you," she countered. She could feel his gaze following her, reading her movements. She sat quickly to hide the shaking of her legs. Her heart pounded in excitement, the kind of excitement brought forth from extreme terror. "I was finished. So why don't you leave."

"Doesn't anyone say please anymore?" he grumbled. His brows furrowed in concentration. "I do confess politeness must be an antiquated custom, but surely the world has not lost it completely."

"*Please* leave," she muttered with a heavenward roll to her eyes. She pulled her hair free and ran the brush through it. She ignored the fervent pounding in her chest as she did her best to be nonchalant towards him.

"No," he answered with a half smile, full of charm. He leaned back in easy repose.

Jaden shivered at the change in him. He seemed almost nice. Not one to mince words, she said, "Stop being … pleasant. I much preferred your indifferent disdain. Niceties don't suit your kind, vampire."

That stopped him. The smile faded from his features. "You are a harsh judge, m'lady."

"Yes, I am. And quit calling me m'lady. It gives away your age, bloodsucker." Jaden purposefully batted her eyelashes coquettishly at him in mocking. He sat up straighter in the chair. Slowly, he came to his feet. The effort took no strain as if he floated more than stood.

Tyr did not like the scornful tone to her voice or the displeasure in her face as she stared at him. He knew she was afraid of him, could feel it easily though she hid it well. Her dark reddish-brown hair spilled prettily over her shoulders, cupping around her bruised jaw. He eyed the wound, surprised to see it healing so quickly. There was a lot of power in this woman. It was a wonder she wasn't mad with it.

Parting his lips so she could see his fangs, he whispered, "I have ways of quieting your foolish mortal tongue and taking the information I seek from you by force. I do not need this aggravation. I can control you."

Jaden shivered. All thoughts of Rick faded from her as her primeval lust transferred itself easily from the man to the vampire. Her eyes dipped to his mouth as he loomed closer. She could see the firm set of his mouth, a hardness that would only go away when he smiled. His were lips that would move with tantalizing expertise if he let them. His whole body had the gift of time when it came to control. Tyr knew himself, knew his power and wore it comfortably.

Unbidden, her head cocked to the side. She stepped close. The brush slipped from her grasp, falling forgotten to the floor. The thin sliver of air between them heated with the sparks of their bodies. Electricity flowed, joining their chests with gossamer strands that attracted the two together with the driving force of high powered magnets. She resisted the pull, refusing to sway into the last breadth of their separation. Jaden wavered on her legs. The two wounds on her lip throbbed. Raising her hands, she hesitated slightly before reaching to touch his cheek.

His face was smooth and cool. A jolt ran down her fingers. Panting breathlessly, her stomach trembled. Her fingertips grazed over the length of his eyebrow, stopping gently to tremble at the arch before moving on. The ice melted from his gaze, capturing her with the beauty of it. Regarding him through the veil of her heavy lashes, Jaden tried to urge him forward with the tips of her fingers.

Tyr didn't move, didn't touch her. Jaden didn't care. Lifting up on her toes, she breathed in the intoxicating scent of him. It was so unlike the contrived smell of cologne. It was natural, fresh, earthy. Her eyes stayed trained on his face, studying him for a response, feeling him for emotion where there was none. Her head fell to the side. Her body brushed lightly next to him. She could detect the beginning press of hardened muscle to her sensitive skin.

Closing her eyes, her lips drew forward. Her nose angled next to his. Her lips brushed lightly along the natural path carved in his skin. She felt breath echoing in harsh pants from his mouth. For all his cold stillness, he could've been a sculpture.

Her mouth ventured forward, parting wider as her lips slid and molded around his bottom lip to suck gently. Her insides shook with insecurity. She knew what she wanted from him. Wasn't her own existence proof that he could answer her request? That he was fully shaped as a man should be? She didn't want a child by the vampire. She didn't want to curse another with her existence. Besides, Jaden knew she would never be fit as a mother. However, the nervous shaking in her limbs told her she wanted something from him.

She felt him smile as she held him firmly in place. A breathless suspension of time cocooned her. She waited for the response that had to come--that must come. She waited for his mouth to part, to lay claim as it surely ought to. She waited for the feel of his tongue, wondering how it would taste, how it would feel, how precisely it could move under his command. And his strong hands, how they must know the inner working of the female body. Jaden's fingers curled, dipping into the overlong streaks of blond hair. And then he spoke. The spell was broken.

"I told you I could control you, m'lady," he whispered in aggravating confidence. The low sound of his voice was tortured, as he whispered, "I can make you love me."

The words didn't come out as Tyr intended. He wondered why they would've slipped in such a way. Still, he did not take them back. They were said and would remain so.

Jaden's jaw dropped open in a gasp of agonizing pain. His words slapped her, the ultimate rejection to her vulnerable state. Never had she opened herself up in such a way. Normally, she knew the man wanted her before she tried. She could lie and make them believe what she wanted them to believe. But Tyr was different. He could feel inside of her, could control her. And, yes, he could make her love him if she allowed him access to the last bit of her control and defenses. The love would be a lie, a ruse brought forth from the brainwashing power of his mind, but she would be convinced of it nonetheless. And a lie, when believed, became the truth.

Jaden pulled away from him on trembling limbs. Her eyes burned to release a dam of moisture she held at bay. *Rejection.* The word echoed harshly in her brain. The desire within her wasn't completely of his doing. He only pushed her over the edge to make her react to it. His gaze was cold, unfeeling.

This creature could never truly return the passion she felt building within her at his nearness. She threw his face away with a hard push. His head snapped to the side, but his body didn't move. Tyr closed his eyes to her anger, not allowing himself to react to it.

Shaking with indignation, she said, "I could never love a creature like you, vampire. You couldn't even know the feeling. A creature like you would never be able to touch my heart, not with all the tricks in your book." Her words dropped to a mere, cruel whisper, "I loathe you. I hate you. I despise your very existence."

Tyr felt a piece of himself crumble. His jaw tightened but his expression otherwise stayed intact. Jaden flung herself away from him and stormed over to the bed. Sitting down, she glared at him with a huff.

Tyr forced a cold, crackling laugh at her tantrum. When he turned to look at her, his smile faded. Back was the cold employment of his visit.

"Get on with it then," she whispered. Her words carried a sinister purpose. "I'll waste no more of my time on you. I have a real man waiting for me. A man of flesh and blood, a man of fire and heat--"

"It's getting late," he interrupted gently, pretending as if her declaration didn't sting. His thumb ran absentmindedly over the coolness of his own hand. Only after eating did he feel warm. "Maybe we should go."

"I'm not going with you," she resolved through gritted teeth. Tilting her chin up nobly, she sighed, "Tell me what it is you want from me."

"What were you doing tonight?" he asked. He thought of Rick. A wave of displeasure crossed over his face. Was that the lover she spoke of? He shook his head, trying to clear his thoughts. He didn't like his brain muddled. The long years had taught him that everything works itself out given enough time, and some things would always be the way that fate wishes them to be.

Jaden wondered at the curious frown. Carefully, she said, "You should know. You were there."

"Ah," he mused silently, remembering why he was sent for her. "Then you are a part of it."

"A part of what?" she snapped in scathing aggravation. "Tell me what it is you think is going on."

"I know what is going on," he murmured. "I just want to know your part in it."

Jaden shivered. His eyes were no longer kind or placid. They swirled violently as he stared at her. Shakily, though she wasn't sure she would like the answer, she questioned, "What happened in the park tonight? Do you know where they took that vampire?"

"Did you ask your uncle about it?" he wondered aloud.

"He's gone," she admitted. Jaden forgot her anger as she studied him. Biting her lips meditatively, she ordered, "You tell me."

Tyr ignored the command. Thoughtfully, he turned from her. He paced to the window to look out over the city. His fingers threaded behind his back. Jaden started to move forward, her hand reaching to touch him from the distance. Catching herself, she pulled back. Her hands balled into fists.

He isn't your friend! She reminded herself. *You hate him.*

"How long will Mack be gone?" he asked. Jaden heard the words clearly in her head. She wondered if he spoke or merely directed his thoughts at her. She had heard that some of the old had very powerful gifts, though she herself had never experienced such things as mental telepathy. It was said that all vampires could converse amongst themselves by such means, but only some of them with humans. The problem with the facts she had been given was that she never knew when they would be exaggerated as a means to frighten her and others like her.

"Can't you tell, o mighty one?" she jibed. Tyr glanced over his shoulder, shooting her an unamused grimace. With a sigh, she answered in dejection, "Three days."

"Fine. You have three days to find out what you don't know or to try and hide what you do. But remember, Miss MacNaughton, the vampire council does not need evidence of the deed, only my word in the matter." Tyr came around to study her face. With swift precision, he was by her side, holding her face tenderly in his large hands. His eyes glistened and pulled. "I could be your best friend or your worst enemy. I could bring them your heart and they wouldn't question it."

"Am I on trial?" she asked in a whisper.

"You have been on trial since before our first meeting in the alley," he said softly down to her. "You have been on trial your whole life. And do not think you can escape me. The world is too small to hide you and my reach too long. I'll find you wherever you are."

"And if I kill myself before then?" she asked in low tones. She hid her passionate jade gaze beneath her lashes. "Not even you can find me in death."

"If you were going to do the deed yourself, you would've done so before now," he answered logically. His thumb stroked over her cheek. "Do not be in such a hurry to die. You life is short enough as it is."

"Release me," she beseeched him. Tyr knew what she was asking. Still, he wasn't sure of why.

"I cannot."

"End me," she continued her plea. "Give me peace. Tell your council what you will about me. I don't care. If you do it, it will make your job easier."

"Why do you wish it so?" he asked, unable to stop the question. His eyes fell to her lips, watching the birth of her answer. Her eyes clouded briefly.

"Don't ask that. You have no right." Jaden pulled away from him. He let her go. Her stomach tightened.

"I am your master, dhampir. I have every right to you." Tyr's words dropped and Jaden couldn't mistake what he meant by *every right*. His claim on her body burned brightly in his eyes. He was only biding his time until he would obtain her completely.

Turning her back, she said boldly, "Judge me then, Dark Knight, and be done with it. Don't wait for your answers. Decide now."

"Three days," he whispered. His lids fell listlessly over his eyes. When they again opened he was no longer looking at her. Jaden didn't notice.

Jaden felt him leave before she had a chance to protest. The devilishly strange sensations he aroused went with him, leaving her to a bitter ache of despair. She said nothing to stop him. On the verge of tears, she touched her bottom lip. Her fingers slid onto his mark. She wondered if they would leave a scar. It would be only a small one in her long history of collecting. She didn't care. Their maker wounded her more purposefully than a small physical scrape.

She waited until she was sure he was gone. Jaden shook her head, her lips letting loose a trembling sigh. Her body ached, wanting desperately to be held in a tender embrace, to be protected. But she wasn't the protected kind. She was the warrior, the brave soldier who needed no one.

Jaden quivered. When would someone finally discover her shameful lie? That she wasn't as strong as she pretended to be. She choked back a stray tear that threatened to fall from her eye. Tyr was right. Rick would never understand and didn't deserve to be involved in her disastrous life-- not even to be used for physical pleasure. Quietly, she crawled into bed alone. The end was near, she could feel it. All she could do was wait for it to come.

Chapter Five

The sun streamed in through a crack in Jaden's curtain. She held still, her eyes closed as she pretended to sleep. The nightmares of her dreams faded into reality. She waited. Her lungs filled with soft falls of air, her body alert as she listened for another sound. All around her was perfect silence.

Without warning her skin felt alive with fire. Jaden kicked viciously at the covers, rolling over as a blade swished past her ear. Feathers flew up from the pillow floating gently around the bed in the sunlight. Untangling her feet, she jumped onto the floor. Her breath came hard as her eyes focused on her attacker. She had little time to think as a sword flew through the air at her head.

Lifting her hand, Jaden swung to the side, missing the point and catching the handle. The action spun her about until she completed a circle.

"You're a little sluggish this morning," Rick teased. He tossed his matching blade from one hand to the other. "I thought you said we could practice."

Jaden snarled. Suppressing a yawn, she slowly made her way around the bed frame. She jutted her chin in greeting, all the time cursing him for his rude awakening. The steel glinted sharply as it passed the stream of light. She pointed it daringly at Rick's chest.

"You slept in your clothes," he noticed. His eyes swept over her disheveled hair, her wrinkled attire. She was sensational. She made him want to grab her up into his arms and cart her away--at least as far as her bed. His blade didn't move to defend. His hand fell to the side, his chest open and trusting. Her jade eyes were brilliantly alive and on fire. "Would you like time to change?"

"Coffee," she growled viciously. With the deadly accuracy of a snake, she flung her wrist, sending the blade flying through the air to stick into the wood of the door. Rick gasped, jumping out of the way. The metal vibrated loudly before settling into its new home.

Rick chuckled as he stood. Lowering his sword arm, he bowed gallantly. "Yes, Jade, coffee."

"Now," she said, unamused. Spinning on her heels, she strode over to her dresser. She began yanking out her workout shorts and T-shirts and flinging them violently onto the bed.

Rick watched her and gave a humored laugh. As he opened her door, his eyes fell on the blade. It was embedded all the way through the thick wood. Sheepishly, he said, "I'll just leave this here for you."

He was rewarded with a growl followed by a curse. Shutting her in with her anger, he smiled gleefully at a maid as she passed by. The woman's mouth fell open as she witnessed the deadly weapon's tip protruding from Jaden's door.

"Coffee for two in the dining room, please," Rick ordered, as he moved to the stairs. His hand struck out to pluck a fresh flower thoughtfully from a vase as he passed. "Miss MacNaughton will be down in a moment. And I would stay out of her way if I were you. She's a little testy this morning."

"Yes, Mr. Fletcher," the stunned woman mumbled before hurrying about her duties.

* * * *

Three days passed and Jaden was exhausted. Mack sent word that he was going to be late and Rick gallantly declared that he would stay with her until Mack's return. Rick not only attacked her by sword, but by fist and knife. She was sure he thought fighting romantic and at one time she might have been inclined to agree with him. But, nowadays, it just wore her out. She had enough fighting in her life. All she wanted to do now was sleep.

Rick never let her out of his sight. Jaden suspected he was wearing her out on purpose to keep her from leaving the apartment. Little did he know that keeping her indoors didn't protect her. The one she should fear the most proved he had no problem getting to her. There was nowhere to run.

Tyr didn't return, though he did find himself a comfortable place within her thoughts. Sometimes she would imagine she was attacking him and go at Rick full force. Luckily she remembered the man she fought, though Rick never once asked for mercy, and let up before she hurt him.

Slipping undetected into Mack's library Jaden sighed with relief. Rick was out of the house. She sent him on an errand across the city to a small bakery to pick up sandwiches. It was a needless task, but it bought her enough time to snoop through Mack's library. With the ambiguous directions she gave it would take him at least two hours to find the place and get back.

Jaden ignored the smell of her sweat-drenched shirt. She flipped on the light. Her feet were silent as she moved over the carpet. Coming to the desk, she laid her latest weapon, a knife, on top. Mack was a paranoid man, but also a prudent one. He wouldn't put cameras anywhere he did business and Jaden wasn't afraid of being discovered snooping. The servants had finished with the upstairs cleaning that very morning.

Within moments Jaden riffled through his desk, using the tip of her knife to pick the locks. There was nothing terribly interesting hidden in the drawers. A few folders with weapon speculations--from the mundane to the fantastic--were on top. Financial statements, business proposals, boring rows of number-filled ledgers fitted into the others. Leaving the desk as she found it, Jaden ignored the computer.

Mack only used his computer for research, often claiming not to trust his line of work to the susceptibility of hackers. Beyond a few simple texts, the system would be empty.

Jaden ran her eyes over the bookshelves, freezing as she listened to a maid pass by her door. To her relief, she felt the woman move on without stopping.

Jaden turned to the sundial behind the desk. Running her fingers over the top, she frowned. The safe didn't move. She continued on over the room, running her hands lightly over the walls and under paintings, lifting the edges of the rug for clues. She even scanned the bookshelf, knowing from the hours that she spent pulling books from it that there would be no secrets hidden there.

She paused in her investigation only to pull down the book on Dark Knights from the top. Within seconds she copied the foreign description of Tyr onto a piece of paper and shoved it in her pocket. She planned on translating it later.

Jaden found nothing else to capture her interest and sunk wearily into her uncle's thick leather chair. Leaning forward, she poured herself a glass of scotch from his decanter and swallowed it in several long gulps. The liquid burned pleasantly down her throat. She blinked heavily to keep her thoughts clear. She refilled her glass and rested it on her stomach as she spun her heels into the ground. The chair turned slowly until she faced the safe.

She eyed the large base carefully, looking for grooves in the plain design. She saw nothing. Then, standing, she took a quick drink before setting the glass behind her. Pushing at the dial, she jumped as it clicked. The top piece was the lock. Jaden smiled. She figured it out. Now all she had to do was think of the combination.

Trying a few numbers and receiving no reward for her effort, she grimaced with sudden insight. Attempting the lock again, she turned the dial around--seven, one, nineteen, seventy-eight. The latch clicked open and the top fell to the side. It was the day her mother had died, July 1, 1978.

Rhona's death was the whole reason Mack began hunting vampires. Her uncle had never forgiven Jaden's father for impregnating his sister and ruining her reputation. Mack had been very close to his sister, taking in her only daughter when she died.

Jaden refused to think of the mother she didn't remember. She had been a year old when Rhona had died. And though she resented her vampire roots, she never blamed the woman for falling in love with her father. A handsome immortal would be a hard thing to resist by a normal mortal woman. Their gaze alone could strike up the most fascinating feelings inside a person. Jaden thought of Tyr and frowned. He was her proof of that.

Her fingers trembled as she opened the top latch. Inside, tucked within the depths of the pedestal were a bound folder and a box. Jaden lifted them from the depths. Her breath caught in her throat as she felt the smooth box. Her mother's name was carved intricately in the top of the wood. She set it aside, unable to open it.

With a heavy, slow breath, she placed the folder on the desk. Seeing her liquor, she took another drink. The liquid didn't burn nearly as bad as the first time. It landed thickly in her stomach, numbing invitingly against the pain that threatened her chest.

She unbound the string around the folder, opening it to the front page. The words were written in French. Jaden sighed in weary frustration. Her uncle spoke the language fluently, having been raised partially by a French nanny when he was young. She didn't know why, but Mack had never taught her the language. She always assumed it was because he was too busy training her to be a warrior.

"You never write in French," Jaden muttered, thinking of her uncle. "What do you have to hide?"

Flipping through the file, she saw scientific charts and graphs and what looked like an endless line of medical sheets and blood work-ups. All was written in French. Halfway through the folder, she paused. Paper clipped to one of the pages was a photograph. The image was turned away, pressed into the sheet. On the back it read, *Sydney, 103, 1984.* Jaden recognized the slanted fall of her uncle's precise penmanship.

Jaden slowly turned the photo over. Her heart fell into her stomach. The image was of a young woman tied to a gurney. She looked scared, her eyes frozen in panic as she stared out from the slip of photographic paper. Her wide brown eyes begged for release, for help. At the same time, they admitted defeat. Jaden quickly turned the image back around. She couldn't look at the wounded stare.

Then, turning to the next page, she saw a manila envelope. The front again bore the number *103* in tight script. Unwinding the threaded latch, Jaden pulled the stack of photos from within. They were of the same woman only with a number of days penned on the edges. The first, bearing the title *Day One*, showed her neck gouged by familiar markings. She had been bitten by a vampire. As the days progressed, the woman's cruel change became evident. She was denied blood. Her face contorted with first anger, then tears, and then lunacy until finally, at the end, there was a skeletal figure of the same person. The woman's eyes still shone with life, an eerie discovery in such a withered and rotted frame. She was tied to the same bed with the notation, *Day Forty-three, External Termination.*

Jaden pressed her lips together. A sensation of dread overcame her senses as she put the photos back into their place. Behind the envelope was another picture turned upside down. And, behind that, another envelope filled with photographs. This one read, *Henry, 296, 1986.* Looking at the pictures, Jaden discovered that it was pretty much more of the same thing, but with other notations as well. The subject had been given a serum of sorts, which appeared to prolong the agony of starvation. But the subject ultimately died the same as the other--by an outside hand and in much pain.

Jaden stared at the skeletal face in horror. It was obvious that Henry had been tested upon most cruelly. Cuts were made on his arms until the wounds no longer had the power to heal themselves. Some of them went as deep as the bone. At one point, the arm had been sawed nearly off above the wrist. The only question was, by whom? And why did Mack have these pictures? What exactly did the experimenters have to gain by such tests? It was already common enough knowledge that it took only a few days for most vampires to go crazy when denied blood. And there was no cure to be had.

Did those who had done this think that they could find a cure? Or was a much worse experiment going on? Without reading the details, it was hard to say. And, the most damning of all questions, why was it Mack's handwriting on the back of the first photograph?

Seeing that there were more cases behind Henry's, Jaden refused to look at anymore. She wasn't sure how long she had been in the library and didn't want Rick to catch her. Rick was loyal to her uncle and she wasn't sure if he was to be trusted.

Jaden thought of Tyr. Was this what he thought her uncle to be involved in? No, she couldn't believe it. Mack might harbor a lot of hatred for creatures of the night, but she had to believe he would never be capable of such atrocities.

Slamming the folder shut, she turned to the box. Her fingers lingered on the carved swirl of her mother's name. Lifting the lid, she peered into the shallow depths. Inside was a piece of folded parchment, yellowed by age and tattered by time. Jaden lifted it, opening what looked to be a letter. She couldn't read the finely laid scrawling, not recognizing the language but knowing it to be old. Folding it carefully, she laid it aside. Beneath was a picture of her mother and a locket.

Jaden studied the black and white face that mirrored her own. Rhona had been a beautiful woman, glamorous and feminine in a way her daughter wasn't. Touching the face, all Jaden could feel was a sense of sadness at never having known the woman. She pressed her lips together and looked thoughtfully around the room. She had to get the file translated so she could read what was inside. Except whom could she trust?

Jaden thought instantly of Tyr. Surely, having lived so long, he would be able to speak almost every language. He might be able to even translate the letter she found. Her finger's trembled. What if the file incriminated her uncle? Tyr seemed to have already judged Mack without a trial. Did she dare hand the evidence over to her enemy? No. She would have to bide her time. But then did she ask Mack about what she had found? What would he say? Should she even trust him?

Jaden felt her body quake with apprehension. Carefully, she laid the picture and locket into the box and placed it back into Mack's safe. She could trust no one. Going to the bookshelf, she pulled a thick volume from the top ledge. The book looked old and carried with it a small cache that kept the pages together.

She felt only a moment's regret as she picked up her knife and cut into the binding. Stripping out the pages, she swapped the inside of the book with the inside of the folder. Closing the leather binding over the folder's contents, she latched up the book and set it aside. Then, taking the folder, she placed it back into the safe. She made sure everything was as she found it.

Hugging the newly rendered book to her chest, Jaden grabbed the yellowed letter before she strode to the door. She clutched her knife in her hand. Pulling the heavy oak open, she froze. Her eyes instantly met with Rick's. He was on the stairs, his hands laden with a brown paper bag. Cocking his head to the side, he eyed her burden.

Slowly, he continued forward. "I got the sandwiches."

"Oh," Jaden gasped. She hugged the book closer. She forced a smile to her lips, as she grumbled, "Good. I'm starving. Why don't you put them downstairs? I'll shower and be right down."

"Need any help?"

"Excuse me?" she gasped in affront. She spun on her heels to force a glare on him.

Rick laughed, holding up his free hand. "I meant with the book. What are you doing? Research?"

"Ah," Jaden felt her chest tighten with relief. Quietly, she mumbled, "The book."

"Are you all right?" he asked carefully. His head tilted in concern. "You look a little pale."

"I'm just tired from our workout," she lied. Rick saw right through it. Jaden had the stamina of an immortal.

"How about we do something else tonight? A movie maybe?" he offered with a boyish grin.

"No," she mumbled, backing away. "I'm beat. I think I'll just sleep tonight." Jaden forced a yawn. Again Rick saw through her. She hadn't slept a full night since she was a child. Mack made mention of it more than once.

"Fine," he answered, shading his eyes from her. "You'll still join me for dinner though, right? You did send me halfway across the state for these things."

Rick impishly waved the sandwich bag at her.

"Of course," she said. Rushing towards her room, she yelled over her shoulder, "I'll be right down. And you won't be sorry. Those are the best sandwiches in New York."

"Can I get you anything to drink?" he called after her.

"Ah, no!" she yelled in distraction. "I have a water bottle in my room."

Rick let her leave him, watching until her door closed firmly behind her. He knew there was something she was hiding from him. He wished with all his heart that she would confide in him. But past experience told him that she would try and face it alone--*and with a book on witchcraft, no less!* With a shake of his head and a frown on his face, Rick made his way to the dining room. Jaden was in over her head and it was up to him to save her.

* * * *

Jaden studied her half-eaten sandwich as she rubbed the back of her neck. Smiling politely, she pretended to listen to Rick. She couldn't concentrate. Her mind kept wandering back to the impression of ice blue eyes. A few short days hadn't lessened her longing for the disapproving vampire. In fact, despite the direness of Tyr's impending visit, Jaden found she was almost looking forward to seeing him. Such a development did not sit lightly with her conscience. Since he first started aggravating her, she had stopped dwelling as intently on wanting to die. His arrogance lit within her a fighting spirit until she almost felt alive again.

Smirking to herself, she thought of his overbearing presence. Sure, she was alive with hatred, but it was better than feeling nothing.

The dining room consisted of a long table surrounded by hand carved chairs and a matching elegant sideboard. The easeful decorations made the imposing room feel more intimate than should have been possible, with low lighting and soft, warm colors painted onto the paneled woodwork.

Jaden reached for her sandwich, taking it to her mouth. Her limbs felt a strange lethargy as she tried to bite. Setting it down untouched, she looked at her plate. Her teeth felt oddly numb, her gums lost the ability to feel the poke of her tongue. Rolling her neck on her shoulders, she blinked heavily. Rick's face danced before her eyes.

"Jaden?" Rick questioned, stopping in mid-sentence. He watched as she ambled to her feet. She swayed slightly, her eyes turning dull as she looked at him.

Jaden stumbled to the dining room door, ignoring the sparkling light as it rained down from the chandelier. The wiggling spots waltzed across Rick's tilting face. She saw his hands reaching for her. She shooed them back with a quick snap. Her aim missed, falling far to the right. Growling in dismay, she demanded, "What did you do?"

Rick tried not to take exception to her accusing tone. Reaching for her again, he was surprised when she darted past. He heard her footsteps bounding up the stairs, tripping over the hard steps as she moved. Jogging, he followed cautiously behind her.

"Jade," he began as amiable as he could muster. "Wait a minute."

She circled around to face him as she reached the top. Holding onto the rail, she backed away. Raising her voice, she yelled, "What did you do, Rick?"

"Jade, please," he begged. His guilt played all over his features. He became aware of the gathering servants behind him. They stared at Jaden and at him, though none moved to help her as she stumbled. Rick shooed them away with a deft wave of his hand. They immediately obeyed. Lifting his hands towards Jaden as he approached, he said, "It is just to help you sleep."

"You drugged me?" she cracked sharply. Reaching her bedroom door, her quaking fingers reached for the knob.

"You gave me no choice," he defended. A frown pulled at the lines between his narrowing eyes.

"You deceitful," she began. Her speech became slurred. Her ears echoed strange and hollow. Jaden stumbled into her bedroom. A glaze clouded her eyes.

"Me?" Rick scowled. "You've been lying to me for the last three days, Jade! I know you are up to something. I can read it plainly in your face." His words became desperate, as he begged, "Tell me what is bothering you. Trust me. Let me help. I can take care of you. Please, Jade."

"I don't need taken care of," she hissed. "I don't need anything from you."

Rick barged into her room, staying close enough to catch her if she fell and far enough that she couldn't hit him until she did.

"How?" she whispered. "When?"

"Your sandwich," he admitted through his shame. His eyes didn't leave her. "Your uncle left me some po--"

"I don't believe you! Mack would never!" she screeched with a crazed shake of her head. But then a memory from childhood surfaced, a dim memory she never visited. It was the same feeling now swimming in her limbs, slowing her blood. Then her arms had been small and Mack's voice had been soothing, begging her to sleep, to rest without nightmares.

Jaden's neck swung back on her shoulders. She fell roughly into the side of the bed. Using all her strength, she pushed herself to standing. Her fingers twined around the post for support. Her thoughts danced haphazardly in her head--a laugh from childhood, the voice of an unimportant tutor lecturing algebra to a ten year old girl who wanted nothing of it, the clang of swords, a line from a Broadway play shouted by painted actors. Rick's face danced and she tried to focus on it, blocking out the sounds. Hoarsely, she denied, "I am up to nothing."

"Well, I don't believe you," Rick countered easily. "I can see the packed bag you've hidden under your bed. Where are you going?"

"You don't know what you have done," she mumbled. A trail of spit slid over her wan complexion, down the side of her jaw and throat. Jaden could no longer stand. She sunk to her knees, powerless against the tide of the drug as it drowned her in its languid pool. Her mind reeled. "He's coming here … for me … tonight. You don't know what you have done."

Rick barely heard her words, but what he understood was enough. Going to her, he gathered her in his arms. His hands were tender as they stroked over her. "Who, Jade? Who's coming?"

"The devil," she muttered feebly, trying in vain to hold onto sanity. Her eyes rolled in her head. A blue gaze stared into her mind, filling with blood, dripping wet crimson tears. Spit continued to trail over the side of her cheek. Her mouth fell slack, as she said, "He's come to collect. He's come to judge."

"I'll take care of you, Jade. I'll always take care of you," Rick whispered. Jaden didn't hear him. Her mind collapsed into blackness.

Rick hugged Jaden's pliant body to his chest. He felt her strength weaken until she was a moldable mass within his arms. Her mouth opened in even breath. He reached for her pulse. It was steady and sure. Adjusting her in his arms, he lifted her from the floor. Her limbs flopped as he cradled her carefully before him.

Kicking her black bag from beneath the bed with his foot, he leaned over and picked it up. He angled the heavy duffel bag over his shoulder, keeping Jaden held fast in his arms. It was too late to take her to a safe house, but first thing in the morning he was going to get her out of New York. Tonight they would just have to make due with his apartment.

"I won't let him take you," Rick whispered when she fussed in his arms. Even in sleep she was fighting the effects of the drug. Or was she fighting him? He studied her restless features. The bruise was almost faded. Her clear skin was soft and free of makeup. She was so pale, the sensitive skin a gift from her father. Along her eyes he could see the purpling shadows of little sleep. She looked peaceful and so vulnerable. Knowing that he may never again get the nerve, he murmured, "I love you."

Jaden moaned as he bounced her body in his embrace. Her lips parted with a sigh. Rick leaned over, his heart in his throat, to hear her soft whimper.

"The devil is going to take me for my sins," she wheezed, half asleep. Her eyes opened once, the lashes too weak to remain so as they fell over her pin-pointed eyes. "And I am going to let him."

* * * *

London, England

"Why are we meeting in London?" Mack asked, breaking into a long silence. He hunched forward, leaning partly over the small round table of the café. His elbows pressed into the wood, feeling the imprint of the rough-hewn top. The opulent cut of his suit was sorely out of place in the literary atmosphere of the dark café. Someone spouted poetry into a microphone, annoying him with the college-boy whining. The kid really knew nothing of suffering.

Mack stared into the cold eyes that bore from the depth of an ageless face. Skin that was once dark glowed with a ghostly undertone. At Mack's words unlit eyes rose unwaveringly to search the mortal man's face. Mack turned his gaze away, pretending to look for a waitress in the dank room.

Stagnant air curled with smoke from burning cigarettes. When the old vampire didn't answer, Mack dared a glance at him. The face hadn't moved. Mack made out the flatness of the creature's nose and the thinness of his lips more from memory than the light afforded him in the dark corner.

"Has something happened, Pietro?" Mack whispered, growing alarmed. He did his best to sound calm, but his words were a bit rushed.

No," Pietro answered evenly. His words were thick in his Albanian accent, though his English was flawless. He didn't move, taking no enjoyment from their surroundings. He looked out from the straight length of his dark brown hair, the eternally graying temples hugged to his cheeks, snuffing his ears from view. "I am monitoring a situation here."

"What situation?" Mack demanded. Even though his tone was forceful, he still didn't meet the vampire's eyes. He knew better than to study the old gaze too long.

"It is nothing to be concerned over," the ancient voice allowed. "Just a vampire and his club."

"Fine." Mack waved his hand in distraction. Balling his fist, he pressed it hard into his lips, sighing heavily from his nose. The nostrils flared like an angry bull.

"What urgency forces you to seek me out?" Pietro asked at length. He lifted his hand absently as a woman tried to near the table. She turned around, taking her tray with her. The microphone crackled in the background as a new speaker cleared his throat.

"Is the list you gave me accurate?" Mack queried. Finally getting the nerve to look Pietro in the eyes, he studied the humorless expression.

"Yes," Pietro drew out with a rustling to his word. A woman with pink hair passed their table, her bangs pulled high off her head. She didn't pay any mind to the vampire and his mortal companion as she led her lover away. Pietro waited for her to pass, glancing briefly at her back, sensing she was undead. Then, smiling enigmatically, he added, "As complete as you need it to be."

"Then you have left some names off," Mack concluded. "I thought as much. Why? Who are you protecting?"

Pietro's lips tilted. He didn't answer.

"You promised that Jade and I would be protected," Mack exerted. His breath left his throat in a hiss. His eyes glared in helplessness as he waited for Pietro to answer.

"And so you have been," Pietro responded. "Here you sit before me-- protected."

"Jaden has been marked," Mack insisted.

"Then she was careless," the ancient vampire shrugged. "You should have trained her better. I told you all she would need to know. Methinks it is you who cannot control her."

"She is trained," Mack defended. "And she is loyal to me. She listens to me. You wanted proof of it so I gave you proof. Bhaltair is dead, is he not? Dead by her hand."

"Mmm," Pietro hummed wisely. His eyes closed. Before opening them, he said, "You tricked her."

Mack ignored the accusation. Frustrated, he said, "She was attacked by an aged vampire. One she was not prepared to fight."

"If she was not prepared, she shouldn't have sought him out," the creature said evenly. He held no sympathy for the mortal dhampir.

"She did not seek him out," Mack retorted in mounting frustration. He pounded his fist on the table in anger. Pietro raised a brow in warning. Mack knew well that Pietro didn't like tempers. Mack raised his hands in apology. Softening his tone, he managed through his frustration, "She was sought out. I believe the one that has sought her is named Tyr. The only reference I can find for such a creature is in a book of myths. It is said he is a legendary Dark Knight."

"He is," Pietro said evenly.

"Then it is true," Mack whispered, shaking his head. "There is no hope for Jaden. She can't possibly defeat one so strong."

Pietro shrugged, unconcerned.

"You sent him after her," Mack accused fervently. "Why? We had a deal. I have kept my end of the bargain. I have killed who you've asked me to kill. And I have done what you have asked me to do. Our plans are so close to becoming a reality."

"Not I," he responded, "but the council. They caught wind of her activities. They sent him to investigate her."

"So you knew?" Mack asked. "You knew they would send Tyr after her if she killed Bhaltair."

"I knew only that he was watching her," Pietro answered. "But I didn't know he would mark her--such a curious thing that, but hardly worth noting."

"I won't lose Jaden like I lost her mother," Mack swore. "You promised me protection. Call Tyr off. Get rid of him."

"Mayhap, you won't have to lose anyone," Pietro murmured. His eyes lit with a devious charm.

"What do you mean?" Mack asked, inspired by the familiar look in his companion's features.

"Use the Dark Knight to your advantage," Pietro answered. "His blood is strong and pure. It is second to only that of the tribal leaders. It will help you in your cause."

"And how do I capture him?" Mack gulped. His brain formed around the idea greedily. His heart pounded with excitement.

"You have an expendable army," Pietro shrugged. "And you have your niece. If he has marked her, he will come for her."

"You mean use her as bait?" Mack murmured, part in disgust and part in uneasy consideration.

Pietro nodded once.

"Maybe he only tracks her," Mack mumbled, doubtful. "What if he doesn't come for her at all?"

"Vampires are drawn to those they mark. And I have seen the beauty your niece was in her youth. If the rumors of it are now true, he will go to her again. The *Draugers*," Pietro stopped with a look of disgust as he mentioned the tribe, "are vain in that way. Beauty and youth sway them. You should use her as bait. Then, when he comes, trap him."

"But he may kill her," Mack protested, torn between his ambition and his love for his only family.

"Yes," Pietro said without sympathy or pity, "he may kill her either way."

Mack turned his gaze away, knowing he would do as Pietro said. He always did as Pietro said. He didn't have a choice. It tore at his gut to use Jaden, but he had done it her whole life. Soon though, his work would pay off. Then Jaden would understand the sacrifices they both had to make. She would be happy then. He would make her happy.

"I am famished," Pietro said quietly. His gaze traveled down to the table.

Mack visibly swallowed before jostling out of his jacket. Rolling up his sleeve, he laid out his arm across the table. Bracing himself for the first sting of pain, he didn't have to wait long. Pietro leaned forward, his fangs biting into the flesh offered him. Mack turned his gaze away, staring at the stage. His jaw hardened at the feel of cold fingers wrapping around his forearm. He felt teeth moving within him, lips sucking the fresh wound.

Soon it was over. Pietro didn't bother to stay around. Within a blink he was gone. Mack grimaced, reaching to a nearby table to grab a napkin. He pushed it to his opened wound and bent his elbow to apply pressure. Glancing around to make sure no one saw the interaction, he waved a waitress for a drink.

Soon, he thought. Soon it will be all over. And I'll finally be free.

Chapter Six

New York City, New York

Rick sighed nervously, laying Jaden down gently on his bed. Drawing his hands out from underneath her unmoving body, he tenderly pushed the hair back from her face. Her head rolled to the side, limp. He maneuvered it back onto the pillow.

"Don't worry, Jade," he whispered softly as he adjusted her limbs. He knew she couldn't hear him, but he talked anyway. "You'll be safe here. I'll keep you safe."

Rick watched her face carefully, hearing the even fall of her breath. The sound was only outdone by the loud hum of the refrigerator coming from the other room.

There were no windows in his bedroom. A single thread of light made its way from a lamp in his living room, giving her pale cheek a soft glow. Taking a quilt from the end of his bed, he covered her up and tucked the edges around her slender frame. Still she didn't move.

Rick let loose a deep breath as he touched her motionless cheek one last time. The longing he felt for her welled inside his chest. He'd loved her for a long time and part of him believed that if he just waited long enough, she would come to feel the same way for him. He had felt it in her when they first met--before the reality of their worlds collided. He could give her space, because he knew she had a hard life. Mack MacNaughton wasn't exactly the most affectionate of father figures.

Stretching his neck, Rick wearily rubbed the tension from his muscles as he stood. He made his way to his living room, leaving the door cracked so he could listen for her as he lay on the couch.

Picking her duffel bag up as he walked, he dropped it unceremoniously on his metal coffee table. His feet didn't break stride as he retrieved a bottle of beer from his kitchen. Twisting the cap, he threw it in the general direction of the wastebasket. It bounced off the wall, landing neatly in its target.

Rick didn't wait to watch it. Going to Jaden's bag, he took a long pull off of his beer, wiping his lips on the back of his hand. He studied the bag for a moment, debating with himself. Then, his decision made, he sat on the couch.

Rick unzipped the bag, looking in over the content. It had been so heavy that he expected to see an arsenal of weaponry within. Instead, he found her clothes. He smiled slightly, seeing the haphazard way they were thrown into the bag. She hadn't stopped to fold them. Snagging the strap of her underwear with the corner of his pinkie, he lifted it up into the light. He grinned sheepishly, gazing at the fine lace panties. He couldn't stop his mind from picturing them on her. Wearily, he glanced at the door to his bedroom. How he wished things were different between them.

Dropping the panties back inside the bag, he dipped his hand in after them to feel around. His fingers met the bottom. Just as they began to curl around the book's edges, a deadly voice intruded his thoughts.

"Did you think you could protect her from me?"

Rick startled. His hand hit his beer, pouring the content onto the floor, the liquid dumping and gurgling until empty. The glass rolled off the table with a crash. Rick ignored it. He stared at the large vampire before him. Behind the intruder, the door was still locked, his windows undisturbed.

"You're him, aren't you?" Rick asked, his mouth hard. He expected to face Jaden's devil some night. He just didn't expect it to be so soon.

Tyr watched the man in displeasure. He could hear Rick's mortal heart beating violently, though his body was calm. He smelled the strength in his blood, a strong life full of potent health.

"I have come for Miss MacNaughton. Step aside," Tyr ordered. He moved forward. To his pleasure, the man didn't move. He was glad he didn't. He wanted to fight him. He wanted to hit him for presuming to take Jaden away. He wanted to hit him because Jaden went with him. Tyr could detect her sleeping in the man's bedroom.

"She won't leave here," Rick said forcefully. The blond giant in front of him chuckled. "State your business."

"My business?" Tyr chuckled, a humorless sound meant to install fear. "You know what I am, mortal. I am her master and I have come for her. You have no business trying to stop me."

"Jaden has no master," Rick took a step back, keeping his body between the mysterious vampire and the door. He knew if the vampire got past him, Jaden would be helpless to fight him off. And he was the one who drugged her and left her vulnerable. He had to protect her. It was his duty.

"Do you think you are good enough for her, mortal? Do you think you can understand her?" He felt the feelings the man possessed and hated them. He tried to block them from his body, not wanting to feel the other man's love within him. Taunting where he knew he would do the most damage, Tyr continued, "You'll never be worthy of her. She knows it, too. I can feel inside of her. I feel everything inside of her. I know her better than you ever could. She is beyond you, mortal."

Rick shivered at the low whisper. The words gave him pause, denting the hope he clung to for so long. The vampire's strike was deep.

"She won't have you," Tyr whispered. The ice blue of his eyes glazed in emotionless candor. "And she does not love you."

"And you won't have her." Rick growled, darting forward to attack the gigantic enemy. Bravely, he struck out. He couldn't listen anymore.

Tyr let him punch his jaw, feeling the hard snap of it glancing off his chin. His lips opened. A thin trail of blood dripped where his bottom fang tore open the delicate tissue of his lip. Licking the bloody wound, his gaze bore into Rick's. The gashed closed, healing shut. Rick hesitated. The two stared at each other for a long, silent moment. Then suddenly, with a snap of his hand, Tyr hit him. Rick went flying across the room, banging loudly into the plaster wall. His body dented into it before crumbling on the ground.

Tyr frowned. Rick was a strong man, one that would be a great human warrior. But he was no match for a Dark Knight. An army would be no match for him. Tyr knew mortals couldn't kill him. They had tried and they always failed.

Tyr stalked to the fallen soldier. Rick groaned, looking up at him weakly. Tyr grabbed the man by the collar. Hatred and jealousy seethed in the vampire's breast. Tyr acted on animal instinct, his fangs straining to bite into the man's neck. Rick moaned, feeling the sharp pierce gouging into his artery. The fangs sliced through flesh like it was water. Rick's lips parted to draw a ragged breath. Spit gurgled up from his throat. He was helpless against the monster sucking and drinking along his skin.

Tyr swallowed with blind abandon, unmindful of what he did. He felt the man's life slipping away. He felt death coming swiftly as he stole the man's existence. Rick's power flooded him. Suddenly, Tyr stopped. He pulled back, his eyes tortured with what he was doing. Rick hung limp, passed out from the rapid blood loss. Blue lines edged the man's lips. Blood trailed from four puncture marks on his thick neck.

Tyr felt the heady energy life swirling in his head. He felt it in his eyes, filling them with the power of bloodlust. His mouth opened wide, wanting to continue, wanting to taste, glorifying in the pureness of the man's heart, the pureness of his blood. Rick was untainted by the normal human failings. His story was in the flavor of his life's essence. He was a good soldier, doing what he thought was best for the world.

Tyr's mouth closed as he fought to gain control over his greedy hunger. Pushing his lips to his teeth, he swallowed the remaining drops of blood lingering in his mouth.

Slowly, Tyr lowered the man to the ground. Rick wasn't dead, but if he lost any more blood he would be soon. Tortured by what he had almost done out of jealously, Tyr bit his finger, drawing a droplet of his own. Swiping the wound on his victim's neck, he watched as his blood sealed the holes. Rick might live, but he would be weak for some time if he did.

Without a backward glance, Tyr went to Jaden. He saw her sleeping peacefully on the bed. She didn't move. Her heartbeat was steady, too steady for a dhampir. Her power was dulled. He couldn't wake her.

Crossing to her with boneless grace, Tyr leaned the back of his hand to whisk past her face. Her eyes opened briefly to stare at him. Her pupils were small pin-pointed dots of black.

*Jaden? H*e whispered into her mind, his lips not moving.

"There are too many secrets, devil. You cannot hope to discover them all," she hissed, before falling into the lethargy of sleep once more. The flash of awareness was enough. Tyr knew she was drugged.

He had no choice but to take her with him. In her condition, there was no way for him to discover what she knew. Her eyes would be unreadable, clouded as they were with the haze of sleep. Her mind would be numbed from the forced slumber. As she dreamt, her thoughts would scatter, making the leftover fragments hard to decipher. It would take too long for him to probe within the muddled depths. Tyr cursed. He wouldn't have his answers tonight.

Scooping her up into the fold of his arms, he rested her cheek against his chest. She mumbled lightly before settling next to him. Her hand twitched, pressing against his heartbeat before falling to her stomach. Going to the living room window, he stepped dispassionately over Rick. The man didn't move, barely breathed.

Tyr jerked open the window with one hand, unable to form into mist with his burden. On last impulse, he grabbed the duffel bag laden with feminine clothing and slung it over his shoulder. If Rick recovered he didn't want the man fingering Jaden's intimates again. He didn't want the mortal to have anything of her. Tyr had little time to wonder at the jealous act as he left. Within a blink, he was gone, flying effortlessly through the night with Jaden in his arms.

* * * *

Mack pulled the mauve privacy curtains along the metal track to block out the insufferable sounds of misery. The thick material was no match for the howls of pain escaping the lips of a man withdrawing from heroin. Directing a scowl at Tom, he ordered, "For goodness sake, Carter! Get this man a private room."

Tom nodded, hurrying to do as he was commanded.

Mack wrinkled his nose, sniffing in protest against the disinfectant smell of the hospital. The intensive care unit was unusually lively due to the man hollering obscenities at passing nurses as his body thrashed against restraints. One moment he was begging for drugs, the next he was cursing the world for his misfortune. Mack had no pity for the man. He had no compassion for the weakness of addicts.

Eyeing Rick's pale form on the bed, he met the man's wakening gaze. His cheeks were starting to flush from the four units of blood he had been given, but Mack could tell the man was still weak from his ordeal. Absently, he tossed his leather briefcase and coat in a chair.

Going to the bed, he looked at the large IV in the man's arm. The clear plastic tube led up to a hydrating bag of saline. Rick's skin was clammy, his face taut against his cheekbones.

"What happened?" Mack asked in his ever matter-of-fact tone. The man next to them yelled in pain, again demanding drugs. Rick flinched.

Mack frowned. Turning, he disappeared behind the curtain. Rick heard a loud smack and then silence. When Mack came around the corner, he was wiping his knuckles on a handkerchief. Drawing closer to the bed, Mack laid his hand on the railing.

"There, I daresay he won't be bothering anyone for a spell," Mack said by way of explanation. Rick smiled in tired gratitude. He hadn't enjoyed wakening to the sounds of the irritating man.

"What did the doctor say?" Rick queried in a soft voice, mindful of eavesdroppers. "Did you talk to them?"

"They don't know what to think," the man admitted. "At first they thought it a suicide attempt or internal bleeding, but they didn't find any wounds. They said you lost a lot of blood and was given a transfusion."

"How long have I been out?" Rick wondered aloud, moving as if to sit up.

"Two days," Mack answered. "They gave you something to sleep at Tom's request. He signed you in. He would've taken you to our personal facility but there was no time. Don't worry. I'll take care of the doctors. They won't be asking you anymore questions."

"Two days?" Rick groaned in exasperation. He tried to push himself up only to fall back again with a shiver. "We have to go. I can't stay here."

"What happened, Rick? Where's Jaden?" Mack's watched the man carefully, hating to see him in such a sorry state. Inside, his stomach knotted.

"She wasn't found?" Rick said sharply. His head began to clear. "He must have taken her. He said he was coming to take her."

"Who said?" Mack asked, though he was scared he already knew.

"Some vampire," Rick mumbled. Mack lowered the railing on the bed as Rick tried to sit up. The sick man swung his legs over the edge. Grimacing at the annoying needle stuck in his arm, he pulled it out with a hard yank. "He was strong, Mack. Unlike any I've seen before."

Rick's arm trickled with blood. Mack handed him his handkerchief.

"I tried to fight him. I couldn't. His mind was like a black hole that sucks you in. I have never seen anything like this creature. I doubt a hundred men could've stopped him." Rick absently blotted his small wound. Silently, he added, *let alone one lone woman.*

"Tyr," Mack whispered.

"What is this Tyr?" Rick glanced up. "I heard Jaden mention it."

"It is the demon you fought and lived, son," Mack said with a pat to the man's shoulder. "You're very lucky. He is not known for his mercy."

"The devil," Rick muttered, shaking his head. "I should have listened to her. Jade tried to warn me. God help me, Mack, I drugged her like you ordered. She was planning on running away. I should have just let her go. Instead, I left her helpless at that monster's mercy."

"It's not your fault. None of us could've known what was coming." Mack stood, turning at the sound of an entering nurse. The woman pulled back the curtain.

"Mr. Fletcher?" The woman stopped cold, gasping in dismay to see her patient sitting up in bed, his discarded IV hanging to the floor. The light blue scrubs she wore shook and swished as she rushed forward. "You're not to be out of bed."

Rick grimaced, ignoring the woman. Looking pointedly at Mack, he said, "Get me discharged."

Mack nodded as he gathered his briefcase in hand. Throwing his jacket over his arm, he strode from the room.

The nurse placed her hands on her hips. Her wide brown eyes tried not to laugh as she kept her face dutiful. "You are not going anywhere for a couple days, Mr. Fletcher. The doctor will never allow it."

"Hum," Rick answered. He laid back at her insistence, feeling a little weak and not completely averse to the pampering. "My friend is very persuasive."

"So am I," she challenged. Rick smiled at her, his eyes roaming naturally over her small frame. She placed her hands on her hips. Cocking her head to the side, she asked coyly, "Finished?"

Rick chuckled to be caught staring like a fool. With a groan, he closed his eyes. "I need to get out of here. I've been in bed too long."

* * * *

Island of Delos, Cyclades

The carved stone chamber of the council was imbedded far beneath the surface of the small island, hidden away from human eyes and the ferocity of the Aegean sun. A large stone table, circular in shape with a large hollow center, graced the middle of the council hall. In the middle of the unbroken circle, in the hollow, the floor was sunken a few feet below the table's legs with a short pedestal in the direct center holding a lighted torch for illumination. It was not a place that immortals and mortals alike would be fond of finding themselves. Once someone entered the circle to be judged, it was rare that they were allowed back out alive.

High-backed chairs surround the table in eight spots, all but one occupied by leaders of the tribes. The Moroi chair stood empty. It was well known and pitied that Vladamir, tribal leader of the Moroi, was in a *sopor*. He did not partake of human blood, only rested in his unnatural sleep. It was not known why the Moroi leader had chosen such a life only that it had been so for a long time. Another vampire of the same tribe, Jirí, ruled in his place. Jirí was a loyal tribesman, but not fully trusted by the other council leaders. They often omitted him, without his knowledge, from talks of old things.

Colorful mosaics decorated the walls depicting the bites of vampires, legendary and real. Around the doors, dark red draperies hung, framing the thick old wood. The round table dominated the rectangular room, its legs and edges hand carved with old designs. The floors were formed with gray marble slats, a black impression of the tribal symbols carved into the stone behind each of the eight chairs. In front of each chair was again imprinted the symbol of the tribe within the wood tabletop.

The firelight from the center torch cast its ghoulish contrast on the seven faces of the attending leaders. Every tribe originated from different regions across Europe and Asia, each leader officially in charge of their region of descent. Though, in the old days, before the time of an organized council, there had been more of them. Warring and petty jealousy had driven tribes to conquer tribes--much like the human forces conquered other weaker nations. It had been a glorious time for the vampire--the bloodshed and anguish of the old days.

The remaining eight formed the council, each possessing their own unique abilities. They all excelled in certain powers, passing on the strong force to their benighted children. But for all their differences, they were ultimately descendent from the same true bloodline.

Theophania of the Vrykolatios was keeper of the island and of all vampiric secrets. She lounged lazily in her high-backed chair, her legs and arms draped with the seductive allure of an ancient queen, her straight black hair flowing over her shoulders to her waist. She had a face that could lure men to their deaths, even without her vampiric powers. Often servants would crowd her, fanning her body with large palms. They would bring her mortals to eat upon like grapes. Theophania found herself above the hunt for food, not liking to waste the energy it took to capture her prey. Her place was acknowledged as the head of the circle though in truth it was the same. She lived an isolated existence, away from the influence of modern life, thriving on the old ways. Because of her isolation, she was respected and looked to preside over the gathering.

Her sister, Chara of the Vrykolakas tribe, was at her side. Both sisters were dark and beautiful, and although they were not twins, they could easily pass as such with little effort. Whereas Theophania dressed as an ancient, showing a large amount of her skin beneath her metal bodice, Chara was more contemporary in her tastes with a revealing dress of thin black and lips painted the color of blood. She'd often slick back her black hair, wearing large amounts of dark eye makeup. When she smiled, she exposed the tips of her fangs with the practiced ease of endless centuries.

Andrei of the Myertovjec was placed alongside Chara. His flirtatious eyes and lust for living, though he was dead, made him a charming companion but highly unreliable. He, too, had dark hair and a face so beautiful women ached to look at him. The Myertovjec's appetite for sex was only to be outdone by their craving for drink. His kind often threw compulsive parties, feasting on whole families in a single night with the vigor of an all out orgy.

Ragnhild of the Drauger clan made his place at the left side of Theophania. He too had a taste for the old ways, missing the lusty lifestyle of the old Norseman. His weathered voice boomed when he spoke like the dictating lord over his manor. Long braids bound through his blond hair at his temples and he was the only vampire with a beard. How he managed to keep it was a mystery to even the council. And Ragnhild, in his vanity over the trim whiskers, was not telling his secret.

Ragnhild was seated next to Vishnu of the Rakshasa. Vishnu carried herself as the Indian princess she had been. The richness of her clothing wrapped around her slender body in silken grace. Her temper was short and her patience constantly tried, much like the God she had been named for. Her arms were adorned with bracelets. The long locks of her black hair parted in the middle to spill about her shoulders to frame her wide almond-shaped eyes. Her gaze sought those around her with a keen, dark gray beauty.

Amon, leader of the Impudula, carefully beheld all those around him. When he sat, he had a tendency to lean towards Vishnu. They shared a common bond of blatant, unashamed self-indulgence. His black skin shone almost gold as he threw out the presence of a supreme being. It was only for the council that he left his homeland of Africa where he lived a quiet existence in a grand palace.

Pietro of the Llugut was the last of the seven. He had been chosen for the dark gift past the prime of his youth, which often gave his handsome features the appearance of knowledge and grace. His chair stood opposite Theophania, which was to his liking. He didn't care for the immortal woman and his feelings were well acknowledged and returned. Pietro was the last of his line and refused to make more of his kind. He sat brooding in his silence, ignoring all but the torch as it caught his attention.

As the leaders talked amongst themselves, Pietro listened intently to all their words, his ears perking up beneath his dark veil of permanently graying hair. His fingers curled, settling beneath his flat nose.

Completing the circle, between Andrei and Pietro, was Jirí's appointed seat. It stayed empty.

"Ragnhild," Chara began. She looked at her sister, both of them exchanging secretive sulks. Ragnhild turned his Viking blue eyes to the women. Chara smiled a seductively sweet smile that made Andrei frown. "What have you heard from your knight?"

"He's in the New World," Ragnhild answered gruffly. The leaders' noses wrinkled in distaste. None of them found a liking for the Americas. It was too far to travel for too little reward. The Drauger's voice rose as he spoke, divulging his information for all to hear, "I have been sent documents."

A stern quietness fell over the leaders as Ragnhild paused. He reached into his tunic shirt to pull out a tattered piece of paper from within.

"This is a document of Alan MacNaughton's," he continued. "It was taken off of one of his men. It's a work detail for one of his *excursions*."

Pietro's head snapped up to study the page. The word 'excursions' had been said with supreme disdain. All other eyes were turned the same way.

"Would MacNaughton be so foolish as to write down his deeds?" Chara questioned aloud. Pietro nodded in agreement.

"He is overbold," Amon said quietly. "He would dare much."

"Excursions," Vishnu said with disgust, her tone mimicking Ragnhild's. Amon glanced regally at her, sharing the sentiment but keeping quiet. Hissing between her teeth, she said, "I do not need to hear more. Order Tyr to kill him. Mortals are too tiresome."

"He's a hard man to get to," Ragnhild said, not liking the interruption.

"If your Tyr is not up to the challenge of a mere mortal, then I'll be happy to send Shiva. He will make MacNaughton suffer." Vishnu smiled at the prospect.

"I didn't say he couldn't do it. He will kill the man soon enough. But right now he is carrying out his orders to discover what he can of the dhampir Jaden MacNaughton." Ragnhild's anger dissolved quickly at the look the sisters gave him. "It is too soon to act so impulsive. There is too much that needs to be learned first."

"And what of the rumors?" Pietro asked quietly.

All eyes turned to him in amazement. He hardly ever deemed to speak.

"What rumors?" Andrei asked, ready to steal some of Chara's attention back to himself.

"That he has made the dhampir his indicium," Pietro replied quietly. "Mayhap he cannot be trusted."

"What are you implying--" Ragnhild began, rising to his feet in anger. He levitated over his chair. Blood swirled dangerously in his eyes, his fangs extending in caution, as his face contorted into a dark look of forewarning.

"Sh, Ragnhild," Theophania whispered. She waved her hand through the air. "No one is insulting the cleverness or strength of your tribe."

Ragnhild sat but directed a hard glare at Pietro. Pietro returned his look with one of his own before growing bored with the battle and turning away.

"Continue," Theophania instructed.

"I only wondered at the rumor," Pietro shrugged as if it were no big deal. The old Albanian again found renewed interest in the flames. He was done talking.

The attention on Pietro turned dismissive. Soon what he said was forgotten.

"The document," Ragnhild started anew, "describes that a woman is to be turned by an unnamed vampire working for MacNaughton. The new vampire is then taken, strapped down and left to the whims of MacNaughton's patron. Ultimately the vampire is done to death. From what Tyr has gathered it seems sometimes the vampires are raped by the patrons, or by his men in front of the patrons. They can be cut, tortured-- whatever has been paid for."

The leaders' eyes became livid with volcanic rage. Ragnhild dropped the paper before him in the table. Standing, Theophania screeched, "Who dares defy our laws? Which vampire turns for such purposes? It matters not what has been done with a mortal woman. But once she is turned she is ours. I want the traitorous vampire brought here to face judgment."

"To help a blood being use our kind for sport!" Amon said in disgust.

"No one makes sport with our kind, but us," Vishnu added, with a stiff nod to Amon. None of them cared to mention that their kind had done worse to humans since the dawn of time. To them, it wasn't the same thing. Humans were beneath them--like cattle grazing in the field, waiting to be slaughtered.

"This," Ragnhild said with a glare at Vishnu, "is why I have not ordered Tyr to kill MacNaughton. I have ordered that he find out who is helping him. Then all parties will be brought here for us to feast upon. We will show these transgressors the true meaning of pain. Their last lesson on this earth with be--"

"--of anguish," Chara murmured, a sparkle in her deadly eyes. A slow breath slid from beneath her widely parted mouth. Slowly, her crimson lips curled into a smile. The remembrance of spilled blood entered lustfully into her eyes.

Pietro snorted. The others ignored him, nodding their approval. When the murmuring died down, Pietro questioned, "And the dhampir?"

"Bring her too," Andrei said to Ragnhild. "Let us judge her for ourselves."

Ragnhild nodded and it was agreed. Suddenly, all eyes turned to a cobwebbed hole high in the ceiling. All talk of Tyr ceased. Ragnhild pulled the paper from the table, slipping it back into his tunic.

"Jirí's report is of little importance," Vishnu murmured. "I don't care about a club of London young ones. Let them kill themselves."

A figure fell down from the ceiling, landing neatly on his feet. He folded his hands elegantly in front of him, standing tall as if the descent took no effort. His long, wavy brown hair landed gently on his shoulders. Smiling politely, he respectfully met the eyes of the others gathered, nodding his head to all around.

"Jirí of the Moroi," Ragnhild's weathered voice acknowledged. His old, blue eyes glowed slightly yellow from his handsome Nordic face. "Has Vladamir not risen from his rest to take his rightful place in the chair?"

"Nay, he has not. But his body is safe, buried deep," the new arrival allowed, as he had every meeting since his first.

When Jirí was seated at his chair, Theophania silently raised her delicate fingers. One of the four corner doors burst open revealing a line of eight beautiful, young women in white shrouds, each a human native of their respective vampire. The women walked dutifully to their designated master or mistress to stand by the sides of their chairs.

The leaders could smell the rare ethnic purity of the offering's blood as it flowed in their veins. Their eyes were clouded with a fine mist. Their bodies glowed with warm brilliance. Pulling up their sleeves, the women held an arm out for the vampires to drink. And, as the leaders partook of their meals, all hid their thoughts, suspiciously wary of the motives of others.

Chapter Seven

Jotunheimen Mountain Range, Norway

"I'm going to butcher him." Jaden's foot tapped in irritation. Her jaw tightened, worked and pulsated with all the pent up frustration four, long days could bring. Her eyes saw red. Her heart hammered the color until blood flooded her face, neck and body. Outrage poured out over her like a rockslide from the highest cliff on a mountain top. Only her rocks had nowhere to land, no ground to pummel and crack against with a satisfying burst of destruction. She was trapped with her anger, imprisoned with her outrage.

She remembered Rick drugging her sandwich and she remembered wanting to kill him for it as she collapsed on the floor. However, when she awoke, ready to strike out though her mind was hazy, her fists met with air not flesh and her eyes met with the solemn color of a gray-green stone prison. From her estimation, it had been at least four days since she awoke in the dark tomb. But who could tell how long she slept before then? Her dreams had been long and endless, but were impossible to keep time by. They could've lasted a night or a month.

She knew who had her. Tyr. He spoke with her through the thick iron door, pushing food beneath the little swing gate for her. As for the fare, it wasn't very inventive--cold meats and cheeses, bread and fruit. More humiliating than that was the linen covered chamber pot he allowed her for her more personal needs. Each night he came, he offered to let her out if she would be willing to 'behave'. She offered to smash his face into the back of his skull when he did. Needless to say, he left her alone with her anger--and oh how her anger did seethe!

Jaden could feel him outside her door. It was the only diversion her mind was afforded, aside from staring mindlessly at the dancing flicker of a candle flame and plotting her revenge. She had smashed the first candle given her, only too late realizing her mistake. The darkness surrounded her like a crypt. A straw mat lay on the hard floor as a bed. The stone wall and ceiling were constructed so thick that Jaden realized the sound proof walls were more than likely underground, as they weren't bricked around, but hollowed out.

After careful examination, she discovered claw marks dug into the stone. No mortal could've made such a marking on the walls. The prison was originally constructed to keep a more dangerous breed within. It was made to hold vampires. Jaden smiled, longing to lock Tyr within these silent walls. But if her fantasy was ever going to be close to becoming a reality, she would have to bide her time and she would have to let her anger go. He could smell it too easily on her.

Standing, she went over to the door, greeting the oblong shape of her shadow as it crept before her. Glancing at the food door, she grimaced. Already, she knew it couldn't be opened from the inside. She had bloodied her hands trying.

Turning her back to the iron door, Jaden kicked the metal in steady thumps with the back of her heel. She hated to admit that she was starting to waver. How men spent years in such isolated prisons, she had no idea. Four days and she was already loosing her mind. Her limbs longed to stretch out and her skin begged for the feel of the open night air.

Any truce she called would be temporary--as temporary as it took for her to walk out the door. Surely it wouldn't be too hard to discover what part of the states she was in. They couldn't have gotten too far out of New York.

"I'm going to kill him," she hissed under her breath, repeating the words like a mantra. As she felt him draw near, she stopped pounding.

"*Argh*," Tyr growled. A door slammed with a heavily muffled thud. It sounded like a trunk or coffin lid. She couldn't be sure. Without a window, it was hard to tell if it was night or day. "What is it woman? For the sake of Odin! Stop that blasted noise!"

"Good morning," she called with as much sugary sweetness as she could muster. She pasted a false smile on her face so that her words would sound properly concerned and contrite. "Did I wake you?"

Jaden felt him falter outside the door. She could almost see the question in his ice blue eyes as he tried to discern what she was up to now. Hiding her laugh, she waited.

"What is it?" he asked at last.

"My, my," she said with a playfully scolding tsk. "Aren't we the grumpy little vamp?"

"Are you … pouting?" His words were filled with the beguiling affects of a stupor.

Jaden's grin widened. She had never thought sweetness would send this vampire off guard so much quicker than fighting. "I do have quite a lot to be upset about. I'm in jail. I have been kidnapped, wrongly accused--"

"Jaden--"

"--of a crime that remains unnamed and I am in need of a hot bath," she finished triumphantly. Wrinkling her nose at the all too pungent truth of her words, she mumbled, "badly."

"It's not a jail," he said quietly, his tone belying the matter-of-fact statement of his words. Jaden didn't have to strain to hear his low, pointed answer as it came in an aggravatingly reasonable tone. "It is more like a dungeon. And I did try to free you, but you refused to come out. As to the bath, I have been able to smell you for days. Only I figured that if you didn't mind smelling that way, I shouldn't mind it either."

Jaden's expression fell with scathing insecurity only to be replaced by the more biddable sensation of her outrage. With sudden insight, she realized he was having fun at her expense. "Why, you--!"

"Tsk, tsk, now who is the grumpy one?" he taunted with even assurance.

"Just let me out," she growled. She gave the door a vicious kick. Snapping back her foot, she grabbed it, hopping as she tried to rub out the stinger. Jaden let loose a dark curse. Liking the feel of it on her tongue, she followed it with a few more, each growing in intensity.

"Ah, I think you are forgetting one thing," Tyr reminded her composedly through her tantrum. He smiled at her hushed venom. He had been trying to illicit her promise not to try and escape him--not that such a thing as escape would be possible. He would find her wherever she went. There was no evading him. Part of him hated the fact that he must force her cooperation in such away. But no, the council's orders had been clear and Jaden MacNaughton hadn't given him much of a choice or much help.

Tyr wondered if he kept her in there too long. He just wanted her to cool her temper--a task that took a lot longer than he first imagined. Sometimes he forgot that a week was much longer to a human than to a vampire. Shrugging off his guilt, he leaned his head to the door and shut his eyes.

He could feel her moving within. He could always feel her. She surrounded him, haunted him in his dreams. No matter what he did, she was inside of him, stirring emotions and desire where he preferred there to be silence.

"Tyr?" A long moment passed before her voice trailed from within. The word was soft, almost heartbreakingly abandoned. He held silent against the door, knowing she couldn't hear him. He felt her quiver. He felt her heart fall.

*What? H*e thought wearily, allowing her to detect his word within her mind.

"Let me out," she paused. He could hear her breathing become staggered. He felt her hand lay next to his forehead on the door and he jolted back as if it was direct sunlight. Under her pants came a soft, "please."

"I must have your pledge that you'll behave," he said. "I won't have my time done in--"

"I promise," Jaden said, forcing the words to be formed. Her anger faded by small degrees. She still hated him, but she was beginning to hate the encroaching stone walls more. She definitely didn't want to hear his lecture on wasting a vampire's time. In fact, the concept was an oxymoron. All a vampire had was time.

To her relief, a heavy lock was thrown on the door. The iron soundlessly swung open on its hinges. Jaden paused, swallowing, not knowing what she should expect. But, whatever she anticipated seeing, she couldn't have been more wrong.

The prison led out into a stone cavern filled with the natural carvings of rock formations. She had been right. They were under the earth in the belly of a cave. But it wasn't just a cave. It was a home, too. *His home.*

Jaden shook. She panted, trying to force her legs to move. Her mind sung with freedom, only to be frightened in the face of it. Closing her eyes for a split second, she forced herself to move, not knowing what horrors she could possibly find in a vampire's lair.

Jaden slowly took a step forward, terrified of looking too closely at the surreal ambiance of her surrounding. The room was amazedly clean, no spider webs hung from the ceiling, no dust gathered on the walls and furniture. For a vampire's lair it was astonishingly well attended. Thick red rugs lined the smoothed floors. The stone had been worked flat by endless pacing until it was as fine as any marble. At first she didn't detect Tyr watching her carefully. She moved past him, her eyes twitching in one fascinated direction, her head urging her in another.

Anchored into the ceiling hung a bed. Instead of wooden posters there was thin red gauze clinging around chains as they led up, hiding them from view. The gauze swept over the top stone forming a roof of sorts over the mattress. On the bed was a silken coverlet of the deepest red edged and decorated with embroidered gold. The craftsmanship of it was fine, sewn by hand. Matching pillows scattered the top.

Jaden had to turn her eyes away in embarrassment as she thought of Tyr's large body encompassing the span of the mattress. It was a mistake. Her vision took her right to the object of her fantasies. Tyr raised a brow in expectation. He was handsome, dressed all in unforgiving black. His hand lifted with the silent, consuming ease of shadows creeping over the earth.

Jaden shivered, feeling as if he could read the wicked thoughts that swam in her head. She tried to deny her body, but seeing his cool eyes the fire he ignited in her swept over her once more. All anger disappeared, replaced by passion. She resisted the urge to go to him, knowing he must have surely put it in her. When she spoke the words were quiet.

"Where is your coffin?"

"I have no need of one here," was his swift, low response.

Jaden was sorry she asked. It would have been better for her self control to imagine him in a rough pine box. Then a sudden insight hit her. *We must be under a crypt, which means we are in a city.*

"Go ahead," Tyr urged her quietly from behind. His words carried the soft essence of a babbling brook with the hard finality of fire--tender, yet dominating. "Explore. For as long as you are here, my home is your home. But, try and escape, and my home will become your prison."

Jaden glanced at him, seeing the handsomeness of his youthful face, the steadfastness of his firm mouth. The black of his turtleneck sweater and pants contrasted his pale beauty in a most dangerous and delectable fashion. She waited for him to hunch over, his body conforming as he stalked her, attacking like the wild beast she could feel churning beneath his surface. He held flawlessly still.

Seeing the tip of his lip threaten to twitch at her staring, she turned her attention back to the bed. It was the last place she wanted to look. It brought forth images that she tried hard to banish in her dreams. Pride kept her from darting away. She forced herself to resume inspection.

At the end of the bed was a trunk, very large and old in design. Next to the bed a thin table fitted along the wall, its top barren, a single high-back chair pushed up against it. Candles sprinkled in sconces and on surfaces adding a soft glowing light that was very ambient of his whole seductive theme. To her side, close to the prison door, was a wide cushioned chair carved in a style of a throne, but done in such a way that she was sure she had never seen the like of before. Through the dimness of the corner, she detected an unlit fireplace, its stone mantle carved into the wall.

From the bedroom, there was only one escape. Seeing through the soft flickering of firelight, Jaden's feet skirted past the end of the bed, following the carpeted corner of the rug. As she turned the corner, she was forced to take a step down. Jaden gasped. She could feel Tyr moving behind her, studying her carefully for her reaction. But she had little time to wonder why he should care what she thought.

For a man, even an undead one, the home was tastefully done. Jaden was surprised at the continuity of style. The cave was set up like a studio apartment, only there was no kitchen or bathroom, just one long chamber that functioned as a living room.

The oval room fell forward like the hall of a small museum. Couches and chairs were impressed into the stone along the sides, cushions fitted perfectly to the carved inlets in black with red and gold pillows artfully arranged. On the far side, the floor was carpeted completely. The space was left wide and open. Jaden decided it would be the perfect sparring corner. In the far wall she detected a wooden door with large iron hinges.

A stone-based couch sat before a fireplace. The crackling of wood was distinct now that she was before it. One would have to walk down a slight incline to reach the comfortable nook.

She could feel heat pouring over the room in perfect temperature. Hanging from the tallest crevice in the center of the room was a cast iron chandelier with melted candlesticks waiting dormant. Matching candle sconces were set into the walls, the candles unlit.

But Jaden's greatest discovery was the hollowed out spaces along the wall, encasing ancient to not so old artifacts. Where she expected to see only weaponry and torture devices she found paintings and old nobleman clothes. The groupings passed over the walls like a testament of the eras of human growth--and failings. Odd knickknacks found their respective places amidst their brethren. Swords hung next to their respected inlets, the metal gleaming and well kept. A gem encrusted jewelry box settled next to a plain locket resting alongside a metal crown. A silver handled cane rested next to a snuff box and top hat. A rifle met with a leather satchel and silver timepiece. An expensive pistol, available at any American pawn shop, nestled next to a box of ammo. The items were as endless as time itself.

Tyr watched Jaden's expression cautiously. She was the first mortal he'd had in his home. It was strange, watching her eyes, waiting anxiously for her opinion of it. When it came, he felt a little part of him release a nervous hold.

"It's beautiful."

The words were a softened whisper, admitted with reluctance and awe. Tyr nodded his thanks. She didn't see it. Her eyes discovered the oldest collection, the collection from his human past. Following her gaze, the items seemed like a once loved but now worn and forgotten dream.

Jaden slowly made her way forward over the slight incline. Stepping next to the fireplace, she stopped by a lonely inlet. Most predominately displayed was the cross shaped handle of a broadsword. The blade was straight, perfectly even and looked sharp to this day. Jaden leaned forward seeing an old inscription weathered across the tang. Her fingers itched to touch it, to test the mighty weight. A round wood shield rested on the ground, its edges a bit chipped and worn. Next to the sword was a trunk. The edges once tattered were now smoothed and disfigured by time. She reached down to lift the lid and hesitated. Her fingers trembled, afraid to touch it lest it turn to dust.

"Go ahead," Tyr whispered from behind. "It is only clothing and a suit of armor."

Jaden refrained, even with his offer. It didn't seem right disturbing the relics, as if her touch could undue the last centuries and alter time. On its shelf were some crude grooming instruments, bronze artifacts, an amber decorated brooch, a once brightly colored tunic shirt and some leather shoes starting to stiffen and corrode.

Jaden closed her eyes, not turning away. Her breath came in hard gasps. Guilt, thick and choking, surfaced within her. Her nose stung with the need to cry out. She only now realized the true impact of a vampire's life and the length in which Tyr had lived. He had seen so much of life, but even more of death. He had seen countless eras come and go and still he braved forward, forever alone. And here she was ready to give up after a few lousy years. She was a coward.

"Why do you keep these?" she asked hoarsely. She already could guess at his answer. Only a sentimental being would care about such everyday things--things used and discarded by the humans of their respective eras without thought, yet kept and preserved by an immortal who never forgot them. An immortal who loved and cared for them, dusting them off for an eternity, keeping their dead spirits as alive as he--stuck in their immortal tomb never to find the rest everything must eventually seek. Time had no meaning in this cavern of infinite age.

Tyr studied her from behind with the silence of a walking ghost. He saw her shoulders tremble, felt the agony of her grief flowing from her. Her anger slipped, her animosity fleeing with it. Carefully moving forward he hesitated before touching her shoulder.

"It is all the memories I have of the passing time," he answered in a low murmur, surprised that the admission came out. It rested between them, spoken as an answer to her unasked questions.

Jaden stiffened beneath his hand but didn't pull away. She lacked the strength to fight him. She took a deep breath and then another. She couldn't face him. She couldn't face herself. She wanted the floor to open and swallow her up.

When she didn't move, Tyr became alarmed. The feelings stirring from her were not her usual strength and defiance. He forced her around, her body too weakened to protest.

"What?" he urged softly. His eyes ran over her body. "Are you ill?"

The words were a whisper, one she heard but couldn't fathom. So instead of answering, she asked, "Can I have a bath?"

When Tyr hesitated Jaden glanced at his face. It was as pale as she remembered. But the unnatural blue of his eyes was not so cold and unfeeling. They bid her to go to him, to draw comfort from his arms, to lay her head to his chest and confess everything as a small child would to a loving parent.

Jaden drew strength from within, turning her eyes purposefully hard against him. She couldn't tell if it was his power pulling the emotion from her or her own treacherous heart seeking comfort where there could be only a lonely void. Either way, it wasn't in her best interest to indulge. Tyr wanted information from her and would stop at nothing to get it, had kidnapped her to discover what she knew.

She'd be damned before she would incriminate herself or Mack. No matter what Mack was guilty of, she would be the judge of it. She wouldn't turn her only family over to the hands of a professional killer. Faulted or not, Mack was her kin and she loved him as much as she could love anyone. And if not for love, then for loyalty she would act.

Tyr detected the change in her. It came like a sheet of ice announcing a blizzard. His hand dropped away in regret. His offer of comfort had been pure. He wanted to help her, to find her innocent. He wanted it desperately and not so much for her but for himself. He wanted everything he had learned about her to be wrong. But she wasn't helping him and he was too proud to force her before duty demanded it.

With a gruff nod of his head, he turned, spurned by her rejection. The fast gait of his stride took him from her with supernatural speed until she was left alone in his living room. Jaden glanced around. Her eyes fell on the wooden door. She tensed, ready to run for freedom. His words in her head stopped her.

Don't even try it, dhampir, he warned. His tone echoed callously in her head with inflexible authority. *You'll get lost in the maze of the black caves and I'll be forced to put you back within the cell.*

Jaden gulped, the artificial strength draining quickly from her limbs. Her body surged with numbing fear. She couldn't go back in the small prison, not yet. Besides, she could think of nowhere to go. Turning back to the sword, she moved to touch it. Her fingers hesitated, shook and fell away before ever knowing the cold steel of the ancient blade.

* * * *

Steam curled and danced in ethereal patterns up from the portable metal tub to create a soft mist of clouds. They pulled together like the upper reaches of the heavens before dissipating altogether. The mist reflected the softened glow of firelight as it blazed from the bedroom fireplace. Lifting her arm, Jaden watched as the pale cast took over her wet skin and golden rivers of bathwater trailed and beaded on her flesh.

She sighed in momentary contentment and let the heated water warm her blood. It had taken an eternity for Tyr to prepare it, hauling water in buckets to the tub from where they heated on a hook in the living room fireplace. She didn't know where the water came from, only that he hauled it in from behind the mysterious brown door.

Guiltily, she almost offered to help him. But pride and the annoying truth that she was there by force kept her from speaking. Instead, she wandered patiently about his living room, watching and waiting for him to finish. By the time he was done she had fashioned herself a medieval princess--a princess locked in the tower guarded by a terrible dragon, but a princess nonetheless.

Tyr left her alone in his bedroom to bathe. He hadn't spoken to her as he worked, only motioning when he was finished. For a brief instant his cold blue eyes had found her. Jaden imagined she found loathing there.

Next to the bath, on his bed, he left folded linen for drying. The thin material was a far cry from a thick terry cloth towel, but she decided it was a small price to pay for getting clean.

Jaden had literally peeled her clothing from her itching skin, surprised when her shirt didn't crawl away on its own. Her first task had been to wash her hair with a shampoo and conditioner he set out for her. They didn't have any particularly distinct scent to them, but they were clean and that was all that mattered.

Next, she managed to shave with an old straight razor he'd procured. It was a thoughtful gesture, one that was very badly needed. She couldn't even fathom from which decade on the wall he had procured it.

Jaden let the water soak into her skin as she relaxed her tense neck against the edge of the tub. Languidly, she pushed her knees up in the water, letting them bob from beneath the surface as she lowered her shoulders. She could feel the grime soaking from her body. Reaching over the rim, she grabbed a bar of soap. As she worked up lather, she recognized the faint odor of it. It smelled like Tyr.

Unbidden, her hands drew themselves before her nose. She breathed deeply the earthy smell of him. It was strange that he would bathe. Most vampires got out of the habit. The clean potency of the soap encased her senses, making her body shake with longing. The bar slipped from her hands, landing with a splash between her legs. The noise brought her up short. Never had a smell evoked such a compelling reaction inside her stomach. For all that Jaden could remember, never had a man evoked such feelings of lust and power beneath her skin.

"I must be going insane," she fumed in a heated whisper. The sound of crackling wood grew in the silence. Scornfully, she scrubbed her skin raw, refusing to breathe through her nose lest her senses be tempted. Rising, she worked vigorously on her thighs. "It's this damned place, made to make you forget reality. No wonder my senses are going crazy."

"You're finished then?"

Jaden froze, spinning around in horror.

"I apologize," Tyr said quickly. He wasn't quick to turn his back as his eyes roamed over her soapy skin. His blood slowed, filling into his lower extremities. Small scars from many battles lightly puckered her flesh, though they couldn't even begin to mar her beauty. Her flesh was the color of cream with a hint of pink roses. The orange firelight silhouetted her slender form, shadowing her face. But Tyr didn't need the aid of light to mark all of her features, every subtle nuance of her form. He could see her perfectly in the shadows--her parted lips, her pert breasts, her thighs.

His vision took in the wet strands of her washed hair sticking in wild trails to her shoulders, curling just above her collarbone. His eyes followed her hair's direction, sliding easily down the texture of her breasts, large enough to fill his palm but not impedingly so. Suds adhered to her nipples, teasing him as they clung to the puckered tips. Rivets of water trailed in the valley beneath her neck, dragging down in slow motion over the flatness of her finely toned stomach, pooling into her shallow navel, entangling into the short hair of her soapy womanhood. Easily, he saw the breadth of air between her shaved thighs, thighs that were parted naturally as she stood. There was just enough space for him to slip a finger into the lathered folds.

Tyr's hands tensed. Jaden proudly straightened to her full height. She could see his eyes penetrating her hips. The ice blue encompassed her with uncivilized enthusiasm. His lips parted and he worked his jaw with the savagery of a devilish fiend intent on taking what he wanted, as if his lips might sample her true woman's essence. Jaden's chin lifted into the air. If he was tying to make her nervous, she wouldn't succumb to it. She mustn't give in … she wouldn't give in … give in....

Tyr knew that if he wanted, he could move forward faster than her eyes could catch. He could claim her for his own, without giving her time to think or protest. He smelled her readiness as assuredly as an untamed beast senses estrus in his female mate. It called to him--she called to him with everything but her words. Her lips begged to be kissed--her body beseeched him to release it from the primitive longing she tried to deny.

Nevertheless he wouldn't bend her to his will in such a way. When he took a woman to his bed, both before and after his dark rebirth, it was with her willing consent. Not like the others of his village when they went out on scouting parties to defeat the Saxons. Conquering the women, after burning their villages, had been a way of warfare. Tyr had claimed his fair share of feminine plunder, but by the time he bedded them the women were most ready partners.

He shook off the distant memory of the past, letting it slip as he focused on the woman in front of him. She reminded him of the strong women of his human time--women who knew how to fight and to defend themselves, queens who knew how to conquer a nation beside the throne of a king--women who weren't afraid of passion in his arms once it had been learned. Not like the women of modern era. They were weak, pampered, spoiled, and greedy. They didn't know the meaning of turmoil or hard work. They wanted everything handed to them. And the men were just as bad.

"You can't tell me you have never seen a naked woman before," Jaden mused wryly when he continued to stare. If he didn't turn away soon, she would melt.

It's been a long time since I've seen such as you, m'lady, he thought. He refused to let her detect the words. Seeing the bravado on her face wavering slightly, he let the side of his lip curl up. If she wanted to play, he would play. Slowly he skulked forward. His eyes took further possession of her form until she knew he branded her for his own.

Jaden gulped and panted and shivered. She knew the look on his face. She saw the evidence of his meaning in the growing bulge of his tight jeans. It was too late to back down, too late to scream and hide in the depths of the concealing water. Her hands quivered, wanting to shoot up and hide her private areas from view. She felt like a piece of raw meat about to be devoured by the wolves.

"Do you mind?" she asked flippantly. The look didn't hold. Animalistic hunger devoured her. She wanted to jump out and tackle him to the ground. But seeing the silver splinters alighting in his eyes, she held back. It was all a mirage. He was forcing her to feel. She couldn't trust him, couldn't trust herself around him. He was a vampire, an undead being of the night, a nightstalker. His persuasive reaction growing between his thighs was just a primal impulse felt by all things that moved, a need that surged in even the darkest of beings. It didn't mean he could feel. It didn't mean he wanted her in particular. It just meant he wanted to fulfill a basic need, to find a slot in which to do so.

"Not at all," he said, tilting his head irresistibly to the side. He stopped before her. Jaden held still. He leaned forward, his face not touching her flesh as his head moved near her neck. She could feel the push of his breath on her wet skin, chilling it with the breeze of his words. "I would be happy to stand immodestly before you, as you have for me."

Jaden gasped. The audacity of him thinking she put a show on for him! That her bold, brave act of defiance was somehow in those few words torn down as an invitation to his lust. In all her years of training, she did the first thing that popped in her mind. She slapped him across the face with open palm while releasing a feminine sound of affront.

Tyr smiled, amused and unharmed. Jaden quivered before him. Pride kept her from running away. His hand lifted. Inwardly, her hips strained to press against his palm. Outwardly, she didn't move. Without touching her, he traced the angle of her shoulder and arm. His hand rotated, letting the backs of his fingers moving past her hip, over her stomach, down the front of her thighs. It was as if an invisible demon followed him, straining inside of her skin to close the distance. His hand stopped before her womanhood, soaking in the intense heat coming from her and returning it tenfold. His fingers moved slightly and Jaden imagined she could feel him as clearly as if he pushed into her.

"Are you quite finished?" she asked, though her words shook and the forcefulness of her declaration was lost in the panting of her breath.

"If you tell me to be," he whispered. His eyes bore piercingly into her. His lips formed over his words seductively. "Or I could only be starting. Just ask me and I'll show you untold pleasure."

Jaden had never heard the offer made in such bold terms, demanding such a clear cut answer from her. There was a confidence to him, a swarthy assurance that he could make her scream in ecstasy for hours. Jaden couldn't ask. She never once asked with words. Usually it only took a look and then nothing was at stake. If the man refused, no harm was done. No sense of rejection or loss, because hey, it had only been a look. But with Tyr, she would have to say the words. She would have to ask him. It was something she vowed never to do. She didn't need his attentions, handed down like a God bestowing favors on his lowly subjects.

Tyr could feel that she wanted him, as badly as he wanted her. He could feel her blood racing in her veins, pumping furiously. He could hear the rhythm of her heart in his ears. He could feel the heat radiating off of her sweet smelling womanhood. And something inside of him urged him to provoke her, to taunt her, to tease her relentlessly until she lost all self control.

Jaden waited, wishing he would just force himself on her so she could pretend to protest. Then later, she could hate him for doing it to her. She could take the pleasure and retain the pride.

Tyr's mouth came forward, his eyes closed as he narrowed in on her neck. Jaden's head fell to the side, unafraid of his bite. Her skin begged to be touched, to be set free of all her damnable principles. Her eyes met with the bed. Her body instantly wanted to test the softness of it, to test the strength of the chains against their thrusting weight.

"Ask," his breath urged, causing gooseflesh to sprinkle on her chest.

Jaden caught herself, knowing those were words she could never utter. She could never beg a vampire into her bed. He was the enemy.

"I'm cold," she whispered with a stiff jerk of her head. Her eyes closed briefly and she swallowed. Tyr's eyes rose to her in surprise. He didn't think she would ask him. Pleasure swam unexpectedly in him, anticipating her acceptance of him. His body lurched with need. Jaden bit her lip, before saying faintly, "Could you hand me a towel so I could get dressed?"

Tyr felt as if a boulder landed on his immortal head. His face became a hard mask, blocking all emotion from her. With a tense nod, he smiled through his tightly pressed lips. Disappointment coursed inside his arduously tested loins.

Tyr strode past the towel, not handing it to her. Instead, he went to the corner of the room. Picking up her duffel bag, he dropped it on the bed. Turning to her, he said, "I brought this along. I saw Rick going through it and knew it was yours."

Jaden paled. Her eyes darted to the bag. The way it landed, she could tell the papers were still in there. Had Tyr looked inside? Had he seen the papers tucked within the hollowed out book? Eyeing him carefully she nodded. By the impassive look on his face it was hard to tell if he knew what was hiding within.

Observing her with a vacant look, Tyr disappeared in a blink. Jaden gasped, holding her breath as she looked around the room. He was gone. With shaking fingers, she carefully rinsed the drying soap from her tingling body before stepping gingerly from the tepid water. Wrapping the linen around her still sensitive skin, she tiptoed over to peek into the living room. Tyr was nowhere to be seen.

Jaden couldn't stop trembling as she pulled her bag from the bed. Pressing it to her chest, she hauled it into the prison. She dressed hastily, pulling on the clothes with a haphazard grace. Then, hair still clinging to her back from inside her shirt, she pulled out the book from the bottom. The latch was still caught, but that didn't mean anything. The papers weren't as neatly stacked, but they could've been jostled in travel. Jaden shivered, pulling the little note describing Tyr into her pocket. Maybe he couldn't even read French, but there was one way of finding out.

Concealing the book beneath her clothes, she shoved the bag into the dark corner. If Tyr hadn't seen the documents, she would make sure it stayed that way. She wouldn't condemn Mack to the vampire council's judgment. For a moment, she considered burning the documents in the bedroom fireplace. But something stopped her. She had to know the truth for herself. And somehow, some way, she had to find a way to escape the prison Tyr kept her in.

Chapter Eight

The fire rustled pleasantly before the stone couch. Surprising to Jaden, the cushions provided ample padding to the stone and she was induced to snuggle into their depths. She rested her head on a thick pillow, hugging another to her stomach as she lay halfway over and awaited Tyr's return. It occurred to her she could try to escape despite his warning of getting lost, but she knew Tyr would never have left her if escape was possible.

Even if she did manage to find her way from the cave, she had no idea where she was. She could be in a crypt below some mausoleum in New York, or she could be in the middle of Arkansas in Ozark country. One phone call and she could ask Mack to come and get her. But she wasn't ready to call her uncle, not until she figured out what was in the file.

Part of her tried to admit she stayed because she was drawn to Tyr. She hated the small voice and squelched it instantly before it could give birth to other ideas. Her body stung with resentment at being so thoroughly aroused and then neglected. But her mind knew it was for the best. When the pleasure had faded, she would only hate herself for being weak. Tyr could feel nothing for her. She detected the void of his emotions within him and never had the curse of her gifts been such a burden. To know that he could never prefer her over another, that he could never pick her, pricked irritatingly at her insides. But it made it easier too. She knew not to expect anything from him.

"I am a job," she reminded herself. "And I have a job to do."

When had her job become secondary? She must have been cooped in his home longer than she thought. She needed to get out. The tomblike walls of the cavern beat into her, blocking out all outside conflict and allowing her to focus within. With sudden insight, she sat up. That was it. She couldn't feel anyone else but herself and Tyr. And reading Tyr's emotions were like communicating with a rock. He was empty.

It was the first time in her life that she couldn't sense outside herself and she wasn't sure she was ready to go where her emotions led her. The walls of the cave pressed in on her senses. The stone was too quiet, the fire becoming too loud.

"I got to get out of here," she whispered, rising to her feet. She panted and panicked. Her senses reeled to pick up something other than herself. Her eyes darted around to the brown door. Warning or not, she had to try. Why was she hesitating? Where had all her fight gone? The question was answered with the calm accent of a bored voice.

"Where are you going?"

Tyr moved so stealthily that she didn't know he was there. Chills racked her spine as she spun around. He was behind her. The panic subsided the moment she saw his calming eyes.

"How long have you been standing there?" she asked with an undercurrent of wonder, trying to remember what she muttered under her breath. She really needed to stop talking aloud to herself. It was bad enough the Tyr could read most of her thoughts anyway, without her saying them aloud for him.

"Why?" he said effortlessly. His face showed no strain of their previous encounter. His blue orbs were as clear as a summer sky but with none of the gentle promises. When she didn't answer, only stared, he lowered his words to a murmur, "Why? Did you miss me, princess?"

Jaden groaned, rolling her eyes heavenward. She refused to answer his baiting. Ruefully, she wrinkled her nose and met his jeering expression with one of her own. Her words dripped wryly out of her mouth. "No, I just wondered how many hapless New Yorkers you managed to kill."

Her eyes searched his, waiting and hoping for him to slip and tell her where she was. Tyr placed his hands on the back of the couch, leaning over to press his face towards hers. She hoped he might kiss her, but instead his lip twisted into sinister darkness.

"That would be difficult," he said lowly, "even for me."

"Then…?" Her eyes hid beneath the silken length of her dark lashes.

"If you want to know, Miss MacNaughton, ask." Tyr moved around the back of the couch, sitting easily on his chair before the fire. Leaning back in repose, he watched her expectantly. His fingers steepled, tapered fingernails meeting beneath his chin. Jaden met the challenge in his gaze. Would he never give her an inch?

"Fine," she seethed, sitting down to face him. "Where are we? And for God's sake quit calling me Miss MacNaughton. It is very annoying."

"All right, princess." He shot her a charmingly arrogant grin. His voice was so seductive and soft, low and erotic. Jaden knew he was using the pet name to aggravate her. It did a good job of that, as was evident by the chill of pleasure that worked its way up her spine.

"So?" Shaken, she could almost feel him pressed against her.

"We are in my homeland," he murmured quietly. His eyes watched her face. They didn't seem as cold as before. Maybe he found peace from the raging feelings of others in his home. Jaden only found insecurity. It was hard to be left alone with herself after a lifetime of other people.

"Homeland?" Jaden screeched in sudden weariness. Her wide eyes looked around her as if the stone walls could answer her. "I don't understand. Are you trying to make a joke? You mean in the grave?"

"It's called Norway now," he said, amused by her puzzled look.

"Norway? As in the country Norway?" Jaden gaped in skepticism.

"Mm," was the only reply.

"But how?" Her mouth worked violently, near speechlessness. "Th--that isn't possible. I--I...."

"You what?" he prompted arrogantly, helping her along.

"I--I," she stuttered again.

"Oh, you mean that your lover only drugged you once and you don't remember the journey over here." Tyr hid his bitterness at the words. He looked thoughtfully at his hand, wondering for the hundredth time why he hadn't let the man die.

"Yes," Jaden frowned at his offhanded reference to Rick. Not wanting to deal with that topic right now, she said, "You couldn't have gotten me here in one night."

"You're right," he said, undaunted by her pale face and growing anger beneath the surface of confusion. What did bother him was that she didn't deny her relationship with the mortal he'd allowed to live. "I didn't. But I did keep you locked in your drugged state, so to speak, until we did arrive--a little over a week later. Do you not remember lying with me in my coffin, eating fruit from my hand?"

"I've been gone for nearly two weeks?" she said incredulously, not daring to think of the erotic images he put into her head with that last remark. She closed her eyes briefly, before growling, "Are you mad, vampire? My uncle will be searching for me. He will find you. *Two weeks...?*"

"Nearly," he chuckled, absently leaning his temple on his fingers. His eyes glanced so quickly over her that she didn't see them move. She was lovely. "No, princess, you've been gone for well over two weeks."

"What?" Jaden shook her head. Holding out her fingers she began adding days on her fingers in an exaggerated manner for his benefit. "Check your math, immortal. One week to get here, four days in pr--"

"Eight," he inserted coolly for her, "not counting tonight."

Jaden got to her feet in anger. Placing her hands on her hips, she glared, "You kept me locked up in that prison for eight days! Are you insane?"

Not to be outdone, Tyr stood, gracefully towering over her to his full height. The suddenness of it caused Jaden to step back so she didn't ram into his rock-hard chest.

"Now, princess," he tried to soothe.

"*Argh!*" she yelled, shaking her fists. "Quit calling me princess!"

"All right, sweetheart," he began, moving as if to touch her face. She jerked back from him and he let the hand drop. His eyes bore mischievously into hers.

"No."

"Sweetling?"

"No!"

"Darling?"

"No!"

"Baby?"

"*No!*"

"*Ma chère,*" he whispered with a cocky half smile forming his mouth. He was thoroughly enjoying her anger.

"No, no, no!" she shrieked. "I am not your girlfriend or your lover or your anything! I am your hostage. Treat me as such!"

Tyr met the contempt in her gaze. Lowering his jaw, he leaned forward. His eyes glittered dangerously. His lips parted, revealing his fang points. Jaden took an involuntary step back and then another. Tyr was fast behind her, pursuing her on feet that glided more than walked.

"Shall I show you, Jaden," he questioned on a low growl, her name sounding more intimate than his other half-hearted endearments. "Shall I show you how I was raised in my human days to treat female prisoners? Men were not like you know now. We took what we wanted without consequence. We conquered nations, villages and even women. Would you like me to show it to you, Jaden? Would you like to be conquered?"

"You're not a man," she said weakly. "You're a vampire."

"Ah, but I am a Dark Knight," he whispered, his low words dangerously seductive her core. She trembled violently with need. "And I still know all my lessons. My warrior instincts have been honed and trained over the last thousand years. Is that what you want? You want me to show you the nature of the beast, the nightstalker, the Nordic warrior?"

Jaden shivered at the very notion, not completely adverse to its implications. But the obscurity in his gaze stopped her from answering. Coming to the end of the couch, she spun around intent on fleeing. Tyr caught her before she even reached his bedroom door. His hands twined around her elbows in a forceful grip, holding her steady. His words rasped low and hot and sharp along the back of her ear.

"Why are you running, prisoner?" he growled, rumbling with the thundering hooves of a thousand rampant mustangs. "Isn't this what you wanted? I offer you civility and you scoff at it. So should I grant you your wish, Jade? Should I act like the beast you insist on thinking me?"

"Please," she begged softly, frightened and aroused by his power. She hated being out of control. Even with Rick things happened when and how she wanted them to. No man ever had the strength or the skill to overpower her. But this vampire behind her held the demonic power of a devil and the heart-stabbing physique to back it up. His soft, firm grip held her steadfastly with the gentleness of steel. And it was the nature of that very gentleness she found impossible to fight.

"Please?" he repeated softly, turning her word from a plea to a seductive whimper. His breath caressed the back of her ear.

Jaden stiffened. His arms pulled her into his chest. She could feel the fiery length of him pressed along her back. His hands were warm as if he had just fed. When she would pull away, he stepped forward, forcing her into the stone of the wall. Her breasts met with stone, flattening as her cheek was forced to turn to the side.

Tyr pulled her elbow, arching her back forward, pressing her breasts hard into the wall, forcing her bottom into his male sex. He let her feel what she did to him, rubbing his length to her backside in an even stroke. Jaden's breath shuddered from her mouth as he mimicked another slow thrust. His wide open lips hissed by her ear.

Tyr drew forward letting his mouth settle by the pulse in her throat. He lapped her skin. He felt her pulse speed beneath his wet caresses, heard the matching rhythm in his ears. He could smell her blood filling with ripening passion and her womanhood with a downpour of desire. Grazing his sharpened teeth over her skin, he didn't harm her, but showed her how much he could hurt her. He let her feel his strength, his power, his complete control over the situation.

And when he was sure she knew that he could take anything he wanted from her by force or otherwise, he whispered against the sweat beading on her flesh, "Say it again, Jade. Say please. Ask me to do it."

Before she could answer, Tyr swung her around. Jaden gasped at the sudden release, only to be caught and steadied by his embrace. Everything became a dim haze as her vision sought only him. He leaned over her, not touching except for the exploring of his little finger trailing from beneath her chin down her throat in slow circles. His free hand pressed to the wall behind her head, trapping her within his reach.

Jaden couldn't speak. The impression of his need still burned into her buttocks. Her gaze drifted to his chest, afraid to meet his eyes. She couldn't chance his gaze. If his voice and his touch evoked such longing, his eyes would be the kiss of death to her composure.

His mouth came forward gently. Her eyes fluttered closed, anticipating his touch. His tongue darted to trace the seam between her lips without deepening the gesture into a kiss. Jaden felt her knees weaken. Her hands wrestled with the air, clenching and unclenching in an effort to remain calm. Finally, she found a secure anchor in the thin sweater covering his waist.

"Ask," he whispered, urging her to answer him. His lips brushed her tenderly with the word. His mouth captured her breath.

"I--I can't," she panted. She turned her face away. She knew if he touched her, tried to force her as he claimed he might, she would succumb to him--willingly. Her body screamed for fulfillment. Her lips pulsed, swollen as if she had been kissed hard and long. Tyr drew back, his eyes seemed to glint with sadness at her refusal but the emotion was gone before Jaden could focus her thoughts enough to study him.

Seeing his face, his painful withdrawal, Jaden realized that he couldn't force her. For all his power and natural primal instincts, he couldn't ravish her. It wasn't in him. Straightening, he said, "Sit down. I have no need for a standoffish mortal in my bed when I can seek a willing one out with ease."

The jibe was like a well placed smack across her face. Jaden took a slow breath, waiting until he was once again seated before following. Taking her placing far away from him, she turned. Nervously, she waited for him to speak.

Tyr's eyes stared blindly into the fire, seeming to get lost in time. She watched the orange glow bathing his pale skin, reflecting off the deep dark blond of his head. Her eyes measured the width of the black turtleneck, detecting folds of muscles in the chest. And beneath the sleeves, she was held breathless by the size of his large arms--arms that could crush a person into the ground, arms that could wrap around a body and hold it tight, arms that could control.

Jaden shivered, tearing her gaze away to the safety of the flames. Her body raged with emotion. She hated the baseness of her passion, the persistence of her hunger. After some time passed, each gathering their wits to continue the game of deceit set before them, Tyr deemed himself ready to speak.

"What did you learn of your uncle?" he asked quietly.

"Am I on trial now?" she asked sharply. Her eyes snapped to his. She looked for any sign of what transpired between them. There was nothing. He looked completely unaffected by her. "It hardly seems fair. I have yet to be charged."

"Your uncle has secrets," he murmured, thinking of the night he found her drugged on Rick's bed.

"Everyone has secrets," she answered tersely. "It isn't a crime. And I have none I wish to tell you."

Tyr allowed a rueful smile. He had to give it to her. She was strong and she fought him relentlessly at every turn. However, it would be easier for him if she just told him what he needed to know. Fighting the barriers in her mind would be very draining.

"It seems we are at an impasse," he sighed.

"Then let me go. Let me just walk out of here."

"I can't do that," he denied with a glance to her solemn face.

"Why? The council?" she asked, frightened by the prospect.

"Yes, among other things. This place is in the middle of the Jotunheimen mountain range, the Norwegian wilderness. We are twenty miles from the nearest town. Beyond this cave even though it is still summer there is the snow, unexpected fog so dense you can't see your hand, and rain. And if you don't freeze, you may just get lost long enough in the wilderness to starve."

"Then take me to a city," she pleaded. "Any city. I can disappear from there. You'll have no reason to come for me again."

"I cannot. The long summer daylight makes this a prison for my kind. The dawn and dusk peek out from the heavens all night around."

"But, you're here now," she said, not trusting his words. "Can you not go out at night at all? And where is your coffin? You must go somewhere to sleep."

"I sleep on the bed. This place has been consecrated as a tomb so I may rest at leisure. As to the Norwegian nights, I am so old that I have built a tolerance to the dusk and dawn when the sun has yet to show. Though it is draining, I can survive. And these tunnels lead all through the mountains."

"You must have someone helping you," Jaden said logically.

"I do."

Jaden shivered. He would only reveal such information if he wasn't worried about her revealing it to anyone else. Had her fate been sealed then? Was he just biding his time with her until the tribal council ordered him to bring her forth to them? Shivering, she had to change the subject. She had to concentrate on finding out what he knew without revealing herself to him, without admitting to the full extent of her crimes.

"Well," she began, twisting her mouth dryly, "since you are so talkative tonight, why don't you see if you can translate this? If anything, it might prove amusing to you."

"What is it?" he wondered aloud, reaching out for the paper she offered from her front pocket.

"You tell me," she countered

Tyr look took the paper in his hand and laughed. "It is very amusing, is it not? Where did you find it?"

"In a book," she said blandly. "So you can read it?"

"I can read many languages and speak almost all. It was part of my training," said Tyr. "If you wanted to know all you had to do was ask. This test wasn't necessary."

"Prove it." Her face was blank as he turned to her. She refused to admit she didn't know herself. "How do I know if you are bluffing? Translate if for me. Say the words."

"Tyr," he began reading his name in her hurried script, "of the Dark Knights, tribe of Drauger."

Jaden leaned closer to hear his low words, scooting towards him on the couch. His accent became thick as he spoke. Her eyes studied his lips as they moved, turning over each word in a taunting caress of air. When he stopped and glanced at her in curiosity, she urged, "Go on."

"This fearsome warrior is widely known." Tyr stopped again, looking at her inquisitively. Jaden swallowed, nodding for him to continue. A strange sensation curled within him, reading the legend his name had become. Quietly, he murmured, "I am known as a heartless and cruel warrior. I use my massive strength to crush my victims and I do my duty to obtain whatever information I am sent to acquire."

Jaden nodded. It was pretty much what Mack had told her except for the crushing part. She leaned back, stopping when he continued on.

"I never fail in my duty," his eyes meaningfully lifted from the page, the rest memorized, "and I am a great punisher of *vampijorivic* crimes. The council sends me to watch and to judge. I have sexual prowess irresistible to women. They cannot deny me."

There it is, Tyr thought a bit cynically. *All my years narrowed down to a few cold sentences.*

Jaden shivered. A roguish smirk threatened the side of his face, as he added, "And I am a great lover."

"It doesn't say that," she denied with bated breath, not knowing if it was true.

He smiled and shrugged sheepishly. The paper dropped from his hand as he made a move to crawl towards her. Whispering, he asked, "Are you asking me if it is true?"

Jaden trembled violently. She couldn't move away from him. Her body stung too disobediently with need. Her vampire tormenter ran so hot and cold. His mood could turn from leisure to passion and back again in an instant and it was wreaking havoc on her senses. Her body couldn't keep up. At his dark look, all the passion she had spent the last half hour smothering alighted anew. She didn't answer.

"Are you asking me?" he growled again, his body drawing nearer. His piercing eyes demanded an answer she was too afraid to give.

* * * *

New York City, New York

"Jade is dead. I know that bastard killed her, sir." Rick rubbed the back of his neck wearily, his finger unconsciously going to the invisible wound on his throat. There was no sign of the vampire's bite. It was almost as if it had never happened. He was still weak from the blood loss, but his strength was coming back in great strides. Thoughts of revenge were the greatest fuel for his improvement. Nevertheless, he couldn't help the small curiosity of why he was left alive. He placed his hands on Mack's desk. Leaning over, he vowed, "I'll avenge Jaden or die trying."

Mack studied Rick carefully. He wasn't as sure as the soldier was about Jaden's fate. Dead, she would be no use to Tyr or the vampire council.

Pietro assured him that she was unharmed for the time being. If Mack ensnared Tyr at the right moment then Jaden would be safe and he would have everything he had ever worked for.

Eyeing the young man's face, red with bloodlust and determination, he nodded. "Be ready in five minutes. I'll meet you downstairs in the car."

Rick strode from the room to pack a bag. Mack leaned back, watching where the soldier disappeared through the doorway. Lighting a cigar, he rolled it between his lips as he moved to open his sun dial safe. Rick would be a good man to have along on this trip. His anger and desire for vengeance would make him a stronger warrior and greater ally. Angry men with a purpose were easier to manipulate.

Lifting the folder from the safe, he dropped it on the desk. The insides shifted, showing a page number in the upper right corner. Mack frowned, tearing the front flap of the folder open. His eyes flew to the bookcase, to the vacant space on the highest shelf.

With an angry howl, his teeth bit through the end of his cigar. The tobacco fell unheeded to the floor to sprinkle burning ash beneath the desk. Mack spit out the tip and stomped the ash out with his heel. Grabbing the folder, he threw it against the wall. Papers skidded and spilled over the floor. Rick had told him everything that happened, even discovering the large book in Jaden's missing bag. He'd never dreamt that Jaden would've deceived him. Never had he expected this betrayal.

"My God, Jaden," he growled. He knew his niece couldn't understand what was written in the folder and wanted to believe she took it only to hide it and keep it safe. But, without knowing what she carried, would she be tempted to hand it to the dark knight for translation? Would she give it to the council? Mack trembled, feeling the rare instance of fear at the thought. Staring at the mess of papers on his floor, he shook his head. "What have you done?"

* * * *

Jotunheimen Mountain Range, Norway

Ask me.

Jaden's mouth went dry. Tyr's demanding tone echoed in her head. His eyes pierced with the fierceness of demons as he continued forward. His hands crawled over her legs, reaching with tiger-like paws to fit beside her body on the couch. He kept his weight above her, trapping her slender body beneath him. His expression was a mere look, steaming with possibilities.

"I grow weary of these games," he said aloud, his face above hers. His self control was pushed to the limit. He could only cool his ardor so much. And knowing she wanted him, smelling that she did, didn't make his struggle easier. If she would just forget her damned pride for the moment and beg him, all would be settled and then maybe he could concentrate on doing his duty.

"Who's playing games?" she whispered. "I find no enjoyment being on trial for my life."

"No enjoyment," he chuckled, his eyes devouring her where his fangs longed to. In a low murmur, full of masculine promise, he answered, "That is no fault of mine."

"I don't want you," she denied. Her heart lurched treacherously. Her stomach ached and throbbed its potent acquiescence to his offer. "I can't want you. And you don't want me."

At the obvious lie of her words, his eyebrow raised in question. Her body said very differently.

"You cannot want me, vampire. You cannot want anyone. To truly want means you have to feel. And you don't feel. You are an empty vessel, a timeless piece of driftwood sucking on humanity, watching us from afar, but never feeling. These relics of yours hanging on the wall are just relics--something that meant something to someone else, the skeletal remains of past humanity. That thing growing between your legs is just instinct, a bitter part of you that refuses to die like your soul. You cling onto it, envious of the life you snuff out. You're pathetic and I don't sleep with losers." Jaden glared, purposefully cruel. It was her only defense left. She had to keep him at arm's length.

Tyr retracted as if burnt. His body tensed and filled with outrage. He rose onto his knees with a swift, graceful pull.

"And you are a killer! You have no conscience!" she said, emboldened by his withdrawal.

Red veins gathered in his eyes, spreading like a demonic plague until the white completely disappeared. Jaden struggled for breath. She had never seen him so angry. She was afraid to move, afraid he would pounce and devour her if she dared.

Tyr's body slammed with impulse. His fingers tightened into fists. He wanted to kill, to hit her until she shut up. But he couldn't strike her. He couldn't hurt her. Her words weren't entirely a lie. He did envy mortals. He envied their laughter and free flowing smiles. He envied their ability to love and be loved. All he was left with was duty, and he buried himself in it, refusing to get attached, never finding anyone he'd bring to be with him. Even if he wanted to turn someone to share his pain, he couldn't.

Dark Knights were not allowed to procreate. Passing the gift on weakened the blood and interfered with his responsibility. He couldn't even find solace with his own kind. Though he could mingle within them, he couldn't talk to them--tell them who he was because someday he might be called to kill them. It had happened before. It was easier not to form attachments. Tyr accepted this, understood it, and lived by it.

And this mere slip of a mortal was challenging everything he was allowed to hold dear.

Tyr jerked away from her, dashing swiftly to put distance between their bodies. He moved with unnatural speed, rotating around to direct his stiff back to her. There was nowhere to run. He felt her inside himself, curling comfortably in his brain, driving him past the point of reason. He fought the beast within, fought the torment of his dark soul. Manipulating himself so that he could again look at her, he turned back to bear witness to her wan complexion.

Jaden was shocked by his sudden withdrawal. His eyes had been so intense it hurt her to look at him. Now, they were emotionless masks hiding whatever it was that floated in his head. The red was still tingeing the sides, but the blue once again dominated the orbs.

"We are the same," he said at last, the tone hostile and dark. "You are a bloodstalker. I am a nightstalker."

"There is a world of difference between us, Tyr," she denied weakly. She stood up from the couch holding on to the side, not trusting her legs to support her. She shook violently under his inspecting gaze.

"Why?" he asked sharply. "We both kill."

"You kill innocent...." Jaden couldn't finish the words. She was as guilty as he and she knew it. Well, maybe not on the same level. She thought she might be forced to explain her hesitance, but didn't have to. He interrupted before she had a chance to retract.

"And you kill vampires," he said enigmatically, his eyes threatening to fill again. Jaden had seen the red rage before, had been attacked by it. But never had she seen a creature keep it at bay. His accented words came in a low growl, strained by time and death, as he said, "Death is death. Your hands are stained red, as are mine. Death is the life that has chosen us."

"Chosen us?" she squeaked, faced with his convictions when she no longer had any. She was frightened by the truth in his words, frightened by the thoughts she had and never said. Frightened that he may say them for her and force her to face what she couldn't. Frightened by how much of the damning truth he might know.

"Did you ask to be dhampir?" he continued, his head cocking to the side. The unnervingly calm creature was completely gone, replaced by a barely contained monster.

"You're all powerful," she sneered. "You should be able to tell."

"Dhampirs are hard to read correctly," he admitted. Then, repeating in a softer tone, he asked again, "Did you ask to be a dhampir?"

"No," she said vehemently. "I hate what I am."

"I did not ask to be a knight," he said with a grunt. "Though our difference is, I no longer hate myself for being."

"You can't hate," she hissed. She was angry. He made her angry. The anger felt good. She embraced it. Lashing out, she said, "At your age, you can feel nothing."

At that Tyr smiled, a small unhappy smile that seemed to cause his taut face pain. Bitterly, he hissed, "You cannot know what I feel."

"That is where you are wrong." Jaden didn't notice that he dared to move closer. Her eyes glared out from beneath silky lashes. Her pale cheeks flushed with red. "It is my curse to feel inside your kind. I felt it since I was a child. But, unlike you, I feel remorse for the endless deaths I can't stop. You can't know what it is like to feel the things I do, and with a human heart."

"Tell me," he demanded coldly. He stirred with an unearthly speed, appearing before her partly dissipated into mist. As he moved, he tore the shirt from his back, revealing his chest. Jaden's eyes took him in like a drunkard to wine. He was as smooth and glorious as she could've ever imaged. His chest stopped before her nose. He was well upon her, blocking the flames with his body as it solidified, towering over her in intimidation, engulfing her with the exhilarating musk of his body. "What do you feel within me?"

Jaden forced him back with her hands. They fitted neatly inside the unforgiving valleys of his chest. His pale skin was tepid warmth to her darker palms. The texture pressed intimately to her, making her shiver. Tyr proudly held still. She closed her eyes, searching with every fiber to see what she could find. Trembling, her fingers brushed over his heart. It pounded even and strong, willing hers to make time. As she concentrated, her heart picked up his beat until they were one. She searched him, every crevice he allowed her. His soul was a blank void, a blackened pit of unemotional depths. Glancing up at him, she replied darkly, "Like I said, nothing. You are hollow."

"You're sure of that?"

"Yes." Her breath came harder to her, partly due to his nearness, partly due to the energy it took to search him so deeply. "I'm sure."

Even as she said the words, she wished they weren't true. Within a flash, his hand moved, striking out faster than she could predict. His nail slashed against his chest, drawing a thin line of blood before she managed to blink. Jaden gasped. His hand caught hers before she could pull away. He held her fast in his tight grip.

"There are no sureties, dhampir," he whispered. Then, slowly so that her eyes could watch, he lifted his other hand to the back of her head. His eyes bore into her, mesmerizing her with his will. "If I have learned anything in an eternity, it is that."

Jaden knew what he was doing. He was giving her a look inside himself with the taste of his ancient blood. She tried to resist, but his pull on her was too strong. His will overpowered hers. Weakly, she was forced forward. Closing her eyes, she hesitated.

"Open your mouth, dhampir," he ordered. Jaden couldn't stop herself. She obeyed. A frail sound escaped Tyr. He pulled her into his chest, folding his arms around her trembling form. Her slight body became engulfed in the volumes of his hold. Jaden's lips touched cooling flesh. The steady beat of a heart met her in confident strokes. With a rough growl, he hoarsely commanded her, "*Taste.*"

Instantly, her tongue darted out to lick him in a long sure line over the gash. She didn't stop to think that it was blood she took like wet silk into her mouth. She didn't think to disobey. In fact, she didn't think at all-- only saw what he willed her to see.

Within him she felt more controlled emotion and power than she had ever felt in her short life. She felt decades of turmoil, peace, understanding, regret. She detected the effects of a human life, repeated endlessly throughout time and age. She had been very wrong. Tyr was not emotionless. He felt a great deal. He suffered a great deal.

The overwhelming pull was more than she could bear. If she was wrong about him then what about the others? Had her whole life been built on a lie? Tearing herself away, she kept her eyes closed. She didn't want to face the pain of the next heartbeat. "Kill me."

Tyr pulled back, dropping his hold. The wound on his chest sealed shut, leaving only the smallest smears of blood from her lips. Her reaction confused him. "Why? Because I have proven you wrong?"

"No, because I am tired of living. I don't want to see or feel anymore of you or your damned kind. I want rest." Jaden hid her thoughts from him. She couldn't tell him that his feelings only compounded her regret and guilt over the life she had lived. She felt other things in him, other damning truths she couldn't longer deny. Her uncle used her to kill for his own gain. He had tricked her. In some ways she had suspected it for a long time, but she never stopped, never dared to question. And was Mack's kind of evil any less horrible than those he condemned to death?

At one time she had thought she understood her place, had known the path she was to follow. It was simple then. She was ridding the world of evil and in doing so the personal sacrifices she had to make were worth it. But since then she learned that life wasn't simply black or white, good or evil. The truth of the reality was still staining her lips, rolling saltily in her mouth. It was in the long history of his blood.

Weakly, Jaden touched her bottom lip. Tyr didn't need the mark to brand her. Even if he released her from his binding, he would still haunt her. She would never be free of him, of what he showed her. The truth pounded in her bloodstream, swirled dangerously in her head. Now that she felt the full force of what he was, she would never be able to get the purity of emotion--raw and unfettered--out of her head or her soul.

The hunt was over for her. Everything she touched had been a lie. She no longer knew if she could trust her emotions or her inherent senses. Jaden felt the strings of her heart pull violently. A pain seared out from the organ, flooding her body. Lowering her head, she was ashamed. The long line of destruction she wrought weighed heavily upon her. She no longer knew if she punished the right vampires. Maybe they didn't need punishing at all. But of one thing she was certain. She would never hunt again. And if she wasn't a hunter, she was nothing.

Tyr felt the outpouring of her soul, flowing over to his like a blast of a desert storm. He knew her self-torment, her grief. But he was ill fitted to comfort her. For all his years on the earth, he'd forgotten the ability to express tender sentiment with words. His hand trembled. He saw a tear brim her lashes. It didn't fall. She refused to cry. His arm lowered, uncertain. Then all of a sudden the feelings hammering from her stopped. Her shoulder's no longer shook. Her breath became deep and even.

Tyr's gaze swung up to her. She was calm and cold. Jaden's eyes pierced him with dangerous accuracy. A slow cryptic smile found her features.

"What?" Tyr hesitated.

"I want to fight," she answered in a low tone. It was all she knew. It was the only thing she had left that was hers. Lowering her chin, her eyes bore forward. Her hands lifted from her side. She backed away from him, stealthily moving with the deadly intent of a fourteenth century ninja. "I *need* to fight you."

Tyr cocked his head to the side in question, not moving from his spot. Only his eyes deigned it necessary to follow her. And then, seeing her face struggling for control, he understood.

"I need to hit something," she murmured quietly. "I challenge you, Tyr of the Dark Knights. I challenge--"

"I won't kill you," he set forth. He couldn't kill her and not only because it was the order of the council. His voice sounded indifferent and bored, but Jaden could tell otherwise. She felt otherwise inside. With the single taste, he had opened the dam between them. It wouldn't be so easy to close. As she circled around him, eyeing him from head to toe, he was forced to turn his head to watch her approach from his other side.

"Fine," she expressed, getting ready to attack. Fighting was the one thing she knew how to do. It was the one thing solid she could face and cling to. And if she must feel pain, then let it be physical. Scowling in grim determination, she charged forward, yelling, "You might not be able to kill me, Tyr, but don't hold back."

Chapter Nine

Two and a half hours passed with the slinging of fists, the darting of hands, the cracking of flesh against bruised flesh. Feet kicked, bodies arced, arms and legs soared. Little breaks were taken between bouts, Tyr allowing Jaden to catch her breath as they discussed technique in a most business-like fashion. Jaden once mentioned swords, but Tyr denied her request. He didn't have two of anything and he wasn't sure it was in his best interest to give a legendary vampire hunter a blade.

Jaden's breath came in ragged pants and sweat beaded her flushed skin. She could feel her heart pounding so hard against her back that her whole body shook with the force of it. Every muscle in her body was fatigued, bruises were starting to form on her skin, she ached in ways she never dreamt possible, and she'd never felt better in her life. With a deep sigh, she eyed the iron chandelier from the flat of her back.

Tyr leaned over her, his mouth pressed in quizzical worry. His blond hair fell forward framing his devilishly handsome face. His skin was slightly flushed from the sparring, but he didn't have breath and his lungs didn't gasp or tire as hers did.

"Did I hurt you?" he asked at length, referring to his last defensive move that sent her flying to the floor. He hid his smile. For a mortal, she was well trained. Tyr reached out his hand to her. Jaden ignored it, rolling onto her side. She shot him an unexpected smile before pushing to her hands and knees.

"Where did you study?" she huffed, pulling back on her haunches. She peeled her sweaty hair off her forehead, throwing it back to look at him.

"Everywhere," he answered, drawing his rejected hand back from her.

Jaden chuckled. A sense of comradeship overcame her. For a moment, she allowed herself to forget who he was. She forgot about the vampire council, her impending trial. They were just two people trapped in a cave, sparring.

Tyr heard her laughter, free of mocking and bitterness. It struck a chord deep within. He held onto that laughter, capturing it in his memory, hoping to never let it go or let it fade. But, given enough time, he knew that would become dim as everything in his life must. Its memory would distort until it wasn't real but an imagined realness. He would forget the lines of her face when she smiled, and beyond that, he might even forget her name. Suddenly, their time together seemed too brief--her mortality too short. He didn't want to forget, didn't want to lose another memory to his eternity. The realization stung--a deep, wretched ache that bittered the taste in his mouth and soured the calmness of his stomach.

Jaden's smile faltered, disappearing as she watched for his answer expectantly. She couldn't feel the sadness in him, though there were other things she tried her best to ignore. At last, he broke the uneasy silence.

"All knights were trained for hundreds of years. At first we studied with humans, learning of martial arts, weaponry, warfare, books, languages, cultures." He shrugged, leaning leisurely against the back of the couch. "As our skills grew, we studied with the council."

"Oh," her expression wavered as she thought of the legendary tribal council. Jaden had always been aware of their existence, even when a young child. When other children got sweet tales of fairies and dream worlds, she got a lesson in horror and madness, descriptions of torture devices and the hell their world could be. It wasn't Mack's fault. He did his best by her. Even without his bedtime stories, she would've known the truth of it. She could feel the silent spider-like strand of fear the vampiric elders instilled inside their benighted children. It was like a part of nature, holding the dark world together. It was a dark fairytale told and retold, distorted and changed, forever real and true. But never did she feel so close to meeting the council as she did now. Part of her never imagined that the day would come--all of her had prayed that it wouldn't, all of her knew that it would.

"What about before?" Jaden moved to lean next to him. She rolled her head on her neck, taking one last deep breath as she calmed. "What about your human life? Do you remember it at all?"

"As a human, I was a great warrior. I fought in many battles under King Guthrum." Tyr became lost in thought. It was so long ago, none of the ideals he had clung to even mattered anymore. Most humans didn't even know of the old king.

"And he was a Viking?"

"A Dane, yes," he answered.

"Did he win?" she wondered aloud, enthralled with his voice as he spoke his tale.

"Yes and then no. He was defeated by King Alfred of Wessex. A treaty was signed and he was given what was then referred to as the Danelaw."

"And that was…?"

"In Britain."

"I couldn't imagine such a life. I don't think I would've done very well in it," she murmured. Realizing what she said, she blushed.

"Ach, nay, m'lady. 'Tis a fine Dane ye wouldst have made," he murmured in the soft Norse burr of his mortal youth. Tyr winked at her, an incorrigible act that warred with the undead of his gaze. Turning to the side, he leaned his hip to the back of the couch and faced her. "Methinks ye wouldst have been the prize o' the battle, after we conquered yer people, that is."

Jaden's blush deepened, but she couldn't look away. "It'd be something to see, I give you that. All you barbarians dressed in tunics--"

"--yelling to Odin--" he added.

"--brandishing your broadsword in long swings to hack off the heads of your enemies, sticking them with your anlace, and then finishing off the wounded with the humane misericord," Jaden finished with a wrinkle to her nose.

Tyr eyed her. She almost seemed relaxed. The tension eased from her body as she spoke of weaponry and battles. He saw the interest in her eyes and felt the excitement in her limbs. This was no usual woman. But, then, he had known that from the beginning. Had he known the secret to unlocking her, he would've beaten on her a long time ago.

"Ye know yer weaponry, m'lady," he nodded in approval.

"Though, being a woman," she put in wryly. "I would probably never have seen such a thing from the right end. I'd be at home with twelve brats, sleeping with the livestock."

"Not you. You would be a noblewoman, married to a great king."

Jaden swallowed nervously and she looked away. A noblewoman? It wasn't likely. There was nothing noble about who she was.

"Would you like to see it?" he asked carefully, almost shyly.

"What?" she turned to face him in confusion.

"It won't be real, but it will feel real if you let it."

"What?"

"I can show you a bit of the past. Just a glimpse, a feel," he turned to her. "When the Dark Knights were made, we were turned by our tribal leader and thus we belonged to that certain tribe, but we were also given the blood of each leader during the rebirth. It strengthened our power and our bond. But it also gave a few of us some additional gifts, if you will."

Jaden had never heard of such a thing. She blinked heavily, waiting for him to continue. Her limbs shook and she wasn't sure she could believe him. But every sense she had said he was telling the truth.

"I can go into a trance and remember my human past--a field, a hall filled with my people, riding atop my horse beside a castle. Other memories are vaguer. It is what has kept me sane over the years, kept me connected. We all must find ways to stay connected." Tyr swallowed visibly. He had never shown anyone before. He had never told such personal details of his human past. No one had ever asked. Almost timidly, he took up her hand. "Come on."

Jaden followed before shrinking back in uncertainty. "I shouldn't--"

"You'll be safe. It is only in my mind," he whispered. "I give you my word that I'll let no harm befall you."

"But--"

"And I promise not to pry into your thoughts just this once, if that is what concerns you. No tricks, just a glimpse." Tyr turned, pulling her toward his bed. He wanted her to trust him--needed her to. Only then could they find their way out of the clutter of deceit between them.

"Where--?" she asked, but didn't finish . Jaden's insides shook. As he held her hand in his cool grip, pulling her behind him, the vulnerability glowing gently in his eyes, he almost felt like a real man.

"It's best if we lay down. That way, if we fall from a horse or jump from the edge of a castle we won't actually fall." His voice was soft and persuasive. His eyes glimmered ever so slightly.

Tyr led her to the bed. Stopping, he turned to her and motioned her onto the mattress.

"I should clean up." She protested weakly, trying to pull back. He refused to let her go. "I'm sweating."

"You'll be fine," he promised, coming close. The back of his hand touched her cheek, the long nails grazing past her temple, down her jaw. His gaze shifted and glowed in the dim light, seeming to whisper, *Lie down. Trust me.*

Jaden nervously crawled onto the bed and faced him. Tyr came over her with the stalking grace of a beast after its prey. His teeth glinted sharply as his mouth parted. His fingernails dug like claws into the bedding. His head fell to the side, drawing his hair gently over his sinewy shoulders so the strands reached to touch her.

Jaden was forced to lie down so that their bodies wouldn't touch. Her arms trembled and weakened, as they lay helpless at her sides. Her heart fluttered faster than the thumping wings of a hummingbird--beating in her chest, her throat. The sound echoed in her head. She knew he could hear it.

Tyr looked down at her body nestled beneath his on his mattress. It beckoned him, warm and inviting and very much alive. He was so cool compared to it.

"Close your eyes," he ordered in a husky murmur. Jaden obeyed. Her limbs were weak from their sparring and her body throbbed with unfulfilled needs. The mattress was chilly against her back, warring with the heat of her skin. The softness of it nestled beneath her like a cloud.

She peeked up at him. His chest was bare, unmarred and perfect, ashen and smooth. When his eyes looked into her, she felt as if he really looked, as if he saw her for who she was and accepted it. She wanted to believe that he understood. But deep inside, she knew what he was. She knew that there could never be anything between them. Their worlds wouldn't accept it. Her eyes drifted closed once more.

Tyr couldn't resist the parted ridge of her mouth, panting softly. Leaning his weight on his arms, he moved down so his lips hovered above hers, whispering next to her mouth.

"I'm going to kiss you," he said boldly. "Tell me you want me to."

"Yes," she said weakly, not looking. The fight was gone, expended in their exercise. Her body quivered in anticipation--in something more that she didn't want explained. "I want you to."

Tyr concealed his fangs beneath his lips. Slowly he lowered his arms, moving to his elbows to close the distance. The first brush of velvety softness was like a match to dry tender. A flame struck up between them sending passion throughout their extremities. Each fed off the other. Tyr mouth parted instantly, diving forward to stake claim with a deep, probing kiss that left them both weak. Though his kiss was deep, he kept his teeth back, artfully refusing to cut into her skin.

When she moaned, a soft and truly feminine sound, Tyr answered her with a heartfelt growl of his own. His knees threaded into her legs, urging her legs to part and accept his weight. His hand cupped her face, trying in vain to deepen a kiss that couldn't be deepened. Jaden's hands worked their way up to touch him. He tasted of mint. He smelled of earth and he felt of rigid, hard man.

Their lips broke for a moment as Tyr lifted her shirt over her head in a single motion, throwing it to the floor. Then his fingers began an exploration of discovery, gliding over the cleft in her throat, beyond the collarbone, over her side to her waist only to draw back to the swollen mounds of her breasts. He took her fully in hand, massaging through her bra, urging with his thumb so that her nipple would slip from behind its lacy curtain into his mouth.

Jaden's hands found hold on his smooth chest, rubbing insistently over his rigid skin. Once she explored every crevice of his neck, shoulders and chest, her hands ran over his nipples, teasing them into hard nubs. Tyr groaned, grinding his hips fully against her clothed womanhood.

His hands became demanding in their search. Threading his fingers into hers, he lifted one of her arms above her head to arch her breasts towards him. Jaden felt the intimate connection of their palms as he held her down. Her head thrashed to the side as his lips slid from her mouth to taste the tender flesh of her neck. Jaden peered at their intertwined hands from beneath the slit of her eyelids. The scar on his forearm danced before her, the brand of a shield with a bar down the center. It reminded her of what he was, who he was, why they had met. At that moment she didn't care--about any of it. This moment, Tyr, was what she wanted more than anything. Jaden knew she would be selfish and take it.

Tyr's jaw worked against her throat, along the fragile beat of her pulse that unwittingly urged him to bite into her, to really taste her. Pulling away from the temptation, he sat up.

Jaden's eyes flew open in panic at his quick withdrawal. She saw the red lining his gaze, the monstrous tilt of his seductive brow. He chuckled, a low throaty sound as he whispered, "It is too late to stop."

Jaden stared into his eyes, her gaze seeming to answer, *I know*. The ice blue orbs swirled with an array of emotion, making them gleam in unearthly splinters of purple and silver. His hands went to her jeans, tugging violently to part the denim. His eyes stayed fixed.

"But what about showing me?" she began only to gasp as he whipped the jeans from her hips and legs in one smooth motion. Those too ended up on the floor.

"I've something much more urgent to show you, m'lady," he whispered, coming on top of her. Jaden liked the way he said, *m'lady*. It made her feel special, unique. The word was as natural as the vampire who spoke it. His hands worked quickly on his own waistband. "And something much more pleasurable to give to you."

As he audaciously said the last, he managed to free himself from the prison of his black pants. Jaden gasped, feeling the hard length of his naked member scolding her thigh. Without looking, she could feel that his male sex was as demanding and big as the rest of him.

Jaden gulped for air, feeling him rub against her thigh. It was as if they had been waiting for this moment since their first meeting. Everything that was said and done could only lead to this one grand conclusion. No matter how wrong coming together was, it felt right, and they were no match to fight their shared destiny.

Her hands greedily ran over his back, reveling in the strong, tense muscles before dipping over the firm hills of his buttocks to pull him closer. He wore no underwear, so it was easy to venture beneath the tight black material.

Tyr growled, leaving her to strip out of his pants with a supernatural speed. Completely naked, he once more rose above her, unashamed. His lips dipped to take her nipple into his mouth. The rough texture of her bra ground against them. Tyr lifted his hands to the bra as he kissed her, pulling viciously at the material from both ends, ripping it in two. Jaden's back tensed in delight of his effortless power. Wondrous sensations flowed through her blood. Tyr's mouth claimed one breast and then the other. His sharp teeth grazed, dangerous and delightful, grazing her flesh.

Her hand moved in hastened curiosity to find his shaft. Stroking it, she marveled at the hot size of him. She fondled the length of it from base to tip, running her finger over the smooth head before reaching lower to cup the contrasting softness of the two globes underneath.

"I want to explore every inch of your flesh with my hands and mouth. But you have toyed with me too long," he growled like a wild beast against her flesh. "We must slow, lest I cannot keep myself from claiming you."

Lifting his mouth he moved to look her in the face. Jaden returned his look of passion, only wavering when his gaze began to soften. Insecure about seeing his tenderness, uncertain if she could handle softness from him, she lifted her knee to massage his outer thigh, opening herself up for his taking. His hand in hers, she led it beneath her panties. She pressed his fingers into her awaiting moisture.

Hungrily, she asked, "Does this feel like I want you to slow?"

Tyr groaned as she thrust herself boldly into his hand. He allowed a finger to test the slickness of her opened depths. Her essence flowed over him like warm honey. But as he moved inside, her cavern was tight, like a woman held long from the pleasure of a man. Knowing she hadn't recently coupled with Rick, or any other, pushed him over the edge. His eyes glinted with a dangerously possessive fire.

Tyr turned his hand, slicing her constrictive panties with his nails and tossing them out of his way. His mouth brought kisses to her breast, circling her nipples with his expert tongue. Her hips searched for him, but he held back.

"Oh," Jaden gasped, tortured beyond control. Her hips sought the air for him, for release, scooting down on the bed as she searched for his touch. "Tyr, please … *please!*"

He ignored her pleas, delighted that she reacted to him with such honesty. Her passion was her own doing, he refused to enhance or force it with his abilities. He wanted to see her pure response to him, wanted to know that she was with him because it was of her choosing. He wanted her to know it as well.

"Tyr," she cried out with more insistence, weak, breathless, begging and pleading for him to end it.

"I want to taste you," he growled.

"I want you inside of me," she countered.

Tyr, with his superior strength, won. Jaden thought her body might explode, but seeing the determination in his eyes when he looked up at her through the valley of her breasts, she didn't stop him. Her legs spread in offering. Her hips lifted up to eagerly meet his caressing mouth.

Jaden gasped, panted, heaved for air. Tyr's expert tongue circled her navel. His teeth grazed the tender skin of her belly. With one bite he could've ripped her in two. Jaden wasn't frightened. She liked to feel his power over her. She liked feeling as if he could control her. Never had a man or vampire been able to beat her, conquer her.

Dragging his hands possessively to rest on her hips, his mouth came to the center of her torment. He breathed hotly against her. His tongue flicked over the sensitive nub once, twice, a third time. Grabbing her by the backs of the knees, he forced her open wide. His lips parted, his kisses drew to the fold that joined her inner thigh to her loins. Smelling the sweet, aroused perfume of her blood, Tyr couldn't resist. He bit into her flesh.

Jaden bucked in delight. She could feel his teeth anchoring into her, could feel the deepened suck of his kiss as he truly tasted her. It was more intimate than she could've ever dreamt. Not to be outdone, his fingers found comfort in the wet folds of her tight holding.

Tyr tasted her, feeling the passion inside of her enhance his. Unlatching his mouth with a groan, he drew his head away in ecstasy, rolling it back on his shoulders. Blood trickled from the wound, staining his lips crimson. It swirled with the dangerous passion in his eyes.

"Now you," he urged. His piercingly erotic gaze filled with lines of red. The low accent of his Nordic speech became thicker, as he urged, "Taste me."

Tyr came up next to her. He drew his fingernail over the side of his neck, cutting into his flesh without flinching. Blood trickled from the wound, flowing like little rivers over the ravines of his shoulder. His body tensed, waiting for her to obey.

Leaning over, he drew Jaden's mouth to the wound. Quietly, he urged, "Taste my passion for you, let it flow inside of you."

Jaden shivered in ecstasy. The prudent voice in the back of her mind was unable to remind her of how forbidden being with a vampire was. Her mouth greedily licked the opening of his self-inflicted cut, kissing deeply as she drank from his flesh. Her tongue lapped in the taste of him. Tyr groaned in delight at her acceptance, feeling her joining him. The vampiric essence made her body sing with fire and need. His blood had the power to heal, the power to enhance, the power to make her lose all control.

"Yes," he whispered. The words were low and brutal sounding, as if he was pushed beyond the threshold of his pleasure. "That's it. Take me within you."

Just then, he parted her body to him. With a quick flex of his hips he pushed into her awaiting fold. Jaden cried out as he filled her completely. It had been so long since she'd been touched that her muscles screamed with the pleasure-pain of his girth. Her loins convulsed and she accepted him into her depths. His touch was stiff and hard and so very deep as if he claimed her very soul. She screamed again against his neck. His blood flowed into her mouth, onto her chest to stain her smooth skin.

Tyr reveled in the burning acceptance of her need, pausing to feel her body convulse around him, adjusting to his size. Jaden growled when he didn't move, demandingly bucking her body against him.

Grabbing her hips, he rode her hard with mindless abandonment of pure gratification. The sensation of Tyr's seething hardness rubbing against her sweet, tender flesh drove them mad until they couldn't stop the delving of their bodies. They greedily searched for satisfaction for their shared desires. In that insanity, they knew that this very thing was why they had met--to be together, to come together, to share, to feel something so much richer than agony and death, to become one being joined in ecstasy.

The plunging of his thrusting member strove for complete conquest, staking Tyr's mystical claim to her flesh. Jaden moaned, whimpered, and yelled him on. He was just as loud in his passion, as he pushed faster, deeper, striking at her core with supernatural speed. Jaden's body felt as if she were on fire. Nothing mattered but the vampire before her. Her blood swam with the sensation of him. His taste was in her mouth. She couldn't resist moving to taste more of him. She kissed him deeply, nicking her lips on his fangs.

They couldn't reason beyond the beatings of their hearts, the pounding need of their fevered flesh. Jaden suddenly tensed, shivers racking her body in violent completion. She screamed, clutching at his strong shoulders, throwing her head back, straining beautifully beneath him. Tyr couldn't resist the call of her taut, quivering body. He too yelled in dominate pleasure as he thrust himself hard a last time only to release his seed within her.

When the final spasms of passion died into soft quakes, Tyr fell against her sweat laden body. Jaden's breath gasped loudly under him, bringing him pleasure at her breathless recovery. Both of them trembled in unison, completely sated. For the barest of moments, they were completely free and neither of them felt quite as alone.

* * * *

Jaden sighed in her sleep as she drifted in peaceful dreams. Her limbs were heavy and calm. She could feel a breeze moving tantalizingly over her skin and the strange, uneven texture of grass beneath it. She could detect the warmth of the sun shining brightly on her face, kissing her warmed flesh. In the distance a bird sang a cheerful summer song.

A cheerful song she thought skeptically. A frown marred deeply on her brow as anger seeped in. *A bird!*

Her eyes popped open. Jaden sat up from her grassy bed in trepidation. Before her was a land blanketed with rolling grasses and swaying weeds. Beneath her was the cushioned bed of a field. The perfumed scent of wildflowers wafted on the temperate wind, their color dotting the ground all around her. It was daytime. The sun was bright--too bright for an old vampire to venture into--and she was alone.

Darting to her feet, Jaden spun in circles. A forest stood nearby, no sign of fences or roads or people. In the distance, she thought she heard the hooves of horses, but the sound was so faint she couldn't be sure. Tyr was nowhere to be found. Had he let her go? Did he decide she was innocent and that was that? Did he abandon her in the middle of Norway without a word?

Anger at being discarded like a cheap whore bubbled inside of her. Her fists balled in outrage until she realized that something wasn't quite right. She wasn't in the mountains, and what the devil was she wearing!

Looking down in amazement, she saw a long, heavy gown of dark blue. Beneath the gown was an undertunic of cream, tightly fitted to her frame. Tiny buttons decorated up the length of the tight, long sleeves. The skirts constricted her legs as she tried to move beneath the unfamiliar weight of the cumbersome dress. The dark blue overtunic gown hung open at the sleeves, arcing like a giant tank top beneath her armpit to her hips. Gold embroidery laid thick over the square neckline and hems and a gold cord draped around her fitted waist, swinging as she moved to touch just below the knee.

Looking around, she felt a fluttering at her neck. Thinking it to be a bug, she wrinkled her nose and jumped to the air. She frantically swatted the dangerous creature away. Instead of smashing an insect, she managed to tear a wimple and veil from over her face. They fluttered to the ground, discarded. Taking a deep breath, she jumped again as the overly long lengths of her hair blew into her vision. The ends reached a good distance past her waist.

"Uh," she said, trying to clear the long locks from her mouth and eyes. Finally, managing to tame the wild tresses back, she held them to the nape of her neck in a fierce grip. She instantly looked around for a knife so she could cut them off.

"Tyr!" she screeched.

"Yea, m'lady," he bowed gallantly. Jaden spun around to face him. He wore a black turtle neck and his matching pants. "Don't you like the open field? Very medieval, is it not?"

Jaden gasped, staring at him in the sunlight. The rays hit upon his face, making his pale skin glow with life. His hair radiated as if on fire. The daylight gave texture to his lips, red from within by the help of her blood. When he smiled, she saw that his fangs were not as sharp.

Jaden swallowed, remembering all too well how he felt next to her. Her breasts felt swollen. She wanted to kiss him, to hold him, make love to him again in this damned field. But he was an enemy and now that the fevered need of their bodies was tempered back to a reasonable pitch, it was time they faced what they must.

"It is not," she belatedly growled, doing her best to ignore his playful mood. "It looks like any other field. And how come you get to wear that and I am stuck in this? And why aren't you dead from the sunlight?"

Tyr cleared his throat, his eyes grinning unabashedly. He almost seemed disappointed by her last question. His gaze moved with a rekindling of longing over her form. He liked her as she was, missed seeing woman as she was now before him--feminine and yet strong. As she had slept next to him, he couldn't find rest. He had stared at her until the overwhelming urge to see her in sunlight prevailed over him. This was the only way he ever could.

"My apologies," he shrugged, none too apologetic. "It is my mind. I tend to put things as I want them. And you did say you wished you could see this time. Well that dress is part of it."

"I meant the battles, Tyr, not these pre-feminism torture devices. What is with all this blasted hair? And what the devil was on my head?"

"I could take the clothes off," he offered, his eyes turning naughtily up and down her slender frame. He enjoyed her in the dress, the tight fitted waist, the feminine neckline that hugged so perfectly across her breasts, pushing them up for ample display. However, he could also tell she was uncomfortable in it.

"If I have to wear something, make it battle gear," she said, grinning impishly as she warmed to the idea. She rubbed her hands thoughtfully, as she added, "And give me a giant sword."

Tyr nodded, mildly disappointed. In a blink, her arms became slanted down in armor. Beneath the press of unexpected metal, Jaden hollered in surprise as she fell backwards, weighted down. She landed with a thud in the cushioning of grass. A sword dropped from her hand, falling softly beside her. Tyr chuckled and leaned over her. His hands threaded behind his back as he gave her an innocent grin.

With a huff, Jaden pushed the face plate of the helmet up from her eyes. She could feel her body was completely naked under the metal. The dress was gone. Glaring at him with feigned anger, she growled, "Get me out of this nightmare, Tyr. I don't like being in your mind. And I think you should know that you aren't the least bit funny."

Tyr shrugged, his look disagreeing with her.

"Come on," she urged, threatened by the softness in him. "Take me back."

"You'll have to give me a kiss first."

Jaden pursed her lips together in mock defiance. Tyr fell to his knees. Leaning over, he didn't give her time to protest as he pushed his lips to hers. Jaden laughed lightly and instantly melted, remembering the all too recent, familiar feel of him. The armor seemed to melt from her skin, replaced by his hand on the curve of her hip. Just as swiftly, he pulled away.

"Open," he commanded her softly.

Jaden moaned, opening her eyes as if from a dream. Wearily, she yawned asking, "Did that happen?"

Tyr nodded and responded quietly, "I told you I would show you."

"But all I saw was trees," she pouted. Suddenly, she realized she was laying naked beside him in full view. She sat up on the bed, remembering herself. Feeling a twinge in her inner thigh, she glanced down. A bruise formed around two puncture marks where he had bit her. She got up from the bed. A sickening dread overcame her with shame.

"Would you like to go somewhere else?" he offered roguishly. "Come lay down, I'll show you a castle. Sometimes the knighted men can be convinced into fighting."

"No, thanks, I'll stay in this century for now." Under her breath, she added, "I don't like you having that kind of control."

Tyr watched Jaden get dressed. His good humor went with her nakedness. He felt her stiffen towards him and was helpless to stop it.

"Come back and lay down," he urged quietly, his gaze watchful and unrevealing. "I can heal that bruise for you."

"Ah, no, I shouldn't. In fact, we need to get a few things straight."

He said nothing. Jaden finished pulling up her jeans and turned to him. She winced at the pain in her leg.

Weakly, she said, "That is to say we shouldn't have done this and it won't be happening again. You are a vampire and I am a dhampir. It's wrong."

"Do you never grow tired of that song?" he murmured menacingly. She felt the mild wave of displeasure her words caused him. A brow rose over his unyielding blue eyes. Jaden couldn't deal with his emotions at the moment. She did her best to block them and he tried to keep them from her. Her mind reeled, tipping back and forth in near hysteria. Her heart thudded at a dangerous pace. She endeavored to remain completely calm, but it was hard.

"We are enemies," she said, mostly to remind herself. She erased the kindness of his expressions from her mind. It was easy, staring at the icy mask he now presented her. Her voice did not rise, but became fevered, as she said, "The truce is gone and there is nothing we could ever do to get it back. We made a mistake, one that we won't make again. We are enemies! This isn't right. It should never have happened!"

Tyr stayed quiet, his head cocked to the side as he studied her.

"Don't look at me like that! You know what I say is true!" she hissed, a part of her nearing hysteria. Tyr knew the emotion in her kind well, but it was the first sense of it he had gotten from her. Growing frustrated, she charged, "Don't forget why you have brought me here. You have your duty and I have mine. Every moment is a test. Even now I can feel you judging me. Well, it won't work. If anything, I am good at my job. My flesh may be weak, but my will is strong."

"Then are you admitting to the crimes for which your uncle stands accused. You know of what he has done?" Tyr sat before her completely naked, his body in easy repose. He was unashamed of himself, despite the unnerved way her disconcerting eyes tried too hard not to look at him. If this was the way she wanted it, then so be it. "You are admitting it?"

Blinking heavily, Jaden realized he was livid.

"No," she said in confusion. She tried to focus. Maybe if she gave him something, he would return the favor. Afterward she could work her way out of the mess she was in. "I found something, but.... I don't know. I couldn't read it. Can't you tell me what it is you think Mack has done? Just tell me and let me go. I'll ask him about it myself. I'll find out the truth. Let me deal with it."

Tyr eyed her carefully. He ignored the insult of her rejection for the moment. Lowering his jaw, he questioned, "What did you find?"

Jaden's gaze turned wide. All softness was gone from his tone. By looking at his stony features, she couldn't tell anything had passed between them. She detected a bit of crimson near his male sex. It echoed the taste of his blood in her mouth. What had she done?

Jaden hastened to her bag. Then, a sudden doubt crept into her mind. He had used her. He had been horny and she was closest thing available to slake his lust and she had put up a pitiful, weak fight. She shuddered violently. He wasn't her friend. He was her jailer. There could be no truce in this war.

She hesitated as she touched the book. As an alternative, she grabbed the yellowed piece of paper she'd discovered in her mother's box. With a heavy heart, she pulled it out and went back out into the room to discover Tyr was completely dressed. With trembling fingers, she lied, "I looked around like you suggested and this was all that I found."

Tyr reached out. Her look stopped him.

"If I show you this, then you must share with me what you know also."

Tyr nodded firmly. He took the paper from her with steady fingers. Inside he seethed at her indifferent dismissal of him. She used him to get what she wanted and now she was done with him. A wall went up between them, neither of them facing the feelings that tried to surface. It was easier to concentrate on work and it was definitely easier to their natures to fight.

"I can't read it." Her body fluttered with insecurities and doubt. She waited for a tender sentiment and found only hardness. Her body was still loose with the pleasure his gave her. "I don't understand the words. I'm not even sure what language it is in."

"Gaelic," he answered. Scanning the paper, he frowned.

"Where did you get this?"

"In a box next to a picture of my mother." Chills ran over her. "What is it? Can you tell me?"

"It's an incantation of the old magic to get a female human pregnant with a vampire baby. It explains how your mother got pregnant. These were supposed to be destroyed long ago. The only known copy was traced to a French family of witches in the fourteenth century. It was assumed their copy was lost to time."

"My uncle's tutor was French. Maybe she gave it to him. He said she was like a mother to him," Jaden offered, trying to sound confident. She swayed on her feet. She couldn't believe that Mack knew all these years how it was she was born. By all research, it should never have been possible and he told her that he didn't know. She remembered asking him endlessly as a young girl, searching for answers to her past.

"It makes sense," Tyr mumbled, lost in thought. "Mack must have discovered Bhaltair and Rhona were lovers and used this incantation on them."

Jaden paled, turning white to hear her father's name said out loud and from Tyr's precise lips. Her stomach folded in on itself, twisting into horrible knots. Her mind flashed, flooding her with memories of his death. The torrent of emotion and regret hit her like a mace. In her current state of insecurity the rush was hard to fathom.

Gulping, she said, "Maybe it was not Mack who used it. Maybe he only found it later and kept it."

"No," Tyr denied absently. His finger ran over the words. "This particular recipe calls for the blood of a human brother and MacNaughton would've had to perform the ceremony."

"Oh," Jaden breathed, growing nauseous.

"Bhaltair already made known his intent to turn Rhona to be with him to the council," the dark knight continued, pacing as he pieced the puzzle together. "And Rhona was most willing until she got pregnant. They must have decided that she would wait and bear the child because if she was a vampire the child would never exist. You would never exist."

Tyr turned triumphantly to Jaden, a large part of his puzzle solved. The council had debated for years how it was Bhaltair got the human woman pregnant. Charts of cosmic alignment had been pondered over, Rhona's diet, her lineage. All came to nothing.

Jaden swayed on her feet. Tyr, in his preoccupation, didn't notice.

"But your mother was killed when you were only a year," he said.

"And she was never turned," Jaden offered insipidly. "Her death was an accident. She fell off a horse."

"She was stabbed," Tyr debated, his brow furrowing as he absently disputed Jaden's claim. "I've seen the official report of the body from the investigating vampire's own file. I was sent to see what would happen to the dhampir child. You were given to your uncle. But why would Mack need you? It doesn't make sense."

Jaden's eyes clouded. She couldn't get Bhaltair's face from her mind. She couldn't focus past the lies her uncle had told her. For when she looked at Tyr, she knew he spoke the truth.

"Something's missing from the story, though," Tyr mused. His eyes scanned the paper. He was lost in deep thought. "Mack took you away, trained you. For awhile you were lost to us, even Bhaltair. He petitioned the council for help several times. When we finally located you, you were full grown. Bhaltair tried to approach you once, I'm told."

"Yes," Jaden said, remembering the man who stood before her, arms open wide, a smile across his undead face. She remembered every detail of the encounter, every heated word. Oh, how she hated him then. How she despised him for her existence! "I sent him away. I told him I never wanted to see him again."

"Yes, he came back to Europe and spoke on your behalf to the tribal council. Due to your upbringing, they had decided to kill you if you didn't accept your father's offer to join him. He begged them to give you another chance. They granted his request to wait a few years so that your anger was given time to lessen. Then, this past spring, he went back over to meet with you and–"

"I killed him," she whispered. Her heart broke into a thousand pieces. She always regretted that night she sent her father away. She always prayed he'd come back for her, take her away with him. Her dreams had been answered--only she botched them.

Tyr's face snapped sharply to hers, seeing the pale line of her ashen features. Tears welled in her gaze, dripping softly over the edge. She swayed, sinking to the floor.

"That is my crime, isn't it?" she questioned in a growing daze. She had known all along. She had waited for someone to come and punish her and here he was. Staring blankly at the floor, she began sinking into the abyss of insanity. The punishment was a grand one. He made her live to face it. He refused to kill her for it. She could no longer live with what happened. The memory haunted her dreams. She saw her father's face, disappearing into ash, blowing over her skin. It covered her flesh until she was mad to scrub it from every crevice of her body and hack it out of her lungs. It had taken weeks of showers until she was satisfied the ash was gone and even then, she could still see it on her if she looked hard enough.

Mumbling to herself, she rocked. "You were supposed to kill me. I went to you so you could kill me. You were supposed to be young. I made sure of it. A young one can't sense me. That is what Mack says. A young one is perfect. He doesn't know it's me. He'll kill me and then it will be over. A young one won't report it. He won't know to. No one will ever know. I'll die undisturbed. No one will ever know."

Tyr felt the slipping of her reason. It was the curse of the dhampir. One small thing and they could snap. Only what she confessed to was no small thing. She had murdered her own father--a father that had changed his undead life around because of her existence, a father who refused to kill even the smallest of insects as he waited for his daughter to grow. Setting his mouth in a tight line, Tyr went to her. He couldn't stand to feel her pain, her deeply wounding shame. Duty warred within him. He wasn't meant to comfort the guilty. He was meant to watch her and discover the truth and when he had her confession, once he knew the truth, he was to take her to be punished.

Glancing at him, she grimaced in confusion, "You're old."

"Jaden!" Tyr growled, taking her about the shoulders and roughly shaking her. Her head snapped back and forth. Emotion and duty clashed inside of him. She wasn't responding. His voice was low, harsh, as he yelled at her. "Damn it, Jaden! Come back!"

Tyr raised his hand as if to backhand her. He hesitated. A frown conquered his face. His hand turned into a clenched fist. He couldn't strike her. Easing his grip on her shoulders, he pulled her into his embrace. Stroking her hair, he cradled her into his arms. He ignored her repeated rambling about their first meeting in the alleyway.

Jaden settled into his comforting embrace, her words drifted to an incoherent mumble before stopping. Tyr lifted her jaw, forcing her blank eyes to look at him. She stared past him, through him. Seeing her lips so close to his, he leaned down to gently kiss her.

"It's all right, Jaden," he whispered into her mouth, as he soothingly touched her. His mind delved into hers, leading her back to him. His thumb worked over her face, brushing aside her tears.

Jaden felt the movement on her mouth, the tugging in her mind that urged her out of the stupor she fell into. Her fingers twitched, clinging to the comfort of a warm chest. Tyr's nearness engulfed her. His steady strength was a balm that stung her soul. She didn't deserve his kindness. Her mind jolted to awareness. She pulled away from him with a gasp.

Her eyes clear, her mind once more her own, she recoiled from him. Tyr had no choice but to release his hold. It tore at his chest to see her so broken. Hot tears poured anew down her face, staining her cheek.

Vehemently, Jaden demanded, "Dispense your justice, Tyr. Kill the murderer. It is what your people believed, is it not--an eye for an eye, a life for a life? Do what you were sent to do, Tyr. Finish me. I plead guilty."

Chapter Ten

Time rolled by slowly in the cave home. Jaden slept throughout the day in Tyr's bed, keeping with his vampiric schedule. Tyr rested on his couch, leaving her alone in his room. During the long nights, they didn't speak. Silence was marred only by the subtle shuffle of Jaden's feet, the crinkling page from some old book Tyr read, and most predominately by the popping wood burning in the fireplace.

After Jaden's plea for death was again denied, Tyr carried her protesting body to the bed. Her anger at his refusal lasted only a moment before he drifted his hand before her face and forced her into a deep sleep.

He had then sat across from her, watching her in her slumber. He examined the soft glow of orange on her skin as it faded to becoming shades of darkness. And when she finally awoke, he was still there watching. She'd hardly spoken since. The part of her soul that glistened normally in her expressive eyes was dead.

Jaden suppressed a yawn, staring blankly at the licking flames. Nothing seemed to catch her attention, but in truth, she felt herself most inclined to stare at the little arrangements of history nestled into Tyr's walls. Her mind reeled with her past, her uncertain future, her confusion over her captor and his motives. He had seen her in her weakest moment, the point where her fragile sanity broke into a thousand glass shards. No one had ever seen her brought low. She was mortified that it had been him. He now knew her weakness. The question was would he exploit it? Sighing again, deep and long, she closed her eyes.

Tyr had watched her silently from his chair for most of the night, leaving to disappear out of the side entrance of the cave when he could take no more of her stillness. The questions he needed answered swam in his head, trying to find their way out from his brain. He suppressed them, as he suppressed any tenderness that tried to escape him for her. He couldn't allow himself to be weakened by her. She was his assignment. Somehow things had gotten messy, but she was still a duty he must perform. He wouldn't risk his very existence for a mere slip of a human, no matter how alluring the package.

Occasionally over the long silence Tyr coerced her into eating. A few times Jaden would get up to relieve herself, or to take a quick bath out of a chilled water basin he got at her request, or to change her clothing. For the most part, he let her be, knowing she had a lot on her mind. And what were a few days to a creature that had lived so many? Even with the thought swimming in his head, Tyr was impatient.

He sorted the facts slowly in his mind. If she collapsed when confronted with the result of her actions, then surely she was not in league with her uncle. Though an angry woman by nature, she didn't have a heart for pure cruelty--and Tyr had seen the numerous faces of pure cruelty.

On the other end, maybe it was only the result of her crimes having been discovered. Any mortal who knew the existence of the tribal council would break under the prospect of being brought before them. If the mortal was guilty, then it was only a matter of time before they cracked.

"You don't eat. How do you resist the hunger?"

Tyr's head snapped up, turning from his chair to her clear jade eyes. Her face was calm, under complete control. Her voice was coherent. The fog around her had suddenly and unexplainably lifted.

"I eat," he answered quietly. His eyes narrowed in suspicion. "I've a storage of blood in this cave. It sustains me."

"Oh," she mumbled. "Then you don't kill?"

"Only for duty." He leaned forward, easing his elbows onto his knees. His tapered fingers tapped lightly in hidden thought.

Jaden's eyes roamed over his masculine form. A chill swept over her spine. She'd spent many hours contemplating her deeds, but even more time was spent under the spell his touch had wrought into her skin. He didn't touch her, didn't try to kiss her again, and she didn't go to him. But she wanted to.

"The night I met you in the alley," she said calmly, trying to focus her thoughts outside herself. "That was duty?"

"Yes," he answered. His eyes were blank, carefully taking her in. "He was a vampire I was sent to deal with."

"I though you were sent to deal with me," she wrinkled her nose ruefully. Her guarded laugh followed.

"You are one of my duties," he said.

Only a duty? she thought before adding aloud, "Oh."

"I had several others to contend with in New York."

"That is why I thought you were young," she sighed in sudden understanding. "I was reading him not you."

"Yes," he admitted. "And then I blocked my age from you to confuse you."

"And what did this vampire do? What constitutes a crime to the council?" she asked quietly.

"He tried to frighten a woman into labor and when he succeeded, he tried to make a vampire mother and baby." The assertion was dispassionate. His eyes cold as he recalled.

"Duncan," Jaden said with a shake of her dark auburn hair. She ran her fingers through the locks, pulling them absently back from her face. She stared into the flames in awe.

"You knew him?" Tyr questioned, growing cautious. He watched every subtle movement carefully.

"I killed the mother and child after he left them in the alley." The task still made her gag to think on it. She saw the baby's purple face, still squirming and wet from its birth, its skin paling from its sudden rebirth. "I thought I was hunting him in New Orleans. It's where...."

"Your uncle sent you to look," Tyr concluded. He predicted as much. He didn't want to believe Jaden could kill her own father, even if he was a vampire and her technical enemy. Despite his facts, he wanted to believe the best in her.

"And Duncan?" she queried softly, still refusing to look at him. "Did he get away?"

"No," Tyr murmured. "I found him again. He is dead."

"Well, that is one thing solved, isn't it?" Jaden whispered. She was glad to hear it.

"The woman and child were not your fault. You did what you had to do. I was sent to do the same thing, if they were still alive," he said. It was the truth. A baby couldn't take care of itself. That is why the sacred laws forbade the changing of children and helpless ones. The mother would've gone mad at such a loss that she would've been a wild vampiress, unable to show control. Experience taught that it was better that she joined her infant.

Jaden nodded, not answering. She looked at her hands, hands that had held so much ash and death in them. A moment of silence passed, marked by the crackling of fire. Suddenly, she said, "You know you should have some music or something in here. It is much too quiet."

"Mmm."

"I am tired of these games," she admitted at last. She thought of the file. Her decision made, she knew she would show it to him. She had to know the truth of what Mack had done and what she had been involved with. "You already know the worst of what I have done. Let's come clean and be honest. Then maybe both our lives can get past this disruption. You can go back to your council and I'll go back to doing whatever it is I do."

"Honest," he repeated softly, very much liking the idea in its simplicity. The steady tips of his fingers brushed lightly over his bottom lip in thought. The ice seemed to melt a bit from the blue of his eyes. He wanted desperately for there to be honesty between them. It was so much simpler than the deceit they had been practicing.

"Yes, I'll tell you what you want to know, if you tell me what you'll do with me."

"I have been ordered to study you and, in a few days, I'll bring you to the council with what I have learned. They wish to meet you." He watched her face to see how she would take the news.

"What?" Jaden gasped in surprise. She was to meet the council? Be set before them? Suddenly all the stories she'd read about what was done to captured bloodstalkers entered her mind--the countless years of pain, being brought to near death only to be saved and tortured again and again until the vampires grew bored with your screams. An involuntary shiver racked her body. With years of learning patience, it could be a very long time until a vampire grew bored.

"If you are innocent enough, they won't harm you," he said.

But I'm not innocent! she screamed silently. Now she couldn't show him the file. What if they thought she was involved? She didn't know what the files said, but she was sure it would be incriminating.

Even after all she learned of her uncle, she wasn't sure she wanted him harmed. He was her only family. He was the only one who ever really cared for her. He deserved a chance to explain himself to her before she turned him over to the tribal leaders.

"Now, it is your turn." His dark eyes swam with dangerous emotions, daring her to defy his claim. "First, what happened in New Orleans?

Jaden gulped. Her eyes started to haze and Tyr was afraid she wouldn't be able to answer. Her gaze focused on his old claymore. But, to his surprise, she told him the whole story with monotone precision, not leaving out one detail. When she finished she inaudibly added, her voice close to choking, "He could've fought me. He didn't even try to defend himself and I delivered him into death. I stalked him and captured him so that the others could take him."

"But you didn't know the other's were there," he said reasonably.

"Thinking back, I had sensed them. I should have been more cautious. It was my carelessness that did it. Now my father is dead and I--I'll never be able to beg his forgiveness. He was my father, my blood, and I destroyed him." Jaden took a deep breath, letting it escape her slowly. She hoped some of her pain would go out with it. Tyr watched her, knowing she needed to talk of something else.

"What do you know of your uncle's dealings?"

Jaden wavered uncertainly, thinking again of the file hidden in her bag. Clearing it from her mind, she couldn't meet his eyes. Tyr saw her falter.

"He tracks vampires," she said softly, staring at her lap. "He tracks those who commit atrocities against humans. Sometimes families who have lost a loved one donate money to the cause and then Mack tracks the vampire who killed their loved one. He sends the guys out after them."

"And then what does he do with them once he captures them," Tyr asked, already suspecting the truth.

Jaden looked at him in confusion. "They are killed. We never 'capture' them."

"What about the one in the park?" he probed. "She wasn't killed. In fact, she had never killed herself. She was newly turned."

"I--I," Jaden scratched her brow thoughtfully. "I don't know. I have never taken a prisoner. There would be no reason to. Your disease can't be cured."

"And what about the ones you track?" he continued, darkening as he thought, *Disease?*

"They are like Duncan," she spoke softly. Her eyes bore piercingly at her thigh, as if she might set it on fire with her turmoil. The bruise was all but faded from it.

"Are they?"

"Yes," Jaden gulped.

"And you've witnessed all of their crimes? You know for certain?" Tyr probed. His eyes dug intently into her.

"No, I--" she paused. Her gaze darted helplessly to his.

"You what?" he demanded. "You said you wanted honesty."

"I took Mack's word for it," she whispered. "Most of them I could sense once I had them down. But, occasionally, Mack showed me their file and I went off of that."

"So you don't know that all the ones you killed deserved it?"

"Yes, no I mean, I did when it happened. I could feel the death on them. I could smell it. Sometimes I could even taste it. And vampires are evil, were evil. You kill to live," she muttered vulnerably. "I really thought I was doing the right thing. This is a war against species and I have my side."

"Thought?" he questioned sharply. "You said you thought you were doing the right thing."

"I don't know anymore. I don't know anything anymore," she allowed. Tyr was confusing her. When she looked at his face, it wasn't the passionate lover of a few days ago. It wasn't even a friend. It was her interrogator, her punisher. She was a fool for ever daring to hope in the briefest moment of weakness that he could be anything else to her. He didn't feel, just faked it really well by mimicking the emotion he had seen in his victims. All vampires learned the trick. Stiffening her resolve, she determined that she would never be a fool again. If she was attracted to Tyr, she was only attracted to an illusion.

"So you don't know what Mack does with the women he captures? You've never heard talk, seen pictures, heard a rumor?" Tyr watched her carefully. He knew she was going to lie before she even spoke. He could feel it and still he waited in anticipation, hoping for the first time in centuries that he would be wrong. He wasn't.

"No," she answered furtively. She shaded her gaze from his.

"You're sure?" he asked, giving her another chance. He knew what was coming, but part of him wanted to deny it. His eyes glazed as he waited for her to speak.

"Yes, I'm sure." She lifted her chin, turning her eyes coldly to his. "I don't even know if Mack is aware of the captured woman. You took me away before I had a chance to ask him. The capture was Tom's doing. Maybe you should ask him. Mack would never be involved in anything remotely unseemly."

"I think I've learned all I need to know," he said after a long moment of studying her. He didn't like what he found. The disappointment strangled him. The tale of her father's death, though horrible, could've been forgiven. But for her to cover and lie about her uncle's crimes made her just a big a part of them as Mack was.

"And what about me?" she whispered. "What are you going to do with me?"

"I've already told you. In a few days, you'll meet with the council." Tyr stood, moving away, out the side of the cave. His movements were stiff, losing some of the grace she had grown to know in him.

When Jaden was all alone, emptiness surrounded her. It went against her instincts to lie to Tyr. But she couldn't trust her instincts anymore. She had to trust her brain. Emotion only got in the way and she couldn't be sure her innermost feelings were not of Tyr's evoking. The Dark Knight was a powerful being. She had felt it in him many times.

But, even as she was certain of it, she prayed she'd done the right thing in keeping the file from Tyr and thus protecting her uncle. She considered burning its contents, but it would be a risky endeavor to do so without being caught in the act. Tyr would be able to smell the burning paper almost immediately and with his ability to control fire at will, he could smother the flames before they did their work. Or, if he chose, he could reach into the fire and pluck the paper from its heat. Either way, the potential for him to discover their contents was great.

Defending Mack wasn't a hard call, logically. She was more a human than a vampire's daughter and she would have to pick the side of her people. She easily rationalized that she had no way of telling what was inside the mysterious folder. Warring with her gut, Jaden tried to convince herself that the pictures only told a half-truth that would make complete and perfect sense once explained.

If Tyr did evoke her into feeling more in him than there was, then everything she felt was a lie. Logic told her it was a lie. Logic was cold comfort to a bleeding and broken heart. Moisture burned inside her eyes and stung her nose. She repressed it down into the pit of her stomach. She couldn't trust him and she couldn't trust herself since meeting him. There was only one thing for her to do. The very thing she set out to do in the first place.

* * * *

Island of Mykonos, Cyclades

The metropolitan island club of Mykonos thrived with the ambiance of drunken drag queens with high-spun hair of all colors and carousing businessmen, with discarded jackets and rolled up sleeves, on their luxury yachts. It was an odd mixture of subcultures, blended into the ancient land of the Greek Gods, backdropped by whitewashed buildings created by unknown folk artists, sandy beaches, water that was bright and clear during the day but now the blue-black of a starry night. Narrow pathways weaved intricately through nightclubs and churches, homes and shopping nooks.

Music poured out into the streets, following patrons as they hopped from one nightclub to the next. Drunken humans stumbled around, thinking the undead gazes in their midst were just more of the same eccentric travelers, blending in with the beautiful surrounding, beckoning a drunk mate for just 'one night of naughty pleasure.' And the travelers would say to themselves, *Why not? It is a vacation,* before falling prey to the deepest of unearthly kisses.

It was easy pickings for the vampires who inhabited the sacred land of Delos only eleven miles away by boat. No human ferries left for Delos after dusk or before dawn as it was illegal to stay on the ancient island over night--and for good reason. The hot daylight might be a time of exploration to the tourists seeking out Greek history. But the night belonged to the vampire and they didn't appreciate intruders.

The night provided safe passing for the undead. Their arranged crafts blended into the dark waters, mixing with the yachts docked into harbor. Mykonos was a natural stop for any vampire traveling to meet with the council hidden beneath Delos' surface.

The council's whereabouts was not common knowledge amongst the undead and the island's vampire population was kept on close watch by the Vrykolatios to make sure such secrets were not discovered. But, for the rare human knowing of the island secrets, Mykonos was a perfect place to hide. The rowdy crowds thronged the streets, making disguises various and easy to come by. Besides, one human smelled as ripe as the next to those who watched from shadows.

Mack strode easily through the crowd, wearing a cardigan sweater with his jacket and slacks, a smile pasted plainly on his face, creasing the lines next to his elegant mouth. Occasionally, he would laugh, turning his head to some alcohol induced antic. Inside, he didn't feel the joy, concentration burning deep as he plotted and schemed. Behind him, strolling as unknown passer-bys trailed Rick and Tom, pretending to enjoy each other's company with easy smiles and hard, watchful eyes.

Stepping over the cobblestone streets, Mack turned past one of the noisy clubs boasting an awful rendition of karaoke music. The surrounding crowd cheered the hapless singer on. Coming to a darker corner hidden from the busy streets, Mack stopped. Looking over his shoulder, he saw Tom and Rick stride past. Neither one of them stopped or acknowledged they saw him turn.

"You are late," Pietro's voice said from within the darkness.

"It couldn't be helped," Mack answered in low tones before turning around. Grabbing a handkerchief from his front jacket pocket, he blotted the sweat from his brow. "I wanted to be sure I wasn't followed."

"You were not," Pietro said. His stood still, his hands folded before his stomach, his fingers pressed thoughtfully against each other. At length, he said, "It is a wonder that you are so cautious, being as a document of yours was taken from one of your men."

"What document?" Mack asked, swallowing to hide his fear. He thought of Jaden.

"No, not the dhampir," Pietro said, reading the thought. Mack cleared his mind. "It was a directive stating a client's wishes to bed a chained vampire woman. It was very careless of you, MacNaughton, to leave a trail. I should expect better from you in the future."

"You have no proof that it is mine," Mack began in weak defense. He never wrote down orders … unless it was one of his men.

Pietro grimaced, holding up his hands to stop any protest that Mack might make. He didn't care about the atrocities of the human race. "I care not how you make your fortune for it suits me that you have it."

Brusquely, Mack nodded. Pietro never asked the details of what he did, but deep down he had a feeling the vampire knew. Lowering his eyes in respect, he asked softly, "What news of my niece? Is Jaden safe?"

"For the time being," Pietro said, giving the man neither hope nor comfort. He drew back as a noisy throng stalled near the alcove's entrance. Mack ducked into the shadows. They waited as a woman crawled on the ground looking for her lost earring. A man came up behind her. Sweeping her up by the waist, he carried her away amidst the clamor of tumultuous laughter and promises of more jewels to replace the one she dropped.

When they were once again relatively alone, Pietro added, "Tyr still has her. Their location is only known to a few. In three nights, the council has ordered that she be brought to them for questioning. They are very curious as to your business practices."

"Jaden doesn't know a thing," Mack said, veiling his emotions. Pietro had no desire to read him and that suited Mack's purpose just fine.

"Good," Pietro said. "If you fail, there will be no answers she can give."

"Fail?" Mack asked.

"In rescuing her, you'll have one chance to liberate your precious dhampir and capture the elusive Tyr. When they come to the island to cross over to Delos, you must have your men ready. And you must kill the boatman. There can be no witnesses. I'll take care of the council. I'll tell them Tyr never delivered the girl. They will think he betrayed them. It is important that you do not let him escape. When you are done with the knight's blood, kill him."

It was the most Mack had ever heard Pietro utter in one grouping. Mack shivered, feeling the coldness of the old vampire's gaze, the hatred he had for his own kind.

Taking a deep breath, Mack answered, "It will be as you say."

"Make it so." Pietro lowered his head.

Mack, knowing what was to come next shrugged out of his jacket and began rolling up his sleeve. He glanced over his shoulder to make sure no one watched before lifting his arm to Pietro's mouth in offering. Pietro reached for him, his cold fingers snapping out like the brittle limbs of fall trees. He stopped to glance over the mortal's shoulder.

Mack turned, seeing Rick standing in the entryway. A scowl etched the soldier's questioning features as he came forward. His eyes darted from Mack's offered arm to the vampire disappearing above them.

Mack turned, his eyes moving above his head to look at the night sky. Tugging down his sleeve, he pulled on his jacket. Rick watched carefully, his chest fuming, his jaw working in mounting anger and suspicion. He glared in barely tempered warning.

"Are we consorting with vampires now, Mack?" he said. His hatred for the undead etched into every word.

Tom came running around the corner. He skidded to a halt seeing Mack's calm face confronted with Rick's anger. Tom hesitated. Then, glancing guiltily at Mack, he said, "I'm sorry, Mack. He got away from me in the crowd."

"You knew about this, Tom?" Rick asked, backing away from both of them in disbelief. "You knew he was consorting with the enemy? What the hell is going on?"

"Mack--" Tom began in protest. He nodded aggressively at Rick's back, willing to take the man out at his boss' command.

"Don't worry about it Tom. Head back to the hotel. We'll be right behind you." Mack brushed off the front of his jacket. When Tom had done what was bid of him, Mack turned his kind, understanding smile to

Rick. Rick watched him in growing confusion.

"What's going on here?" Rick persisted coldly. "What were you doing with that--that vampire?"

"I care for Jade, too," Mack said softly, allowing his eyes to show his stress. He knew that Rick would misdirect the cause of that emotion. In a fevered pant, he hastened, "But I won't be ruled by fear. I won't let my emotions rule my head. And I'll do what I must to obtain information about her--even if that means letting a vampire suck on my arm. This is not a white and black business we are in. There are messy shades of crimson haunting us in everything we do. If I must consort with the enemy to save my niece, then so be it. I would face the devil himself to have her back into the safety of my fold."

Rick watched the older man's controlled expressions. Suspicions and doubt clouded the back of his mind, but mention of Jaden took precedence over his feelings. There would be plenty of time to figure out Mack once Jaden was avenged. His first duty was to her.

"What did you discover?" Rick asked, his tone sharp from aggravation.

"She's alive," Mack said woefully.

"Where?" Rick didn't dare to hope. His heart raced, his mind darted frantically trying to formulate a plan with no facts. "Are you sure?"

"Yes." Mack turned his eyes away so the young soldier couldn't read his expression.

"What is it? What has happened?" Rick demanded, his words sharp with worry. He crossed to Mack, forcing the older man around to face him. Desperately, he said, "You must tell me."

"It isn't good," Mack pronounced like a minister at a funeral. His words dropped to a whisper. "She's been--ill used."

Rick felt his stomach drop. His heart beat in awful thumps, dreading the man's next words. He thought of Jaden's face, the hard lines softened with laughter, a memory he carried from their first night together. He remembered her face in slumber, lying in his bed, made peaceful from the potent drugs he had dosed her with. He loved her and whatever happened to her would be his fault. He had left her helpless. Rage worked inside of him, swallowing the sickening terror of what he was about to learn.

Mack saw the look, the raw guilt and passion the man carried for his niece. He had suspected it before, but never knew for sure. Now he had his answer shining like a dying beacon in the soldier's eyes. Rick's breaking heart was in that look and Mack took full advantage.

"Tyr has made use of her, Rick," Mack said gravely. "She has been tortured and abused most viciously. I can't even begin to describe for you the liberties that undead bastard has taken with her."

"No," Rick whispered, his hard face growing pale, his steady eyes wavering. His large body quivered in fear. He forced himself to listen. It was his self-punishment that he should hear everything and his redemption would be making it right.

"God in heaven, it must be killing her to be that undead monster's--" Mack let his words trail off with a tortured breath. Rick looked helplessly at him, urging him to finish the sentence and at the same time praying that he wouldn't. In a low voice, Mack whispered, "--whore."

"He's--he's touched her then?" Rick queried. "You're sure of it?"

Mack snorted, his only answer.

"I'll kill him," Rick swore in a growing frenzy.

"I know Jade," Mack said, with a comforting pat. "She is a tough girl. She will get over this in time. But I know something we can do to help her recover."

"What?" Rick expressed in anguish. His words were hoarse as he promised, "I'll do anything. Just tell me."

"We must capture Tyr," Mack said.

"Capture?" Rick asked in outrage. His eyes rounded in disbelief that Mack could even say such words to him. "Don't you mean kill?"

"No. I mean *capture*. We let Jaden do what she will with him. Let her kill him. Let her know for sure he is dead by seeing his death, by causing it. It is the only way to help her. Otherwise, she might always be fearful and then she will be no good to us or the cause."

"I don't give a damn about the cause," Rick said.

"At this moment neither do I," Mack said with more control. Another wave of night-clubbers passed by in reckless abandonment, their laughter sent a chill through Rick. How naive they were of the world. Their only care was finding the directions to the next bar. Mack lowered his voice to a low murmur. "But Jaden does care about the cause. Without the fight, she could never be whole."

Rick slowly nodded in agreement, his mind unable to argue with the point. Jaden's whole life was fighting vampires. She even sacrificed personal happiness and companionship for it.

"Will you help me?" Mack asked fervently. "Can I count on you to lead the men? Can I count on you to have a clear head about this?"

"Yes," Rick answered. "Just tell me what needs to be done."

Mack smiled, knowing the man was in his pocket. Rick would be like putty to his molding fingers. If all went well, his putty would be brought in from the dark and offered a place at his side. With a careful smile, he walked back to the hotel. He nodded for Rick to follow him. The young man did, lost in torturous thought. As they moved, Mack began laying voice to his plan, "They will arrive in three night's time...."

Chapter Eleven

Jotunheimen Mountain Range, Norway

Tyr stared at the sealed pouch of blood gripped in his hand. The contents were tepid, unappetizing on the best of nights, but necessary to live. Tonight he couldn't find the hunger for it. His stomach tightened in anger each time he thought of drinking and his mouth twitched in protest, ferociously urging for a warmer fluid to fill his palate. Only one drink would do--only one person's blood would satisfy him. Jaden's.

His body wanted her, craved her, and needed her. He knew she was a liar, a deceitful wench sent by Odin to torment him. He knew that when he stood before the council and told the truth about what he had learned, she most certainly would be sentenced to death. If only she hadn't lied to him, he could've protected her. If she only told him what she knew of Mack and his business, no matter how big or small. If only she trusted him, he could save her. But she didn't trust him. He couldn't blame her. With the life she had lived, he wouldn't trust anyone either if he were in her position. It didn't change the facts.

Jaden would never come to feel anything but disgust for his kind. She even abhorred herself for desiring him, had fought her lust till the bitter end. She thought he was a disease, a curse, a maggot to be squished under her mortal boot. Had she not said as much on many occasions? Her defiance was one of the things that drew him to her. She was tough and reckless. And, in his bed, she had been most passionate. There was no denying the ardor jumping back and forth between their bodies. Reviled or not, their obsession was as hot as molten metal and her body burned just as brightly as his.

How was it he could spurn and distrust someone so much, yet physically fit into her as if she were shaped to be his? It was a force they couldn't control and he felt it building between them once more. They might have been able to temper their longing, but they would never restrain it. Already Tyr could feel the temptation cutting heavily into his blood and he knew that she would respond to it as much she resisted. The more they fought and the longer they hated, the stronger their yearning became until it exploded. Once tasted, the bitter-sweetness of it would only tempt again and again … and again.

Groaning, the thought brought Tyr up short. He could admit that he had become attached to the reckless dhampir, but he didn't wish to discover how deeply those feelings ran. He couldn't care for someone who lied to him to protect the guilty. He couldn't feel for a woman who didn't trust him, and in all probability didn't like him. But, despite all of what he couldn't do, he found himself doing just that. He wanted her, wanted to claim her and possess her. He wanted to control her and be controlled by her. He wanted this nightmare of their own making to be over.

Tyr threw the package of blood against the storage wall. He watched with satisfaction as it splattered on the gray rock, dripping down the sides of the dark stone to pool onto the floor. His body clung to anger. He spun around, navigating his way through the dark tunnels with ease. Seeing the light of his fireplace beckoning him from beneath a heavy door, he slowed. His body dissolved into mist, shirking around the edges as he passed through the barrier.

Jaden was still on the couch, her face turned towards the flames in deep contemplation. He could feel the torment in her, the rage. He wanted to erase it from her. Like the brief moment he had her in the field of his mind, lying on the soft grass, weighed down by armor. For a moment, right before he kissed her, he felt happiness, tentative and pure and new within her. She had given him a willing smile and a chuckle. His soul ached that it should be so again.

But this deceitful creature before him now, spouting half-truths about honesty, was not that same woman. She was his prisoner, his obligation. And, so help him, he was going to do his duty. Honor forbade anything else. Striding into the room, he looked her up and down. Her face turned to him in horror before she jumped to her feet.

He felt her clearing her thoughts, though he hadn't been reading into them. Seething with growing outrage, he watched her. Her eyes glanced briefly at the fireplace, but he was too angry to detect the faint smell that came from there. Her chest rose and fell with fragile breath. His fist pulled at his side, clenching and unclenching with the desire to strike out, to make her tell him the truth. He took a step forward and then another. His eyes glared out from under sunken brows.

"Tyr," she hesitated. Jaden's heart fluttered. He looked livid. Could it be that he knew her lie? Did he come to drag her to the council now? Jaden panicked. Her hands reached absently behind her as she sought composure. Finding the reality of the wall behind her, she lifted her jaw rebelliously.

"I shouldn't want you," he swore, dark with assuaged sincerity. "I shouldn't want to touch you."

For all his words, they didn't sound like a compliment to Jaden. They sounded like a curse. She trembled, not answering. Her eyes took in the raw exposure of his face, the raging lines that threatened the whites of his eyes with red.

"What are you doing to me?" he continued, with a nebulous stare. His old Nordic accent cracked over her like a striking whip. Chills ran up her spine.

"I'm doing nothing to you. I don't even like you," she gasped, eyes wide and round. "I hate you. We are enemies!"

That caused a chuckle, mysterious and wicked, to escape Tyr's throat. *More lies, princess? Will there ever be truth in your words? Has there ever been truth in your words?*

He was in front of her within a blink. Jaden gasped at the potent force of his inspection. His face came into hers, the tip of his nose touching her as he probed her eyes. Jaden saw a dark war waging within him, felt the confusion of his soul. She tried to ignore it, tried to block it. She told herself it wasn't real. That it was all a trick to confuse her, to keep her off guard. How could a vampire's soul be tormented when they didn't have one?

"You don't hate me," he whispered ardently. His hands flexed and faltered before finally reaching to stroke her arms in rough impassioned massages that ran the entire length of her limbs from shoulder to wrist. "You only tell yourself you do. Feel inside yourself. I've sensed it in you the first night in the alley. I can feel you, Jade, as sure as I feel myself. Never, in all my years, have I felt such strength in one mortal person. Never have I felt such turmoil as to match my own."

Jaden panted in wonder at the quiet, passionate declaration. Tears came to her eyes at the gentle fierceness of his words. Weakly, she whispered in nervousness, "You're wrong. We're not alike."

Jaden tried to deny him. She tried to deny herself. She didn't want there to be truth in his words. But as she looked into his eyes, free of the coldness, swirling with passion for her, she knew he was right. She swallowed against the strangling closing of her throat. It was the final torment of her suffering. She loved a vampire--not only a vampire, a Dark Knight, a creature bred an eternity to punish and kill.

Seeing the realization crossing her face, he nodded. "You can't run from me any longer. You can't lie to me. You can't escape. I won't let you go."

Jaden was trapped against the wall. But even if she could find freedom, she wasn't sure she would seek it. His hands stopped their reckless course over her skin. His fingers cupped her chin, turning so that her eyes were forced to meet with his. In a low murmur, he declared against her lips, "You are mine. You belong to me. And you'll never escape me. I'll never give you your freedom."

Jaden felt herself tremble. His lips dared her to deny his heated claim as he stole her breath with a deep kiss. She hated the beating of her heart, thudding out his name in a frantic rhythm. She could see the hunger he had for her, the longing his body didn't try to deny. He wanted her, pure animalistic physical lust. But he said nothing of emotion, nothing of love.

Jaden's mind screamed for order, but her body ran its own rampant, wayward route. She was like a vulnerable ship, crashed against the rocks, riding on the whim of a treacherous black ocean. She could no sooner deny him or change her course.

A weak moan escaped her. Her resistance faded. She hated herself for the vulnerability, tried her damnedest to deny him. It was no use. Her fingers wound into the silken locks of his blond hair, pulling him close. She had her future charted, whether the vampire in her arms realized it or not. Her path was sealed. It had been since that night in the alley. He didn't spare her life, only delayed her death. She knew that now.

One last time, she thought, *one last surge of feeling before the endlessness of eternal sleep.*

Jaden poured all of herself into the kiss. Knowing the end was near, she didn't hold back. Tyr moaned against her, his body alighting with the fire of her raw, unfettered response to him. Grabbing her beneath the buttocks, he lifted her into his embrace. Her back slammed against the stone wall. Her legs wound around him, pulling his hardened erection to her heated core.

Jaden tore her lips away for breath, her hands eagerly sought to strip him of his shirt. The dark material ripped beneath her impatient fingers. Tyr growled and moaned, devoured and conquered. His lips found her neck, the sweet base of her pulse. Seizing her to him, he sped with supernatural speed to the bed, laying her softly onto the mattress as his mouth kissed viciously at her body.

Within moments, his deft fingers freed them of their clothing. Jaden shivered in the coolness of his touch. Not taking his lips from her neck, Tyr levitated her from the bed, using his will to direct the heavy silk coverlet down beneath them so she could lie on the satin sheets instead. He lowered her down. Jaden's thighs rubbed against his muscled hips, intertwining with his legs in precarious passions. Tyr let the coverlet slide up his back, offering her warmth with the covering.

The sensual slide of silk on her skin contrasted with the hair roughened length of his calves. Her mouth tasted his mouth, his neck, his chest. Growing wildly impatient, she rolled him onto his back. She sought to devour him with her body. Her hands couldn't feel enough. If she had one thought that lasted with her into death, she wanted it to be the memory off his flesh, the way he made her soar at this very moment.

Tyr growled in mild surprise at her complete surrender. He let her explore him, her hands taking in the fields of his body, her mouth trailing behind them. Her tongue flicked over the rigid erection of his nipples as her hand found the matching hardness between his legs. She fondled him, stroking the length, driving him mad with urgent need.

Tyr returned her enthusiasm tenfold. His large hands cupped her breasts, massaging the tips into aching peaks that taunted his mouth from the distance. He found the softness of her hips, the hardness of her muscled stomach and thighs. His fingers glided over her skin, liking the practice she had of shaving the area smooth.

Tyr urged her to sit. His hands played with the rise of her breasts, the bottom curve of her swollen globes. Jaden stroked against the probing heat of his leg as it pushed up into her. Tyr could feel her hot wetness on him, burning his skin. Jaden looked into the passionate vault of his swirling eyes, the parted seam of his lips.

Leaning over him, she whispered hotly, "Let me taste you."

Tyr again hid his astonishment. Obeying her request, he drew his nail over his neck in a slow line. Jaden watched, pausing slightly to see the blood beading on his flesh. It beckoned her lips like wine. She looked at Tyr's eyes, ice blue orbs that watched her closely. With the attention of a worshipper, she lowered her lashes and moved her tongue over the wound. Tyr gasped, throwing his head back in ecstasy as they connected.

Having licked her fill, she lifted her face to stare down at him. His blood stained her white chin, smeared over her breasts, and puckered her kiss-swollen lips to crimson perfection. His wound healed itself shut. Her eyes glowed with an inner light of their own as she lifted her wrist to his mouth. Tyr watched her, knowing she was offering herself to him, knowing that she was allowing him to taste her passion. The willingness in her was like an acceptance of him and it forced a part of his spirit to surrender to her.

Tyr grabbed her wrist, keeping his eyes steadily on her face. She watched him in eager anticipation. Adjusting her hips over his legs, she slowly embedded his member within her. Tyr paused in his bite, his teeth grazing the skin as he rose up into her. The fit of her hot center, as it took him in, was perfection.

Jaden mooved on top of him with heated abandon. Her head fell back, her hair dipping behind her slender back. Tyr dropped her wrist, leaving it unharmed. He watched her face, his body enjoying her rough ride. But something inside him pulled.

Touching her on the side of the face, he ran his fingers behind her ear. Jaden looked at him in surprise. Tyr flipped her beneath him, stopping the wild stroking of her hips. Staying embedded and unmoving within her, he forced her to look into his eyes. She did so shyly, the confusion of his actions making her uncertain.

Keeping his eyes trained on her, he kept his touch to her cheek. Jaden swallowed nervously, her eyes trying to move away but unable to. Slowly, Tyr began to move in measured strokes that pushed her core deeply in a shallow rhythm. Jaden again tried to speed their pace to a frenzied release, but Tyr stayed strong to his purpose. He knew she was trying to hide herself in the abandonment of her passion. He wouldn't allow her to. He wanted her to see what she did to him, remember how he felt inside of her.

Soon, the bittersweet pleasure built within her. Jaden lifted her hand to Tyr's chest. Her eyes drifted close out of pure rapture. Tyr took her hand in his, lifting it to his mouth. He kissed her palm, licked the pulse at her wrist. Then, leaning over, he allowed her hand to drape across his shoulder as he leaned to drink from her neck.

Tyr bit her gently, letting his mouth fulfill the second most urgent need of his body. Her life's blood, warm and wet, entranced his senses. Jaden gasped in delight, brought to a straining pinnacle of pain and desire.

The motion of his hips grew stronger, the gentleness he was capable of like nothing she had ever known. It threatened to rock her soul, drown her heart. Her back arched, his lips broke free from her neck. Their bodies strained together, pulling and pushing, pushing and pulling until the tension and primal need took over and they were slaves to each other and their desires.

Tyr rose up on his arms, delving with sweet surrender. Their voices sung out in primitive moans and grunts, their mouths fell open in silent screams. He pushed her to the edge of sanity, riding them both over the brink until they were falling into a river of pure emotion, pure desertion of reality. Jaden tensed, bucking up against him as he brought her to her peak. The sweet call of her body was too much for him and he soon joined her in earth-shattering release.

In the immediate aftermath, their bodies trembled weakly, their minds joined, showering full of glistening colors. Jaden closed her eyes tightly, blocking out the sight of the handsome vampire. He had been so tender, so sweetly giving that her heart broke with it. He was nothing like she expected, nothing like she was trained to face. She was as helpless as a babe in his arms.

Tyr withdrew himself from her body, easing on the bed next to her. Feeling her shiver, he beckoned the coverlet over them. Jaden began to sit up. Tyr reached out, stopping her firmly as he pulled her into the cradle of his arms. Seeing the wound purpling on her neck, he sighed and bit his finger to rub his blood over the puncture marks left by his teeth. Jaden shivered, feeling the skin close under his administrations.

Jaden drank in the comfort of his arms. Her body still ached with melodious release and contentment. She felt his lips move over her neck, nestling her skin from behind. What was he doing to her? She shivered, wanting to cry out. Closing her eyes, she let him touch her. Her lips parted with a sigh.

"I'm in love with you." Jaden froze. She was amazed the words had come out. She refused to move. She refused to breathe. She waited for the pits of hell to open up. The admission tore through her like a machete. Sick with herself, she tried to pull away. The emotion brought her no pleasure, for it could never be.

Tyr stiffened next to her, his lips still affixed to her skin. He waited, the words rolling in his head. He didn't dare believe them. Gradually, he pulled back to study her face. He expected to find her mocking ill-humor.

"Jaden…?" he began but couldn't finish. He wanted to believe her, but her actions didn't back up the deployment of her words.

Jaden knew what she had to do. Not meeting his eyes, she turned her face down to the pillow. She let her body soak in one last bit of pleasure before speaking.

"Can you please go get my bag?" she voiced quietly. "There is something I have to show you."

Jaden allowed her body to quiver. She breathed deeply, waiting for his answer, hoping he couldn't read her intent. Tyr turned her face to his. There was something in the back of her jade gaze he couldn't describe. His instincts told him to deny her the request. But before he could act on instinct, she spoke again.

"Trust me," she whispered, her eyes begging him. She let him feel her emotion. Tyr nodded, against his better judgment. What harm was there in just retrieving her bag?

"Where is it?"

"There," she pointed, shading her eyes beneath lashes with a delicate sniff, "in the prison cell."

Tyr rose up on his arms, crawling over her from the bed. Her soft vulnerability confused and elated him.

Jaden was aware of his scar as his forearm passed by her face. Gulping, she couldn't keep from watching the play of his nakedness as he crossed over the bedroom unashamed. Jaden sat up, crawling quietly off the mattress.

Tyr walked boldly into the stone chamber. His eyes scanned over the stone. Seeing her bag in the far corner, he leaned over to pick it up.

"There is no--" His words were cut off by the latching of the iron door behind him. Tyr dropped the bag, spinning around on his heels. He heard the stout locks sliding into place. He narrowed his eyes in disbelief, not even trying to push his way out. He was trapped, naked. Inside her words echoed like a jeering irritation, *Trust me. I'm in love with you.* He was a fool to have ever dared to hope.

Jaden stared fixedly at the locked door. Her breath came in pants through trembling lips. Tears fell silently from her eyes. Her knees weakened and she fell heedless to the floor. She had done it. Tyr was trapped within.

Crawling on her hands and knees, she didn't bother to hide her nakedness as she huddled into a corner. Her limbs shook with fear and regret. Only at the last minute had she seen the prison door and decided to trap him inside the stone walls. She knew what he would find in her bag. She wanted him to find it.

Jaden waited a breathless eternity for his anger to show itself. Her gaze bore into the iron door until her vision blurred, waiting to see if he would break free of the prison. But the door didn't move and inside the cell was dead silence.

* * * *

Island of Delos, Cyclades

"My queen," Shiva bowed low to the ground, lying almost prone at Vishnu's feet. His words were muted and precise, clipped short from unnecessary lengthiness. Lifting her hand regally, Vishnu silently bid the knight to stand. He did easily, showing no effort in his slender, lithe body as he hopped up to his feet. He stood at attention, his dark gaze steadily forward, not looking Vishnu directly in the eye.

Vishnu lounged back on the dark blue and green silk trappings of her large rectangle bed. The silk of her robes hugged along her skin, blending into the silk of the coverlet. Her look was soft and inviting, not at all like the heartless queen that presided within the council. Leaning absently on her arm, she glanced at Amon in the doorway. She beckoned him in with a brief, sultry smile.

Amon entered, taking his place at her feet on the bed. He leaned over to hide part of her body from view as he lay in front of her. Vishnu absently patted Amon's bald head, rubbing her fingernails idly over his flesh, to trail over the breadth of his naked black-gold shoulder. Amon rested comfortably in his white linen loincloth, preferring the simple garb to modern day embellishments and well aware of the aura he put out by showing the sinew in his chest and legs.

Shiva waited patiently for his orders. His body didn't move. Vishnu sighed, rolling onto her back. Her arms drifted above her in the air, as she lazily commanded Shiva, "Speak, my knight."

Shiva nodded once before answering, "The hunter Alan MacNaughton's men have been seen wandering in Mykonos. It is possible they are looking for the entrance to council chamber. My bound one has reported their presence during the human day tour here on Delos."

This brought Vishnu's attention back up. She pulled onto her arm, sharing a humorless glance with Amon.

Composedly, Amon asked, "And MacNaughton himself?"

"I have not seen him," Shiva responded. "But I follow his men in hopes of locating him. If he is on Mykonos, I'll find him."

Amon nodded. Turning his eyes to Vishnu, he said, "Tyr has not yet arrived with the dhampir. And he has not sent word of her."

"Do you suspect--" Vishnu began, only to finish through their minds, *Ragnhild?*

"No," Amon answered aloud. He turned his eyes back to Shiva. "Not yet. There is no reason to believe he would've betrayed us."

Are the rumors true then? Vishnu thought to Amon. *Has Tyr marked the dhampir? Has he slipped?*

He would be a fool, Amon answered.

"Shiva," Vishnu said aloud so the knight could hear her. Her face became pouty, her lips pursing seductively. Her hand found its way back to Amon's head. "Leave the others to look for MacNaughton. Go to the homeland of your old friend. Gather him back to us and make sure he has the bloodstalker with him."

"Yes, my queen." Shiva bowed, leaving immediately amidst a flash of his ghostly skin.

When they were alone, Vishnu pulled herself to sitting and clipped, "I do not trust Ragnhild. Bid Osiris to find this Alan MacNaughton and discover who has been helping him. We cannot allow this insolence to go unpunished. We must know who is betraying the council."

Amon nodded in agreement. Laying his head into Vishnu's lap, he said, "Aleksander and Hades are near. I'll send orders to all three. Tyr is a good knight. He has never betrayed us before. If he has not come it is because it is not safe to do so. I'll have the knights watch the docks and report as soon as he arrives."

"So be it," Vishnu said quietly as she leaned over to press her lips to Amon's. Her hands slid over his cool cheeks in a tender caress. Before she kissed him, she whispered, "But don't speak of it to the others. Not until we know more. I have a feeling the truce of this council is about to run its course."

* * * *

Island of Mykonos, Cyclades

"Where is she, Mack?" Rick sat forward in his chair. The bright sun bounced off the walls of the whitewashed hotel and the blue waters of the swimming pool, stinging his sleep deprived eyes. His sockets were sunken into his face from a night spent watching the water for signs of a boatman. The boatman hadn't come--again. "Are you sure your source can be trusted? I fear we may be getting set up for a trap."

"Yes," Mack answered. He didn't feel as confident as he sounded. He too was beginning to have doubts, though Pietro assured him it was only a small delay. Thinking of the old vampire, he scratched the scab forming on his arm beneath his white hotel robe. Pietro had nearly drained him last night, leaving him weak and dizzy. Taking his drink off of the table next to him, he finished the straight scotch with one gulp. "Trust me, Rick. I have it on the highest of vampire authorities."

"But how can you know?" the man persisted, his voice rising slightly in his ire. He was growing weary of Mack's lack of emotion when it came to rescuing Jaden.

"Because I know," Mack hissed, leaning forward to the young man with a scowl. "Listen to me. This goes nowhere. The vampire council is on the verge of restructuring. They are falling apart."

"What does this have to do with Jade?" Rick questioned sharply.

"Nothing," Mack said. He twisted his fingers wildly into his hair in frustration. Rick was taken aback by the man's nervousness. His eyes narrowed, watching him carefully. "It is just that everyone is backstabbing everyone. Take my word for it, the information is correct. Tyr and Jaden will come here. When they arrive, we must be waiting. We will only have one shot at this. If we fail, Jaden dies."

Rick leaned forward, placing a hand on Mack's arm briefly before letting go. Under his breath, he whispered, "We will be ready."

"Good, good," Mack whispered, returning to his old calm. Rubbing the back of his neck, he leaned into the lounge seat. "But, if something should go wrong and she can't be rescued. You know what you have to do. We can't allow the council to take her alive. It would be hell for her."

Rick couldn't answer. He refused to conceive the possibility.

"Rick," Mack warned. "It's important that you realize what they will do to her. She knows all the locations of the safe houses. She knows how we do things, where we hide, who the men are."

"She won't tell," Rick said.

"Once they get inside her head, she won't have to tell," Mack said. "Promise me that they won't take her alive. It is what she would want."

"Yes," Rick whispered. He understood the order perfectly. "I promise."

"Very well," Mack answered, sure the man knew what had to be done. Jaden couldn't be allowed to go before the tribal elders. Mack had no way of knowing how much she really knew about his business. If the council could get inside her head and dig out all her secrets, his whole organization--his whole plan--would be lost. Closing his eyes, he ordered, "Now go and get some rest. You look like crap. I'll meet you in my room an hour before dusk."

Rick stood. Walking slowly back to his room, he knew there was nothing else he could do at the moment but go to sleep and wait for another night to fall.

Chapter Twelve

Jotunheimen Mountain Range, Norway

Her fingernail split into two jagged pieces, as she withdrew her pinkie from her mouth. She spit the broken nail onto the floor. Paying no mind to the ripped edge left, Jaden began chewing nervously on the next one. Guilt plagued her, gnawing her stomach raw. She couldn't eat, could barely sleep, and had scarcely enough inclination to keep the fire burning hot.

She gave up on escape. Tyr hadn't lied. The cave that extended out past the wooden door was as dark as it had to be long. It twisted and curled in strange erratic patterns, a virtual maze of underground tunnel systems. She had taken a candle and lighted it in the fireplace before braving the darkness. The candle glow reflected eerie patterns onto the jagged rock walls and uneven floors. She managed to find a small room with Tyr's blood supply stored coolly inside and even some fruit for herself. But whenever she tried to move past it, a breeze would blow the candle out and she would be trapped in a tomb of darkness, forced to crawl her way back into Tyr's home.

Working a third fingernail the same as she had the first two, Jaden stared at the iron door. Restlessness came from within, the strange psychic link unbreakable between her and her prisoner.

She tapped her bare feet silently on the edge of the bed. She couldn't rest, knowing Tyr was in there. He was so quiet, never speaking to her when she called. If not for the link of emotion between them and the steady stream of animosity that flooded her from behind the door, she would have thought him dead.

Days passed with him locked inside the prison. After hours of worry, she finally relaxed enough to believe he couldn't escape the stone. Her bag was trapped with him. She knew he must have already dug through it, finding the file she hid from him. After careful deliberation, she decided it didn't matter. That if he read it, it would only fuel his anger and help her cause. Once she dared to ask him to pass her clothing through the food bin in exchange for some of his own. She was rewarded with a snort and silence.

Purposefully, she hadn't fed him, letting the blood hunger settle deep in his blood, making him ravenous with need until the red rage overtook him and he couldn't think straight. Already she could feel him pacing the length of his prison like a madman.

It is only fair to end this way, Jaden thought. She remembered her father, helplessly brought low by her doing. Continuing, she vowed, *Justice will be done.*

Jaden gulped, hearing the scraping of nails against the iron door. That must have been what awakened her from sleep. She swallowed nervously. The sound became more insistent, fevered. She crawled from the bed, tugging anxiously at the hem of her white T-shirt. Chills ran up her spine and she hesitated. Her course was set and she wouldn't back down.

Closing her eyes, she stepped forward. The scratching stopped. She could feel the beast within. Gone were all coherent thoughts, leaving nothing but the hungry monster. She reached out. Her hand touched the cold iron. *Smack!* Tyr hit the door from behind, making Jaden jump back with a start. The door vibrated loudly but didn't open.

Calming her racing heart, she again moved forward. Coming close to the door, she refused to touch it. Lightly, she called, "Tyr?"

Nothing.

Again, she tried, "Tyr, are you listening? Are you hungry?"

A paper slid from underneath the door. Jaden caught it up. The frightened brown eyes were very familiar. Quietly, she whispered without looking at the back, "Sydney, 103, 1984."

The photograph slipped out of her shaking fingers. Shame welled within her, thick and choking. Her entire body quivered. Tyr would be good and mad with only those photographs as company the last week. And his bloodlust should be near the point of insanity. It was time.

Jaden stood, taking a deep breath. She lifted her chin with a bravery she didn't feel inside. Her eyes closed, her hand lifted to the latch. The wild pounding she felt in Tyr's heart heightened her own. She wavered with all the jittering of a leaf ready to fall dead from the tree, clinging to one last moment.

"Forgive me," she whispered as the latch slid out of place.

* * * *

Tyr's eyes wildly rolled about in his head. Hunger chewed at his insides. His body started to turn on itself as his skin grayed and sunk into his frame. He was too proud to beg Jaden for blood, too proud to ask for release. He'd held off longer than most of his kind, of that he was certain. An uncanny sense of betrayal and deceit kept him focused in the first days until the need for blood became so strong he was reduced to a pacing animal.

His jaw worked violently, the tempting perfume of Jaden's blood moving outside his door to torment him, along with the soft rhythm of her deceitful heart. The hated memory of her gentleness of emotions--all of them a lie--was cold comfort in a barren cell. And her declaration of love, so taunting and tormenting to his damned soul! It was unforgivable.

He found the files hidden in her bag the first night. She didn't give him light, but he didn't need it to see the words clearly. Her having the files only proved that she knew the contents within--every damning word. Endless faces haunted him, vampires tortured before being done to death, experimented on like lab rats. Tyr knew she never intended for him to have the files. She had been hiding them with Rick. Only chance, and a momentary jealousy, caused him to grab the bag and bring it with him. Where did she think to hide them from him? And did she really think drugging herself would mask her location from his senses? The bloodstalker had sorely underestimated her foe.

But, Tyr thought bitterly, *I sorely underestimated her.*

Obviously Jaden's inherent talents as a dhampir were greater than any had ever expected. She masked her emotions, putting out just the right amount of pain and hatred at just the right time, and forcing vulnerability and lust and desire to seep at the most poignant moments. She was good, he'd give her that. But he wouldn't be fooled by her again.

Tyr grunted, slamming his fist on the door in disquiet, wishing he could strike her instead of metal. He felt the deceitful dhampir everywhere.

The woman he thought to have found inside her was a figment of her doing and his hopeful imagination. But now her true nature was known. She was a manipulative, hateful, deceitful, lying bitch and she would pay for her crimes. The council sent him to gather information and that's exactly what he had done. It might have been a sloppy investigation, one highly unworthy of a Dark Knight of his age and skill. But it was done and now so was Jaden. He wouldn't let this embarrassment haunt his perfect record. He wouldn't let her haunt anymore of his nights.

Tyr?

Tyr froze in his frantic thoughts. He scratched his hair back from his face, noticing he had been scratching at the iron door, as if he could gouge her eyes from the unforgiving metal. He eyed the claw marks and then his hands, not remembering having done it. But the metal shards beneath his nail beds said otherwise. His fingertips bled, not healing as quickly in his weakened state. Putting his ear to the door, his eyes shot wildly around in the darkness. His lips parted. He listened.

"Tyr, are you listening? Are you hungry?"

That time the words were clear. Was she taunting him? Angrily, he grabbed a photograph from the floor, sliding it under the door's edge. That would be his answer. Let her be reminded of her deeds. Let her know that he would come for her soon. The demon inside him would grow. Soon his body would rip through the iron door.

Sydney, 103, 1984.

What? What was that? Tyr leaned to the door again, sniffing the air like a feral dog. He caught her aromatic scent, her warm blood. His mouth parted, baring fangs in an insatiable effort to bite her with his mind. He couldn't control it. His hands flexed and fidgeted. The bloodlust took over him. His heart pounded and his hands shook in anticipation. He licked his dry lips. He could feel her moving, standing, coming. He tensed, waiting to strike.

Forgive me.

The whisper was lost on Tyr. He'd been reduced to a beast, stripped naked, trapped, starved. The latch moved, the agonizing slowness of it suspended by his need to pounce, to seek life, *to drink*.

Tyr knew the instant the door was released. He charged forward, hitting the metal with his arm. His flesh scraped on the jagged edge, ripping open a bloody wound. Tyr ignored it, beyond pain. Seeing flesh, warm and waiting before him, he instinctively seized upon it.

Jaden screamed in terror as the naked vampire leapt out of the darkness onto her thin frame. Tyr's skeletal gray flesh appeared to be covered with a thin, white powder-like decay. She lifted her hands in a naturally feeble effort to stop him from pouncing, but nothing could've stopped him. Her body slammed into the ground. Instinct made her squirm but his strength overpowered her weaker protest. His teeth were bared. His eyes were filled with the reddish cast of hell. His nose wrinkled on his once handsome face, gruesome and cruel.

Tyr crouched above her, pawing her shoulders with his claws, digging restlessly into her shoulders. Leaning over, he sniffed her neck, her breasts. His mouth opened, ready to bite. Then he saw her jade eyes, frightened, terrified of him. A last thread of sanity stopped him. He looked over to the living room, his body tensing to take off for the blood supply.

"It's gone," Jaden whispered, unable to take the suspense and waiting. Tyr's head snapped back to hers. Groaning, she whispered, "All of it-- gone. I smashed your stock pile and it has long dried on the stone. Mine is the only blood for miles. Kill me, Tyr. You have no choice."

She was right. His animal self knew it and took over. Viciously, he growled, slashing at her throat with his bared teeth, tearing the flesh like a wolf on his prey. Pain shot though her like a white fire blazing a sticky trail through her neck and shoulder. Jaden's eyes became wide, the agony worse than she imagined. His bite was not the gentle kiss of the lover she remembered. There was no longing or passion in his touch-- only pain and need and torment.

Jaden gasped. Her throat constricted. Tyr sucked hungrily against her. A gurgle escaped her opened mouth. Blood trailed from her lips, leaving a crimson trail over her fast paling skin. Weak, she hit Tyr's shoulders in a last, natural defense. Her fist bounced off of him, only to land with open palm. Her fingers slid over his muscular arm in a strangely forgiving caress. Her finger pulled lightly at his elbow, soaking in one last feel of him.

Tears rolled silently out of Jaden's listless eyes. Her body jerked. Her hands fell in insipid masses to the ground. Her fingers twitched. Her mouth gaped open, wheezed. Her heartbeat slowed with nothing to pump. This was it. She was dying. Then, unexpectedly, the pain was gone and there was nothing but the oddest sensation of warmth.

Tyr pulled back with a howl, pleasure rippling throughout him as potent as an orgasm. Sanity was once more his. His eyes cleared back to white, ringed with blood. His flesh filled in, growing young and handsome, hiding the outlines of his bones. Blood dripped over his chin, down his naked chest. The sweetness of Jaden flowed through him, saving him.

Sweetness? Jaden!

Realization hit. Tyr looked down at what he had done. Jaden's chest didn't move. Her eyes stared lifelessly at the ceiling, the green orbs faded and dull. Below her slack, blue lips he saw the horror of his attack. Her throat stuck out of her flesh, ripped free, the skin peeled back to expose the inside strings of veins and arteries. Her body lay cold and lifeless beneath his heated one. Panic rose inside of him, outweighed by the outrage of what she had forced him to do. She'd forced his hand, taken the choice away from him, and he had killed her.

"You are not going to win!" he growled, willing her to cling to the last bit of life swirling her body.

Biting his wrist, he gashed it open. Jaden's essence flowed out of him. Grabbing her roughly by the hair, he tilted her head back. Blood gushed from him to her tattered throat, dripping onto her chin and cheeks. He viciously forced her lips to his wound.

"Drink, damn you!" he yelled at her, following his words by a string of black curses, damning her, coercing her, daring her to be reborn. His heart nearly stopped beating as he waited, suspended in time and agony. He couldn't lose her. Not like this. Not yet. Not yet.

At first there was no change, but slowly the skin on her neck began to heal itself, closing little by little. Then her lips faded from blue to a cherry, the color seeping in from the sides in aimless swirling paths across her face. Gradually, her mouth moved against him, swallowing what he forced down her, moaning ever so lightly into his bleeding skin. Tyr relaxed, growing weak as he gave her back what he so viciously took.

Jaden coughed, spitting blood out of her mouth. It ran over her skin, streaking the new paleness with crimson rivers, matting her hair. Tyr tightened his grip on her tender scalp, pressing her more firmly so she couldn't refuse to drink. She had started this madness. He would make sure she finished it.

Suddenly, her eyes burst wide open, the jade and white completely done in with tell-tale scarlet. Her gaze darted in protest, warring through their ecstasy for him--begging him to stop, to never stop. She tried to fight it, but his will was too strong. She continued to swallow, drinking greedily to his flesh. Her body tingled with life, aching and straining delicately.

When he was satisfied she had taken enough, Tyr let go of her and backed away. The pleasure stopped. Jaden wheezed violently. Her eyes shot around in blinding confusion. Her mouth worked angrily as her organs continued to die only to be reborn. She could feel her body's death. Her muscles tightened with newfound strength. The hair on her head grew about her face, falling into her eyes. She felt her nails growing, a strange sensation as her fingers strained against it.

Looking frantically at Tyr's blood-tainted face blurred by her unclear vision, Jaden gasped and gurgled and rasped. A resounding cry left her in a hoarse whisper, "No!"

She felt all of her little scars from past battles tingling, smoothing and stretching themselves out as they disappeared beneath the surface. As her gaze began to clear, so did the smug countenance of Tyr as he watched her with unfeeling eyes.

Jaden sat up with a groan. Again she cried out in despair, "No! Ty--"

Her words ended on a gulp as the contents of her stomach came rushing forward. Tyr reacted with the speed of a striking snake, sticking the water bucket under her head. Jaden puked into the pail. When she finished, she fell back to the floor. Her panting breath had left her. She lay as still as a corpse, except for the glaring accusation of her expression as she gaped disbelieving at Tyr.

"I was finished," she mumbled weakly, her lips barely moving as the dark rebirth took complete control. She knew what she had become. She knew what he'd done and she hated him for it. Fangs grew out from her gums to match his, two longer on top, two smaller on bottom. They felt strange brushing up against her mouth, poking the sensitive skin of her inner lip, as she said, "Damn you."

"You begged for death so desperately," he chuckled, the menacing sound matching the hatred in her words. The relief he felt at seeing her back was bittersweet. "Well, now you have your wish. Welcome to death, m'lady. How do you like it?"

"You bastard," she swore, trying to sit up and failing. She relaxed against the carpet, unable to force her limbs to move. "I never asked for this!"

"Tsk, tsk," he sneered, "such a temper. Is that anyway to treat your master?"

"You'll never be my master, Tyr," she hissed, glad to have enough strength to put venom in her words. His face was so cruel, so unmoving. Her body still ached for what it couldn't have--it burned for him. If he would but look at her with caring, touch her face with reassurance then she could forgive him instantly. But he neither comforted nor touched her.

"You are mistaken," he whispered. Crawling forward, he came above her. He looked down on her sullen, hate-ridden face. Jaden could find no pleasure in the sight of his naked body. She saw his face clearer with her vampire eyes. She saw the texture of his skin, the firmness of his hard mouth, the stiff resolve of his expression. Her skin tingled with the nearness of his flesh, drawn to it as never before. Her eyes even detected each line of resentment in his shallow gaze. Coming down so his face was next to hers, he whispered into her ear, "I gave you the dark gift. You are mine until I let you go."

"Then you are letting me go right now," she ordered, her voice growing by degrees with each word. She focused all her energy to push at him. Her arms lifted to strike his chest. It was a weak effort and he caught up her fingers easily. Knowing it to be a lie, she demanded, "Give me a stake. I'll end this myself."

"So bloodthirsty," he hissed. "Haven't you had enough of death for one evening?"

"End it!"

"Never." He forced her palm to feel his heart. He was warm from her blood. "I'll never let you go."

"There is nothing you can teach me of your kind," she said. "That is what a master does. He teaches the student."

"Our kind," he interjected softly when she finished her raspy declaration. His eyes softened for an instant only to harden with her decree. "Your fate has been decided dhampir. You are no longer human."

"I'll never be one of you!"

"You are like me! You were like me even before I gave you my blood. You hunt, you punish the guilty. You thrive on the blood and ash of others." Tyr rose above her, gloating bitterly. Her hand flopped down on her chest, sliding to the floor. Sneering, he added, "Only that isn't all you did, was it little Jaden? You've been a very naughty mortal."

"I am nothing like you," she denied vehemently, knowing his words to be true. "I'll run and you'll never find me. I'll keep running."

"Where will you go, little vampire?" he queried sharply. His lips turned up in cruel mocking. "Back to your uncle? Do you think he will take back his little vampiric niece with open arms or ready stake?"

Jaden paled. He was right. She had no one, nothing but him, and Tyr was cold comfort at the moment. She had died once and wasn't so eager to face the pain of it again. She was tired. She saw an eternity of hate and torture stretch out before her. She felt a never-ending wave of heartache and hell.

In a whisper she heard as loud as a scream, he added, "Do you think he would spare you? When he stabbed his own vampiric sister?"

Jaden's throat tightened in horror. What game was this? Her mother had never been turned. Mack told her she had never been turned. Mack told her a lot of things. Were they all lies? And didn't Tyr say Rhona was never turned or had he just let her assume she wasn't? Hadn't he said he saw the vampire's report? Had he lied to her too? She was so confused. She couldn't think, couldn't reason.

Tyr watched her with unbearable superiority. His mouth opened again to speak and she couldn't stop him, couldn't block him out.

"Or will he use you like he did the others?" Tyr whispered. Jaden blinked in confusion, but he didn't notice as he strode away from her. When he returned, he dumped the heavy file on her chest with a thud. Jaden moaned, pushing the weight to the side. The folder slid to rest beside her on the floor. "Will he do to you what was done to them?"

"No," she moaned. "Please, Tyr, end it now. Finish me or let me go."

"Who better to keep you than the vampire you love?" His eyes still did not lessen in their icy rage. "Does not your heart sing that we should spend eternity together?"

Jaden flinched to hear her words thrown back at her so hatefully.

"The council--" she began. Tyr ignored her as he raged on.

"And I am going to punish you, naughty vampire, for your mortal sins." Tyr put his hands on his hips. She really was his now.

"The council will find me guilty," she broke in. Her laughter that followed was hard and humorless and a bit wild. "You'll never have me for an eternity."

Forebodingly, he answered, "Yes, it is possible that you will know the death you've dealt so much of."

Suddenly, feeling another presence, Tyr whipped his neck around to the bedroom entryway. His old friend Shiva stood quietly in the entrance watching. His eyes roamed briefly over Tyr's lack of attire before glinting with great amusement. Then, Shiva's gaze went to the newly turned woman on the ground. Coming to Tyr's side, he looked down his nose at Jaden. Jaden stared fearfully back.

"Is this the dhampir, then?" Shiva asked quietly, cocking his head to the side. He studied the woman carefully before turning away with a dismissive shrug.

"Yes," Tyr whispered. He too left her, turning his back on her helpless state. Her eyes roamed his naked backside, unable to see aught else.

"Get dressed," Shiva said with a small chuckle, though he was hardly affected by the sight of his naked friend. "I'll get food. You must be hungry after such a rough turning."

Tyr watched the knight leave his bedroom. He quickly donned his clothes, ignoring the solemn eyes that followed every moment from the bedroom floor. His stomach tightened. His heart lurched. He realized he was late in delivering the dhampir and that the council had sent Shiva to check up on him. He grimaced with annoyance over it. If the deceitful wench had only left well enough alone!

"Yes," Shiva said from the door, holding two bags. He tossed one to Tyr. His slender body held still as Tyr set the blood packet aside. It would seem his blood supply was well intact. Just one more detail Jaden had lied about. The Rakshasa knight continued, "They did send me after you. What has happened here? Why is the guilty one turned?"

Tyr frowned, taking more care with his thoughts. He didn't like Shiva referring to Jaden in such a way, but he didn't correct him. How could he? It was true. She was guilty.

Tyr changed his language, speaking in Shiva's native tongue. All the knights taught each other their culture and language so they could speak without being detected. Shiva glanced quizzically at the change but easily slipped into the old words. Tyr gave a condensed version of what transpired, leaving out their passion. Bitterly, he finished with, "She tricked me into the prison and locked me in. That is why we're late. You'll have to watch this one. She is cunning beyond measure and she is deceitful beyond imagination."

"Ah," Shiva said in understanding. His body moved across the room with the graceful steps of a dancer. "She forced you to attack. Then you did right in changing her. Otherwise, you would have failed in your mission to bring her to the council and you cannot glean information from the mind of a dead human."

Tyr knew that Shiva's acceptance of his story would hold weight with the elders. The word of two Dark Knights would be beyond question.

Shiva glanced to the folder at Jaden's side. Picking it up, he thumbed through it. Tyr's first impulse was to stop him. He didn't. He held back. Laying the folder on the table, Shiva read a page as he sucked thoughtfully on a bag of human blood.

Finishing the drink, he threw it into the puke bucket. Motioning to the page, he questioned, slipping back into English, "Her?"

Tyr nodded. Shiva glared down at Jaden with a look of utter disgust. Jaden tried to shake her head. Shiva dispassionately ignored her.

Throwing his empty bag next to Shiva's, Tyr picked up the bucket. He whisked it from the room, discarding it away from his home. When they were alone, Shiva came over Jaden. Reaching down, he touched her face, turning it from one side to the other in inspection.

"I have heard many things of you dhampir," he said, "but none as fierce as this."

Jaden marveled at his meditative demeanor, but was too weak to ask. Shiva pulled back her gums to inspect her teeth. Jaden knocked her head back, trying to escape his hand. He followed her shaky movements with ease. Satisfied with what he saw, he stood.

Tyr strode back into the room with a show of dominance. Grabbing his jacket from his trunk, he slid it stiffly over his broad shoulders.

"Come, Shiva, the night is young. Let us begin our journey." His gaze was cold as he directed it briefly at Jaden. She could detect no emotion in him, despite her blood within his veins, despite the intimacy of their past and the profound gift he had just bestowed upon her--asked for or not. Jaden's mouth opened to speak. She felt her new heart beating, the ache in it worse than before. She wanted to cry, but tears wouldn't fall. Tyr turned contemptuously away. "And grab that one there. I wouldn't want her to miss it."

Tyr didn't wait to see if Shiva listened. As he strode past the fireplace, he squelched the flames with a wave of his hand, throwing the cave into completely tomb-like darkness. The knights were fine without the light and Jaden was afforded a chance to test her new vision, as Shiva dragged her by the delicate strands of her hair out of Tyr's cave home.

* * * *

The trio traveled south through Norway, taking a night ferry across the water to Denmark. Tyr barely looked at her, except to shoot her evil glares of dominance. Jaden's vampiric strength grew after her first day of sleep. Though, she had the distinct feeling that, without her, Tyr and Shiva could've moved faster across the earth.

Shiva bound and gagged her at Tyr's request to keep her from exploring her newfound powers. Once Shiva had her limbs bound, she caught a small glimmer of manly interest in Tyr as he studied her in her restraints. The glimpse sent a rush of excitement through her. The look faded so quickly she began to doubt it was there at all. Her hands had been left to dangle above her head. She fought the ties but could no more cut through them than she could cut through Tyr's blatant hatred of her.

At the first of the night, Tyr and Shiva would leave her to feed. When they returned, Tyr would tear off her gag and shove a squirming rat dispassionately into her face. In the beginning Jaden tried to resist, but the pull was too strong and she was forced to bite into the hairy creature to eat. The stiff fur poked at her lips as the animal squirmed against her mouth. Her eyes shot daggers into Tyr's, refusing to be subdued by him.

Tyr's gently mocking laughter stung, holding no affection, only scorn. Shiva blinked heavily in disgust, turning his back on her, unable to watch.

During the feared daylight, they would sleep in old crypts, surrounded by skeletal bodies and musty clothes. Jaden was glad she wasn't forced to breathe in the stagnant dust. Although she had the eerie sensation that other vampires were around, they didn't seek them out. In fact, Jaden could feel Shiva and Tyr cloaking their presence from the others.

From Denmark they traveled by the top of train through Germany. In Germany, Tyr arranged for a private plane to fly them over most of Eastern Europe. They landed in an empty field in Macedonia. The pilot glanced only once at Jaden, not showing the bound woman any concern. Tyr directed him in German so she couldn't understand how it was he explained her presence.

Tyr refused to speak directly to her, though she caught him staring at her with a deep-seated abhorrence. His dislike made her skin crawl and the pain in her chest intensify tenfold. Shiva was more benevolent with his words, ordering her quietly in one direction and then the other as he led her about on a rope. He too would stare at her, his eyes roaming curiously over her disheveled hair and dirt smudged face. She wondered if Shiva detected Tyr's scent on her. It would have explained his interest in her.

Jaden was forced to piece together the new abilities of her vampire body alone. As she slept in a smelly Macedonian crypt next to her guards, she awoke in a panic to find herself levitating next to the ceiling. Her struggles alerted Shiva and Tyr. The former who laughed in amusement, the latter who grunted and pulled so hard on her ropes that she was forced helplessly into the ground with a hard smack to the concrete earth. The landing left her dazed, her eyes rolling in her head.

Even under the stress of her dire treatment, the nights moved too quickly for Jaden. As they crossed the border into Greece, her heart fell from her chest to the pit of her stomach. Part of her waited, hoping to hear a tender word from Tyr, some gentle reassurance that he would take care of her. Her body longed for his like before, only worse now that she had the passionate nature of the beast so newly developed in her. There were times when she felt so needy of him, she was sure she could break through her binds and ravish him in front of Shiva as witness. But, then, his eyes would turn to her, probing and dark as if he read her longing for him, and she'd force the temptation aside. There was only cold emptiness inside of Tyr when he looked at her. Tears wouldn't come to her eyes, though her nose burned with them. Inside her chest there was a deep physical ache that made her want to retch with the force of her unreturned feelings.

On the last night before they would take a boat over to the Island of Mykonos to meet the vampire council's boatman, Jaden was released from her bonds. Shiva cut them from her with his fingernails, pulling them apart with his strength when they would hold true. Jaden looked at him, blinking in surprise.

Seeing her fear, he didn't comment, but handed her a large fish plucked from the sea. His body was still wet from his swim in the cold ocean, the little beads of water glistening on his skin. Jaden bit hungrily into it as he watched. His eyes didn't judge her as she ate her unappetizing meal. When she finished, she tossed it aside. Resentment warred within her, as she managed a grudging, "Thanks."

"Come," Shiva bid her, standing. He began walking through sand to the edge of the ocean.

Jaden followed him, dread poking in her stomach. Her limbs were a little weak from malnourishment, but she didn't complain as she trailed over the beach. Shiva led her to the calm rolling waters. Pointing out over the dark depths lighted by a round bright moon, he bid her, "Look."

Jaden did. She fell to her knees in the white sand, transfixed by the celestial orb. She saw it so clearly, her vision picking out craters and valleys in the bright blue light. The sight entranced her into mindless wonder.

"It is the vampire sun," Shiva said, kneeling next to her.

Jaden turned to look at him. His hand touched the white sand, letting it fall through his fingers. The wind picked up the grains, blowing them across Jaden's lap. She watched the tiny granules glistening with a silvery white cast all around her.

"And these," Shiva said, waving his hand to encompass the endless beach, "are the sands of a vampire's life."

Jaden swallowed, not sure she got his meaning. She blinked, studying his solemn, pale face. He was so slender, so beautiful to behold. His dark eyes were nearly black and beckoned without intending to. She became entranced by him.

Shiva didn't pay attention to her enthralled look, pretending not to notice how she stared at his face, his lips, in total fascination as if she could suddenly kiss him. He knew well she felt no real desire for him, above the basest of desires all recently turned felt in their new forms. Taking a handful of sand, he let it fall again, drawing her attention away from his mouth. "This was your mortal life--short, over. You are now like this beach, as are we all--long and unending. No longer can you predict the number of grains in your life for they cannot be counted. And, when you do reach the end of them, the ocean will just wash more up for you."

Jaden read the meaning in his eyes, the obscure coming into reason.

She was one of them, like it or not. He was telling her to accept it, to choose a new alliance. She felt a peace inside of him. He was giving her hope, comfort, in the only way he could.

Turning to look up the beach at Tyr, he sighed. Glancing back to her, he whispered thoughtfully, "And, like us, you have an eternity to right a wrong."

Jaden shivered, knowing this knight knew much more than he let on. Shiva stood, leaving her alone on the sand. Jaden turned to watch Tyr. His strong, proud face glowed dully in the moonlight. Her love for him hit her like an impacting wave--powerful and all consuming. If she could feel it after her change, then maybe Tyr was capable of feeling it too. Maybe she had been blind. Maybe she had misjudged him.

Needing to tell him, she shot to her feet. Weakly, she stumbled across the deserted beach to reach him. Tyr didn't move to help her. His eyes stayed steadily focused on her every movement. Jaden came to stand just below him. She looked up into his masked features. A vague hope struggled for life within her chest.

"Tyr, I--" she began in a rush. His hard look cut off her words. The ice blue of his eyes sliced through her as if he could cut her in half.

"Tomorrow we meet with the council," he said. "I have received word that the boatman will be ready."

Jaden nodded. Her body trembled in fear. For a moment, she thought she felt Tyr soften towards her. If he would just hold her she could face anything--her uncle, the council, eternity. She waited breathlessly, unable to speak, unable to sing the joy choking to life in her chest. Her lips parted. Tyr turned away. Her hope withered. The joy died.

Jaden watched the hard line of his back, knowing automatically that she was to follow behind. Her eyes worked wildly over his long hair. The blond locks were tied back, away from his handsome face. She tried in vain to reason with her sorrow. Her heart sunk deeper into the pit of despair. After tomorrow she might not have an eternity. For, if Tyr wouldn't champion her, the council would be sure to vote against her. However, if she did by some miracle survive, she doubted forever was enough time to make Tyr realize she was sorry and that he truly did love her.

Chapter Thirteen

Island of Mykonos, Cyclades

Tyr sensed Jaden shivering beside him. He knew it wasn't the cool island night that made her tremble. She was scared. She had been ever since they left his cave. He tried to block her from him, like he had most of the trip, not trusting her emotions as genuine. But, as they stood on the silent beach, the partying crowd of Mykonos' nightlife behind them, he couldn't help but hear the strained beating of her heart.

Every fiber inside of him urged him to touch her. His lips begged him for her kisses. But his mind held firm, knowing that he must hide his feelings well before they were detected by the elders. He knew Shiva already had a suspicion.

Besides, Tyr couldn't forget Jaden's deceptions. Time hadn't lessened the pain of her lies. She had rekindled emotions inside of him that were long dead, only to dash them into an earthen tomb once more. In centuries he hadn't dared to feel tenderness of such a magnitude and she used it to trick him.

Trust me. I love you. The words morphed in his head until they blended into a silent song of uneding torment.

Centuries had passed and no one had loved him. They'd been enthralled by him, enchanted. He'd been desired, lusted for in many ways. He'd even been pursued by women who didn't know his secrets. More than that, he had been feared, despised, revered, but never loved. And for her to pretend such a cruel thing, to make him hope only to take it away was a brutality much worse than that of endless time.

Jaden shivered again. She glanced at Shiva standing several yards away, nearly hidden by shadows. The slender knight paid them no mind. She dared a glance at Tyr. He was so strong and proud and he had lived through so much. She knew she was a fool for daring to hope that he could think more tenderly of her than the centuries of others that came before her. She loved him so much, and yet she was nothing to him.

Tyr saw Jaden eyeing him from the corner of his gaze. He pretended to ignore her.

"Tyr?" she questioned softly. Tyr kept his eyes on the water, waiting for the boatman to come. The sooner the boat came, the sooner it was over. "Won't you talk to me?"

"And what would you have me say, princess?" he murmured quietly.

The endearment was not tender. It hung between them like a bitter irony choking in the bowels of the underworld.

"What will they do to me?" she couldn't keep from asking. Jaden's fingers lifted absently to her mouth, feeling the sharp fangs. They were still so new to her.

"Are you scared they will treat you as you have treated others?" he questioned, the bitterness returning as he thought of the folder in the satchel behind him.

Jaden's mouth trembled. She pressed them firmly together, pinning her lips closed with her fangs. The salty tang of her blood ran into her mouth. She ignored it. She didn't answer as her eyes turned to follow his. She was scared of facing them. Who knew what heartless beings they might be? And why should they show her mercy? She was their enemy, the killer of their benighted children.

"Tyr, I have to explain," Jaden began urgently. As she spoke a thin trail of her blood passed over her lips, dripping off her chin. "I have to explain to you about the photographs you found. It's not what you think."

Tyr glanced down to her and was about to answer, but his body prickled in warning. He slashed a hand before her ordering silence. Jaden blinked, startled. She felt the warm stickiness on her lips and absently rubbed it away. Tyr's eyes went first over the distance, but there was no boat. He looked for Shiva in the shadows, the vampire had disappeared.

Suddenly, a battle cry went out over the beach. Jaden's eyes widened in horror as she spun around, turning her back on the water. An army clad in black rushed forward over the sand. Jaden instantly recognized their attire and detected their mortality.

Glancing fearfully at Tyr, she saw his body postured for a fight. She had to choose--and fast. Loyalty to the humans surged within her, but her heart beat for Tyr. She was no longer mortal, but she didn't feel like a vampire. She had never belonged in any of their worlds. Now was her chance to choose a side. What should she do? But, the choice had been taken from her. She knew that. Hadn't Shiva said she needed to choose a new alliance? Would her uncle's men stop at her, knowing what she had become? Would Mack?

She closed her eyes. Her fang bit again into the tender flesh of her lips as a reminder. There was no going back to mortality. She chose Tyr.

Tyr stepped in front of her, shielding her with his body. Jaden growled, darting past his side to lunge at a man in the forefront. She thumped against his chest, tackling him to the ground. Her hand snapped to his throat in a choking hold.

"Jade," the man gasped in terrified surprise.

Jaden recognized the voice. Ripping the mask from the man's head, she threw it aside. She saw the fair locks of Tom's hair drifting in the breeze before she focused on his sharp features. The man gasped, panicked by her sudden assault. His fingers clawed the backs of her hands, digging into the flesh of her knuckles. Again, she pressed her hand around about his neck.

"Jade," he whispered again, desperate to get her attention. An overly relieved smile came to his face when she lessened her hold. "Thank God you're alive! We've come to save you!"

"Save me," she said, her eyes glowing hotly with her immortal powers, "Or kill me?"

Tom saw her undead face and squirmed. Her skin was flushed with a ghostly pale beauty. Her lips were tinged with the subtlest shades of blue and crimson. When she spoke, she displayed sharp white teeth that glinted in the moonlight. Kicking his leg around, Tom knocked Jaden in the back of her head. Her body jolted, falling to the sand. Tom sprang to his feet. Jaden was quick to follow. Her eyes turned wide before narrowing dangerously on his retreating back. She could smell Tom's fear—not only of her, but of all things unknown. She detected intolerance and savagery and she hated him, more so than when she was human.

Tyr saw Jaden fighting Mack's soldier. She handled herself well as they exchanged punches. He grudgingly respected her skill, recognizing moves she had used against him while they sparred. Why was she fighting the man? Tyr half expected her to help them. He had little time to ponder it as he turned to face the dozen men encircling him. One carried a net, others brandished stakes and swords.

Above them on the road leading past the beach, Mack sat in his car watching, puffing quietly on his cigar. He clutched a phone in his hands, ready to call a gunman he had waiting in the trees. It was so dark he couldn't see who was who, except for the gigantic creature surrounded by his men. Mack knew that was Tyr. His body jolted with eagerness as the circle enclosed around the knight. He scanned the beach for Jaden.

Jaden flew at Tom, empowered by the endurance of her rebirth. His fist met her jaw, her stomach, her temple. His feet kicked at her legs knocking them out from under her. Jaden jumped right back up. A smile played over her features. Tom froze, knowing suddenly that she toyed with him. A demonic light had entered her eyes as she studied him. Jaden pounced, tackling him to the ground. She pinned his body beneath her. Her mouth opened to bite him.

"No, Jade," Tom wheezed. "You don't want to do this. We're friends!"

"Friends?" she asked. Jaden's lip curled. The beast inside of her took over. She had been feasting on rodents and fish for so long that her body instinctively craved a real meal. Her mouth opened. Her head sank.

"Jade!"

Jaden froze. The sound of childhood broke through the fog in her brain.

Her eyes darted to see her uncle standing on the dock above. His arms were widespread for her. The fire and blood in her eyes lessened to see him there, waiting for her, calling her. Her eyes tilted, seeing the smile on his face as he sought her in the darkness. He was relieved. He was calling to her, but she couldn't hear the words as blood rushed in her ears. Beneath her, Tom sighed in relief.

"Go to Mack," Tom urged. "He will help you. He has a plan."

"He will kill me," Jaden growled. "I'm not like you, not anymore. I won't be a part of it anymore."

"No, Jade," Tom eased, growing empowered. "You don't understand. It'll be fine. Mack will understand. He will take care of you."

"Like he took care of the others?" she said, her fury growing by bounds to think of it.

"Go to him," Tom insisted. "Please, Jade."

Jaden snorted and ignored the advice. Feeling a strange pull, her eyes darted to Tyr. Something was wrong. A net was cast over his back. Ten men held him down. She saw Rick wielding a stake. It was aimed at Tyr's turned back. Tyr flung an attacker off and then another.

Jaden let Tom go. Tom waved frantically over his head at Mack. Mack's arms fell to his sides at the signal. His smile faded. Jaden left the man on the beach and dashed with all her speed to rescue Tyr.

Mack lifted his phone and pushed a button. The call was immediately answered.

"What's happening? Can you see her?" Mack rushed.

"She is helping him," the gunman whispered. "The creature is almost free. What do you want me to do?"

There was silence as Mack watched his niece's figure dart over the sand to help Tyr. His gut tightened and his heart sank. Matter-of-factly, he whispered, "Take your shot."

Tom began crawling along the beach towards Mack, his face hanging low to the ground. All of a sudden he stopped, a heavy boot appearing before his nose. The silver buckles gleamed in the moonlight. Tom shivered. Looking up, he stared into the motionless gaze of the undead. The creature shot forward, his pale hands grabbing the mortal man's throat. The vampire hauled Tom up to his awaiting mouth.

A shot rang out, whizzing past Jaden's shoulder. It burned into her, causing her to pause in her progress across the beach. In the distance, she heard a man scream as he was tossed down from a tree. She knew instinctively that the gunman was dead.

As Tom died, he watched a small horde of dark beings come out from the shadows. They passed by, going to the other soldiers around Tyr, grabbing their victims to drink. The vampire at his neck tore, sucking before tossing him to the ground like garbage. Tom wheezed in dying horror, his eyes focusing forward to the back taillights of Mack's car as the man abandoned them.

"No!" Jaden yelled, throwing herself at Rick. Rick swung down, his stake hitting her in the shoulder above her heart. Jaden gasped with the pain of it. Rick's eyes cleared from the battle haze. He paled, pulling his mask from his features. Reaching out, he caught her to his chest.

"Jade," he began confused. Rick eased her tenderly to the ground. Desperately, he tried to stem the flow of her blood. "What have you done?"

Tyr felt the stake inside of her as if it had been his own body. The hands of the ambush weighed in on him only to be suddenly lifted by an unseen force. Tyr tore the net from his back. He scanned the distance. Before him was Shiva, leading Ares, Osiris, and Aleksander into battle. They fought the mortals, killing them easily, littering the beach with the dead. The battle was won before it really started.

The echoing pain in his shoulder drew his eyes down to Jaden. Rick was next to her, cradling her head in his lap. Tyr growled, sensing the blood that was coming from the wound.

Rick glanced around in horror. He'd seen Mack abandon his niece, abandon them all. He'd heard the shot and saw the bloody streak of it across Jaden's arm. Leaning protectively over Jaden, he silently swore not to let her get taken again by the undead monsters that surrounded them.

"Pull it out," Jaden demanded, her voice hoarse with pain.

"No," Rick whispered, glancing down at her in surprise. "You might bleed to death."

Jaden chuckled bitterly. The sound caught his attention and he looked fully at her. Her eyes glowed up at him. Rick froze, seeing the truth of what she had become. He pushed her from his lap and scrambled away.

"Oh, no," he murmured, desperate, pleading at the injustice of what she had become. "No, Jade."

"Pull it out," she demanded again. When he didn't move, she grabbed the stake herself, trying to weakly paw at it. A hand reached from above, lifting it from her skin. The wound began to close. She saw Tyr throw the bloody stake aside. His eyes bore angrily into her.

Hiding his torment at seeing her hurt and knowing she had taken the stake meant for him, he said bitterly, "Damn it, you fool! Do you think to get out of your judgment so easily?"

Rick backed away. The undead victors gathered silently around Tyr and the fallen young one. One by one their eyes turned to the mortal man.

"What of him?" Aleksander asked with a sneer. His straight, black hair blended perfectly with the night. His teeth parted, ready to bite on command.

"Take him," Tyr ordered. "He is one of MacNaughton's leaders. The council might want to question him."

Rick tried to protest, but his lips never opened. Aleksander swiftly moved forward, knocking the mortal over the head with his fist. Rick's world went black. Aleksander tossed the man over his strong shoulder as if he weighed no more than a child's rag doll.

"The boatman," Shiva said, his chin jutting down the coast. "His throat is slit."

"There is another," Ares said, coming forward. His dark blue eyes glittered with the light of battle. "Come. We will reach the council tonight."

"And what of this one?" Aleksander whispered, motioning down to Jaden. Her eyes were closed, but she was still awake. Hearing the words, she blinked, looking up at them.

Tyr lifted his hand over Jaden's face. Her eyes rounded in horror as the others did the same. They leaned over her, blocking out the stars with their unsympathetic expressions.

"She will sleep," Tyr stated, "so that she may never find her way back here."

* * * *

Mack frantically paced the length of his immense hotel suite, marching to the dresser and then back to his suitcase with an armload of clothing. Feeling Pietro on the balcony, he stiffened and turned his stricken face to the thin glass door. He saw movement through the white gauze of the curtains. The lock unlatched in the breeze, the door coming slowly open with a measured creak.

Pietro glided forward, his eyes taking in the suitcase and Mack's agitated frown. Lifting his hand, the door shut behind him without touching it, leaving them alone in the room.

"All my men are dead," Mack whispered. He went to the dresser for another load of clothing. "I am getting off this island."

"What of your niece?" Pietro questioned.

A wave of guilt racked Mack's body, forcing him to close his eyes. Sniffing, he wiped his nose. "She's dead. I kno--"

"She lives," Pietro broke in.

Mack gulped in surprise. Shaking his head, he said, "There is nothing I can do for her. She is within that fortress. She is as good as dead."

Pietro didn't argue. Lightly, he admitted, "It is likely she will be tortured and killed."

Mack stiffened. Turning his hateful gaze on the old vampire, he scowled, "How did this happen? I did everything you told me!"

"The Dark Knights interference was an unfortunate--"

"Unfortunate?" Mack yelped in ire. "It was more than unfortunate!

Why didn't you warn me? I could've been killed and then our plans ruined. Why did you betray me?"

"I had no time to warn," Pietro said, his lifeless eyes stating that if Mack died, his plans would go on without him.

"Then you did know," the man accused

"I was told, yes," Pietro said. He watched Mack slam his suitcase shut and begin to latch it. His dark eyes narrowed, as he said, "You are not leaving. Jaden might be lost, but our plan continues."

"What about Tyr?" Mack cried. "What about the others? You never warned me of them! They slaughtered my men within seconds."

"Yes," Pietro said calmly. "I imagine they would have."

Mack fumed. Falling wearily, he sank onto the bed and abandoned his packing. He realized he had no choice. If he defied Pietro he wouldn't last the night. It was only with the vampire's warnings that he lasted so many years.

"What will they do to her?" he asked, thinking of Jaden.

"They will judge her," Pietro answered. "And they will more than likely kill her."

"Will you help her?" Mack asked in dejection. "Can you bring her back to me?"

"I'll try," Pietro promised coolly. "When it becomes time to decide, I'll vote for life. Now, prepare yourself. I'll come back for you, but for now I must join the council. They will be expecting me."

* * * *

The boat rocked on the choppy sea as the knights made the passage to Delos. The bound boatman stood at the helm, used to the vampiric passengers. He ignored them, though they were an imposing sight-- standing stock still on the uneven water. Their vampiric eyes glittered in the silver of the moonlight, their hair lifted gently in unison on the breeze, and their black clothing clung to their bodies like second skins to hide the tell-tale paleness beneath.

The boatman's old knobby fingers ran over the smoothed wood of his boat, his thin legs planted unfalteringly on the deck. He knew better than to ask questions of the strangers at his back, having ridden them on the water most of his life. During the day, he was allowed to ferry humans to the sacred island and at night he was roused from bed to do the same for his vampiric masters. It was the lot of his family line to serve the dark ones, and they did so without complaint for they had been well rewarded and taken care of in return.

The Dark Knights in turn ignored the loyal servant. They rode noiselessly over the short distance, each keeping their thoughts in their own heads. The dhampir and mortal captives laid quietly by their feet. Their bodies were for the most part motionless, though they rolled and swayed quietly on the deck with the waves.

Tyr let his eyes drift downward. Jaden's face was turned away from him, pressing close to Rick's side. The man's arm arched over her head. The waves scooted them intimately together until they looked to be lying peacefully. Tyr didn't need to see her features to recall every detail of her fine appearance or the legendary jade of her gaze--a gaze made all the more potent by the accursed gift he had given her.

The wound on her shoulder was healing, the worst of it over. Tyr stared at it and felt his stomach tighten. Instantly, his companion's heads turned to him, sensing his torment in a brief anguished moment he forgot to hide. Tyr forced all feeling out of his chest, leaving in it a cold numbness. He lifted his passionless eyes to the approaching dock emerging out of the night, refusing to answer their unspoken inquiry. He didn't deem to look at her again and his quiet companions turned their curiosity away.

* * * *

Jaden awoke with a start from the strange sleep induced by the power of the knights. She was surrounded by stone walls. Her lungs softly panted with breath out of human habit until she realized they didn't need the air. She stopped breathing, sitting in the surreal shadow casting of light coming dimly from a narrow slit at the bottom of the door. The tiny edge allowed a thin beam to illuminate within. She was again in a prison cell, a dark dungeon in the vampire council hall.

Her vampiric eyes cut through the darkness with ease. She still hadn't grown used to trusting them. Her vision focused too quickly and she shut her eyes to stop them from wavering. Her other enhanced senses had been easier to handle, since being a dhampir had given Jaden a lesser degree of them her whole life.

Peering into the door, she knew the tribal council was close. She could feel the concentrated energy of the tribes thumping all around her, pumping in her veins, flowing like electricity from the old stones. It made her shiver with the coldness of it and she was very afraid.

Tyr was gone. She couldn't detect him beyond the thick metal. Her body contracted with a sob that found no release. Her limbs quivered violently. Death was all around her, had become part of her. All she wanted was one last smile from Tyr, one last gentle touch of his hand, the press of his body.

Hearing someone else's breath in the darkness, Jaden paused. Her eyes closed in languid pleasure. She realized a mortal shared her cell. The smell of blood curled in her nose with a predator's accuracy. A faint heartbeat unfurled in her head. Her lips parted with new-found instinct, begging her to eat, to bite, to drink. The meals of rats and fish swam inside of her. The borrowed life in her blood was painfully inadequate.

Jaden cracked open her eyes. She wondered if a meal was left for her.

Turning her attention to the ground, she saw Rick. His body was still, his chest falling in even sleep. She forced the bloodlust to subside and her fangs back behind her lips.

Going to the immobile man, she touched his cheek lightly. Rick jolted awake as if burnt. His eyes darted open. Seeing her, he weakly scrambled away.

"Rick," she began softly, unaware of how her eyes glowed with an eerie green light.

He shook his head, squinting into the dimmed light. "Stay back, Jaden."

"Rick," she continued with a soft plea. She moved to reach out to him, but pulled back when he flinched. "Don't be scared of me."

"You're one of them," he defended wearily. Proudly lifting his chin, he knew he could never fight her. He saw her eyes and knew he could never hurt her, not even now. "You're dead."

"Yes." Her gaze fell mournfully to the ground.

"How could you do it, Jade?" he hissed in aggravation. "How could you have allowed it to happen?"

"I--I didn't allow it to happen," she defended halfheartedly, thinking of how she trapped Tyr in the cave and forced him to bite her. Looking back, what exactly had she expected him to do? Let her die? She should have known better.

"You could've resisted. You could've refused to drink his blood."

Jaden looked at him. A dark, bitter chuckle escaped her tired throat. She wouldn't defend herself to him. He would never be able to understand the body's forceful cling to life in that last instant of death.

Bitterly, she countered, "You drugged me, left me helpless. If not for you, I wouldn't have been in the position I was in."

Rick choked with guilt. "Then it is true? Oh, God, Jaden! I am so sorry. Mack said that he ill-used you and--"

Jaden softened. She shook her head. "No, I was treated better than could be expected."

He shot her a look of utter disbelief.

"It's not your fault, Rick," she amended, sorry that she had lashed her anger out at him. She could never hate Rick, could never blame him. "He was coming for me that night. I wouldn't have been able to fight him off. You saved me the humiliation of trying. I should thank you."

"But, both of us--together," he offered.

"No." Rick couldn't see her sad smile in the darkness. "Not a whole army of us. Whatever has happened, will happen, you must promise me not to blame yourself. My fate was sealed long before we met."

"What happened to you, Jade? What changed between us?" Rick bemoaned the loss of his love. "I could've made you happy."

"I can't make myself happy," Jaden said under her breath. "What makes you think you could've done so?"

"I--"

"No," she broke in. "My whole life has been a mistake. Mack tricked my mother into becoming pregnant with me and then he killed her when she turned into a vampire to be with my father. My uncle has manipulated my entire life. He hasn't allowed happiness in it. He took my family from me. You couldn't have changed all of that, Rick."

"We should have never trusted Mack," Rick stated in dejection. Seeing that she didn't move to bite him, he relaxed. Rubbing his head, he drew up to sit against the hard, damp wall.

"I know," she said sadly. "I, too, foolishly trusted him. He is the reason I am. He is the reason I was born. He worked a spell over my parents and he has molded and raised me to do his bidding. Out of all of us, I am his most favorite puppet. And like a puppet, I was led like a child by my strings."

"When did you start to suspect?" Rick grunted, pressing his fingers into his temple. When he drew them back, he saw drying blood.

"New Orleans," she whispered, crawling close to him. Rick eyed her cautiously, but allowed her to sit next to him. There was no warmth in her, just the coolness of the stone reflected from her skin. "I knew I couldn't trust him in New Orleans."

"What did happen that night?" Rick asked. He watched her suspiciously, flinching when she lifted her fingers to touch his wound. Gingerly, she probed it. "You changed so much after that. Were you truly so mad at me for stomping on your turf? I've racked my brain a thousand times and so help me I can't figure it out. Duncan was a loser. He deserved to die."

"Yes," she agreed. "Duncan was a loser and did deserve to die. But he didn't die in New Orleans. He died later in New York."

"Then--"

"My father," she whispered. "I killed my father in New Orleans."

"Oh," Rick blew softly in surprise. He let the news sink in. It made sense. Mack had been so insistent that they go and help her. Giving them a load of crap about her getting emotionally involved. "Jade, I'm so sorry. But you didn't kill him. Mack did. I did. I am the one who didn't listen. I'm the one who called for the sunlight."

Jaden swallowed. Wearily, she laughed through her unending pain. Rick narrowed his eyes, trying to see her clearly in the darkness. His reward was the sinister toss of her tongue, as she queried, "Trying to comfort the vampire, Rick? That isn't like you."

Rick reached for her, pulling her to his chest against his better judgment. Jaden drank in his comfort, feeling nothing beyond friendship in his hold. Rick squashed his feelings, finally realizing that what he wanted could never be. Jaden was lost to him. Lightly stroking her hair, he said, "We've been in many scrapes, you and I. So how are we going to get out of this one?"

"I don't think we are," Jaden whispered. "It's already too late for me."

Rick nodded in understanding. He knew there was no escape from this hell. They weren't fit to fight the council and Mack wouldn't be coming for them. Easily, the vampires had overtaken the best of Mack's mortal army. They had been foolish to think they could make a difference under such unfair odds. Until now, they had been fighting vampire babies--weak newborns without the eternity of skill the older ones possessed. Only horrors awaited them outside their prison walls--torment and pain. Death was preferable to both.

"But if I can help it, your end will be easy," Jaden whispered soothingly. She felt Rick's sudden turmoil.

"You won't let them turn me."

It wasn't a question, not even a request. Jaden felt his heart beat speed beneath her cheek. She felt his strength that he was trying hard to cling onto. Rick was a good man. He deserved better than this. If he hadn't come after her, he wouldn't have been captured, waiting for the end like a wrongly accused prisoner on death row.

"Promise me that you'll kill me. I'd prefer it if it was you."

"Yes," she agreed. Her lips opened to bite. Rick knew what was coming, could sense it in her gaze as she lifted up from his arms. He closed his eyes, letting his head fall back to expose his neck to her. Jaden cupped his face, gentle and soothing to his warm skin.

Inside, they felt their heartbeats joining. Jaden's lips caressed his hot skin in a tender kiss, not hurting him as she ran her lips and tongue over his neck, relaxing him. His hand lifted to her waist, smoothing over her hip. She felt his throat working. Rick shivered beneath her, tensing slightly as he awaited her bite. Whispering against his skin, she vowed, "I won't let them turn you."

* * * *

Tyr rose from his knees, having bowed gracefully before the council, as was the long clung-to tradition from the time of his turning. Walking to Ragnhild, he placed his hand on the old vampire's shoulder. The greeting was returned by his maker.

Ragnhild's eyes glowed softly as he nodded in approval of his knight. In truth, their ages were separated by only a few hundred years. At the time of Tyr's making, it had made all the difference. But now, after they both traveled the centuries well past a millennium, the age difference was minuscule and they held each other in the well tried affection of brothers.

After a similar greeting had passed with the other attending knights to their respective tribal leaders, the vampire soldiers moved to face the council, standing at attention behind Pietro. Tyr held rigid between Shiva and Ares. His undead eyes stared forward with detached responsibility. He didn't look over the familiar old stones, having stood thus many times over the years in judgment of mortals and immortals alike. Never before had his stomach tightened in repulsion of that duty. Never had he felt anything for the one standing trial. Before now, it was only a job he had done. He knew what was to come. But knowing didn't make it easier.

"You have brought the dhampir?" Theophania asked quietly. Though her lips moved as she spoke, it wouldn't have been necessary. They could all hear her well in their heads.

"Yes," Tyr answered in an even tone. No sentiment showed on the contrasted faces in the chamber. The unearthly gazes, embedded within statuesque features that echoed an aching beauty, beheld the knights with a strange mix of boredom and anticipation. "And one of MacNaughton's mortal soldiers."

"What has taken you so long?" Pietro growled, his eyes narrowing as he spun in his chair to glare at Tyr and the others. "Why are you late?"

"All in due time, Pietro," Theophania scolded with a pretty pout on her crimson stained lips. She looked around the table. The Moroi were not represented, but all others were present. Amon and Vishnu nodded in silent agreement of her decree. Pietro turned his eyes to the center flame to brood. They dismissed him easily. Ragnhild lifted his chin with pride.

"Tyr's delay is not important," the Drauger leader said in a stern tone. "His loyalty shouldn't be questioned. Nor should his judgment."

"It is not," Chara said easily with a purse of her cherry lips. Andrei smiled adorningly at her, reaching absently in her direction as if he could touch her over the distance. Ragnhild shot Pietro a challenging glare.

Pietro met the yellowish cast eyes focusing on him as they awaited his response. Grimly, he muttered, "My apologies, Tyr. You are a faithful servant to the tribes."

Tyr nodded in acceptance of the old vampire's words. Pietro didn't turn to watch, unconcerned with the knight's thoughts.

"Continue," Ragnhild directed.

"As ordered, I have been trying to discover which vampires have been assisting MacNaughton in his crimes against our tribes," Tyr said.

"And," Theophania urged.

"The one called Duncan was helping him to change mortals into vampires for a fee. He also assisted MacNaughton's men in capturing and tracking other young ones. I read it in him and put him to death," Tyr said quietly.

"Good," Chara murmured in approval.

"Was he alone in it?" Vishnu asked, her words clipped short.

"He was the one turning mortals for MacNaughton's pleasure," Tyr restated. The council nodded. The other knights held still. "And he was not aware of any others that MacNaughton might have employed. He thought himself to be a God. I showed him how little he truly was."

"And what do you suspect, Tyr?" Theophania asked quietly.

"Yes," Chara added. "Do you think Duncan was alone in his deceit?"

"No." Tyr's admission was soft. He couldn't avoid answering the direct question, but didn't feel the need to elaborate.

"Before we send for the dhampir," Amon said with a stark bite to his tone. His low voice rumbled with the primitive beat of his homeland. "What is your judgment of her? What have you discovered?"

"As suspected, she is responsible for the death of Bhaltair," Tyr said. His eyes looked coldly at each of the leaders in turn as he spoke. His stomach twitched. He refused to let them feel his turmoil. He swallowed it into his gut. He felt Shiva's eyes on him as he spoke. Tyr ignored his friend's mild disapproval in the curtness of his tale. Tyr had revealed to him the whole story while they traveled. Unable to bear Shiva's continued censure, he added, "She didn't kill him, but she did track him and stake him in the chest to slow him for others."

"Then she shall be executed," Vishnu acknowledged with ease. Tyr stiffened at the vampiress' easy dismal of Jaden's life. It was as he had expected, but he was not ready to hear the words. "And what of Alan MacNaughton?"

"No, Vishnu," Amon whispered. She turned surprisingly to him. "Let us hear from the dhampir before we condemn her. I am very curious what she has to say for herself."

Amon's keen senses had picked up on the underlying thread of emotion passing between Shiva and Tyr. He didn't trust the complete lack of sentiment coming from the Drauger knight. It was unusual for even the hardest of them to feel so little. Tyr was hiding something and Amon was determined to discover what that was.

Tyr kept his eyes sightlessly forward. He felt himself being probed.

"Yes," Ragnhild said quietly. He sensed something amiss as well. "The reports about her have been conflicted. It is said she spares as much as she kills."

"And," Theophania added, "She might know more of her uncle. We should at least explore her before we kill her."

"Osiris," Amon commanded. "What happened on the beach tonight?"

Osiris quickly gave an accounting of the brief battle. The leaders nodded in approval. All except for Pietro, who stared lifelessly at the center flame. Finishing, Osiris said, "MacNaughton was not with them."

"Well done," Theophania said. "Your loyalty is duly noted by this council."

"Yes," Chara said, her eyes roaming over the handsome vampire knights. Licking her lips like a kitten contemplating which saucer of milk to drink from, she murmured seductively, "Well done."

"Ares, Aleksander," Amon said "Your duty is done this night. You may go and seek your leisure. After meeting with Chara and Pietro, you may leave the island."

The two knights nodded, gliding effortlessly from the room. Amon turned his attention to Osiris.

"Osiris," Amon ordered. "Gather the dhampir. Bring her here and then you too may retire."

Osiris nodded, before he too strode from the council hall in a flash of black clothing.

"Tyr, Shiva," Amon acknowledged when the others had gone, "You shall stay to add insight to this judgment. You have been in the company of this woman and surely have read her. Dhampirs can be deceitful in their emotions and thoughts. Reading them is tricky until you learn their manner."

Tyr and Shiva bowed their heads in concurrence and didn't move. Tyr felt his pulse slowed as he forced his eyes from the door from whence Jaden would come. His mind told him that he didn't care about her, that she was already dead to him, as she would surely soon be to the world. His mind was answered by his heart that it was all a lie.

* * * *

"Someone is coming. I think it's time." Jaden whispered to herself. She lifted her head from Rick's shoulder. The man didn't attempt to stop her. His arms lay completely motionless at his sides.

Standing, she lightly closed her lips over her teeth, as she blocked Rick from view. She could feel his shallow breathing behind her. She didn't have it in her to kill him quite yet, so she used all her strength to lull him to sleep. A knight she recognized from the skirmish on the beach threw open the door. Reaching his hand to her, he motioned lightly with his fingers that she was to follow him.

"Come, dhampir," he ordered coldly.

Jaden stepped forward, obeying the beckoning of his golden hand. His tightly curled black hair was bound back at his neck, threaded tight with black beadwork so it didn't fall. She entered an old stone passageway. The prison door shut firmly behind her with a clink. She blinked slowly, her only reaction to the chilling noise. Torches gave the old hall light. Spiders spun webs over the iron sconces, so thick it was as if they alone held the metal into place. The patterns fluttered aimlessly in the stagnant air as the immortals passed, holding tight ageless dust in their fold.

Her feet echoed softly on the irregular rock, the only noise as the knight moved silently before her. His feet touched the ground but his gait was so unusually light for one of his size that it whispered softly over the stone. Self consciously, she moved her fingers through her hair, trying to smooth the tangled, wayward length. Tucking her longer tresses behind her ear, she wiped at her cheeks, hoping to add a semi-pleasing hue to the ashen features. She knew she looked a fright.

At the end of the long tunnel, past numerous unmarked doors that resembled the one Rick was behind, the knight stopped. Jaden could feel a presence behind some of the prison doors. She knew that only a vampire with honed senses could pull apart the emotions coming from within--some angry, some desperate, some dying and already dead. For a vampire there was no need to mark the doors. Each scent that wafted vividly from the prisoners marked its owner as no word could.

Pulling open a thick oak door at the end of the passageway, the dark knight stepped aside to let her pass. The entryway was blocked by thick velvet drapes, ironically dyed to the bloodiest of reds. Jaden hesitated, glancing at the vampire's immoveable face and dispassionate eyes before turning back to the doorway.

Jaden gulped. Her legs turned to jelly, her stomach filled with immovable lead. The knight's golden features showed a whispering movement as he nodded toward the drapery. His hand swept forward slowly, beckoning her to move on alone.

Closing her eyes, Jaden pushed forward. Her hand fervently sought the soft red only to slide through the velvet, hitting cooler air. Leading with her hand, she stepped between the soft barriers as they brushed erotically over her heightened skin. Her gaze drifted open, unable to remain shut at such a dire time. She was met with the soft orange glow of firelight on gray stone. Across the way, her eyes focused on a mosaic of a medieval vampire amidst his bite.

She could sense eyes focusing in on her, knew that if she turned only slightly she would see the faces holding those dangerous eyes. She refused to look. Guilt overwhelmed her as she thought of her father, of her life. She tried to fight it, tried her best to hide it away, but the council leaders sensed it easily. Just as she knew they found the emotions in her, she also knew that they would never be able to understand them.

Bowing her head, Jaden stepped forward. She was in the most sacred hall of the vampire, the hall of wisdom and centuries. She was to have her life torn apart and analyzed, summed up and judged. She was set out to slaughter before the dreaded tribal elders, the oldest known killers in existence. And not one of them was happy to see her.

Chapter Fourteen

The tribal elders held quiet in the great hall, each studying and probing the accused dhampir before them. They waited for her to react, unwilling to break her telling silence. Part of their curious pleasure was waiting to see if she would break as so many before her had.

Jaden took a steadying breath. The stagnant air did her no good and sounded abnormally odd in the silent chamber. Feeling many but not hearing anyone, she finally managed to lift her eyes to take in the vampire hall.

Jaden shivered, knowing that salvation for the moment wouldn't come. She could feel Tyr's nearness as she stepped into the ring of light that glowed from a torch stand levitating in the middle of a round table. Seven pairs of hostile faces examined her. She stopped. Her blood ran cold in her veins. She searched frantically for Tyr, not seeing him at first. Then, detecting Shiva on the far side of the oversized room, she took another hesitant step forward. Tyr appeared within her vision from behind a brooding tribal leader's face. Her heart leapt only to fall and crash. He refused to look at her. He was as emotionless as the rest.

Jaden stopped once more. Watching as, one by one, the inspecting faces turned from their detached mask to grim frowns of disapproval. Her eyes darted about, desperate to find deliverance. All she found was unwavering contempt.

She could feel them on her, as if they reached cold invisible hands from the distance to push and probe at her body, to poke at the inner working of her mind. She forced her mind to be blank, dropping her gaze down at the floor to avoid being mesmerized by their eyes.

Black symbols swam before her in a gray stone sea. She felt so alone, so lost. The cold hands wouldn't stop their inspection. She could feel the tribal leaders sniffing her, touching her most intimately. She was like a helpless sacrifice, tied to a cliff and left to the whim of the kraken, as if the stone would soon part beneath her feet and the mythical sea beast would swallow her whole.

When silence prevailed in the chamber, Tyr finally turned his eyes to the pitiful creature before them. Her frame was thin, her features sunken into the depths of her bony face. The ashen skin pulled skeletal around her cheekbones. Her dark auburn hair was matted, long and thin like a corpse growing old in its coffin.

Blood stained her once white shirt from the wound he inflicted on her neck, reminding him of the elation he had felt when he killed her--the passionate orgasm of her death and rebirth, however bittersweet. Its seeping red pattern edged eerily from the gaping hole in her chest, rewarded to her when she jumped before Rick's stake aimed for his back. The man had come close to killing her. Dirt and grime from her nights on the floors of crypts stained that which wasn't dried red. Even under the swaying of her wan body, she was beautiful to him.

She is a liar, a deceiver, a heartlessly cruel wench who is only now remorseful that she is caught, Tyr assured himself with a cool numbness. He refused to feel anything for her, forcing his mind to remember the folder, to remember her deceit, to remember her false words of love. What did either of them know of love? Theirs were lives filled with many things, many undeniable passions and lusts, but never love. Such sweetness would be wasted on them. They could never hold onto it, understand it. Her deceit was a cruel reminder, but effective in its unintentional aim. The memory would serve as a harsh lesson never to crave laughter and light in an endless abyss of black. Hardening, he added silently, *And she is a coward, choosing death instead of facing her fate! She will reap the rewards of her deceitful, black heart! If it is in my power, she will live only to feel regret.*

Then her eyes lifted from the floor to look at him, detecting his gaze in the oceanic flow of her pain. Tyr's mind went blank, forgetting the revenge he had just sworn to. His body convulsed under the dull glaze in her jade eyes. They peered helplessly at him through the tattered depths of her long dark hair. His mind rebelled with the bitter stirrings of pride and reminiscent thoughts of duty and honor. But such things paled in importance. The seam of her lips parted showing her fangs. It was like a kick to his already damned soul. He could've let her die there on the floor of his cave. He could've spared her this torment, and thus spared himself the torture of inevitability. No matter what she had done, his body still craved to protect her.

But it was too late. She had constructed her prison of fate with her own bloodied hands. Her lies, the actions of her mortal life were laid out before her, carved into the proverbial granite of her past deeds. Although she quaked in the hell of her own making, he wished there was a way he could lift her out of it.

But what could he do? Lie to the council? Lie to the vampire nation he served for so long? And what honor was there in deceit? Could he really sacrifice his morals, his very nature to save her? And if he did, would he lose that last bit of humanity he still carried inside of him? It was that shred of humanity that kept him alive in death. Could he live without resenting her for an eternity? Even as he thought it, he knew he wouldn't lie to save her. For, to sacrifice his honor, he would sacrifice everything in him worth keeping. No, he wouldn't lie. He could only wait for a miracle that would never come.

When it was evident no amount of time was going to give Jaden the courage to continue forward, Tyr stepped around the table. She watched him come for her, unable to help the glimmer of hope shining in the dull pools of her eyes. Tyr stopped under the watchful veil of the council, in the drowning of her pitiful expression. His eyes traveled briefly over her face before he reached out and roughly grabbed her arm.

Jaden trembled as he hauled her behind him. There was no love in his chilled touch, but she desperately drank in the feel of his palm to her skin. He stopped before an empty chair around the center circle. Taking her by her slender shoulders, he held her firmly in his grasp. Jaden's face lifted, catching his passionless eyes with her own. A shock fell over her, a powerless urge to kiss his disapproving lips. He didn't return her look as he levitated her above the ground. Tyr brought her into the center circle, landing on the lowered ring beneath the floating torch stand. Letting her go, he stepped away.

Jaden shuddered weakly. Her eyes automatically looked up to see if the torch would fall. It held steady. To her great relief, Tyr didn't fly away but stayed beside her. She unconsciously leaned towards him. The council's eye became more intense, prickling like needles to the flesh.

Jaden jolted slightly as Shiva landed noiselessly next to her. Her round eyes sought him in surprise. He stiffly nodded before turning forward, the friendliest gesture she had yet to receive.

Jaden jolted again as Tyr spoke. The low, accented tone of his words reminded her of how much they had been through together in only a short time. Lifting his hand, his low voice quietly introduced her to the leaders. She managed a weak nod to each as she stepped around full circle. She hesitated only once, seeing Pietro's face. It tugged at the back of her mind like a far away dream. He didn't acknowledge her as he turned his expression to the floor. In an instant the sensation was gone and she again faced the vampiress lounging decadently in her chair. The council stayed quiet through the formality of introductions, not making her welcome with words or expressions.

"What is this you bring us?" Theophania asked after a long silence.

"This is Jaden MacNaughton," Tyr answered. Jaden glanced at his face to see if any softness invaded him as he said her name. There was none. He ignored her. Jaden turned her eyes forward, lifting her chin. She drew strength from Tyr's nearness, whether it was his intent or not. A shiver racked her, as Tyr added cryptically, "the dhampir."

"She is no mortal," Chara stated with a tap of her fingers on the wooden table before her. She glanced at Andrei for needless confirmation.

"The bloodstalker," Andrei said. "The one who killed her father."

"Ungrateful child," Chara pouted with a sneer to her full lips.

Jaden lowered her head, the memory of it hitting her fresh, like ice water to the skin. To hear them dispassionately speak of it, as if it was nothing to her, cut deeply. Not even Rick's soft assurances whispered in the dark cell could convince her it wasn't her fault.

"And who changed this dhampir?" Amon asked.

Tyr turned slightly to acknowledge the vampire leader. "I did."

That statement caused a look of speculation to rise between the elders. Amon nodded, pressing his lips together thoughtfully.

"And you remember, Dark Knight," Vishnu said coolly. "That you are not to make more of yourself. Your blood is not to be passed on."

"Yes," Tyr said. His expression became tight.

"Then do you mean to disregard our laws?" Vishnu queried, daringly. "Do you no longer obey them?"

"I understand and respect our laws," answered Tyr.

"And you made her anyway?" Ragnhild asked in surprise. Tyr turned back around to face him and nodded.

"Yes. I invoke the right of the knights, the right to break a law for the greater purpose of the council. This dhampir was dying. My order was to bring her in. I thought it best, save the circumstances, to do so."

"And how was she dying?" Theophania questioned, straightening her limbs only to rearrange them and lounge in the opposite direction of her sister. She, like the others, already knew part of the answer. Only by Tyr's bite could she have been dying, for his blood to have changed her. "You could've given her your blood and saved her mortal coil."

Tyr's cheeks would've stained with embarrassment if he hadn't been practiced at hiding it. He tried to block Jaden's trembling from his mind. She stood beside him, shaking like paper in the wind.

"I was--" Tyr began.

"He was trapped inside a chamber while retrieving documents," Shiva said. "By the time Jaden released him, the bloodlust transformed him. He attacked her in his frenzy, drinking her blood. Then, when sanity returned and he had seen what he'd done, he turned her. I saw the change and wouldn't have acted differently."

Tyr glanced briefly at Shiva, nodding his head in quick thanks.

"Very well," Theophania said. "It is done and matters little to me."

"She is sickly," Andrei whispered good-naturedly to break the bleak ambiance. Chara giggled. Andrei made a great show of sniffing the air. "What have you been feeding her, Tyr? Rats?"

Jaden gulped and looked at the ground in embarrassment. Her bony hands wove together, the knuckles sticking out of the skin. Theophania and Ragnhild's chuckles joined Chara and Andrei's. Even Vishnu and

Amon managed small smiles of amusement.

"I know you've never been a father, Tyr, but surely you could manage to better care for your benighted child," Chara teased with approval. "You must feed them if they are to survive. Why deny her the thrill of human blood? Let her taste the other side of things."

"Bloodstalker turned nightstalker," Andrei crowed in a sanctimonious cry. "What a perfect irony!"

"Do you know why we call you bloodstalkers?" Chara asked.

"We call you bloodstalkers, because you stalk your own blood," Andrei continued. "Because you take with you a part of the vampire's remaining humanity and then use it to destroy us. To vampires, dhampirs who hunt are less desirable than living with a festering corpse."

"And now you are what you hate," Chara finished happily.

Jaden had no defense. She pressed her protruding knuckles to her mouth, a look of agony marking her wan features. She bit her flesh, a droplet of blood running over the back of her pale hand. Tyr smelled the blood and jerked his eyes about to her. At his direct look, she dropped her knuckle to her side and hid the wound beside her leg. Blood trailed down her finger and dripped onto the floor. The droplet resounded like a loud splash in vampire ears. Jaden grimaced like a scolded child. Her bottom lip pulled out a fraction. Tyr blinked heavily, looking away.

"And what of the documents," Ragnhild said, eager to resume the judgment. His eyes narrowed carefully on Tyr, able to feel the torment wafting through him. Tyr was connected to all the elders, but was felt by his true father the most.

Tyr peered coldly at Jaden, lifelessly taking her in. Jaden's lips parted as if she would speak to him. She pressed them shut, unable to tell him what she must. Her heart ached for him. Her body longed for him. She was in love with him. She loved him. Her heart exploded with it. But she couldn't say it, not here. And if she could, if she froze time and it was just the two of them, would he even believe her or care?

No, Jaden thought in dejection. *It doesn't matter. None of it matters. They might as well kill me. Without Tyr I am nothing.*

Inside she wavered, her stomach turning with hunger and defeat. Healing her shoulder had taken a lot out of her. Even the small puncture wound on her finger refused to heal itself shut. The hunger made it hard to concentrate, to focus on what was being said. She closed her eyes, swooning slightly with the desire to bite something. But there was nothing around but the smell of the grave--no fresh blood to ease the ache. She felt the bloodlust swimming in her eyes. She wondered if the orbs were pulling red as she had seen Tyr's do.

What a fright I must be! She snorted wildly to herself. At the sound all eyes turned suspiciously to her. Tyr's words shook her from her trance.

"I have them," Tyr said sternly. Jaden saw his look of warning and wrinkled her brow in confusion. With an effortless bend of his legs, he leapt over the table only to leap back with the folder. Jaden gulped, wishing more than ever she had discovered what was inside. How could she defend what she didn't know? Tyr lifted up the files for all to see before setting them before Ragnhild.

"They are in French," Ragnhild said. Changing his tone, he began to read. Jaden studied his lips--enthralled by the way they moved and formed. She couldn't make out the foreign words but she listened to the low rumbling voice. A trance came over her senses, like a babe listening to a lullaby. Her numbed mind floated with her eyes, over rocks and symbols, torches and pale flesh. Ragnhild's song lingered on for a long moment. The words were fast but melded into a complete rhythm. All of a sudden, she felt sick. Tyr and Shiva visibly stiffened. Eyes slowly turned to glare at her.

Stopping after reading a few pages, Ragnhild frowned. Out of deference to Jaden, he spoke again in English. "There are pictures within and many more documents. I have no wish to waste the council's time reading them all here. Let me take them tonight and tomorrow I'll report on the evidence within."

The council nodded in agreement, trusting Ragnhild to see to it.

"So be it," Theophania said. She then turned her attention to Jaden. Looking down her nose at the young one, she said, "We will read this file and tomorrow we will make judgment. We know you worked for Alan MacNaughton, your human uncle. We know that he has been involved in numerous crimes against the vampire as well as smaller, less important crimes against humans. He has made vampires only to watch them die. He has extorted money by helping humans avenge themselves against each other, by making the enemy one of our kind and allowing the patron to torture said enemy at his leisure."

Jaden became pale. She saw the truth in all of them and they believed she had something to do with it. Her mind numbed, flying rampantly for an excuse, a defense. She came up with nothing. Any argument died in her throat.

"Rape," Theophania continued, "Murder, blackmail, larceny. The list is endless."

Jaden got the impression Theophania liked doling out the charges in detail. Just as she could tell the vampiress cared nothing of Mack's mortal victims. Jaden could see the disdain on the woman's delicate features as she muttered the word, *humans*. Jaden glanced at Tyr. He refused to acknowledge her.

"Many are the MacNaughton family crimes against the vampire," Theophania stated. "You'll be given your chance to answer for them tomorrow. It would be wise of you to consider what you say very carefully. The more you tell us, the more lenient we will be with you."

Silently, Theophania directed, we *want names, dhampir. Expose the others and spare yourself. Either way, we will discover them.*

"Do you understand?" Chara insisted when Jaden didn't move.

Jaden nodded weakly. She felt the black hole of fate beginning to close. She hadn't a thing to say. She knew nothing, could name no one.

"Take her to your chamber, Tyr," Ragnhild said. "Keep her close to you. There you will be fed. Bring her back at dusk."

Tyr nodded. His stomach tightened as he took Jaden's elbow in his tight grip. Jaden winced at the pain of his sharp hold. He couldn't look at her. Couldn't trust himself to get caught in the sorrow her eyes.

"And Tyr," Chara called. Tyr turned to the vampiress, dragging his prisoner with him. "Do clean her up. For, if only briefly, she is one of us. This," Chara waved an appalled hand up and down Jaden's form, "smell will never do. It is too reminiscent of the Barbarian age."

Tyr nodded, "I'll see to it."

Chara nodded, pleased. "I'll have my girl bring her clothes."

Jaden watched on silently. Tyr turned to her in warning, squeezing her arm in expectation.

"Ow," Jaden gasped, glaring at Tyr. Seeing his ice blue eyes, she calmed. She bowed her head at the vampiress. "Thank you."

Chara smiled benevolently. Then, wrinkling her nose, she waved them away with wiggling fingers. Her amused giggle followed.

Shiva followed as Tyr escorted Jaden over the table. Their feet landed with a soft thud and Tyr continued walking. The three left out one of the doors. Jaden sighed with relief once they were out of the council hall. Her body swayed as if she would collapse.

"You did well," Shiva murmured in mild approval.

Tyr glared at him. Shiva shrugged. Without breaking stride, he skirted past them, disappearing down the stone carved hall. Jaden looked after him. The hall was lighted by torches, though it was cleaner than the prison passageway. The stone was smoothed to rectangular perfection, the stones polished to a black gleam.

"Why didn't they put me back in the prison with Rick?" Jaden asked. Tyr growled brutally, forcing her to follow by his grip on her bruised elbow. He hastened through the passage, flying by endless doors in blurring madness. Jaden stumbled behind him, her feet tripping. When he didn't answer, she snapped, "Aren't you going to at least talk to me?"

Tyr stopped. Pushing open a door with the Drauger symbol over a shield that matched his brand, he shoved her inside. The room was dark. Tyr fixed it with a wave of his hand. A fire blazed in a stone hearth, candles lit in an overhead chandelier.

A fur rug covered part of the stone floor, a matching white pelt on the large rectangular bed. Jaden bit her lip. There was only one bed. She guessed she'd be sleeping on the floor.

A writing table was situated against the far wall. Books lined a shelf above it. The room was smaller than his cave, but still very luxuriant in style. Turning, Jaden noticed a large tiled bathtub, minus the nozzles for water. She swallowed, spinning quietly away to watch Tyr.

"You are here because you are mine," he said quietly, answering her question from the hall. Jaden glanced up to study his face. His jaw lowered possessively. His head cocked to the side with seductive precision. "I made you. I am responsible for you."

"Oh," she whispered for lack of a better word. A dim hope tried to light within her, but she was no fool as to fan that flame.

Tyr lifted a hand to her skeletal chin. His thumb stroked her sunken face. He felt the loneliness inside of her, knew her fears. He also knew that this might be her last night. Gently, he said, "You did well in there."

"I did?" Jaden whimpered in awe at the kindness in his voice. She closed her eyes, drawing comfort from his large hand. A part of Tyr's iron control crumbled. It had been so hard to deny the feelings he had for her. Now that they were alone, perhaps for the last time, he couldn't hold himself completely back.

"Yes." Suddenly, as he looked into her jade eyes, her past didn't matter. He didn't want her dead. He didn't want this to be it. Even if he could never forgive her, maybe he could forget. "Character and strength matter to the elders. And you showed much of both."

"No," she mumbled, unable to take his touch, feeling dirty and ugly in her grimy clothes. She pulled back, putting distance between them. She didn't want him to look at her. She didn't want him to see her broken and lost. "I was weak and scared and they know that. I felt them looking inside of me. I felt them searching me, violating me."

"That is part of the test," he answered, spurned by her rejection.

"Then I failed it," she breathed. "I know I did."

"Not everyone can stand before them. I have seen the oldest of vampires brought low by the mere sight of them." Tyr kept his distance. He could hear her heart fluttering like the beating wings of a hummingbird. Lowering his tone, he whispered, "I have seen men cry out with fear and run themselves headlong into the stone walls trying to escape. You stood before them bravely."

"They have already found me guilty," Jaden said. "I could feel their anger."

Tyr said nothing. He had felt it too.

"You think I am guilty, too, don't you?" she whispered remorsefully. Her mournful tone tore at him. Her lips quivered. "I can feel it in you.

You think I'm capable of what is in that f--"

"Don't," he growled. His gaze darkened in anguish. "Let us not speak of it."

Tyr couldn't stand to think of her sins. He couldn't consider them, wanted to forget them. He couldn't bear to hear more of her lies. Even as a vampire, in his centuries of taking life, he had never performed such cruel experiments on humans or immortals. It sickened him that she could've been a part of it. Even in the days when war was all the land knew, the warlords had been merciful enough to let their enemies die.

She was involved in her uncle's business, watching rapes and murders, catering to sick mortal fetishes. By the evidence in the folder, that was only the beginning. That it could've been her hand sawing into flesh countless times, tearing off limbs that would never grow back, torturing vampires and humans on devices meant to kill not prolong agony. That it could've been her finger taking the memento photographs of what was done. It made Tyr sick to think on it.

Only the sickest of minds could perform such atrocities. Only the basest of all creatures would keep the photographs with them. He knew what she was, but when he looked at her, felt inside her, he didn't see it, and that baffled him. He knew she was a talented dhampir and that accounted for the deceitfulness. He wanted to hate her, tried his damnedest to. Faced with only one night, it was more than he could do.

Jaden knew he already condemned her. It tore at her heart to think he believed her capable of something so bad that it turned a hardened vampire's blood cold. She had seen the reaction of the council. She loved Tyr so desperately and he couldn't even believe in her a little. She would've denied everything, fought everyone, if she thought he would believe her.

"Your bath," Tyr said.

Jaden's brows rose in question at the statement. The door to the room opened and a woman entered carrying a basket of towels, perfumed soaps and hair rinses. She was swathed in white from chest to toe. Jaden smelled the mortal woman's blood. Her eyes leapt with hunger. She took an entranced step forward, her eyes greedily scanning over the smooth, brown skin of the woman's neck and arms.

Tyr's hand shot out to stop her. He pulled Jaden to his chest. His arms wrapped about her from behind like a vice, hugging her close to his solid form. The feel of his skin broke through her mind's lethargic hold. Leaning down, he whispered, "Look at her eyes."

Jaden looked at the woman's eyes. They were glazed white and stared out over the room like a zombie. The woman didn't see the two vampires as she set the items on the ledge next to the tub.

"She is a *servitor* of the Vrykolatios." Tyr kept Jaden at bay, still feeling her body straining to eat. Suddenly, he felt bad for having nearly starved her. At the time it had seemed a suitable punishment, now it just seemed cruel. "She has traded years of her life to serve here in return for a gift."

"A gift?" Jaden said softly. The compassion of his words absorbed her senses. She longed for tenderness from him.

"Yes," Tyr said. "These servitors are saved from disease, usually death. In return they spend a portion of their youth, in the flower of their beauty, working willingly. They wait on Theophania. The time passes quickly for them for they are in a trance. They are protected from the bite. To drink from one without permission is to insult Theophania."

"I wouldn't want to do that," she admitted in dejection, licking her lips as the woman left.

Tyr grinned. Touching her cheek, he eased her around to face him. Forgetting himself in her tinged gaze, he said, "The meals will be here soon. I can smell them coming."

"Do I--?" Jaden began weakly.

"Yes, you drink from them," Tyr said. For a heartless killer she seemed to struggle with the idea. "We don't kill them. They too have protection from death. It is hard for the Vrykolatios to find food on this sacred island. The human officials get testy when too many tourists have unfortunate accidents at sea. We feed only. You see, not all vampires are ruthless killers. Some of us do let the victims live. In the old days it was different, the world was different. Like the humans we surrounded, we killed for survival. We hunted and sought to rule over a ruthless and unforgiving land. Life was not valued on a whole as it is now. Now we have evolved as human's have."

"I never knew," she whispered, ashamed for all the times she threw his vampiric nature into his face. She held still as the door opened once more. A line of women carting steaming buckets trailed to the bath. They were dressed as the first, eyes all glazed with a white mist. Jaden sniffed, smelling their blood but held back.

"Don't they knock?"

"The barely see us," Tyr said. "We are like a hazy dream to them."

The women left the same way they came, except for two who stood patiently on the side of the bath. They turned, zombie eyes looking forward as they waited. The women were beautiful, seductive.

"What are they doing now?" Jaden asked, in awe over the strangeness of the council's ways. Ever since she was a girl she had imagine a dark hole full of dust and skeletons, medieval torture devises and impaled humans dying a slow death for the entertainment of the elders.

"That was the old way," Tyr muttered in her ear. Jaden turned around to him, embarrassed that he read the thought.

Well, mostly, he added to himself. There were still a few who tortured humans. But she didn't need to know that. It would only scare her.

"And they are waiting for you," he murmured. Jaden shivered at the seductive pull to his voice. The stress almost seemed to ease out of her at the words to be replaced by longing.

"I--I don't need their help," she denied weakly.

"Leave," Tyr ordered in a strong, strict tone. His eyes didn't leave hers.

The women nodded, filing out of the room. Jaden swallowed, turning her back on him.

"Did you want to spend this night with Rick?" he asked. The phrase *your last night* hung unspoken between them.

Jaden shook her head in denial. No, she didn't want Rick.

Tyr came around her, forcing her to look up at him. His lips parted, his hands lifted to touch her cheek. There was a strangeness to his eyes when he looked at her. Suddenly, he withdrew.

Striding over to the bed, Tyr sat on the end. His gaze turned to the door. Four women walked in. Their gowns were of the same white as the servitors, only golden bands wrapped around their waists and foreheads. Their eyes were glazed, but their bodies moved with more awareness, with a seductive purpose.

All four came to stand before Tyr. They were stunning in their vivid beauty. Upon closer examination, Jaden saw that the linen was almost as thin as gossamer showing off the dusky tips of their nipples and the darkened valley of their womanhoods. She felt a ping of jealousy as the beautiful woman lifted their hands to touch the sultry knight.

The women's fingers ran through the long strands of Tyr's golden hair, skimmed across his beautiful skin in seductive caresses. They moved over his chest, massaging him with intimate promises of more, gliding over his shirt, crumpling the material with their searching fingers.

Jaden's mouth fell open at the blatant display. Tyr's eyes closed briefly in what looked like pleasure. The hands continued to massage him, growing bolder as one knelt before him on the ground. The woman's long, tapering fingers ran over his calves, skimming thoroughly over his inner thighs to his strong hips. She pulled herself forward, rubbing her breast into his firm stomach.

Then a wrist moved across his mouth, brushing over them softly, and held still. Tyr's eyes opened at the woman's offering. He raised his hand to take the woman to his lips as he opened his mouth to drink. For a moment, his eyes flickered across the chamber, seeing Jaden watching him. His eyes fluttered closed, rolling back in his head in pleasure. A wave of anguish accosted Jaden as she watched his lips close around another woman, sucking deep and slow against her warm flesh.

She had no claim to him, could say nothing to stop it. There was nowhere to run, nowhere to hide. If Tyr decided to pull these women into his bed, there would be nothing she could do but watch as they took turns riding him.

Jaden backed away, nauseated. She couldn't watch the temptresses any longer. Her eyes met with the tub. One of the women giggled. It was sultry sound of invitation and desire. With only the thought of escape in her mind, Jaden dove into the bath, clothes and all.

Tyr's head snapped up from his meal in time to see water sloshing over the edge of the bath. Gradually, he realized the hands that were all over him. He detected the bitter sting of jealousy on the air. An animalistic pleasure overwhelmed him. A smile came to his crimson lips, a masculine smile of domination and immense gratification.

His eyes stayed on the tub as he stood. The woman whose wrist bled moved to the side to wait patiently for his return. Tyr grabbed a second woman. He motioned his hand by her face. Her head fell to the side, exposing her neck to him. He bent over to taste, drinking deeply. The mortal gasped as he bit her, feeling no pain, only pleasure. Her arms wrapped around him in invitation to the rest of her body. His eyes stayed focused on the bath. To him it was like a farmer taking milk from a cow. There was no passion in the intimate touch.

Letting his second meal go, he bit his finger and healed the wounds made by his teeth. The women left, leaving two behind. As he stood, the women's hands followed him. Tyr heard Jaden moving beneath the water, but she didn't rise from the tub. Walking over to the edge he looked down at her. Her deathlike features wavered in the rippling surface. A bubble escaped from her parted lips, floated to the surface, and popped. Her eyes stared out angrily, abnormally so in the veneer of a corpse. Seeing him, she stiffened. Her nose wrinkled defiantly.

Unable to resist, Tyr reached a hand in and grabbed her about her jealous neck. He felt the tendons working in her slender throat. She was hungry. He could see the desperation pooling in her eyes even as she fought it. She was tough, tougher than other vampires he had come across, but he also knew that the beast within her was stronger. If she denied herself much longer she wouldn't only disgrace herself but him as well. He couldn't have her attacking, and most probably killing Theophania's servitors in a fit of bloodlust. Such an affront to the vampiress wouldn't be forgiven.

Pulling her up by her neck, he raised a brow in forced amusement. Jaden wrinkled her nose at him. A growl escaped her wet, parted lips. The dirt from her features had dissipated in the water, but her skin was still sunken and a ghastly shade of powdery white. Her fangs bared and slashed as if to bite him. Instantly, her claws swung forward into his flesh, drawing blood from her arms as she scratched pathetically at him.

Her strength was too weak to fend off his hand.

Tyr sighed, watching his blood run down his arm from beneath his sleeve. It slid silently into the bath water. Whispering, he urged her gently, "You must eat."

It wasn't a request but a command. Jaden mouth twisted as she tried to pull back under the water. Her fingers released his arm. It healed instantly, leaving his sleeve soaked with blood. Tyr growled, his fingers slipping in the moisture from her throat. He caught her back up in a locked grip. Yanking her once again above the surface, his eyes met hers in a silent battle.

"Do as I say!" he grunted in frustration. "Why must you always try and fight me?"

Her mouth snarled in defiance. Challenge lit between them like the first calling on the battlefield. Jaden's eyes narrowed. Tyr's matched her look with one of his own.

"You have to eat," he snapped. "You have to calm the bloodlust."

"The only blood I wish to draw is yours," she growled. But, seeing the mortal woman standing behind Tyr, awaiting his command, she tensed. The stark smell of them overwhelmed her and if not for the vice on her throat, she would've torn into them in a frenzy of ecstatic overindulgence. Their heartbeats filled Jaden's head, calling to her. Their bodies looked so soft and warm and so full of blood.

Tyr watched her expression change. Feeling her strain, Tyr shook her hard. Roughly, he growled, "Not like that!"

Still looking at the women, Jaden smiled a cruel and heartless smile. It was a look Tyr knew to be of the bloodlust's making. It was no longer Jaden he held back, but a force that was in them all.

"No, damn you!" He shook her again, harder. Forcing his head before her eyes, he blocked the women from view. They stood quietly behind the vampires, completely unaware of the danger they were in. "You can't hurt them! Don't make things any harder on yourself."

"Let ... me ... go," Jaden whispered.

"Jaden, stop it!" Tyr commanded. In that moment, she controlled the beast within enough to see his face. It was hard and unforgiving. Blinking, she forgot all but what was between them. She forgot the helpless women standing so near. She forgot the bathwater that soaked uncomfortably into her tattered clothes. She even managed to forget her blood craving. But she couldn't forget how she felt about him and how he had treated her. She couldn't forget that he believed the worst in her. And, in that instant, she couldn't forgive him for delivering her into the depths of hell itself.

Sneering dangerously, Jaden said, "Make me."

Chapter Fifteen

Jaden steadily kept her glare on Tyr. A grimace etched her wan expression as she fought him. The wet, brown-red tresses of her hair fell eerily against her pale flesh, but Tyr didn't notice. He couldn't get beyond the green beauty of her eyes as they flashed in hard defiance. He held back his grin, knowing she wouldn't take kindly to his amusement. She was in no condition to fight him and yet, with the odds heavily against her, she was trying to anyway.

"You'll listen to me or I'll make you listen," Tyr stated softly. "Do you understand?"

Insolently, Jaden shook her head. Tyr frowned. Forcing her head underwater to stem her retort, he waited only a second before letting her back up. Water splashed over the sides of the tub at the violent movement. When she surfaced, she audaciously spat up at him. The water splashed back down, hitting her in the face. Tyr smirked as her lids blinked in surprise. The two women remained silently still behind him. He knew that they were not so mesmerized that they couldn't report Jaden's rebelliousness to the council.

"I said eat," he ordered hotly under his breath. His icy blue eyes glowed ardently, begging her to obey him.

"I--I want no part of that," she denied, thinking he meant for her to join the other women on the bed. Fury seeped out of her pores. "You--you can't make me."

"Jaden--" he warned, knowing her words to be an obvious lie. Desperately, he wanted to make her drink while her head was still clear. If she slipped again, he would have to chain her down to calm her and such a stir would surely rouse the others.

"No," she cried. "If you're going to kill me then do it! But do not torture me needlessly."

"Torture you?" he questioned in wonder. "I am only trying to help you and you dare to call it torture?"

"Yes, torture, by making me … with you and those--those *whores,*" Jaden pointed at the bed without looking at it. She tried to sink back under the water. Tyr struck out and grabbed her again. The sleeve of his shirt was weighed down with water and stuck to his skin. This time his hold was gentler.

"You're jealous," he grinned. Pleasure spread out over his face. She tried to shake her head, but he continued unhampered, "You are. You're jealous of them."

"I am not!" she seethed. "I would have to care about you to be jealous. And I hate you. I hate you. I hate you! I should be dead if not for your meddling. It's your fault I'm here. You should have let me die."

Her words stung with venom, but he could tell she didn't mean them. Tyr lifted a hand and motioned for the two remaining women to come forward. He pointed at Jaden.

Before they neared, he leaned down close to her ear. In a heartbreaking murmur, he whispered against her flesh, "I did let you die. I killed you, remember?"

How could she forget? She could still taste the lingering of his blood mixed with hers--possessing her, claiming her, making her. When he pulled away, she could see the torment in his gaze. The look was raw, drowning in a pool of misery and regret and self contempt. The women turned to her before she could respond and began reaching out to her as they had Tyr. Jaden swatted their searching hands away with a sneer.

"Ah," she cried out. "Stop it! Damn you, Tyr! Call them off. I want nothing to do with this!"

"Jaden," Tyr began. His expression cleared as if nothing had transpired over his features. His lips curled in amusement, unable to ignore the comical scene of Jaden fighting off her food.

Jaden disregarded his chuckle, pulling back to the far edge when the women became more persistent. The hands searched blindly for the vampire woman. Their lips parted with bated giggles and pants as if they meant to make love to her.

"Jaden," Tyr said in a firmer tone, though his inner laughter still echoed in its depths. Part of him was tempted to keep quiet and watch the ridiculously seductive performance being played out before him. But he knew that eventually Jaden would hurt the women and he couldn't allow it. With dark warning, he tried again, "Jaden."

"What?" she demanded in irritation, moving to glare briefly at him. One of the women started crawling in after her. Jaden kicked the woman's arm out from under her with the heel of her foot. The woman fell, catching herself at the last minute. She pushed up, unhampered in her cause.

"They are trying to tempt you. If you just let them go and don't fight them, they will let you drink and go away. If you resist, they'll think you'll want to play." Tyr continued to chuckle, the sound grew louder as he tried unsuccessfully to hold it back.

The sight of Jaden, wet and dripping with perfumed water, being attacked by seductresses, was almost more than his undead body could handle. His blood stirred, his loins pulled heavily between his thighs and he wanted nothing more than to jump in the tub and rip the tattered clothing from Jaden's body. If the seductresses wanted to stay and watch, he didn't care, so long as he could possess the aggravating vampiress who fought them.

"Make them stop," Jaden hissed, growing desperate. The women had crawled over the edge and were sinking down into the water. Their wet gossamer gowns floated up around their thighs. As they lowered deeper the material clung indecently to their skin.

"Take her wrist firmly," Tyr ordered Jaden as one of the women passed it by her face.

Jaden roughly grabbed one of them, ready to fling her out on her backside. Her arm tensed with a throw. Heat filled her chilled hand at the touch.

"Now bite," Tyr instructed, his eyes focusing on Jaden's mouth. A sense of primal, lustful anticipation came over him.

Jaden opened her mouth, seeing the pulse beat beneath the skin. The woman didn't struggle. In fact, she moaned loudly and urged Jaden to take her. The woman's fingers lifted to Jaden's neck, caressing her. Jaden opened her mouth and adjusted the wrist before her. She tried to clamp down onto the warm flesh, but couldn't. She could hear the woman's heart with her own, could sense the mortal's emotions stirring in her blood. The salty tang of perfume wafted her senses making her body tense with a desire to bite. With a tortured growl, she hissed, "I can't!"

Tyr sighed. Leaning over, he quickly drew his nail over the woman's flesh. It split open. Blood pooled above the skin. The mortal didn't even flinch.

"Now hurry, before she ruins the water," Tyr commanded with contrived annoyance.

Jaden smelled the blood. She couldn't resist it. She was a vampire, reborn to drink and to live. Hungrily, she pulled the wound to her mouth. The warm nectar of the woman's life flowed into her, sweeter than anything she had ever tasted. Her meals of rats and fish paled in comparison to the life-giving taste of human blood. A slight moan escaped her hungry lips, echoed loudly by her prey.

Tyr swallowed, his gaze darting to the tantalizing pull of Jaden's sucking, crimson lips. Her flesh began to fill with a pale rose. Veins pulsed and cursed over her face, down her neck, spreading life into her undead limbs. Her muscles once again became firm muscle and her hair regained an unearthly shine. His eyes glowed with celestial threads of dark blue and silver. His lips parted, eager to join to hers.

The woman Jaden was latched to gasped and moaned. Tyr saw the mortal's face paling with a dangerous quickness. Gently, he pulled Jaden away from her. Jaden looked at him in surprise, her eyes full of red.

"Enough," he whispered huskily. "You don't want to harm her."

Jaden nodded numbly, not realizing she had even been close to such a thing. It was like she couldn't stop herself. As Jaden watched, Tyr bit his finger and healed the woman's wrist with his blood. The woman bobbed her head like a departing servant and moved to leave the chamber. She wobbled slightly on her feet and closed the door behind her. The remaining mortal held out her hand to touch the vampiress' face. Jaden glanced guiltily at Tyr.

Tyr hid his smile, instead he nodded at her to drink again. Crossing his arms over his chest, he stood above them, watching. Jaden nodded before dipping her head to drink. Without hesitation, she bit into the woman, sinking her teeth for the first time into human flesh. She was struck by how soft it was compared to fish and rat. It was like moving her fingers through warm butter, taking little effort to pierce. Swallowing thoughtfully, she pulled back. In awe, she whispered, "It tastes different."

"Yes," he whispered, nodding for her to get on with it. Jaden again drank.

Tyr watched Jaden's features continue to fill with dazzling beauty. Her lips turned a dark red, her skin a warm pink. Her eyes were closed, but the black lashes that fanned over her cheeks swept dreamily with little quivers. Even her hair looked as if it grew with added fire. Feeling full, Jaden pulled her mouth away and looked at Tyr. The stunning jade of her eyes glittered with the power of sparkling emeralds. His heart skipped in his chest.

When he didn't speak, Jaden bit her finger and rubbed it on the woman. Her previous anger at him subsided with her hunger. The wound on the woman's wrist tried to heal, but continued to ooze. Jaden looked helplessly at Tyr. She began to bite her finger again, when his voice stopped her.

"It will take time for your body to gain strength," he said. Healing the mortal with his own blood, he waited for her to leave. When they were alone, Tyr's eyes dipped over Jaden's wet clothes. His gaze lit with fire. His movements were slow but she could detect every subtle change in him. The meal had revived her senses.

The blood renewed her body with a mysterious force. Suddenly, her skin tingled and her limbs burned. The water became a naughty caress, her clothes felt constrictive and binding. She was sensitive. Every nerve ending inside of her was alive and searching. Wiggling in growing physical distress, she looked at Tyr in astonishment.

"Here," he whispered, knowing what was happening to her. It had happened to him once, though he couldn't remember it. His hand reached out to touch her neck. It slid with the help of beading moisture to caress over her skin and to delve into her hair. Jaden let loose a soft moan. Her lashes fluttered over her eyes as she arched towards his searching hand. His fingers glided down the base of her neck, pulling over the soft indent that guarded the entryway to her chest. In a low, husky murmur, he said, "You still need to bathe."

Jaden nodded in agreement, before uttering, "But I thought vampires didn't need to bathe."

"They don't unless they fall into dirt and blood as you have. Besides, you are newly turned. You must wash off the smell of your human self. The council has ordered you cleaned," he continued drawing forward over the edge. Again she nodded, the motion becoming hurried. Tyr lips barely moved, as he said, "And I am your master. I am responsible for making sure you obey the council's wishes."

"I--I," she tried to protest. She didn't want to clean up. She wanted to end the torment raging within her flesh. She wanted his fingers to rip through her clothing.

"Sh," he said, aroused to the point of explosion. "I am your master. You must obey--"

"I never listened well," she broke in breathlessly.

"Then I'll have to make sure you comply," Tyr murmured, liking his idea very much. Looking over her flushed, warm skin, he pronounced, "First, we must rid you of these offending clothes."

Jaden's eyes turned wide. She saw that Tyr had no intention of leaving. His mouth parted, his eyes fell to her breasts. He could see the line of her bra beneath the wet, stained material.

"Take it off," he ordered. He released her, settling back in preparation of a show. When she hesitated, he said, "You cannot deny me--especially in this place."

Jaden shyly grabbed her shirt but didn't take it off. Tyr smiled a dark grin full of wicked intent.

"Do it," he ordered, low and dark.

Jaden sunk down into the water. Pulling the material over her head she flung it at his arrogant head. He caught it easily, dropping it to the floor without breaking contact with his piercing eyes.

"Now the rest," he ordered hoarsely.

Jaden slowly worked on her jeans. She had never given total control over to someone. The closest she had come was when Tyr made tender love to her in his cave, before everything went to hell. The memory only served her body to course with a yearning need. Her arms trembled. She wanted him, but she was frightened of him.

Tyr enjoyed his role of the master, liking that she had to obey him, for Jaden had never obeyed anyone. It made him heady with power. But with that delicate power he knew he couldn't abuse it. He wasn't going to give her anything she didn't already want.

The jeans flew at his head in the same fashion, followed by a bra. He dodged them with a slight tilt to the side. A smirk lined his features. As underwear soared by, he caught them in his grasp, one arm still resting over his chest. Without looking, he ran his thumb over the wet lacy material in a sensual caress.

Jaden glared rebelliously at him. She could just feel the strokes of his fingers as if he touched her most intimate places. Mustering indignation, she ordered, "Now, go away. I can do the rest myself with no help from you."

"Ah," he began, with a mock sense of sorrow. "It's my duty to see that you comply. I'll have to watch just to make sure."

Jaden's cheeks colored, something very rare in a vampire. She met Tyr's look. Her stomach tensed. Her loins grew hotter beneath the water.

Tyr greedily licked his lips. His eyes glowed fiercely, as he growled, "Now stand up."

Jaden, in all her stubborn pride, ignored the command. Reaching to grab a bar of soap on the edge, she lathered it up and began scrubbing her feet. Tyr feigned a scowl, though it was hard with the heated blood running a fervent course in his body.

When she finished with her calves and moved the soap underwater to work her way up her legs, Tyr narrowed his eyes and said, "I ordered you to stand up."

Jaden smiled to herself, ignoring him again. She pressed her lips together and hummed a solemnly sweet tune. The soap made its way over her arms and neck.

Tyr leaned forward, crawling to the edge of the tub on all fours. Both of them forgot their troubles as they became immersed in their game. Jaden couldn't resist and peeked at him from beneath her lashes. Ducking under the water, she rinsed the suds and rewetted her hair. When she emerged, she continued to hum.

Blinking away water, she broke long enough to say, "Hand me the shampoo."

"Are you trying to command me now?" he asked in bewildered amusement, his eyes dripping with confidence. He shouldn't have been surprised or disappointed, though the feelings were there. He knew Jaden wouldn't take to being ordered about.

Jaden grimaced. She reached over and grabbed it for herself and began lathering her locks. Again she dunked beneath the surface and rinsed the tresses clean. When she resurfaced, Tyr was leaning close. His hands cupped conditioner in his palms. Leaning over, he pushed his fingers into her hair, rubbing the conditioner through her heavy wet length. Jaden kept her gaze focused on his face. Mischievously, he lowered his gaze past her neck to her breasts bobbing on top of the water.

"I've had enough of your disobedience," he growled. "Stand and let me inspect you."

Jaden swallowed, a bit nervous, but too excited by his brashness to deny the command another time. She rinsed her hair quickly. Her legs trembled as she stood before him. His eyes hungrily devoured the look of her. His nostrils flared in animalistic potency. She watched his hands flex with tempered control.

Tyr took in her brilliance. Not even the Norse goddess Freya could've been as beautiful as she was to him. His head tilted to the side. His fingers lifted slowly to her cheek. He searched her eyes, trying to find the truth within her, trying to end the questions of his soul. But what his heart asked, his lips couldn't form.

His finger grazed beneath the soft skin under her eye with the molding precision of a sculpture enamored of his stone. He learned her face, taking each curve to memory. His body ached for her, it always ached for her. But there was more. His heart ached for her too. He could no longer deny it.

"I'll lie for you," he whispered hoarsely, the torment of the admission warring within him. "I'll lie to save you."

His words broke her heart. What was his lie, if he believed it truly to be a lie? He still thought her guilty of crimes she didn't commit. He didn't believe in her. Gulping, she shook her head in denial. Biting her lips together, she bid softly, "No, let only truths as you know them pass by your lips. Don't sacrifice your integrity for me. I have enough that I must live with. Don't add that to my regrets."

"Jaden--" he began. She shook her head, cutting off his words. Pride refused to let her explain or defend herself. Her hand lifted to his parted mouth, blocking off any attempt to convince her otherwise.

Tyr didn't want her to face the judgment of the council. He knew it would be easier for them to just kill her and let that be the end of it. If he pleaded on her behalf or claimed the right of ending her as her maker, then he could assure that the death was painless and swift. But, he didn't want to end her. He wanted her to live.

Her jade eyes glistened as they looked at him. For a moment, as she blinked, he felt the whole realm of her pain. Cocking her head to the side, she managed a smile. Shrugging delicately, she said, "Only the truth. Promise me."

"Yes," he whispered against her fingers. Closing his eyes, he whispered, "I promise."

Satisfied, she tried to pull her hand away. His fingers lifted from her face to grab her departing hand close. His mouth opened, placing a delicately tender kiss on her palm, dragging his pointed fangs over her skin. Jaden shivered.

"Cold?" he asked.

"I'm always cold," she returned impishly. "It is part of the charm of being dead."

"No," he murmured, his hand dipping behind her back to pull her to his chest. He extended her arm to the side in the beginning steps of a dance. Drying beads of moisture on her breasts and stomach soaked into his shirt, heating instantly between their bodies. Leaning to her mouth, he murmured against it, "Not always cold."

His kiss was light, exploring as if he had an eternity to execute it. His hands roamed her, stroking her back in unhurried caresses. His grasp found her buttocks and lifted her with ease. Jaden wrapped her legs around his waist. She felt his bold arousal growing to press into her. She moaned in weak encouragement.

Breaking away, she whispered, "Make love to me, Tyr. I want to feel anything besides fear and uncertainty."

Tyr groaned to hear her say the words of her own free will. He let her slip to the floor. Within seconds he was stripped of his clothing and had her back into his embrace. There flesh became a frenzied playground for the senses. Hands rediscovered hidden crevices. Mouths pressed and teased throats and arms.

Jaden's fingers twined into his long, dry hair. It felt like silk against her skin. His hard flesh molded her body to him, demanding she yield to his hard muscles. Eagerly, she rubbed against him, unable to feel enough of his potent form. His kiss strayed over her shoulder, glancing down the front hollow of her throat. Jaden felt the power in him, felt the primal beast beneath his surface wanting to come out and play.

Jaden's body couldn't process all of the new sensations of her altered form. Tyr lifted her about his waist and began backing towards the bed, carrying her with him. Jaden wanted him too badly. She angled herself above him as he walked, impaling her body deeply onto his hardened member with a scream of delight.

Tyr gasped in mystification as she took instant control. Her long legs wrapped around him, calculating the movements of her hips. Her vampiric strength kept her balanced as she pressed into his shoulders for support. Her fingernails anchored into his flesh to draw blood. He quivered in ecstasy.

Tyr grabbed her hips, encouraging the desperation of her motions. They crashed together, pumping and writhing in elation and enchantment. Both of them had a need to be filled, a desire that needed to be tamed, and a rawness that needed to be explored and conquered. Too much was unsaid, too much had been done. Now was the time for the echoing silence of rumbles and moans. The world and all its woes fell away, blocked out by the thin veil of pleasure that surrounded them. Nothing else mattered, nothing beyond the touch of a hand, a kiss of a mouth, a thrust of two bodies as they became one.

Jaden's hands ran down over Tyr's working buttocks, delighting in the strain of his strong muscles. Tyr growled the sound of a ravishing beast that took what he wanted. Spinning with undead force, he dropped her on the bed, keeping their bodies together. Jaden landed in the soft white fur. It tickled her responsive flesh as she sprawled out beneath him. Her legs draped over the side, wrapping around Tyr as he stood.

Tyr kept his feet on the floor. Lifting her legs over his shoulders, he pumped his hips with abandonment. Through the narrowed slits of his eyes, he saw Jaden's hands grasping the fur above her head. He saw her peaked nipples, erotically hard, bouncing in wicked invitation. He leaned forward and grabbed her shoulders, anchoring his feet to the stone as he drove into her.

Jaden's feet flexed and folded into the air by the side of his head. As he bent over her, he could press deeper into her core. Screaming out in pleasure, her need matched his. The fire built within them, echoing between their bodies as they felt the other's emotions coursing throughout them. They tried to hold onto the moment. They tried to forget the future. They drove it away with their yearning. All they had was now, this one moment when they were together, exploding in unison as a keg of black powder to a match.

Jaden's yell echoed the chamber. Tyr's viciously hollered victory reverberated to join her. They didn't care who heard them, couldn't think to. Tyr released himself into her, pouring out all the emotion he couldn't tell her with words. And Jaden took it, never understanding how he truly felt.

He stood transfixed, thrust wholly inside of her, enjoying the feel of her subsiding quivers, knowing he had done it to her. Jaden gasped, her back arching lightly. Pulling out of her sensitive warmth, he withdrew his member with purposeful slowness. Jaden trembled, feeling every inch of him as he left her.

"Mmm," Jaden hummed for a lack of words, after the shivering subsided enough for her to move. Her mouth parted in a gasp of feminine rapture.

Tyr chuckled, the laugh of a sated being. Jaden weakly clawed her way back on the bed, pulling her weakened legs up to join her. Tyr crawled forward landing at her side.

Looking over at him, she admitted with a catlike purr of contentment, "I feel as if I should be breathless. My heart is beating so fast."

"It takes awhile to get use to it," he said with a predatory grin.

Jaden's face fell. She turned her expression to the ceiling. She might not have awhile.

"No," he whispered. "Don't think about it. Think about me. Think about now."

I always think about you, she admitted silently, though she would never let him hear it. *Since the night I saw you in the alley, you are all I ever think about.*

Tyr's hand roamed to her body. His heart still hammered from their lovemaking, but his body craved her with an urgency that couldn't be filled. Seeing a look in her eyes as they roamed over the ceiling, he asked, "What is it?"

"I was just wondering how it is we can sleep down here and not be in a coffin," she responded as the thought filtered through her head.

"This whole island use to be a burial ground," he answered absently. Kissing her with a devastating thoroughness, he probed in naughty mischief, "You didn't want to sleep, did you?"

Jaden smiled, hiding her fear well within her breast. She never wanted to sleep again. Instead of answering, she kissed him. Her arms wrapped around his body and they made love all through the vampire night. Only near dusk out of sheer exhaustion did they finally drift into sleep, cradled in each other's arms, clinging to the last moments of their time together.

* * * *

The next evening, Jaden was awakened by a servitor. The mortal woman's eyes stared past Jaden's shoulder as she tugged the vampiress' naked body insistently from the bed. Jaden stood, stretching her arms above her head. Turning, she glanced down at Tyr. His face was still, his chest unmoving. She smiled sadly. His hair was disheveled from their lovemaking, scattered majestically over their pillows, and yet he still managed to look perfect.

Jaden stood. Her body stung with sweetened contentment. The servitor handed her clothes. It was a white robe to match those of the servants. Jaden slipped into the fine linen, glad that it was at least thick enough to hide her nakedness.

She began to reach over to wake Tyr, but the hand on her arm stopped her. The servitor shook her head, motioning silently that Jaden was to follow her alone. Jaden gulped, not understanding and not wanting to leave Tyr behind. They hadn't talked of what should happen this day. They hadn't talked of their short future.

The servitor led her from the chamber, moving with the silent presence of a ghost. Jaden trailed behind her, bare feet sweeping in light brushes over the clean floor. The stones were cold against her skin, the flimsy garment offering little in the way of warmth. Jaden smiled ruefully. It was her body that offered little warmth to the garment. Suddenly, the servitor stopped. Turning, she pushed open a solid door affixed with only the Drauger symbol.

"Ragnhild," Jaden whispered, automatically remembering the old

Viking leader.

She followed the lifeless gestures to enter. Hugging the linen over her chest, she suddenly felt naked without undergarments. Resignedly, she looked around the dim chamber. It was laid out much in the same way as Tyr's only with more lavishness to the décor and there were no books. Jaden's eyes instantly found the vampire lounging back amidst brown fur. His bare shoulders peeked out from beneath the coverlet.

"You--you sent for me?" Jaden cleared her throat. Ragnhild threw back his covers revealing a woman hidden beneath, clinging to his waist. The woman yawned, blinking as she looked around in the firelight. Then, with the passionless grace of one of the zombie servants, she slipped on her clothing and left.

Seeing the pale vampire unabashedly naked, Jaden diverted her eyes. The act of modesty amused Ragnhild greatly and he laughed, murmuring in a language too old for her to understand. With no gesture from him, the fireplace blazed at his side with a brighter flame. For a moment, he studied her in the firelight.

"You have eaten," he said matter-of-factly. Appreciation of beauty alighted on his feature in a brief cast. "It has done you very well."

Jaden shivered at his husky tone. She glanced behind her to the closed door. Ragnhild ignored her discomfort as he slipped breeches over his legs, letting the laces hang open at the side. Then, staying bare-chested, he crossed over to the trembling young one.

Jaden's thoughts raced frantically. She hugged her arms about her tighter. She could feel a potent sexuality coming from the ancient Norseman.

Ragnhild leaned over, murmuring into her ear, "I have no use of you that way, little one. As you have seen, I have a servant who sees to those needs."

Jaden jolted, relieved and alarmed. Ragnhild paused to sniff her, sensing Tyr's recent claim. When he had paced fully around her in inspection, he went back to the bed to lean on the end.

"Why have you sent for me?" Jaden managed quietly in growing trepidation.

"*Certainement,*" he murmured quietly in a perfect accent. "*Apprendre vous.*"

Jaden eyed him, unsure how to answer. Weakly, she repeated, "Certainly…?"

"You don't understand me, do you dhampir?" His brows furrowed quizzically on his handsome face.

Jaden shook her head.

"And," Ragnhild began in a murmur. He turned, producing the damning folder from beneath the fur at the end of his bed. He held it up for her inspection. "You cannot read this."

"No," she admitted weakly. "I can't. I don't know what it says."

"I figured as much. But because you cannot read it, does not mean you were not involved with it. Your ties to your uncle run deep, do they not?"

"Yes," she answered honestly. Quietly, she added, "He raised me when my mother died."

"Ah, Rhona, was it not?" Ragnhild asked.

"Yes."

"And Bhaltair?"

"He was my father." Jaden looked him square in the eye. Not waiting to be asked, she said, "His death was my responsibility."

"Ah," Ragnhild said thoughtfully. "Taking full responsibility for it?"

"Yes," she whispered. "I am."

"And do you believe that you should be punished for it?"

Jaden instinctively knew this creature could probe her and find the truth. But instead he waited for her to answer. She didn't dare lie to him. In a solemn whisper, she said, "Yes."

"And the mortal we have captured?"

"He has nothing to do with this and should be set free. He is an honorable man who was only trying to rescue me out of a misplaced sense of duty." Jaden refused to meet Ragnhild's eyes. "If you let me talk to him, I can assure you he will cause you no more harm. He belongs in the human military and I have told him as much. Humans are always on the brink of war. He will be busy and needed."

Ragnhild waved his hand as if unconcerned for their mortal prisoner. His face was blank, not even drawing in thoughtfulness. It was as much of a dismissal as she would get from him. The same servitor who had awakened Jaden opened the door and stepped in. Gently, the woman pulled on Jaden's elbow to signify that she was to follow.

Jaden left, wondering at the strange interview and not knowing if what she had said made a bit of difference. Ragnhild was too old and powerful for her to try and sense. Even her developed dhampir senses wouldn't have detected him unless he so wished it. It was like reading a corpse in the grave--nothing but infinite blackness.

Jaden trailed silently through the hall, making her way back to Tyr's room. The servitor left after opening the door for her. When Jaden walked inside, Tyr was gone.

Chapter Sixteen

Tyr eyes roamed evenly over the council hall. He could still smell the light scent of Jaden's body on his skin--exotic as cinnamon--and he knew that the elders must have detected it also. They didn't question him about it and he didn't offer. Clenching his fists, he could still feel her soft flesh on his palms. The curves of her lip were still imprinted to his mouth.

The door opened and Ragnhild entered. Tyr nodded to the vampire. Ragnhild took his place amongst them, turning to look at Tyr with the same uniformity the others displayed.

"Where is the dhampir?" Tyr asked, unable to resist knowing. His hand trembled and he balled it into a tight fist. "Has she been sent to her punishment?"

"No," Ragnhild clipped evenly.

Tyr felt relief sweep him. He hadn't realized the fear that had overtaken him since discovering Jaden was missing from his bed. He had reached for her before fully waking only to find her gone.

"Let us get to the point," Chara sighed. She cocked her head, her eyes boring into Tyr's. "Do you think she's guilty of killing her father?"

Tyr considered lying. It rose up on his lips. Remembering his promise, he couldn't do it. Nodding his head, he said, "She is inadvertently responsible though she did not deal the death blow. However I do not think she meant it."

"Meant it?" Andrei laughed. "Bhaltair is dead. There's enough meaning in that."

Tyr nodded.

"And of the other crimes, do you think she has committed them?" Ragnhild asked.

"Yes," Tyr answered, his jaw becoming stiff. "She had the folder in her bag. When I abducted her from her uncle's building for questioning I took the bag not knowing its contents. She then later omitted telling me of the existence of the documents on several occasions. I found them."

"And do you *feel* that she has committed these crimes?" Ragnhild asked. To their highly evolved senses, feelings were just as important as logic.

Tyr swallowed. He couldn't keep the truth from being voiced. "No. I don't sense the cruelty in her."

"Is it true," Pietro stated in distaste, "that you have become ... involved with this dhampir?"

"Yes," Tyr answered. There was no point in denying that either. They could smell it on him.

"His judgment is affected by a weakness of the flesh," Pietro muttered cruelly. "I say we kill her and be done with it."

"Pietro," Chara said. "You grow wearisome in your old age. I think you wish for the entire world to die--including yourself. If you are so miserable, why don't you find yourself a nice sunrise to watch? I am sure the brilliant colors will make you happy."

Pietro grumbled and held silent.

"What, no response?" Chara goaded.

"Is your judgment affected?" Theophania asked quietly, readily breaking into her sister's verbal attack on Pietro.

"I do not believe that it is," he answered. Daring to turn his eyes around to Pietro, he whispered, "Duty is duty and I have always done mine. Feel inside me if you think me dishonest."

Pietro waved his hand, disinterested. Tyr nodded and turned back around to Theophania.

"Do you think to love her?" Curiosity burning brightly in Theophania's eyes, as she continued to speak, as if uninterrupted, "Do you remember what love is, Tyr? Can you feel it coursing in your veins? Because what you feel cannot be that human love echoing in your mind. Vampires are not made for love, for the emotion is not made to last for an eternity. The sooner you kill any inkling of it, the sooner you'll find some sort of peace. I have seen the greatest brought low by the memories of it. I had thought you old enough and wise enough to know better. For our kind, especially you my dark knight, it is better to be alone. So, tell me, Tyr of the Drauger. Tell me, do you think to love this dhampir?"

Her words were soft. As she finished, Theophania eyes narrowed in sorrow. Something in her was daring him to deny her, begging him to. Tyr hesitated, not knowing how to answer. Could he lie? Did he even know the truth anymore? The elders watched him carefully for a response. They all knew the myth of the vampire being an unfeeling being was just that, a myth. Vampires were like humans, only more. They were driven by more, felt more, craved more. They could feel and in the beginning did so often, reveling in the pleasure and pain of it all, conquering the world like Gods. But, as it must, time hardens what is left of the soul if ever a soul they had. The only certainty was that time for them would go on. And time held a great many changes. There was no reason to cling to what must inevitably pass.

Tyr's eyes fell to the ground. He knew the council would try to save him from himself. How could he admit what he didn't himself know? If he did think to love her, would they kill her to protect and keep their soldier? Lust, desire, need--these were things he could know for certain.

They were superficial, temporary, readily discovered all over again. As they waited, Tyr didn't speak. There was nothing he could say.

* * * *

Jaden sat alone in Tyr's room, unable to move from her place on the end of the bed. Closing her eyes, she tried to feel him. Her memory sensed him on the coverlet--the scent of him, so familiar. She had no idea how much time passed before she was retrieved by the same servitor. The woman led her needlessly to the hall. Jaden could've found her way. The sensations behind the thick oak door willed her onward.

As she entered the hall, she glanced around. Tyr was gone. Her heart thumped solemnly in her barren chest. Remembering his words about strength, she walked forward, her chin not too proud and not too meek. Looking at the hollow table, she stood on the outside edge.

The tribal leaders stared at her in expectation. Theophania waved her into the middle. Jaden nodded. Going forward, she hesitated before reaching to climb over the Moroi spot on the circle. She struggled with her skirts, trying not to let them ride up as she sat and swung her legs over to the side.

Andrei laughed in self-amusement. He murmured to no one in particular, "He hasn't trained her to her nature at all. So young she is."

Jaden hopped down to the ground, feeling as if she was stepping into a pit of snakes. Facing Theophania, she came to stand by the torch that settled from the ceiling to rest on the floor. She felt Pietro's eyes boring into her back and did her best to keep her mind blank as she waited.

Chara's head cocked to the side and she smiled. Letting her eyes roam sensually over Jaden's body in appreciation, she murmured, "So pretty. So fresh."

Andrei's gaze alighted on her and he gave her a wicked, lopsided grin of appreciation.

"You stand accused of experimenting on defenseless vampires for the sake of human knowledge and gain," Theophania began without preamble. "Name the vampire who helped you in this, and we will be lenient."

"I don't know who did it. But--" Jaden was cut off with a hard look.

"Will you let us inside of your head to prove the answer we seek is not there?" Chara asked.

"I know it's not," Jaden said. She looked at their cold faces. She didn't want them to read inside of her, to invade her. They might find her love for Tyr. They might discover how she fooled him into becoming locked in the prison. She didn't want him hurt. "I didn't know about the experiments until I found that folder."

"Then why did you try to hide the evidence of it?" Amon asked.

Jaden looked around helplessly.

"What are you hiding, dhampir?" Vishnu asked.

"Let us in," Andrei cried.

She felt them all coming at her. She lifted up her hands, fighting off the invisible attacks. Falling to the ground, she lifted her hands over her head and rocked herself.

"Stay out, stay out," she exclaimed desperately. Suddenly, the onslaught stopped. She raised her eyes from her place on the floor. Not bothering to stand, she whispered miserably, "I have killed vampires. I admit to that. I'm a dhampir and bloodstalker. I've sat in judgment of the vampire kind. But I hunt no more and now I've been made one of you. I don't know what it means to be one of you. I never asked to see an eternity. In fact, the night I found Tyr, I only asked for death."

The council held quiet, listening patiently to her words--analyzing them desperately for their answers.

"I don't know anymore if what I have done is just. It isn't in me to decide. I did what I had to. I did my duty." Jaden looked around at the cold, unmoving faces. She saw her guilt reflected in the blank features. They condemned her before they met her. There was nothing she could say to change that. If she couldn't defend herself, then she would just say want she wanted to say. "A human life is nothing to you, a single grain of sand on an endless beach. But the humans were my people, my tribe, and I was protecting them."

"But you have a new tribe," Theophania said. "You are no longer human."

"Yes," she answered. Jaden looked over at Ragnhild's immovable face. "I am vampire, descendent of Ragnhild of the Drauger. But I am also the dhampir, the ex-bloodstalker, daughter of Rhona and Bhaltair. I was once human, as were you all. I have not forgotten that."

"We speak of crimes, dhampir," Chara whispered. "Not loyalty."

"But being a bloodstalker was done out of loyalty," Jaden answered from her place on the floor. "Loyalty to my dead mother and to her people."

"We understand loyalty, dhampir," Ragnhild said. He placed his hand on the thick stack of papers sitting before him. "That does not explain the atrocities shown here."

"We speak of vampires turned and raped repeatedly for cruel pleasure and money--ravished during changing, during death," Theophania put in. "We speak of prolonging the agony of vampiric death by serums and torture. We refer to the denial of blood. These things cannot be tolerated. Humans are beneath us, dhampir. They are cattle to us. Wouldn't your humans seek out and kill the farm animals that ravished and killed mortals? Would you not have them slaughtered?"

"But vampires commit worse crimes unto each other," Jaden answered wisely. "I've seen it."

"That's our business," Chara stated with a hard toss of her head. The others nodded in agreement. "We have our own laws."

"Do you deny you have done these things?" Amon asked pointedly.

"Yes," Jaden answered. "I deny it. I have told you what I have done. I was a hunter. I hunted. I never captured. I never tortured."

"Then you'll let us read you," Ragnhild whispered logically. "If you told us everything, you have nothing to hide."

"Why waste the time?" Pietro bemoaned, secretly fearful of the confidences she might hold within.

"We must know who betrayed us!" Chara growled violently. Her eyes flashed as she stared angrily at Pietro. Her hatred of him bubbled forth.

Jaden watched in fascination. All of a sudden, she understood. The 'trial', the intentionally fearful anticipation of waiting, the little show they put on for her laying out her crimes, it was just a way to get her to confess. It was an elaborate scheme to get her to reveal who they believed her to know. They were fearful of the vampire who dared to betray them, the one who dared to defy the council of vampire elders--the one who evaded them. And being the supreme beings they believed themselves to be, they didn't know how to handle that fear and doubt. They didn't care about her. They didn't care if she lived or died. They just wanted a name, a face that they could go after.

They probably didn't even care about Mack except that he offended their bored pride. And bored they were, these archaic relics gleaning onto the past. Jaden could feel their boredom, their tired eternity. Beyond that, she could feel their dying essence. They were immortal--all powerful beings--and yet they were powerless against the onslaught of ever-changing time. They were lost in a modern world, one they didn't have the energy to understand. And, in being lost, they were immobilized against it. Not even their judgments could assuage their exhausted wisdom of forever. They were beasts that needed to be quickened and yet couldn't find the spring from which to do so.

"Read me," she said finally, knowing that her relationship with Tyr wasn't what they looked for. "Do it and be quick."

Jaden stood. She raised her arms out in offering of her body. She stared directly into Theophania's eyes. The vampiress' orbs glowed with an eerie green. She felt the woman enter her. And Theophania wasn't alone. Amon and Vishnu joined her and then Ragnhild, Chara and Andrei. She could hear them in her head, talking in a dead language, chanting out her secrets. Finally, they were joined by a reluctant Pietro, who seemed to keep his thoughts on the outermost edge of hers. Pietro didn't probe, only watched and listened.

Her head rolled back. Her body suspended off the floor as she was forced up into the air. Her limbs dangled like a rag doll. All her past deeds flashed in an instant, every emotion she had ever felt, every lustful encounter, every embarrassment, catching up to the death of her father. She felt the pain anew, swift and strong and so surprising. She felt as she did in the alley facing Tyr. She felt the lethargic need she had for death and realized that she didn't feel that way anymore. That she hadn't felt like that in a long time--not since meeting him. Tyr made her feel alive.

Unexpectedly, her love for Tyr burst forth like a ray of light. The council drew back almost instantly as they sensed it. Their eyes cleared as Jaden lowered to the floor in exhaustion. Her body shook, violated and cold and so very weak.

Theophania raised a hand. A servitor entered. With a sigh, she voiced lowly, "Call Tyr."

Jaden waited anxiously on the floor. Her eyes stared at the velvet drapes. Her heart thudded with nervous anticipation. She wondered if she had done the right thing.

Then suddenly he was there, striding into the chamber. His eyes found her in the circle. In a flash he was next to her, standing proudly before the council. Jaden wanted to reach out and touch him, to pull his hand into hers. But her body was weak from the elder's intrusion. It took all her will to lift her head to look at him from her place on the floor.

"It is clear you have killed, child, but you are now a vampire and allowed the occasional sin," Theophania began. Jaden didn't dare to hope. She trembled, looking up at Tyr. She no longer wanted death. She wanted to live. She wanted a life--whatever kind of life it may be--with him. She bit her lips, as the vampiress continued, "Mortal laws do not apply to us. Had you been human, we would've killed you instead of bothering with you."

Jaden felt a dim hope forming inside her. She tensed, waiting. Tyr reached down, urging her off the floor to stand.

"We have read you," Ragnhild said. "We know the full truth of what you have done."

Tyr glanced at his leader in question.

For the sake of the knight, Ragnhild continued, "The crimes contained within the MacNaughton documents are not hers. She had no knowledge of them or her part in them."

Tyr felt a relief come over him. He felt Jaden sway at his side. Glancing down at her, he wondered why she hadn't told him herself. He knew the answer. It was her pride.

"However...." Theophania said.

Jaden's hope faltered. Tyr's body stiffened once more. The fluttering of her heart joined his, pounding in his ears.

"...the Dark Knights are a sacred and ancient order. They are a secret, even to the vampire tribes. Knowledge of their existence is forbidden," the vampiress continued.

"As is their procreation," Chara added, with a pointed look directed at Tyr. Tyr held quiet, staring forward. He felt each of Jaden's movements, each nervous quiver.

"Discovering proof of their existence is punishable by death, for both mortals and immortals," Theophania said. "As a knight, you know this is our law. It's important that the secrecy of the order remains for the sake of the vampire tribes. If you were to be discovered Tyr, there would be chaos."

Tyr nodded. He knew it was true. The laws vampires were forced to abide, though few as they were, were still laws. Tyr and his fellow knights had broken almost all of them. To know that the council bade them to do it, the vampire nation would crumble. There would be a rebellion. Whenever war broke out of chaos, there would be many deaths.

Jaden paled, wobbling weakly on her legs, wanting to sink back onto the hard stone. She gazed weakly at Tyr. Only his will kept her on her feet. After all they had put her through they were going to kill her on a technicality.

"You said you know your duty, Try," Pietro mocked from behind. There was a cruel pleasure in his tone.

"I made her," Tyr said with a bravery he didn't feel. Turning his face to hers, he announced, "I'll end her."

Jaden gasped in surprise and stared at him. She could still smell him on her skin and he was talking about killing her now! She didn't want to die, not anymore. She'd been a depressed, lost fool to ask it of him. Then she'd said she wanted death just to aggravate and confuse him. Only too late did she realize that she wanted to live--forever with him.

Tyr kept a straight face out of old habit. Inside a war waged within his chest. All Jaden had ever asked from him was death. He should have given it to her that first night in the alley. Then none of their misfortunes would've come to pass.

If death must be delivered, Tyr knew that he could make sure it would be painless. The tribal council wouldn't be so kind. No, it was his duty to her and to the council. He owed it to her. No matter how distasteful he found it.

"That is how it should be," Pietro said bitterly. "Death."

Jaden trembled. Her gaze darted around to the impassable faces. She'd expected the decision, but part of her always thought she had a chance. As the words were pronounced, she wasn't ready for the verdict.

"Death!" Andrei cried with a jovial wave of his hand.

Jaden's knees weakened. She dropped to the floor once more. Her stomach churned and her mind reeled. In a daze she felt Tyr reaching down to grab her. Her frantic eyes flew to his. She tensed.

Then, seeing the tenderness in his gaze, she reached out to grab his hand. Her body shook as he pulled her to standing with his strength. She could feel his mind trying to take over hers. His strength wavered slightly as he drew her into his chest.

Tenderly, he bent her head to the side. Jaden didn't struggle. His mouth brushed her neck. If she had to die, she could think of no better place than in his arms. Fangs punctured into her flesh setting off a white hot flame. Blood flowed over her neck, staining the front of her white linen gown. Jaden could feel Tyr's lips kiss her deeply as she gave herself over to him. She quivered beneath his touch, the enraptured web of his mind in hers. And then it was over.

"Not so quickly," Theophania said in quiet consideration

The flavor of her vampire blood was in his mouth. Tyr swallowed, drawing slowly away at the vampiress' words.

Jaden was again left weakened, this time from blood loss, and she fell to the floor. She buried her head in her shaking hands. Sticky blood met her fingers. She couldn't do it anymore. Her heart beat slowed. Her mind started to fog. That distant place of insanity called to her, welcoming her back. Jaden tried to fight it, but she hadn't the strength to resist its pull.

The council's eyes turned to Theophania, as she said solicitously, "We may have a use for this dhampir. It may be in undue haste to end her just yet. Besides, anyone of us could kill her at anytime."

Chara nodded in agreement. Tyr held still. He could feel the numbing sensations taking over Jaden. Looking down at her, he drew his mind into hers. Her jade eyes widened in surprise as she gazed up at him. He willed her to stand, using his strength to keep her calm. Then, when she was again at her feet, he turned forward, part of him still keeping inside of her, keeping her sane.

"You are a dhampir, a vampire hunter. Yet you have also shown courage and your leniency with many vampires is well documented. Taking into account your human skill as a hunter," Theophania said, "and your knowledge of the council and the tribes, I am not sure death is our best use of you."

She looked around at the others, some of them giving silent nods of consent. Andrei waved his hand, not caring.

"And she is one of us," Ragnhild whispered in defense of his daughter. Jaden glanced at him in surprise. His face was emotionless, but she felt a rush of pride come from him as he looked at his children in the center of the council. Tyr and Jaden had done him very proud.

"I think we should test her," Chara said.

"Yes," Theophania nodded. Turning to Jaden, she directed a hard stare at her. "If you pass this test, we'll let you live. You'll train as knights before you have. You'll be an apprentice. We could use new blood within our folds and your knowledge of modern human weaponry will no doubt come in most useful for us. It's whispered that humans are harnessing the power of the sun."

Jaden thought of Mack and said nothing.

"And what is this test?" Tyr asked.

"The mortal in the cell," Theophania said simply. "You'll go to him, find out what he knows of MacNaughton and his vampire contact. Kill him if you must. If you get the information from him, you'll live."

Pietro stiffened, thinking of Rick. It was clear that Jaden had no knowledge of his part in Mack's crimes. The others ignored him.

"Tyr, you'll go with her. Her vampire strength is not yet up. You'll be able to detect the man's lies." Ragnhild waved his hand. "Go."

Jaden felt herself being whisked up into Tyr's arms. The elder's faces blurred before her. She had no time to answer. Soon they were in the prison hall, walking towards the cells.

"Wait," Jaden whispered grabbing Tyr's arm. Turning him around, she asked fervently, "What does this mean?"

"They are going to make you a knight," Tyr said evenly. Biting his finger, it shook as he healed her neck. "You'll apprentice under me. Now, come on. The council won't like to be kept waiting."

Jaden felt a smile beginning to spread across her face. Then seeing his dark look of rage, she frowned. "You're angry. You don't want me to be with you?"

"I can't trust you," he said. "You have lied to me endlessly. And if I can't trust you, how can I work with you?"

"But the council said I didn't do it," she whispered. "You know the truth."

"I can't trust you. You lied to me about the folder," Tyr said. *You lied about your love for me.*

"What about last night? What was that?"

"That was last night," he whispered with an unfeeling evenness. He was glad she was given a chance, but he couldn't help his outrage. It was easier than admitting the feelings he was hiding within.

"Then, by all means, take me to Rick," she growled in growing indignation. "Now!"

Tyr nodded, whisking down the hall. Jaden was quick behind him. In her ire, her speed increased to keep up with him until she felt the world blur. Stopping at an unmarked door, Tyr slid the latch and stepped in. Jaden's eyes instantly found Rick in the dark. He looked up at her, blinking heavily.

"Jade?" he whispered.

"Yes, Rick," she ignored Tyr and rushed forward to kneel beside her friend. Touching Rick's face tenderly, she said, "I'm here. I've come to talk to you."

"Who is with you?" Rick asked, squinting to look behind her head. The man was weak from a beating and starved.

"It's not important," she whispered. "I need to talk to you."

"They've come to execute me, haven't they?" Rick nodded, expecting as much.

Looking earnestly at him, Jaden asked, "Were you part of it? Did you know what Mack was up to? Did you know about the experiments he did? About the things he allowed to be done to vampires and humans?"

"No," he gulped. Jaden could see the honesty in his eyes. "They already asked me that, Jade. I didn't do the things they accuse me of."

"Have you ever seen Mack with a vampire?" Jaden asked doubtfully. She detected new welts on his body where a vampire had beaten him. Biting her hand, she rubbed it gingerly over a raw wound on his arm. Rick winced and pulled away. The wound healed slightly but was still red and puffy.

"Yes," he whispered. "Here on the island."

Jaden glanced at Tyr. Under her breath, she said, "He means Mykonos."

Tyr nodded, but held back.

"Yes, Mykonos," Rick whispered. "Why?"

"Do you know who it was? Did you see his face?" Jaden insisted. "This is very important."

"No." Rick shook his head. Rubbing wearily at his temple, he said, "It was dark. Mack was meeting him in an alleyway, letting him drink off his arm. Then later he told me he had a contact. I got the impression the man was higher up. He said the vampire council was going to be restructured."

"That's why the council doesn't care about me," Jaden whispered. "They only want the traitor."

"What?" Rick blinked. Tyr frowned, hearing her words.

"What else?" Jaden persisted. "You have to tell me, Rick."

"The vampire knew the boat schedule and when you should be arriving with Tyr. That is why we were on the beach waiting for you." Rick grunted, as he repositioned himself on the floor. Grabbing his temple he rubbed it and said, "But you know Mack, he's a liar. Who knows if what he says is true?"

"A knight?" Jaden glanced up at Tyr. He didn't answer. "Or someone on the council? Who else would know of such a thing?"

Tyr was reluctant to agree with her assessment, but he couldn't disregard her logic. The elders and the knights were the only ones who knew of his existence. Only they would've had the knowledge to betray. Tyr motioned for her to continue.

"Is that all?" Jaden asked, turning back to Rick. Tyr stared jealously at her gentle hand as it stroked back the man's hair.

Rick nodded. "I only tell you because it's you, Jade. I wouldn't tell the other one they sent. Now, do with the knowledge what you will. I know no more. But you must tell me. What will you do with me?"

Tyr stepped forward. He felt Jaden's kinship to the man. "For your cooperation, you'll be released. But I pledge if you ever hunt again I'll personally come after you. If you are attacked you may defend yourself, but you can never use your knowledge against us."

Rick stood, looking Tyr square in the eyes. "You have my word. My war with you is over. I'm taking some advice and going back into the military. But what about Mack?"

"We will get him," Tyr said.

"I want to go with you," Rick said. He turned his eyes to Jaden, more comfortable facing her than her partner. His eyes glanced briefly over her blood stained shoulder and then her white gown. "I know his homes. I know how he thinks. I can be of service."

"Why?" Jaden questioned. It would be so easy for Rick just to walk away--and safer.

"Because he lied to me, because he has sent men knowingly to their deaths. Because he hurt you--my friend--and because he left us all to die on that beach," Rick said grimly. "A true soldier never leaves his men behind. And a true friend doesn't send them to die."

* * * *

Jaden found herself whisked back to the hall to quietly report what she learned to the council. Tyr confirmed her words with as few of his own as possible. It was no more or less than the leaders had learned from the mortal man themselves, but it was more detailed of an accounting. Granting Tyr's request for leniency, with the plea that Rick's knowledge and skill might still be useful to the Dark Knights and Jaden, they allowed the mortal to live under the same provisions Tyr had laid out.

"You have done well, dhampir," Theophania whispered at last. "I have one more promise to extract from you."

"Yes?" Jaden asked, curious.

"I would have you swear to divulge all knowledge you have of this time to us. Help us to understand the way of the humans," Theophania said.

"I don't know how much I have to divulge. But, what I know of human nature will be yours," Jaden swore.

"Very well," Theophania said.

"Then she shall be my apprentice?" Tyr asked. He waited in tentative pleasure, not knowing how to feel.

"No," Amon said. Tyr's heart stopped. Jaden paled.

"But," Jaden began, "You said--"

"We said you would apprentice. We hold true to our word," Ragnhild said. His eyes stared blankly, refusing to meet the swirling confusion in Tyr's. "You'll apprentice under Osiris."

"But I made her--" Tyr interrupted.

"Your insolence is noted, Tyr," Vishnu said harshly. "And though you have explained it, it cannot be overlooked."

Tyr's mouth snapped shut. He eyed Jaden warily.

"You are too involved with her fate," Ragnhild said quietly. "It's affecting your work and your decisions. From this night, you are forbidden from speaking until the whole of two hundred years has come to pass, including telepathy. And you are forbidden from being in each other's sight until the end of a hundred years--unless so ordered by us. That should be enough time to temper what is between you. If it has not, then at that time you may do with it what you will."

Jaden paled. She looked frantically at Tyr. Her heart thudded low and hard against her breast. She couldn't move. She wanted to scream, to fight. She would never last a hundred years without seeing him, or two hundred without hearing her name called on his lips. It was too much time, too much could happen. But, for all her fears and longing, their proclamations didn't stop.

"Jaden MacNaughton, you will be ordained a knight. You will drink of this council's blood and swear your loyalty to the vampire kind. If you ever deceive us, you will be killed in a most horrible fashion with a death that should last five hundred years long." Theophania's decree was final. Jaden looked around at the council. There was no reprieve from them, no more mercy to be given. She nodded in understanding.

"Tyr," Chara said, her tone sweeter than her sister's. "Go gather the other knights who are on the island and bring them here. She must swear herself onto them and exchange their blood. She has tasted yours. There is no need for you to come back."

Tyr turned to Jaden, his mouth opening as if he would speak. Her eyes darted to the sharp fangs peeking between his lips before seeking out the whole of his face. He couldn't answer her puzzlement--not with them looking on in judgment. All that he would say would only make their fate worse. Slowly, he nodded. His mouth closed without utterance. His eyes stayed upon hers as he bowed his head to her. Then, he blinked, his eyes looking away before opening. He knew this was the last time the council would let him see her for a century. Jaden was being ripped from him. Tyr knew as well as any what a hundred years could do to a vampire.

Questions loomed eagerly in his brain, but he couldn't lay voice to them. He couldn't tell her how he felt. Would Jaden still think of him? Would she wait for him? Osiris was as beautiful and powerful as he. Would she succumb to him? He couldn't bear it. He would never survive without her. He needed her. Remembering the council's decree, he quietly walked away and never said what he had meant to.

Jaden watched him depart through the red velvet drapes. Her heart shattered. She wanted to scream, to fight. She couldn't move. The door closed silently behind him. It was an image she would carry with her forever. Was he still angry? Would he wait? Would he still want her then? Did he want her now?

"Come, dhampir," Theophania ordered, standing as she flew gracefully over the table. The old vampiress landed in the center ring. Holding out her arm to Jaden, she said, "Drink of me and seal your fate."

Jaden gulped. The elders all landed around her. The door opened. Jaden's eyes flew hopefully to look for Tyr. Instead, the other Dark Knights entered. She saw Shiva nod at her in acceptance. A small smile of welcome whispered over his immovable features. Unexpectedly, she knew the old knight had played a small part in the council's decision. She nodded back at him.

One of the knights carried a branding iron. Jaden shivered. The knights crowded into the hollow circle. The one called Aleksander thrust the iron into the torch fire to let it heat. Jaden turned back to Theophania. The vampiress nodded, lifting her arm higher.

"Drink of me," Theophania murmured in command.

Jaden took the cool flesh in her hand. She couldn't think to refuse. It was the only way she'd see Tyr again. If she must wait one hundred years to be with him, then so be it. She would wait. The council only said she couldn't see or speak. They said nothing about the written word. She would find a way. She just had to.

"You may get sick," Theophania said, as Jaden lowered her lips. "Vampires were not meant to drink of it."

Biting into the first bit of flesh, her ordination began--the mixing of ancient blood with her own, the feeding ceremony of fast allies. Tyr did not return, nor was his name mentioned. When she had tasted of her new family's blood and they of hers, the vows of loyalty were spoken and the brand was taken from the flames. Jaden gritted her teeth as she was marked for an eternity, her lips pressed tightly to prevent her agonizing screams. The ceremony lasted throughout the night. And, from beginning to end, her mind focused on the one thing that would forever haunt her--her love for Tyr.

Chapter Seventeen

New York City, New York, December

The city stretched out from the height of Mack's library window. The tall gray buildings stood frozen in the glitter of the falling snow. Lights speckled the landscape, dotting the night like stars. Jaden's face didn't move as she stared out over the city. She could feel the people below her, trudging through the snowy sidewalks, hailing cabs that splashed in the watery streets. It was chaos of emotions and it all hammered within her.

She was learning to control her new powers with the help of Osiris and Shiva. Osiris was a hard teacher, very limited with praise. But his methods were fair. Tyr was not there to help her and she had no choice but to follow him.

Over the months he began to accept her presence amongst them, especially when she didn't complain about the tasks he set out before her. They'd tested her rigorously in those first days--gauging her skills, testing her knowledge, asking questions about her human intelligence. There were many things about the modern age they were curious about but didn't understand.

Shiva hung around following her ordainment into knighthood to help with her training. He even patiently explained the best way to mesmerize and bite a victim so that they would sustain no memory or injury. It had been hard at first to consciously bite into living flesh, learning to temper the need.

Osiris and Shiva were, for the most part, amiable companions and talented instructors. She learned a lot under their tutelage. However, there were things they couldn't teach her. They couldn't teach her how to forget Tyr, how to stop loving him. And they couldn't tell her how to reach him.

That brief moment in the council's hall was the last she saw of him. There were no good-byes, no explanations, and no resolutions. She would have to wait two hundred years before she could try and give them.

"I have the weapons specs," Jaden whispered quietly. Uncrossing her arms, she held up a stack of folders over her shoulder. She didn't need to look at Shiva to know he was there. She felt him behind her, could feel his movements connected to her blood.

It was strange being back in Mack's apartment. Everything looked so familiar and distant. So much had changed since her last visit.

"The council will be glad," Shiva answered. He came up next to her, turning his eyes to the cold outside. Jaden handed him the folders. Then, turning around, she placed a thick book on top of the stack. Shiva glanced at it in mild surprise. "What's this?"

"It's a book that describes the Dark Knights. It's said to be a book of myths, but I thought it would be best to take it back to the council hall. I thought I could leave it for Tyr." Jaden refused to meet Shiva's eyes.

"There is no message within?" Shiva asked lightly. "You wouldn't dare to try their patience by writing?"

"No," Jaden answered. "I know the decree and I know the cost at which I must obey it."

"One hundred years is not so long," he whispered. "Soon they will have passed."

"Two hundred to hear his voice," she said. What she wouldn't give to just hear him.

Changing the subject, Shiva said, "Osiris tells me you finished your ordainment."

"Yes," Jaden finally looked at him. "Morana, Chernobog and Hades met with me yesterday. We exchanged our blood."

Jaden thought of the quiet, albeit somewhat hostile, knights. It had been nothing more than a business transaction. They had disappeared right after without any words beyond the required sacred oath.

"Then it is done, little sister," Shiva whispered proudly. "You are truly one of us."

"All but Vladamir," she said, thinking of the Moroi leader she would probably never know. She had been forbidden from seeking out Jirí, his replacement.

"Jade," Shiva whispered.

"Will I not be ordained with a name of a Goddess?" she broke in, knowing by the knight's tone he was going to mention Tyr. There was nothing he could say to ease the pain inside of her. All she had was her work. She had to cling to her work. If she stopped to think, she would again start counting the days. And then she would be useless--a defeated mass.

"And betray the beauty of your eyes?" Osiris murmured from behind, as if such a thing would be an affront to them all.

Jaden had felt he was there. Turning to him, she managed a small smile of greeting. The pleasure was not in the fading light of her gaze.

"Come," Osiris said. "We have located your uncle."

"Are you ready for this?" Shiva asked.

Jaden hardened her face. She was more than ready. After the file had been translated for her, she couldn't wait to get a piece of her uncle's deviously black heart.

Striding across the library floor, she led the way downstairs. The main hall was dark but they moved through it with soundless ease. Then, stopping in the front hall, she pushed the button on the elevator.

The three of them made quite the invisible group. Jaden had adopted their long black jacket, great for enfolding a victim within. Her clothes were also the matching color of night, tight against her form, the dark contrasting her pale skin. When they walked, it was with a decided purpose to their movements.

It had been amazingly simple to breach her uncle's stronghold. How foolish Mack had been to think his houses safe. She walked right in the front door, greeted kindly by the doorman. Shiva and Osiris took the same approach as Tyr once used. Jaden didn't have the skill as of yet, but was assured it would develop in time.

The doors slid open. Jaden stepped inside and pressed her uncle's code into the key pad. Within moments, the doors opened on the basement level. Jaden felt Mack's presence immediately. Shiva and Osiris slipped into the shadows at her sides.

Lowering her face, she stepped forward, letting her footfall hit softly on the cement floor. The room was no more than a clean warehouse-like basement. Overhead the hum of fluorescent lights cast a yellowish hue over her uncle, giving a ghoulish cast to his features as he sat under their dim rays.

Mack's head whipped around at the noise. His hands rested over a laboratory table filled with strange potions and vials. The sleeves of his linen shirt were rolled up his arm. A machine hummed beside him. Seeing Jaden passing beneath the light, he stiffened.

"Jade?" he panted in awe. Suddenly, a weak smile broke out over his face. As he pushed his arms up and tried to stand, a vial rolled onto the floor, crashing. He immediately settled his arms on the counter, leaned forward, and stared into the shadows trying to see her.

Jaden didn't return the sentiment in his tone. She stayed back from the ring of light thrown out over her uncle. Cocking her face to the side, she studied him. Mack was pale--too pale. His dark hair was disheveled over his head in overlong waves. The shadowing of a beard lined his jaw, sprouting with patches of gray. His arms stayed fixed to the countertop as if he moved, his whole body might fall.

"Rick said you were ali--" Mack began. Her eyes flashed from the darkness, stopping him.

Jaden stepped into the light, letting her uncle take in the paleness of her face, the eerie glowing of her eyes. She knew what Rick had told him. She sent him with the news. Her mortal friend wanted to help out more, but couldn't protest when she told him to go re-enlist in the military.

Mack stiffened before vigorously nodding his head.

"Yes, yes," Mack whispered. "He did say the vampire made you one of his. I'm glad you're all right, Jade. Very glad."

"Murder," Jaden said quietly. "Rape."

Mack blinked. "Wh--what?"

"That is what I was charged with by the council," Jaden said softly. She felt her uncle's panic. She waited for him to deny it. Seeing him again, part of her wanted him to explain it to her--to justify it in terms she could agree with. He said nothing. "Why would they think that of me, uncle? Why would they think I captured vampires and mortals only to let them be abused?"

"Jade," he began. Seeing the warning light in her eyes, he hastened, "You don't understand. I was protecting us. I … I … you don't understand. I can explain."

Jaden stepped around him. Her head tilted. Her eyes held steadily on his face. She didn't give him time to continue rationalizing, before adding, "And why would they say my mother was a vampire? You said she fell off a horse."

"No, no, Jade," Mack began. Jaden raised an emotionless eyebrow up on her face. Mack began to sweat, pulling a moist handkerchief up from the ground. He didn't raise his hand from the table as he used it for support. The action took an abnormally long time. Leaning forward, he huffed for breath, "I've wanted to tell you the truth, Jaden. But I didn't want to hurt you."

"Then tell me the truth now," she whispered under her breath. "For this is the only time I'll listen to what you have to say to me."

"I was in the horse riding accident, not Rhona," Mack explained. He took a deep breath, wrinkling his forehead in concentration. "That is when he found me."

"Who?" Jaden queried softly. "Who found you?"

"I was bleeding to death, lying on the forest floor for a whole of a day. And then a vampire came and offered me salvation for loyalty. You have to understand. I was just a kid. I was scared of dying. I promised him I'd help him. I didn't know what he wanted." Mack's words trailed off. His breath became shallow. Jaden watched him carefully, wondering if it was fright that made him so sickly.

"What did he want?" Jaden questioned. She felt a prickling sensation go up her spine. They weren't alone. She could feel the other knights behind her.

"I don't know. He helped me and disappeared. For months I thought it was a dream. Then Madame Fabienne, our young housekeeper, woke me one night and bid me to Rhona's bedroom. I found my sister fornicating with an ungodly beast. He was drinking from her neck and she was letting him." Mack shuddered. Jaden lowered her gaze briefly, her body swaying with longing for Tyr. She understood well what her mother had felt. But she no longer resented the woman for it.

"Fabienne told me that the creature was a vampire and gave me a potion that was to kill my sister's lover next time he came to her. So I made the potion, gave it to Rhona in her drink and waited. The next night the vampire came, but instead of killing him the potion got her pregnant with you."

Jaden listened to his words. Her heart paced steadily as he admitted the truth. Mack weakened and leaned harder on the countertop. Looking around, he saw a stool behind him. Reaching with his foot, he wheeled it to him and sat.

"I thought the potion worked, fool that I was," Mack continued, growing paler with each word. "But when Rhona told me who the father of her baby was, I knew I had been tricked. By then it was too late. You were born and Rhona was going to take you away with her. I waited for Bhaltair to come for you both, but I could never catch him. I knew he had been there for I would find little flowers from the forest in your crib. Rhona was being locked into her room at night to keep her from the devil's work. It was a different time. Our parents were ashamed to have a bastard child in the family. They knew nothing of your father and died soon after from the heartache, believing Rhona had been taken advantage of by a rogue. You were kept a secret. A year passed after your birth and one night the vampire who saved me came to me. He told me that Rhona was no longer my sister. I...."

Jaden leaned forward to hear his whisper. His words came slower, slurring against each other. Confusion lined his face as he tried to concentrate.

"I didn't know what I do now. I killed her, Jaden. I staked her in the heart. I blamed her for hurting our happy family. I blamed her for the death of your grandparents. But, looking back, it might have been someone else's hand that killed them. Doctors didn't know then what they do now. They couldn't explain it." Mack blinked heavily, his eyes trying to focus on Jaden's unmoving face. "I tried to kill Bhaltair but he was too strong. He got away. Then the first vampire came to me and gave me money. He bid me to go away and to take you with me. I was scared of him, but had no choice. He said Bhaltair would be back for me and for you. I loved your mother. You have to believe that. I never would've harmed her had I known...."

Jaden felt her stomach tightened. She kept her face blank, resisting the urge to beat the mortal before her. Everything he had ever said had been a lie. Closing her eyes briefly to clear her head, she asked, "And who was this vampire that saved you?"

"I--I can't," Mack whispered. "He'd kill me and you. He said he would turn us over to Bhaltair if I ever defied him. I've been his slave--killing--"

"Mack," Jaden demanded, trying to get his attention. It was clear her uncle was sick. "What about the experiments?"

"Experiments?" he echoed weakly. He blinked, his lids heavy. He rested his head on the table.

Jaden shot forward. Grabbing him about the shoulders she hauled him up before her. A scream was on the tip of her tongue, but never reached her mouth. Another closed vial rolled on the table and clanked noisily onto the floor. It hit against her boot. She glanced down. To her horror, she found a thick tube ran into her uncle's arm, sucking out his blood.

"You have to believe I've always loved you, Jade," Mack mumbled, more incoherently.

She dropped him, her fingers unable to stand touching him. Mack stumbled, but caught himself. Reaching over to the machine he was connected to, he pushed a button. The blood in the tubing slowly reversed itself.

"What are you doing?" Jaden asked in sharp suspicion. A curling sense of dread overwhelmed her.

"I am joining you, sweetheart," Mack said in a dying mumble. "I have found a way to harness the power of many."

"What are you talking about?" she demanded hotly. "What do you mean?"

"Those experiments," Mack whispered in breathless confession and pride. "I have discovered all of the vampire's weaknesses. I have purified the blood of many. I'll be powerful, Jade--more powerful than the council, more powerful than all of them. And you'll be with me at my side. We will rule them all. We will be immortal. Nothing will stop us!"

"You're mad!" Jaden hissed. She went to the machine, eyeing it, looking for a plug to disable it.

"No," Mack growled as he latched onto her arm. His grip held surprising strength. "I have worked too hard for this."

"You deserve to die for this," she growled into his ear. She could feel the others watching, waiting silently in the shadows. She was grateful for their presence, just as she was appreciative for their impassiveness at the moment.

"You can't kill me, Jade," Mack whispered. His stomach lurched in pain. He fell to the floor, the tube still trailing out of his arm. Jaden ripped if from him. Blood spilled onto the floor from the tube, pooling around his body. But the action was too late. The rebirth had begun. Jaden watched helpless as Mack writhed in agony. She felt Osiris coming forward. Lifting up her hand, she shook her head, telling him silently to get back.

"I am the only family you have left. I am like a father to you," Mack groaned from the floor. His body twitched in pain. Jaden could sense his death. She could sense the potent blend of vampire blood mixed with his own. He had done it. Somehow, Mack had discovered a way to make a vampire without the drinking of blood and he had killed many to do it.

"I had a father," Jaden said quietly. She leaned over, watching his face. She hardened her heart to him, forcing away all sentiment that still lingered. Her hand reached into the folds of her jacket. "You made me kill him."

"I did it for you. He was ... no good," Mack defended. He gurgled. His eyes pooled with red. His body lurched. Vomit trailed from his lips to splatter onto the floor. Jaden jerked away.

Ignoring the agony of his rebirth, she said, "You are charged, Alan MacNaughton, of performing experiments on humans and vampires. For searching for the fountain of youth at the expense of others and for testing on vampire blood to see how long humans could be kept alive in suffering without turning. I charge you with cruelty rivaling any man in history. I charge you with the death of over four thousand mortals by way of your experiments."

"Jade," Mack gasped. "Don't. I love yo--"

"No," she growled. Her words rose in fury. "I charge you with trying to overthrow the vampire council."

"What do you care about the council?" he whispered up into her hard face.

Jaden gave him a slow smile. Lifting up her jacket sleeve, she showed him the brand on her forearm--the shield with a bar through it. Evenly, she retorted, "I'm one of them now."

"No," Mack whispered in horror. "You can't be serious. Those rapes and murders--I did it for us, you. I did them for you. We had to have money to fund this. It was the only way."

"I find you guilty, Mack," Jaden whispered, a touch of sadness rolling into her eyes. She tried to pretend she didn't feel anything for him. But it wasn't true. A part of her still loved him, as the father she had believed him to be.

As if reading her weakness, he said, "I am your family."

"Bhaltair and Rhona were my family. I have lived as my mother's people. It's time I discovered my father's." Jaden stood. She looked down at the pitiful man on the floor. Slowly, she pulled a stake out from inside her jacket. Mack's eyes rounded in horror. "I have a new family now, Mack."

"I made you what you are!" he hollered. "I gave you everything! You owe me! Bhaltair could never have loved your mother. He was using her for sick pleasure."

"Bhaltair loved Rhona and she willingly loved him," Jaden whispered. She felt a single tear line the edge of her eye. She missed Tyr. She longed for him. Suddenly, nothing else mattered--not vengeance or justice--only Tyr. She wanted the past to be dead. She didn't want to wait for him. She wanted him to be with her now. She wanted to spend an eternity begging his forgiveness for her sins. "And the only thing you taught me was death."

Mack's change was complete. His lungs no longer panted. The wound on his arm healed itself shut. Jaden could feel the strange mixture coursing through his blood like a river of souls squished together, fighting to be released from the coil of one body.

"You're right about one thing," Jaden said. "I couldn't have killed you--as a human. But now you're just a corpse."

She lifted the stake above her head. All of a sudden, Jaden felt Shiva beside her. She turned. Mack kicked up from the floor, jabbing his boot into her stomach, knocking her into Shiva's arms. Jaden pushed to her feet to face Mack. His eyes swirled angrily. The blood was too much for him. It raged inside his body.

Mack scrambled to the dropped stake and lunged at her, aiming for her heart. Unexpectedly, she was whisked to the side. Familiar arms wrapped in protection. Jaden gasped. Her dark gaze instantly found the solid strength of Tyr's blue eyes. Her lips parted, wanting to speak. Sadly, he let her go, spinning around to face Mack. Mack darted forward, stake in hand. Tyr shielded Jaden with his body.

Without warning, Mack stopped. The stake dropped from his fingers. His hands pressed into the sides of his head. He fell to his knees. His mouth opened with a scream only to gush with a torrent of blood. Jaden pushed to Tyr's side. Her arm strayed back to touch him as she stepped forward. She could hear Mack's heart racing in her head and then suddenly the organ exploded. Crimson poured from the man's lips. He fell to the ground with a swooshing of air and splattered blood. Then, with a silent eruption, he exploded into an ashen cloud of grave dust.

Chapter Eighteen

Jaden didn't wait for the dust to settle. She swirled on her feet, flinging her arms around Tyr. Her lips rose naturally to meet his. Tyr pulled back. He looked sadly into her face and shook his head. His blue gaze searched every line of her, like a vampire starved. He'd missed her desperately. When he left her, he left a piece of himself behind. And without her, he wasn't whole. If not for Ragnhild's insistence to the council that he be allowed to come this night to help, he wouldn't be seeing her now.

Knowing the danger of being seen talking to her, he turned to leave. He wouldn't be harmed by such a thing, but Jaden would be killed. He knew the decree, had been reminded of it by the council before coming to her.

"Tyr," Jaden whispered. Her hand shot out to touch him. "Please, don't leave."

Tyr stiffened, hearing the pain in her voice. He could feel the heat of her. Her touch was like fire to his skin. Could it be she missed him as much as he had her? Did he dare to hope such a thing? Her greeting said she did.

Without turning, he whispered, "No, Jaden, don't. We can't be seen talking."

"I don't care," she said, pulling desperately on his arm to get him to look at her. She needed to see the cool, ice blue of his eyes. She needed to know he would wait for her. She needed him to know she was waiting only for him.

"You'll be killed," he said hoarsely. "Will you leave me to live with that?"

Jaden looked desperately at Osiris and Shiva. Her heart poured with longing out of her eyes. Shiva nodded. He and Osiris turned their backs and looked the other way.

Tyr felt it to. Unable to deny her insistent hand, he spun around and gathered her into his arms. Jaden pressed her mouth to his. She sprinkled kisses over his cheeks and lips. Tyr's mouth met her eagerly. He pulled her up into his embrace. His hands wound like iron about her waist, never wanting to let her go. Jaden wrapped her arms about his thick neck, clinging to him for her very existence.

"Jade," Osiris whispered quietly. "You must hurry. We don't have much time."

"I'm sorry," Jaden rushed, pulling back just enough to talk. Her lips moved against his. Her hands pressed into the sides of his face, desperately feeling him. "I'm sorry for my uncle. I'm sorry for everything I've done. I'm sorry you're mad at me. I never meant to deceive you."

Tyr stiffened, but didn't let her go. "Why, Jaden? Why did you lie to me?"

"I was scared. I didn't know what the file said and I was afraid you would think I did--" Jaden's words were stopped by the press of his mouth and the stiffening of his hands.

"Not the damned file! I was a fool for thinking you had anything to do with that," Tyr whispered.

"Then--?" she hesitated, confused. She ran her hands into his hair, sewing her fingers through the locks. She couldn't stop their exploring if she tried. "Why are you angry with me?"

Tyr glanced at Shiva and Osiris' turned backs. Pulling Jaden away from them, into the shadows, he set her down. Lifting his hand to cup her face, he said, "I'm not mad."

"Jaden," Shiva called, persistently. "We have to leave."

"No," she whispered, shaking her head in desperation. Her eyes rounded as she turned her tortured face to Tyr's. "I can't leave you. Not again. These last months have been hell."

"We don't have a choice," Tyr said. "They'll kill you if you disobey."

"I don't want to live if I can't see you," she said angrily.

"Don't say that," he hissed, pushing his face into hers. "Wait for me."

"It isn't fair! Tell them you made me. Make them listen." Jaden felt him pulling away from her. In confusion, she detected Shiva at their side.

"Tyr, you have to go," the knight said. "The others are coming. If they catch you here they will report it."

Tyr nodded. He hated to leave her behind when his entire being begged for her touches, her kisses, and her love. His hand lifted to caress her cheek before pulling away. She tried to grab him, but his hand dissipated into a fine mist she couldn't hold onto. A muffled sound of horror escaped her throat. Tears pooled in her eyes.

Tyr's body disappeared completely, slipping through her frantic grasp. Shiva clutched Jaden to his chest to keep her from trying to follow. A small moan of torture came from her throat as she struggled against her bonds. Her heart tightened in agony. The road before her was long, endless. She could taste him on her lips, feel him inside her blood. But she couldn't hold him, couldn't have him.

Shiva felt her pain wash over him. Her eyes stared beyond him in a liquid daze. Slowly, he forced her to leave with him, back to the elevator. Her body didn't put up a fight. She stared blindly, not noticing that Osiris stayed behind working his way through Mack's machine, taking what little notes there were and destroying all the evidence.

"Come on, Jade," Shiva whispered as the elevator doors closed them in. "All will be well."

* * * *

Island of Delos, Cyclades, Two weeks later....

Jaden was dead inside. She didn't talk, barely fed. She numbly went about her duties, stating only that which was mandatory to her job. She'd been the job before and if she must, she would be it again. But, after having known Tyr, duty was a bitter and cold replacement to her soul.

All necessary reports were made to the council to their reluctant satisfaction. The vampire responsible for helping Mack hadn't been caught and the knights weren't blamed for losing such information because her uncle killed himself with his greed. Jaden didn't care anymore. She was tired of figuring out the past.

Rolling onto her stomach, she looked around the room the council was letting her use. As far as she could fathom, it was a guest chamber of sorts, set aside from the council's bedchamber hall. The bed was thick, comfortable. White fur lined the floor and bed. A desk sat in the corner. It reminded her of Tyr's bedchamber--only barren because he wasn't in it. She got no pleasure from the luxury. She wanted Tyr. She could think of nothing else.

Feeling a presence at her door, she turned her head to the entryway. Shiva stepped inside without knocking. She stared at him. The vampire frowned, coming across the room to sit by her.

"You can't keep doing this," he said. She blinked and turned away without answering. Shiva started to speak and slowly shook his head. "Osiris is complaining that you are lax in your training."

"I have been to every session," she mumbled, not caring.

"But your heart has not." Shiva sighed, placing a hand on the back of her head in a friendly pat. "Without your heart, your fighting is weak and predictable."

"I don't have a heart. The elders ordered it away."

"And what would he say if he saw you moping like this?" Shiva asked angrily.

"If he saw me, I'd see him and I wouldn't be moping," she said. Scooting further away from him, she shrugged off his hand. "Now leave me alone. I do what duties I'm bidden to perform. I answer every question. Not once has it been ordered that I do so happily."

"I can't leave. I have come to bring you to the council." Shiva stood. A frown still marred his elegant face. "The elders wish to test you."

"Again?" Jaden wearily hopped to her feet. "I thought the tests were over."

"Call it a mission then," Shiva stated with an indifferent shrug. "I think it will do you good to leave here. There are still many things you must put into order. Not the first of which is getting your uncle's affairs in line. Technically, you are still his niece and inheritor of his property. I've convinced the elders that you should tend to it after you see to this first mission."

"Oh," Jaden muttered to herself. Maybe a mission is just what she needed to make the time go faster. She doubted it--highly doubted it.

She followed Shiva down the passageway along the now familiar path to the council hall. She had been questioned and tested by them endlessly. What was one more time? Soon she was in front of the tribal elders, waiting like a good soldier for them to speak. Her eyes didn't meet their probing faces as they studied her.

"Dhampir," Theophania said.

Jaden nodded in acknowledgement.

"We have called you here tonight to address a complaint," Ragnhild said. "Osiris says you have been negligent in your training."

"I've been to and completed every training exercise," Jaden said. "I've done everything he has asked of me."

"We think there might be a deeper problem," Chara said quietly.

Jaden didn't answer. The council glanced amongst themselves--all except for Pietro who stared dispassionately beyond them all. He was impassively quiet as of late.

Jaden gulped, her eyes finally moving to gaze at Chara. Her heart thudded nervously, not daring to hope.

"You are bored," Theophania said. "You are a fighter, used to fighting."

"Yes," Andrei added. "You need an assignment--something to do."

Jaden's heart sank. She turned her eyes away. Every one of their damned words was like a kick to the gut.

"There is a disturbance in London," Ragnhild said. "Many of our kind have died. We want you to check it out and report back to us. Then, we wish for you to finish your work collecting any of the remaining MacNaughton personal documents and possessions."

Jaden stiffly nodded. Through tightened lips, she asked, "Shall I get Osiris?"

"No, he will be coming with me to Africa. You will be going there alone," Amon stated. "Consider this another test of your loyalty. And remember, dhampir, you may be alone but it doesn't mean your actions aren't watched."

Jaden dutifully nodded.

"Shiva has your travel plans. When you get there you'll be met by a contact. It has all been arranged," Theophania said. "You have been taught our laws and know what is expected. Your life is yours as much as it is ours, dhampir. We won't coddle and care for you, but we will expect you to report back to us."

* * * *

London, England, December 31

All around Jaden celebration resounded over the city streets. The dark alleyways were not as safe a haven, though there were plenty of meals to choose from. Jaden drank quickly from a passing man before letting him go on his way. The liquor in his blood soothed her some, being as she couldn't consume a stiff glass of scotch on her own.

Turning from the crowd, she made her way through the narrow passageway streets. The chipped cobblestone whispered past her feet as she walked. The breeze swept around her, but didn't stir her spirit. She was glad to be out of the council's hall. She was glad to be out on her own again, though much had happened since she was last alone. The night hours were spent more in contemplation and longing, rather than in hunting.

Her feet moved over the direction memorized by her brain. The council's order had been clear. Her London contact, supposedly a young girl, was to be out this night with her parents. Many vampires from a club of young ones had been killed, dragged out into the early morning sunrise and left for dead. It was said the young child witnessed the massacre and it was Jaden's job to lure the girl away and read her to see if she could discover a name or face.

Jaden couldn't care less. The job was no longer important. She just did it, hoping to pass the endless nights until she could see Tyr again. Nothing mattered anymore.

"That is not the chivalrous attitude of a true knight."

Jaden froze. Her heart didn't dare to beat for fear she'd heard wrong. Her lips trembling, her limbs shaking, she slowly turned around. She gasped, her eyes growing round. Slowly shaking her head, she whispered, "Tyr?"

A slow smile curled over the face she loved. Handsome blue eyes shone with a possessive mischief. His lips formed easily on his face. Jaden took him all in--his Viking blond hair, his piercing eyes, and his kissable mouth. Her hands hung lifeless at her side. Stepping before her in the dark alleyway, Tyr stopped. Jaden didn't dare believe it. She didn't dare to move and spoil the dream.

"I'll admit that I expected a little more of an enthusiastic greeting," he said with a wry smile.

Jaden felt tears in her eyes. She had read somewhere that vampires couldn't cry. A lonely trail of moisture worked its way down her face. It would seem she could only cry for Tyr.

"Jaden?" Tyr asked in concern. His smile faded.

"I can't do this," she cried mournfully. Another tear worked its way out of her eyes. "You'll only leave me again. They'll take you away from me again and each time it gets worse. Each time I die a little more. My heart can't take losing you. I can't do it. It hurts too badly. I--I love you."

The rest of her tearful protest was crushed by the onslaught of his mouth. Jaden couldn't resist the feel of him. It was too precious. Her eyes closed against the pain of eventual suffering. She clung to him. Her lips trembled, unable to return his passionate kiss.

A grin spread across his features. Tyr's entire being exploded with happiness. She loved him. It was all that mattered. Pulling his mouth away, he drew back. Jaden panicked, holding on tighter.

"Not yet," she whispered. Her fingers clutched desperately at his jacket front, before maneuvering over his shoulders to cling to his neck. "You can't leave me yet."

"Say it again," he murmured. His arms stayed steadily along her back.

"What?" she asked in confusion. "I can't think straight. I love you."

Tyr's smile widened. "Again."

"I love you?" she asked, the sound more like a timid question than an assertion.

"Never stop saying it, my love," he whispered, leaning in to kiss her.

"But--" Jaden's weakened protest was cut off by his kiss. She returned his embrace full force. Only when Tyr drew back, did she stop to think.

"I love you, Jaden." Tyr said. "I can't live without you. I can't wait a hundred years to be with you. Without you I can't fight. I can' concentrate. I'm nothing without you."

"But, the council," she began weakly. "They--I'm on assignment. They'll find out. They said they have people watching."

"Who? Someone to watch the dark knights? Don't you realize? There is no one to watch us. We're the only watchers and they know it. We're the council's eyes to the world. Besides, I took care of the council. I told them that you were mine and that I was yours. They would rather recant a decree than have us both defy them."

"But, how?"

"You proved your loyalty when you faced Mack alone," Tyr answered. His hand pressed over her hair, smoothing it back. "I turned you Jaden. That makes me your master in their eyes. And you have made me. Without you I am not whole." Tyr smiled tenderly at her, no walls up between them.

"Wait," she panted though her lungs didn't need the air. "You love me?"

"Yes," he whispered, kissing the trails of her tears.

"And we can be together?" she persisted, not daring to hope, making sure she heard him right.

"Yes."

Jaden squealed in delight, all her dreams coming true. She jumped into the air, wrapping her arms and legs around Tyr's steady form. She pressed kisses all along his face. Eternity no longer seemed so dim.

"That's all I have to know," she whispered.

"Wait," Tyr said, enjoying her eager kisses. "There are a few conditions."

"Hum?" Jaden's lips moved to nestle Tyr's neck, making concentration hard. His hand threaded beneath her backside to support her. "There always are."

"They allow it because you have proven your loyalty. But you're on probation as my apprentice. That makes me responsible for you." Tyr's masculine smile said he was unconcerned. He was just happy to have her where she belonged--in his arms, under his spell.

Jaden chuckled as he walked, carrying her easily with him, her body clutching to his. She leaned over to naughtily lick at his earlobe. A smile crossed her face, as she felt him shiver.

"It means you'll have to listen to me," he said, breathing in her cinnamon scent and angling his head to allow her tender lips greater access to him.

"I've never listened very well."

"Then we are both doomed," he sighed with feigned sorrow, though nothing could wipe the pleasure from his face, "for I am ordered to kill you if you disobey me."

"Really?" she preened. Leaning back, she batted her eyelashes coquettishly at him. "Well you know I stand to inherit a lot of money. What if I pay you off? Would you promise not to tell on me if I was bad?"

"It is not your money I'm after," Tyr growled with a seductive proposition to his low words. His lips devoured her neck with licks and kisses. His fangs brushed over her skin. As he moved, his body pressed against her. His thick arousal stood ready and waiting for her touch. "And I must insist that you are bad. We are vampires after all. We have a reputation to uphold."

"Then get me out of here," Jaden said, her eyes round and serious, but so very pleased. "I can kidnap some child for the council another night."

"With pleasure, m'lady." Tyr sped off into the night, into their eternity, carrying her in his steady arms. "And where would you like me to take you?"

"I know of a sunlit field where no one can find us," she whispered, tenderly stroking his long hair back from his handsome face. "And, if I remember correctly, you know how to get us there. Oh, then we can battle those knights you mentioned. And didn't you say something about jumping off a castle wall and--?"

Tyr's laughter rang out. He cut off her words with a deep kiss that left the vampiress completely breathless, which was hard to do since she didn't need air. The sultry sound of his laughter continued, fading behind them, wicked with intent, full of promise.

"Yes, my love," he murmured into the parting night, planting kisses along her neck. His hands explored up her body, not waiting for the comforts of a bed. They blurred into the surrounding darkness like the wind, as he whispered, "You'll have to close your eyes for I'm going to have to kiss you to get there."

THE END